EQUATOR

Also by Antonin Varenne in English translation

Bed of Nails (2012)

Loser's Corner (2014)

Retribution Road (2017)

ANTONIN VARENNE

EQUATOR

*Translated from the French by
Sam Taylor*

MACLEHOSE PRESS

QUERCUS · LONDON

First published in the French language as *Equateur*
by Editions Albin Michel, Paris, in 2017
First published in Great Britain in 2019 by MacLehose Press

MacLehose Press
An imprint of Quercus Publishing Ltd
Carmelite House
50 Victoria Embankment
London EC4Y 0DZ

An Hachette UK company

A CIP catalogue record for this book is available
from the British Library.

ISBN (HB) 978 0 85705 873 7
ISBN (TPB) 978 0 85705 872 0
ISBN (Ebook) 978 0 85705 871 3

10 9 8 7 6 5 4 3 2 1

Designed and typeset in Haarlemmer by Libanus Press
Printed and bound in Great Britain by Clays Ltd, Elcograf S.p.A

For Liam Maximilien Joe Smith
and
Jones Segundo Pascal,
the Varenne brothers.

I

I

Lincoln, Nebraska, June 1871

They supported the South on this side of the Platte River. The town was still called Lancaster then; it was renamed in honour of Lincoln after the defeat. The city's new name was a humiliation for its inhabitants and they never pronounced it without spitting between their boots, even in their own homes. As far as they were concerned, they were now in enemy territory. If a traveller were to enter a saloon in the city and raise a toast to the liberator of the South, he would finish his drink in silence and leave in a hurry.

Lincoln had become the state capital. The city now had a northern governor, a northern postal service, a northern court, a northern school and the Land Office, which offered a plot of land amounting to 150 acres to any American citizen. Free of charge. On two conditions: the applicant had to be at least twenty-one years old and must never have taken up arms against the government. A Northerner, in other words. Former Confederates were not entitled to this federal generosity. Washington, which claimed to be wiping the Civil War from the collective memory by focusing on the conquest of the West, continued to draw up battle lines on the country's evolving map. Mountains, paths, rivers and grudges all rose up like walls.

Many people in Lincoln dreamed of tearing the Land Office down, plank by plank.

For fifty cents a night, Pete Ferguson was renting a room with a view of this little white wooden house, the black lettering above the door spelling out, "US Land Office. Concessions. Purchase and sale".

After weeks on the road, exposed to prying eyes, it had seemed like

9

a good idea to shut himself up in this boarding house room. Since being here, though, his anxiety had driven him to a sort of paralysis. He had spent days on end sitting in a chair, drinking, lifting up the cotton curtain to peer through the window at the men and women entering the government building across the street. The spectacle of their transformation was the only thing capable of distracting him from his anguish.

Dressed in their Sunday best so they didn't look like the beggars that they were, worried that those promises of free land would turn out to be another scam, they entered the Land Office as though it were a church and today was their wedding day. The little white house even looked a bit like a chapel amid all those shops, the government representative standing in its doorway like a priest waiting to welcome his new flock. The ritual was at once a wedding and a baptism. Sceptical, their shoes white with dust, the pioneers converged on the Land Office from all directions, then re-emerged with a deed of property in their pocket. A handshake with the servant of the State would make them the equal of all those others who possessed something. Then they would get back on their wagons; wives would look at husbands, each would take a deep breath, and, with tears in their eyes, they would head off towards their 150 acres. Gratitude and pride were clearly visible on their faces. That gift was enough to make them eternally loyal citizens. Patriots. Their long journey was over; their sacrifices and hard work had been rewarded. They had earned their land; their good fortune was fully deserved.

Watching this, Pete remembered what Alexandra Desmond had told him about that Indian chief: a Lakota who had tried to pass on his people's wisdom to the white men by declaring that the earth did not belong to men, but that man belonged to the earth. He was wasting his breath, Alexandra said, because white men had only come here to make the earth theirs.

Most of the pioneers were his age, with children clinging to their legs or feeding from their mothers' breasts. Men with puffed-out chests and women with healthy pink cheeks.

When Pete woke, his belongings were already packed. His saddle-bags filled, the blanket wrapped around his Winchester, his trunk and his dog-eared notebook – Arthur Bowman's final gift. He no longer remembered how long he had been here or why he had even chosen this town, only that it was high time he left.

The widow who ran the boarding house counted her money on the living-room table, a flag of the old Confederacy nailed to the wall behind her. She grumbled about all these outsiders taking over the town. She pushed a few cents across the varnished wood towards him: all that remained of his last four dollars.

"Your change, Mr Webb."

Pete left the coins on the table, threw the saddlebags over his shoulder and walked to the stable. His horse, Reunion, snorted when he put the saddle on its back. Pete led the mustang across the street and stopped outside the Land Office. He read the painted letters one last time before putting his foot in the stirrup.

"I was about to close. What can I do for you?"

Pete looked at the tall man standing in the doorway, grinning at him.

"I still have a few minutes, if you'd like to come in."

Pete climbed the front steps and went inside. The man hung his hat on the wall, gestured at a chair facing the desk, then went behind the desk and held out his hand.

"George Emery. How can I help you, Mr . . .?"

"Billy Webb."

George Emery shook his hand so energetically that Pete felt as though his organs had shifted inside him.

"Are you looking for land, Mr Webb? A concession? Are you a farmer? A cattle breeder? A miner? Do you have a family or are you planning to start one? That's your right, a man of your age. Maybe you fought in the war, Mr Webb, so you're even more deserving of one of these plots of land. Did you fight in the war, Mr Webb? What I mean is . . . which side were you on?"

"The winning side."

George Emery blinked.

"Of course! Where are you from, Mr Webb?"

Pete eyed the shelves behind Emery, where maps were rolled up and land registers filed.

"Oregon."

The Land Office employee followed Pete's gaze before turning back to his client.

"A state loyal to the Union. But tell me what you're looking for, Mr Webb, and together we'll work out what the United States government can do for you."

The employee had no doubt that the government would be able to satisfy the desires of a young man like Billy Webb.

"So, you're giving land to anyone?"

"To all those citizens who . . ."

"To anyone at all?"

"I beg your pardon?"

"The whole country is yours?"

Pete walked around the desk and over to the maps. He took one, lifted it to his face and sniffed the paper. Then he put it back in its place and opened a register. George Emery cleared his throat.

"I should make it clear that only the first one hundred and fifty acres are free. And that the plots still available in this county are increasingly distant from the Platte River. There is still good land to be had, but it's not easily accessible. And most of it is not well-irrigated. What exactly are you looking for, Mr Webb?"

Pete put the register on the desk and walked over to the window. He looked outside at his mustang and Lincoln's main street.

"Do you ask them what they're going to do once they're in their new home?"

Emery leaned his neck sideways to loosen his shirt collar.

"I don't understand your question."

"How they treat their wives and children?"

"What do you mean?"

Pete turned to face him.

"Do you ask them who they are?"

"Who they are?"

"About their morality. That's what you're offering here with your property deeds, isn't it? The right to do what they want in their own home."

Emery stood up and spoke in a voice that filled the room.

"Young man, from the smell of your breath I'm guessing that you're not sober. You should probably go get some rest."

"Have you ever lived under the roof of a man who had the right to do anything, Mr Emery?"

"That's enough!"

"Give me your money."

The Land Office employee frowned. The young man facing him was stocky, with round shoulders but a powerful chest.

"Listen, you should leave before you wind up in trouble."

"When I was a kid, I thought that God was on the side of my father because he was strong, and that He would be with me when I grew up."

George Emery opened a drawer in his desk and took out a pistol.

"I don't know what your problem is, son, but you should leave now."

Pete stared at the gun.

"You know, possession of a gun is one of those responsibilities that they shouldn't let just anyone have. Like the right to do what you want in your own home."

He slowly reached inside his jacket and drew out a Colt .45.

"It brings . . . consequences."

He relaxed his arm and let the revolver dangle by his side.

"Mr Emery, do you understand the threat that you represent to us? The courage that we must show to face up to it?"

The Land Office employee raised one hand in a calming gesture while the other held the pistol aimed at Pete. He looked as though he were swearing on a Bible.

"Don't do anything you'll regret, kid. I'm sure we can come to an arrangement."

"I don't like negotiations. You should stop talking. Do something."

"I'll give you the money and that'll be an end of it."

George Emery took a leather wallet from his waistcoat, tossed it onto the desk and took a step backwards.

"I want you to leave me alone now."

"What?"

"Go out the back door and leave me alone."

"I can't do that. Just take the money and go."

"Put down your gun and leave, before we both lose our courage and anger takes hold of us."

George Emery licked his lips with his dry tongue, put his pistol on the desk, took a bunch of keys from his pocket, and unlocked the door next to the shelves full of maps. He turned back to the young man, memorising his face and the details of his clothing.

"They're gonna come for you, son."

He left without closing the door. Pete staggered. He took a flask of whiskey from his jacket and downed it. He pocketed the wallet and went over to the maps. He leaned down to sniff them again, then lit a match on his jacket sleeve and touched the flame to a pile of rolled papers. He watched the flames spread from one map to the next. The wooden rack began to turn black. The office flickered yellow and orange and clouds of smoke rolled up to the ceiling. Tears ran down his cheeks. Outside, his horse became agitated.

He jumped into the saddle, rode down a back alley, and fled Lincoln along a parallel street, a line of small gardens and the backs of shops flashing past. Night fell over the eastern path. His leather waistcoat was still hot from the fire.

The mustang stretched its muscles. It ran more smoothly now, faster, breathing in time with its stride. Horse and rider left the main path and headed through the long grass of the plain, a long grey swell under the first stars. A few black shapes – round hills on the horizon – guided them southwards.

At dawn, exhausted, they came to a stop. Pete drank a flask of water and rolled into the hollow of a depression in the ground, while Reunion grazed on dew-wet plants.

Pete woke, drenched with sweat, under the copper disc of the noonday sun. He stripped down to his trousers and climbed, barefoot, to the top of the highest hill, a bottle of whiskey and George Emery's wallet in his hands. Sitting cross-legged, he contemplated the endless flat landscape. Then he counted his loot, wedging a rock on top of the banknotes to protect them from the wind.

His head fell forwards, his shoulders slumped. The sun burned his back and warmed the whiskey. Pete Ferguson, wanted for theft and arson in Nebraska, wanted for murder in Nevada, was the possessor of a grand total of seventy-eight dollars.

〰〰〰

My brother.

After the Old Man, the person you hated most in Basin was Billy Webb, and you hated him even more once he was dead. Because that little shit had become a hero and nobody would ever say that Billy Webb was a nasty rich kid who spat in the faces of us Ferguson brothers.

The day he died, you wished you were in his place – with the other fathers who went off to avenge the Red Indians who were hunting on our land. But it was Billy who went to the Warm Springs reserve with his new rifle and his horse, while you had neither. The Old Man was part of that expedition. He hitched the cart and, drunk like the rest of them, yelled that they'd need a hearse to bring back the corpses of the Paiutes. They all laughed and fired their guns in the air outside the farmhouse. I was scared and you were mad that you couldn't go with them.

It was young Webb that they brought back in the Ferguson manure cart, all them poor bastards too drunk and too stupid to fight the Indians. They didn't think it was such a great idea then, that stinking cart.

When they got back to Basin that night, after the town had rounded up the sheriff and the soldiers from Fort Dalles, the Old Man stood on the doorstep, swaying, and stared at us. I'll never forget what he said. "Here, we defend our land and our families. You know what they'll say in Basin? They'll say that the Ferguson boys weren't up to the task. That they did nothing to defend our farms and that Billy Webb is a hero."

You stayed at the farm to look after me, Pete, because I was too small and I was scared.

I still have a scar on my head from the beating that the Old Man gave us that night. While he was hitting me, you took his rifle and you put the barrel to the back of his neck to make him stop. Anger made your voice sound strange to me: "Stop hitting him or I'll blow your head off."

The Old Man stood up and you held out as long as you could when he told you to let go of the rifle. You knew you'd let it go and you knew what would happen after. But he had stopped hitting me.

You spent three days in bed after he knocked you out, but nothing was ever the same at the farm after that. All three of us knew that something had changed.

Years later, when we went off to war and Rudy Webb bought what was left of the farm, he got his revenge for that: in the Ferguson family there were two living sons and no father, while in his house there was a father but no son.

Now you have a good horse and a good rifle. That's all you have left.

Wherever you are, I hope you're not alone and that you can find somebody other than Billy Webb you can talk to. He forgave you long ago for wishing him dead the day that the men left for the reserve.

2

Dodge City, Kansas, September 1871

That night, a few soldiers from Fort Dodge stayed in town, at Hoover's Saloon; George Hoover had opened it just for them one year before, when Dodge City was nothing more than a row of stakes in the ground. Not that the bar's owner was such a patriot that he wanted to sell beer to soldiers in the middle of nowhere just to keep their spirits up. No, even then, he knew that the railway would pass through there.

Since then, three more buildings had been constructed in Dodge City. First a general store, then a hotel – whose male population was not yet numerous enough to lure any prostitutes. But they were on their way, along with maybe a few pioneers' daughters who would make good wives. After that, a laundryman, hairdresser and barber moved into town, and he too was hoping that some ladies would arrive so the men in the area would start taking greater care over their appearance.

It was no secret that here in Kansas there were, for as far as the eye could see, green plains that would give harvests worthy of Eden as soon as the first ploughs came along. Pioneers had already passed this way, en route from Missouri and Texas. But the train was something else. A river of steel, sleepers and rocks flowing straight westwards, with farms growing up alongside it instead of trees. The Santa Fe Railway increased the value of the plots of land around it. But for the future of Dodge City, what mattered most was not the farmers. What mattered were the great Texan landowners who would load their cattle onto train carriages to send them off at high speed in all directions. Or, rather, the only two directions that America cared about: east and west. Hundreds, thousands, millions of longhorns would be transported. So Hoover, who had a nose for these things and friends at the Santa Fe Railway, had erected his first whiskey tent five miles from Fort Dodge, where the station was going to be built. One year later, the train stopped directly outside his saloon. People left the saloon and they were right on the platform; they got off the train and went right inside the saloon. The train didn't look like much: a new locomotive, a coal wagon, a passenger carriage, a freight wagon, and that was it.

The five or six soldiers from the fort and the thirty inhabitants of Dodge City would get drunk while choosing – if they had a hundred dollars in their pocket – their future: a hotel, a hardware store, a restaurant, a furniture workshop, or a brothel. George Hoover would soon be offering loans, as the dollars continued pouring into the cash register of his bar. Towns like this had grown up out of nowhere before, and it was always the first man to open a bar who became the mayor, the first to build a fence who became a senator, and the first to sell hammers who ended up owning entire streets.

Hot on the heels of this first wave of inhabitants came men from the east and the south: cattle traders and envoys from the biggest livestock farms. That night in Dodge City, including the railway workers, there were about sixty people packed into Hoover's Saloon. The table where they all wanted a place was presided over by the Santa Fe Railway representative, who had become the King of the West in only a few hours. The meat traders formed the first circle around him, with the discussion swiftly becoming an auction: whoever offered the highest price per pound of merchandise would have his product delivered by the next train. The prices rose faster than a newborn's fever. A trader from the North Western Fur Company elbowed his way through the crowd and finally banged his fist down on the table.

"At that price, there's no point in us even transporting our furs! We'd be better off sticking to our wagons. At fifty cents a fur, we may as well let them rot here!"

The Santa Fe Railway representative crossed his arms over his belly. "It's not our company's fault if you can't pay."

The fur trader turned to the cattle breeders: "You can't hold out for long at those prices and you know it. You're playing the railway's game and it's the small businesses like us who are going to suffer. Either we join together or they're going to bleed us dry!"

The representatives of ranches in Texas and Kansas, bunched around Henry Sitler, the biggest cattle breeder between Dodge and Junction City, could not have cared less what the man from the Fur Company thought. Cattle were worth a lot more than furs, and since the end of the drought and the war, prices had just kept going up. The country was gobbling up more and more meat every year.

The man from the North Western Fur Company shook his head, called them all madmen and left Hoover's Saloon. He went past the train platform towards the hunters' camp, where six-foot-high piles of furs were strapped to the wagons. There were about twenty men there, standing around a campfire. Bob McRae, the oldest among them, asked the trader how things had gone.

"I have no choice. If you want to load your furs on that train, I can't offer you more than two dollars a fur. If I give you three dollars, you'll have to deliver them to Atchinson yourselves."

"At two dollars, we'll go bust. We've got men to pay, equipment to buy for the winter. Even at three dollars, we won't make a single cent in profit."

"Two dollars. That's all I can pay you if you're transporting them by train."

Bob McRae gave it some thought.

"So, it's the cattle guys who are driving up the price?"

"They don't even have anything to send yet, but they're outbidding everyone else to make sure that they have the train to themselves in the future. The guy from the railway just sits there drinking while the prices rise."

"And that carriage on the tracks now is still empty?"

"Yep, and the train leaves tomorrow."

"And it's the cattle guys who are stopping us loading our furs on that train?"

The North Western Fur representative nodded. "Half the town is hoping to work with the guys from Texas and the Sitler ranch. They don't want to get on the wrong side of them."

"How much can you pay for the train?"

"Ten cents a fur max., and I'll pay you two dollars ninety for each."

"Give us three dollars and we'll throw in three extra furs, each one worth at least twenty-five dollars."

The representative held out his hand. "Works for me."

Bob McRae looked at the hunters around him. They understood without him speaking a word. When he set off, the others followed him – managers, butchers, cooks and mule-drivers – towards the lit-up saloon.

On the train platform, under an oil lamp swaying in the wind, a man stood, hands in pockets, eyeing the locomotive. He was a tough-looking young man, with a bowler hat on his head and a fur-collared jacket under one arm.

McRae drew close to him. "Kid, if it's your job to watch over this train, I would advise you to go for a walk."

The man turned to face McRae and the hunters. "I don't work for the railway."

"Well, take a hike anyway."

"I go where I want."

The young man was holding a bottle. He turned away from them to look at the locomotive again. The other hunters went on their way, but McRae remained where he was. He smiled. "You looking for work?"

"Depends."

"What can you do?"

"Jack of all trades, master of none."

"Ha, you really know how to sell yourself! You're hired."

"To do what?"

"Come with me into the saloon."

"And after that?"

"We'll talk about it if you can walk out of there in a straight line."

The young man lifted up the bottle. "I'm not scared of whiskey."

"You won't have time to drink any. It's your muscles I need."

"What are you going to do in there?"

"Negotiate the price of this train that you can't stop looking at."

The hunters shouldered their way through the crowd to the table where the Santa Fe Railway employee sat. Beside him, Henry Sitler had ordered a bottle of Hoover's best whiskey. The negotiations had been completed and they were celebrating. Bob McRae said to the railway representative: "These men and I have a load of furs outside on our wagons and we'd like to know what we can do to get them in your train so we can go home and start working again."

Henry Sitler did not give his neighbour time to respond. "I don't think that should be a problem, Bob. All you have to do is pay and the carriage is yours."

"The train will go faster than our wagons and we're willing to pay the difference. But only at ten cents a fur – not more."

"That wouldn't really be fair, now would it, Bob? Given what we have to pay for our merchandise."

"With all due respect, Mr Sitler, you know we can't afford the prices that you have fixed so high. And who is going to clear your prairies of bison if you put these hunters out of business?"

"You should talk about that with your buyers, Bob. It's nothing to do with us or the railway company."

Bob McRae turned to the Santa Fe representative. "Listen, we have a load ready to go. Your train is about to go off empty. Surely it's better to get paid ten cents a fur?"

"The company has settled on the prices, sir. I can't help you. Mr Sitler is right: this is something you should discuss with your trading partners."

"Our trading partners? Sir, we're offering you three hundred dollars and we'll load the furs on the train ourselves. It's not like we're trying to force you into anything, it's simply a fair price."

Voices rose around them. Some said McRae was right, that it was a fair deal, while others said there was nothing fair about the hunters paying less than everyone else. Sitler stood up and bellowed: "Gentlemen, Dodge City will soon be a major cattle city and it's the market that has fixed the price of transportation. It's the same for everybody. Does Mr Hoover sell his whiskey at different prices to different customers?"

Laughter. More shouting.

"Hell, who do them bison hunters think they are? Why should they get a better deal than us?"

"Throw them out the door!"

"Lower the price of whiskey!"

"McRae is right – nobody else can pay what them big ranches are paying!"

"The train is for everybody!"

"Let them load their furs!"

The saloon was soon divided in two, and each side was yelling at the other. McRae leaned down close to the railway employee. "Three hundred dollars. It's a good deal and you know it."

One of Sitler's men grabbed his sleeve. "We told you to drop it, McRae. You're not welcome at this table."

McRae ignored the man and kept talking to the railway representative. "Alright, this is our last offer: three hundred and twenty dollars."

"Forget it, McRae. You and your scavengers should get the hell out of here!"

The Santa Fe representative no longer knew what to do. The saloon was in a tumult now. Everyone was shouting and the drinkers outside were trying to shove their way in. Hoover, standing behind the bar, yelled at everyone to calm down. The railway workers and the cattle workers rolled up their sleeves. Sitler's employee tried to push McRae away from the table. The tough young man that McRae had just hired knocked him out with a punch to the side of the head and fighting broke out as suddenly as if someone had lit a match in a mine full of gas.

The Fort Dodge soldiers, whom no-one dared attack, stood looking at one another in the middle of this mob, drained their glasses, and then threw themselves into the fray. A few shouts gave a general idea of the two sides' aims: one side wanted to throw the hunters out of the bar, the other wanted to be allowed to load their furs on the train. But the battle was far less clear-cut: fists landed on allies and adversaries alike. The only ones with a defined objective were the cattle workers, who had their sights fixed on the group of hunters standing together in the centre of the saloon. Tables were picked up and passed over heads then thrown into the street along with all the chairs to make space for the fighting. The Santa Fe Railway represen-tative crawled behind the bar, which Hoover and his barman were defending with pickaxe handles. Planks were torn from the walls and floor and transformed into weapons. The ranchers and the hunters finally collided and the violence redoubled in intensity. Heads were split open, ears and calves were bitten. A soldier climbed onto the bar, ran along it and dived into the brawling mass. The hunters formed up in a line and, linking their arms, advanced until they had driven the cattlemen into a corner. Chair legs and planks were raised above heads. The tough young hireling punched his enemies until his knuckles were raw and kicked them once they were down on the floor. The hunters had lost several men but soon they were the only group left standing. Sitler had fled. The door had been torn off its hinges and the building's facade ripped apart. Cold air rushed through the holes in the walls, refreshing those who were still fighting, but punches were missing their targets now, while those attempting headbutts and kicks just fell over. Once half the bar's customers had been knocked out, people started looking around and counting.

Bob McRae, bleeding from his cheek and lips, his nose broken, one eye blacked, strode over the inert bodies and smashed chairs towards the counter. He took the three hundred dollars from his pocket and slammed the cash down on the bar. Then he leaned over and saw the railway employee curled up in a ball under the counter. "The men and I are going to load the furs ourselves. You don't have to worry about a thing."

—⚍—

The next morning, the train headed east with a carriage filled with three thousand bison furs: the first merchandise to leave Dodge City. The convoy of hunters went westwards and the wagons split off in various directions in groups of two or three. Each boss had his own itinerary. Now that there were fewer bison to hunt, Bob McRae explained, everyone had his own idea about where to find them. Some swore by the colour of the grass, others the size of the moon; many relied on tip-offs and hunches.

"In the old days, you could go wherever you wanted – Nebraska, Wyoming, Colorado – and you'd happen upon a herd of two or three hundred. Nowadays you spend more time searching for them than killing them and you're lucky if you get thirty or forty. And there must be a thousand of us, maybe two thousand, all in the same business. Anyway . . . you ever kill any buffalo, son?"

"No."

"What's your name?"

"Billy Webb. And I'd prefer it if you didn't call me son."

"Billy, I tend to think of guys who are twenty years younger than me as children, even if I know you haven't been kids for a long time. Hell, there's probably not a single child left in this country. Did you fight in the war, Billy?"

"Like everybody else."

McRae pointed to the right, indicating a cluster of trees along the Arkansas River. In that plain, any plant higher than the grass was enough to make a man think of starting a family there. Two other groups of hunters had already set up camp under the branches. Fires had been lit and mess tins were warming over the flames. The news about the fist-fight in the saloon had already travelled along the roads and the coming evening was expected to be lively. It was said that never before had there been this many people in Dodge City at the same time, and for the hunters fleeing the cities, this confirmed what they already thought: too many people in the same place and it always ended in a fight.

McRae was not interested in this discussion; sitting aside from the others, he watched the sun set: parallel lines of varying colours that ran all the way along the horizon. Pete went over to join him.

"What exactly will I have to do?"

"Your job will be everything except killing bison. Butchering the bodies. The dumbest, toughest and most repugnant work you'll ever have done. Vimy will bring you up to speed. He's the best at it, even in a place like this where everybody is the best at something – most often talking bullshit. Have you ever seen a tornado, Billy?"

"No."

"There's a hot wind that comes from the desert to the south. From the sea below Texas, there's the humidity, which makes my bones ache. And from up there in the north, there's the cold, which is going to come down on us. It's nearly fall and all those temperatures are going to collide. Which means tornadoes . . ."

"Is that bad?"

"Kid, when you've seen a tornado and you've seen a stampede of bison . . . well, it's basically the same thing."

"So how much do I earn for doing this stupid job?"

"The going rate. It's not only stupid, it's exhausting too. So, you get a dollar a day – and a bonus if you last until the winter and all goes well. You got a problem?"

Pete dug his hands deep in his pockets. "I don't really like it when people talk to me too much."

McRae burst out laughing. "Here in the plains, you won't be bothered by too many conversations. Nor by too many questions."

―⚊―⚊―⚊―

My brother.

Here at the Fitzpatrick ranch, we believe you. But we're the only ones.
There's nobody in Carson City who can say that Lylia was lying and that you didn't kill old Meeks. Everybody says that you beat him to death, and that it was bound to happen one day after all the

problems you caused. Lylia's jealousy towards you has become the city's jealousy towards the ranch. Whatever she says, Carson will believe.

They know we're deserters – it's not a secret anymore. The only thing protecting our lie now is the ranch's money and Arthur Bowman. Some people think we're Arthur's real nephews, because they reckon we look like him. They were afraid of you like they're afraid of him. But the truth is we deserted and that the Meeks boy died in the war while we were hiding out at the ranch.

I know it wasn't easy for you here, a lot of things went wrong. I tell myself it's my fault, that you stayed here too long because of your little brother, that you should have left long before. None of us – not Alexandra nor me nor anyone else – had the courage to tell you that, and you didn't have the courage to make the decision yourself. It was all just left to rot . . . until old Meeks' death. Time was against you in Carson. Now you're on the road, it's on your side: the more time passes, the more it protects you from the city's reprisals.

It snowed a lot this winter. But with the new barn on the meadows to the east, the horses were sheltered and they had enough feed to survive.

Aileen asks where her Uncle Pete is. She often thinks about you. Don't forget her – that little girl truly loves you. She was sad when you weren't there in April to celebrate her ninth birthday. She's old enough now to understand that we're not telling her the truth, but she pretends to believe us because she wants to believe that you've just gone on a trip and you'll be back soon.

Alexandra and Arthur are worried about you.

But the saddest one here is me.

Those plans you had for us – going to California and building a house there – I still think about them, even here at the ranch where I no longer need to imagine because the dream came true without you. Sometimes I get the same feeling I used to get on the farm – that I'm living in the house of a dead man that I daren't even mention.

26

We've never been apart before. That certainty we had – that one of us would see the other one die, that we'd always be together – has gone now.

You need to send somebody to Basin with the money so that Ma can be moved to the cemetery. Rudy Webb must have demolished the house after buying our debts and our land. I can't stop thinking about what's happened to the two graves there.

I'm having those nightmares again. The ones about the barn.

I'm going to talk to Lylia and ask her to change her testimony. I know that's what you would want.

I hope Reunion is fine. The son of Walden and Trigger . . . it's as if the Fitzpatrick ranch were out there with you. I know he's just an animal, but I like to think Reunion is looking after you. When I imagine you out on the great plains, I see you sitting by a campfire, reading a book, with Reunion sleeping beside you. That's how I like to think of you. Be careful, Pete. I hope you're not too cold, that you have enough water and food, and that sometimes, out on the road, you find somebody other than me you can talk to.

3

Vimy was a French-Indian from Canada. He'd worked there as a woodsman until the end of the 1860s, when there were no more beavers to turn into hats and the British took over the Hudson's Bay Company. Instead, he went south and started hunting bison. He met Bob McRae and went into partnership with him. Vimy was not the kind of man to tell anyone else what to do, so McRae acted as the boss. It took Pete Ferguson five days to learn this much, sitting next to Vimy on the bench of the wagon. And even then, it was McRae who told him. In the silence of the prairie, Bob McRae was what passed for a chatterbox.

In addition to the two partners, there was also Ralph, a Civil War veteran who oversaw the supplies, the cooking, the mules and the camps. He was in his mid-thirties and he walked with a limp, after being hit by shrapnel at Appomattox, the battle that had forced Lee and the South to sit down at a table in a small house in Virginia. Ralph was with Custer's regiment, who burned the trains carrying Lee's supplies, and he liked to repeat that it was Custer who won the war for the Union.

"What about you, Billy? You left in, what, '64? Did you get here before the end of the war?"

Pete, sitting with the others around the fire, replied that he didn't want to talk about that. Ralph kept asking, though, until McRae told him to shut his mouth and Pete took his blanket further away.

The large wagon was drawn by ten mules and would remain empty until they had bison furs to fill it. The small wagon, driven by Ralph, carried all the cooking and camping equipment and was drawn by six mules. McRae remained on horseback the whole time and would go off on a reconnaissance mission every morning before dawn in the hope of finding a few stray bison. The herds, in September, were generally further north, but, as McRae said, if you didn't buy a ticket, you couldn't win the lottery.

Five days after leaving Dodge City, they reached Fort Lyon, on the Santa Fe track that the train would soon follow. To the west, behind Fort Lyon, they could see the silhouettes of the Sangre de Cristo mountains, the first peaks before the Rockies. A dozen other hunting teams were already in the fort's square courtyard.

Vimy gestured to Pete and the two of them walked towards a little hut. Other hunters were lined up outside it, and those who came out carried crates on their shoulders.

"What is this?"

"Ammunition."

"The army sells ammunition to the hunters?"

"They don't sell it – they give it to us."

Without spending a cent or even saying thank you, they re-emerged with six hundred cartridges. The soldiers were distributing the crates in silence.

Some old Mexicans from Las Animas – a town a few miles away – had come to sell their products to the hunters, and a small market had formed around the entrance to the fort. Pete wandered past blankets covered with vegetables, bags of flour, bottles of corn whiskey, some dried meat (goat and pork) and a few nuts. Craftsmen sold coloured ponchos, braided leather straps, kitchen utensils made from wood or terracotta. Ralph, a wad of dollars in his hand, bartered for food with some old women.

The camp commander had allowed the hunters to stay in the courtyard for the night. The soldiers mingled and drank with them. The commander walked around the camp and greeted Bob McRae, who invited him to join his group. Ralph saluted the officer, while Vimy and Pete shook his hand.

McRae handed the commander a glass.

"How are things at the moment?"

"There are problems between the Utes and the Cheyennes. Since the size of the reserve was reduced, clashes between tribes have become more frequent. But we still have an agreement with the Utes."

McRae raised his glass. "To the new season. Plenty of bison and no Indians!"

"I can drink to that!"

"So I guess there's no need to send soldiers to Sand Creek anymore? The Utes do the job for you." All eyes turned to Pete Ferguson, who raised his glass. "I can drink to that!"

The commander eyed Pete. "Nobody's forgotten those tragic events, young man."

"Including the Cheyennes, I imagine."

"Need I remind you that Colonel Chivington was tried and has left the army?"

"And been granted amnesty."

McRae snorted with rage. "Apologise to the commander or I'll send you packing right away."

The officer interrupted him. "Let it go, Mr McRae. We all know that Sand Creek has a bad reputation. Colonel Chivington benefited from a general amnesty accorded after the war to all officers from the North and the South. Those amnesties are necessary if we're going to rebuild and heal the wounds of war. But he wasn't pardoned for the massacre of Sand Creek's Cheyenne families."

Pete was about to respond but the commander turned to face the other hunters around the campfire and raised his glass. "Gentlemen, I wish you good hunting!"

Everyone toasted the officer. McRae looked for Pete, but he had disappeared.

The next morning, after stocking up on ammunition and food supplies, the teams of hunters scattered in several directions over the plain, following a variety of clues that McRae considered equally ridiculous. Vimy and Ralph, who had consumed too much whiskey and mezcal the night before, took their time harnessing the mules. They were the last ones left in the Fort Lyon courtyard. Pete gave them a hand. He asked Vimy if the other hunters were not getting a head start on them. Vimy smiled and Ralph sniggered in a way that meant Pete was a greenhorn who knew nothing and would be better off keeping his mouth shut. McRae tied a barrel of flour to the side of the small wagon.

"Half of those imbeciles have gone into hiding so they can see which direction we take. We'll make them wait a while."

When they set off across the fort's courtyard, the commander, drinking from a mug of coffee, watched them pass. He nodded to Pete, who did not return the greeting. McRae grumbled: "For God's sake, kid, you're one stubborn bastard!"

Black clouds moved towards them. As the sky darkened, the grass became greener, whipping the air as it suddenly changed direction. McRae scanned the horizon through his rifle's telescopic sights. He was searching for some sort of hill or valley where they might find shelter.

"Damn! There's a ravine or something ahead, and at least two wagons already there. Crack the whip – there's five or six miles to go and we don't have much time!"

Vimy and Ralph obeyed and the mules sped up. McRae turned back and checked the prairie behind them. Since leaving Fort Lyon, another team had been tracking them. Without knowing whether their pursuers could see him, McRae waved at them to catch up. Then he spurred his horse into a gallop, leaving the wagons behind.

"I'm going to see what it's like over there. You've gotta go faster, boys!"

Vimy made some astounding noises with his mouth and the mules accelerated again. The old Canadian turned to Pete as the wagon squealed and grunted and the two of them were jolted violently by the axles' leather suspension. "You know why the army gives us ammunition?"

"So you can shoot Indians?"

The wagon was going down a small slope and the two men leaned back, their feet wedged against the wooden ledge to prevent their bodies being pitched forwards. Vimy tugged at the reins slightly. He had to shout to make himself heard. "Not exactly! When we've killed all the bison, the Indians in the plains will go to the reserves and make peace with us so we give them something to eat. The free ammunition is Washington's way of helping us get the work done!"

McRae was up ahead of them, waving his arms wildly to show them the way. Above his head, the clouds were twisting like water in a siphon. They skirted the edge of the ravine and descended to the dry riverbed where the two other wagons were parked. The hunters who were already under shelter had had time to unload their carts and wrap up their equipment in canvas. They gave the new arrivals a hand as they did the same thing. The wagons' stripped hoops stood several feet above the rim of the ravine, which was too shallow to offer full protection. They unharnessed the mules.

Vimy, pointing at the sky, shouted to Pete: "It's a big one!"

The spiral seemed to be sucking the whole sky towards it, the clouds coiling and converging on the storm's black eye. McRae quickly climbed up out of the ravine, looked through his rifle's sights towards the south, then came running back.

"It's Rusky's men who are behind us! They've stopped – they knew they didn't have time to get here."

Pete turned to where McRae was pointing. Sand from the ravine was flying up into the black hole that had formed in the centre of the prairie. The clouds were shaped like a knotty vine now, reaching down towards the earth, and the earth rose up to meet it, a cloud of soil and grass spinning in the same direction as the nascent tornado. McRae pushed Pete under the big wagon.

"Get under a blanket! Don't come out till it's over! Here it comes . . ."

Mules galloped past, vanishing down the corridor of the ravine. Canvas sheets snapped, ropes whistled. Pete's blanket swelled and was torn from his grip, disappearing from sight as if carried away by a torrent. He covered his head with his arms and lay flat on the ground. The sand sprayed into his nostrils and his ears. He could hear the wooden wagon creaking above him. The wheels kept rising higher and higher before falling back to earth, then a mighty gust lifted the wagon from the ground and smashed it onto its side. The canvas covering the equipment flew away, and McRae and Vimy threw themselves at it. Pete crawled over to them. The wind died down for a few seconds, then came again even harder, blowing and sucking at the same time. The upended wagon started to shake. Another gust blew it back onto its wheels. All they could hear now was the roar of the tornado, like the shriek of a hawk mixed with the rumble of thunder.

A minute later, the wind died again. The dust and torn-up vegetation continued to follow the grey column as it slid southwards; the sky cleared miraculously behind it and shreds of blue reappeared between the clouds. They climbed out of the ravine and watched as the tornado drifted onwards into the path of Rusky's team. A mile or two further on, it began to grow thinner and, as fast as it had formed, the cloud of debris dropped back to earth; the dark vine fell to pieces, rose into the sky and dissolved. Rusky's wagons were no longer visible, only a curved line of churned-up earth on the prairie, a track thirty feet wide left by the tornado's passage, which ended abruptly in the middle of the grass.

McRae turned around. "Where's Ralph?"

The wheel of the wagon had smashed his skull when it fell back to earth. Ralph had died instantly.

The rest of the day was spent finding the mules. That evening, the three teams made camp together and reviewed the damage they had suffered.

Erdrich's team, the first to arrive in the ravine, had been the luckiest of the three. A few broken pieces of equipment, but nothing essential. The only serious loss was Erdrich's horse, which they couldn't find anywhere. For Rusky, the other hunt leader, the situation was far worse. His food wagon had been lifted from the ground and rolled several times: the wheels and the two axles were broken. They had also lost a lot of equipment and food. Most worryingly, Rusky's arm had been broken when the food wagon had rolled over him. Vimy had made him bite into a belt while he yanked his hand to set the fracture of his forearm, which was bent three inches below the elbow.

As for McRae . . . well, he'd lost a member of his team.

They dug a hole and one of Rusky's butchers used planks from the smashed wagon to fashion a coffin for Ralph. They buried his belongings with him. McRae had to check his account book to find his family name and they quickly wrote it on a plank that they planted in the ground. The team leader took off his hat, as did the others, and he said a few words: "If we ever come across your family, we'll tell them what happened. Amen."

After the funeral, the leaders gathered in the shade of a canvas sheet. They had all suffered losses, they had been hunting bison for ten days and not one of them had a single fur to show for it. They decided to work together this winter. Seven butchers, two cooks, a thirteen-year-old kid (Erdrich's nephew) to look after the mules, five wagons and three hunters who knew better than the others where they would find bison. For a short while, they debated which direction to take. Bob McRae first pointed out that Rusky had been following him for the past three days so his opinion didn't count. Then he told Erdrich, a Texan with a strong German accent, that the southern herd was still migrating northwards in search of cooler air, which meant they would go as far as possible from Texas, that desert where no-one would even spit in a thirsty man's mouth. The nights were growing colder north of the Platte River, so the herd must have started to descend. *Ipso facto*, there was only one place the bison could be: between the Platte in Arkansas and the Brazos in Texas. And the midway point was between the Smoky Hill River and the Republican. Moreover, two days from here was Rose Creek, which later joined the Smoky, and in this little patch of paradise, the bison grass grew so thick that McRae himself would eat it. Rusky called McRae a madman, Erdrich called McRae a madman, and then they both admitted that he was probably right.

They left Ralph's grave behind them, and, during the two-day journey to Rose Creek, the three leaders discussed how they would divide any profits they made. Rusky, who was providing butchers but no shooter, said he would saddle up and spend all his time following bison tracks, meaning that he would be a sort of scout, which would save them a lot of time. The shooters would be Erdrich, McRae and Vimy.

Pete now had to drive the food wagon in Ralph's place.

They arrived in Rose Creek on the day that McRae had predicted. The river was only about fifteen feet wide, but it broadened as it flowed north.

After the tornado and two days of travelling, the men were more relaxed as they sat around the campfire – all except for Erdrich's nephew, who was terrified by the idea that the Indians might attack them at any moment. They reassured him. Since the Sand Creek massacre in '64 and the war against the Cheyennes that had followed it, the situation had calmed down. There remained only a few isolated groups of Indians, and they were not going to attack ten armed men without a very good reason.

Pete sat on his own and smoked, listening to stories about encounters with the Apaches and Comanches in the south, and the Sioux, Arapahos and Blackfeet in the north. From the sounds of their voices it was easy to tell who was making things up and who had actually been frightened. Vimy sat next to him and Pete gestured with his chin at the hunters boasting about shooting Indians. "It doesn't bother you, working with guys like that?"

Vimy tamped the tobacco into his pipe with his finger. "Where are you from, Billy?"

"Oregon."

"Where were you educated?"

"Educated?"

Vimy smiled. "You can read, I've seen you writing in your notebook at night, you can think, and you speak well when you have to."

"I learned on a ranch."

"Not in school?"

35

Pete shook his head. "A ranch where I stayed for a few years."

"Why did you leave?"

"You ask too many questions, Vimy."

Vimy stood up. "Listen, kid, Bob and me, we like you. But we're also keeping an eye on you. And those guys you don't like? We know we can depend on them."

Pete controlled his anger. "I'm not here to make trouble."

"I get the feeling that trouble follows you wherever you go, Billy."

4

The solution to the disappearance of Erdrich's horse was Pete's mustang, an animal that all the others had been coveting for a while. The hunters preferred American horses, but that mustang was really something, and they needed it for Rusky, who had to roam the plain in search of bison. When McRae spoke to him about it, Pete was rubbing down his horse.

"Nobody but me rides Reunion."

"We need a good horse for the scout. You understand what that means?"

"That I should do it instead of Rusky."

"What?"

"That mustang goes nowhere without me."

"For God's sake, Billy, you can't take Rusky's place. That's his job. Besides, what do you know about tracking?"

"Complicated, is it, spotting a herd of bison in a field of grass?"

"If this is about money, we can come to an arrangement. We'll pay you for the mustang."

"I gave you my offer. Take it or leave it."

"Shit . . . Alright, but if you haven't found a bison in four days, you either let Rusky ride your horse or you pack your bags."

Rusky wore a bison skin over his shoulders day and night, all year round; he had a black beard that seemed to blend into the fur and a little bowler hat jammed on top of his head. McRae and Vimy were not especially shrewd businessmen, but bison hunting was a way of life more than a path to wealth. Rusky was in only his third season and still believed he could get rich enough to buy a big house with servants. He walked across the camp towards Pete.

"What's all this about, Webb?"

"Nobody else rides my horse, that's all."

"And you still think you can work for us?"

"I work for McRae and Vimy, not for you."

Everyone in the convoy was watching them.

"It's the same thing now. We're a team and I need your horse."

Vimy cut in. "It's his right, Rusky. It causes a shitload of problems for us, but it's still his right."

"What the hell are you talking about, Vimy? You're defending this arrogant little shit? His right? Screw that . . ."

With his unbroken arm, Rusky grabbed Pete's saddle and was about to put it on the mustang's back when he felt the barrel of a Colt .45 touch the inside of his ear. Pete's hand did not tremble.

"They hang horse thieves in this country."

Rusky must have grown up with a gun in his ear because he showed no more nerves than Pete, despite the fact that he was on the wrong side of the revolver. He dropped the saddle and Pete lowered his gun.

"One tracker more or one tracker less – it's your choice."

That evening, McRae was the first to return to camp. After twelve hours on horseback, he had not seen a single bison. He had travelled east of Rose Creek, while Pete had been sent west. Erdrich, who had followed the river, returned one hour after McRae, his horse covered in foam. McRae was on his feet before the Texan was out of the saddle.

"How many?"

"Fifty! In a big bend of the river, about two hours from here. They weren't there this morning, but when I saw them on my way back, they were settling in for the night."

Rusky fidgeted impatiently. "So what are we gonna do? We could leave right now!"

McRae rubbed his chin. "Erdrich says they're gonna sleep there, so we can wait till tomorrow morning. But, man, the first of the season! I'd hate to miss them. What do you say, Vimy?"

"If we leave three hours before dawn, we can take them by surprise. The shooters will have time to get ready. What's it like there, Erdrich?"

"It's nicely set up. A thousand feet from the other side of the river there's a small hill where we could wait. We'd be downwind."

McRae paced in circles. "Fifty? We should be able to get them all in less than an hour, but we can't afford to lose them. Let's do what Vimy suggests. The wagons will stop a mile away and the shooters can get in position.

Three teams of hunters for an entire winter ought to net at least three thousand furs. Fifty bison in ten days was not much, but they had to start somewhere.

Pete still hadn't come back when it was time to depart. They went on without him and by dawn they had arrived at a landmark left by Erdrich the day before. The wagons came to a halt. McRae, Erdrich and Vimy loaded a mule with their Sharps and ammunition and the three of them set off together on horseback.

When they came close to the spot where Erdrich had seen the bison, they dismounted and continued downwind on foot, bent double at first and finally crawling. As they approached, the three hunters looked at one another. McRae stopped Erdrich and whispered: "Christ! How far away are we now?"

Erdrich hesitated. "At least a quarter of a mile."

Vimy and McRae exchanged a look. The odour that reached them now was too strong to have been produced by only fifty bison. They began crawling as fast as possible.

Rose Creek was a deep bend, half a mile long, covered with grass as green as mint leaves, which ended in a spit of dry mud left by the river. The bison were rolling on the ground, eating, sleeping, standing around daydreaming, and the fifty bison that Erdrich had seen the day before in this paradise had somehow quadrupled in number. McRae gestured at the others to retreat. They could no longer feel the rocks and scrub scraping their bellies.

"We don't have enough bullets!"

They ran the last few hundred feet back to their horses. Pete was there with Reunion.

"What are you doing here?"

"Waiting for you."

They galloped back to the convoy. Pete had got lost on his way back to the camp in the dark. Then he had heard what sounded like a roll of thunder and he'd stopped.

"I didn't realise what it was to start with!" He was shouting over the noise of the horses' hooves. "They stampeded past me, about three hundred feet from where I was. I followed them until they stopped at the river down there!"

Five minutes later they arrived at the convoy, jumped out of the saddles and started filling their pockets with ammunition.

McRae pulled Pete aside. "Billy, can you handle that Winchester?"

"Sure, better than most I reckon."

"Listen carefully. This herd is our big chance, but it's not as simple as it looks. If you're a good shot, you can take down thirty or forty on your own before they start to run, because bison are dumber than rocks. The trick is to hit the old cow that leads the herd first. Without her, the rest of them might stay there for an hour without figuring out what's going on. But with three shooters, there's gonna be so much noise that the bison will run sooner rather than later. So I want you to bring your Yellowboy and come with us. You'll have to get closer than we will because your rifle's not as powerful as our Sharps and you don't have a telescopic sight. Don't shoot so much that the bison move, O.K.? But once they start to get nervous and pace around, you take down as many as you can until they disappear. Got it?"

Pete loaded his Winchester.

"You shoot the old ones. I don't shoot until they start getting jumpy."

"I don't have time to repeat all this, kid, so listen good: you aim for the neck. Even if you don't kill it, the beast won't get far and we'll be able to find it. Not the belly, not the legs, not the head! If you hit one, move onto the next. Never hit the same one twice. You take this

40

rifle stick and you put your Yellowboy on it. You shoot with one knee on the ground. Don't lie flat! It makes a massive echo and the bison will go crazy a lot quicker. Let me see, I don't think I'm forgetting anything..."

They got back in the saddle. As Pete urged his mustang to a gallop, McRae yelled: "Oh! Billy! One more thing: don't shoot the calves. They're not worth the cost of the bullets and it makes the mothers panic!"

The herd had not moved. The wind was still with them, blowing from the east. McRae, Vimy and Erdrich took up their positions while Pete continued crawling. He went so cautiously that it took him a good ten minutes to get ready. From his position, he could hear the shush of the river and the breathing of the bison as they rolled on the ground, raising dust clouds whenever they shook themselves. It was an impressive number of animals. Grazing, their enormous backs and flat snouts made them look stupid. Pete raised his hand to signal to the other shooters that he was in position and then he waited for a moment amid the gentle sounds of the river and the herd.

The detonation of the Sharps behind him made him jump. The herd did not move. Only one animal swayed to the side, took two small steps and then fell to the ground: the first leader. Some of the others sniffed the dead body and started grazing again. Three more rifle shots: the detonations, at this distance, sounded relatively discreet, but Pete clearly heard the bullets whistling over his head. For several minutes he watched as bison startled, as if stung by a hornet, then took a few steps before collapsing. The others, around them, did not react. The shooters concentrated their fire on the densest part of the herd and Pete could no longer tell how many were falling. Suddenly a ripple of panic spread through the animals' ranks, the bison scattered, the shooting stopped, and for two minutes there was silence again. The creatures lifted their heads and slowly calmed down. Forty or fifty of them had died, but the others did not run. When they started grazing again, the shooting recommenced. Pete understood now why the hunters talked about harvesting bison: they killed them as if they were picking fruit from a tree or scything crops in a field.

The carnage continued, but, in the absence of any leaders, none of the other bison fled. More than half the herd was on the ground now. The survivors could smell the blood, but they were paralysed by fear, incomprehension and stupidity. A gust of wind blew just above Pete and for a few moments the sound of gunshots grew louder. The herd shivered like leaves on a tree and the animals stepped back as if preparing to run away from the river. But they stopped again, because the shooting stopped. McRae and his colleagues were good at their jobs. Some of the females moved away, changed their minds and returned; some males stamped at the ground with their hooves. The bison were getting nervous. Pete put one knee on the ground and placed the Winchester's barrel in the fork of the rifle stick. But the animals started grazing again. Pete couldn't believe it. It was as if the bison were deaf and blind, as if someone were telling them something they refused to believe. McRae, Vimy and Erdrich started shooting and the heavy brown bodies began to fall once again. Then one of the calves was hit. Its mother made a lowing noise that echoed for miles across the plain. One cow, hearing this alarm, finally started running eastwards.

Pete aimed for the bison closest to him and squeezed the trigger. In his viewfinder he saw a small cloud of dust fly from the animal's shoulder. He used the lever-action to load a fresh cartridge into the chamber of the Winchester and moved onto the next one. Further off, in the blurred edge of his sights, he noticed the herd starting to run. But he kept going, firing all fourteen bullets in his magazine, activating the lever as fast as he could. He reloaded and some bullets fell to the ground, jangling as they rolled over the rocks. The metal of the gun was hot and Pete's ears were whistling. He emptied another two magazines. The bison were further and further away now, but some strayed from the herd or ran in circles and came within range once again. One last straggler, perhaps already wounded, was moving away slowly. He aimed at its hindquarters and fired six or seven times, until the animal collapsed. Then Pete stood up.

Three hundred bison were lying on the ground in the river's bend. Some of the calves remained, sniffing at their mothers' corpses.

Higher up the hill, the three hunting leaders were shouting with joy and dancing the jig.

McRae ran down to where Pete stood.

"Good work, son! That was a hell of a harvest, and you got more than your share with the Yellowboy! Don't worry about the calves – they won't move from here. We can finish them off when we go down there with the wagons.

Pete contemplated the harvest. Rose Creek ran red with blood and from off in the distance he could still make out the sound of the last remaining bison stampeding.

5

The butchers approached the wagons. The bison lying in the grass, their huge shoulders black and round, looked like rocks in a dried-up lake. McRae, Vimy and Erdrich walked between the corpses to shoot the terrified calves.

They set up the big tripods, and tied ropes to the wagons and the hind legs of the closest animals. Whips cracked and the mules advanced, lifting the corpses from the ground so that they hung suspended in the air. Working in teams of two for each bison, they began by cutting the skin below the hooves and along the feet. They yanked on the hide, slicing the fat off little by little to detach the fur and pull it over the body, slicing open the stomach, until the skin had been stripped from the body all the way to the head. Then they cut it from around the neck. Thousands of flies swarmed around the carcasses and the men, aiming for their eyes, their hands, their hair, their leather aprons smeared with grease and blood. The last part of the operation consisted in cutting out the tongues, each one worth fifty cents. They were thrown into barrels of brine attached to the sides of the wagons, the salt and water both taken from Rose Creek.

"We used to only kill the females," Vimy explained, "because their skin is softer and more in demand, but we do the males too now."

It took two butchers one hour to finish a bison. By the end of the first day, forty-odd furs were stretched out on the grass to dry. The shooters helped out too. They only had a week to butcher the animals they'd killed; beyond that, the furs would be too rotten to sell. The butchers were not all equally good at their job; one fur in three was badly cut and lost almost its entire value. The meat was left to rot, apart from a few choice cuts that were consumed then and there by the teams. The cows weighed over a thousand pounds each on average, and the males about 1,500 pounds, up to a ton for some of the old bulls. By the end of that first day of work, thirty tons of meat had begun decomposing by the river. The teams set up camp further off to escape the stink and the flies.

The next morning, they let off a few shots to disperse a wake of vultures feeding on the corpses; Great Plains wolves retreated too, their mouths and paws dark with blood.

"We'll poison the carcasses with strychnine tonight and tomorrow we'll butcher any wolves that got too greedy. A wolf fur can sell for two dollars."

It was a bright day and by noon the temperature was up to eighty-five degrees. The flies bit the men's skin and the slaughterhouse stink was unbearable. After three days, bathing in Rose Creek made no difference: the smell remained stuck to their skin.

"Anyone who complains about the Indians smelling bad hasn't spent much time with us! Even the Indians think we stink."

After four days, Pete was as fast as the others and had stopped vomiting.

After a week, the butchery was almost done; the skins on the corpses were becoming too fragile. There were more than two hundred furs in the wagons. Vimy thought they could manage another thirty – one more day of work – and that the rest, about fifty furs, would be lost. All was well – except for Rusky's mood. He was brooding over his frustration at not being able to take part in the shooting. He never went within thirty feet of Pete.

They had harvested about twenty wolf furs and Pete negotiated with McRae to keep four for himself, the price being taken from his pay. The boss let him have them in return for five days of work and gave him the choice of the best ones as a reward for his fine shooting.

Pete, who had become a tracker, shooter and butcher all in the same week, went off with McRae and Erdrich in search of the next herd while the others remained behind near Rose Creek to finish skinning the last bison and pile up the furs.

The three trackers rode for a day before setting up camp. They were grateful for the pure air after so long breathing that stink. In the evening, sitting around the campfire, they shared a bottle of corn whiskey. Erdrich asked Pete: "So, Billy, are you going to tell us why you named your mustang Reunion?"

Pete Ferguson sank into one of those silences to which his colleagues had become habituated. Erdrich did not ask the question again and in the end he fell asleep. A few moments later, he was snoring noisily. McRae passed the bottle to Pete.

"Billy, when I hired you I promised you that you wouldn't be bothered by too many questions, but there is one thing I'd like to know. Maybe I'll get used to it, but it still bothers me to call you Billy Webb when I suspect that's not your real name. I was wondering if in the end you won't get tired of nobody knowing who you really are. Because it seems to me that it must be . . . I don't know . . . even lonelier."

Pete took a long swallow of whiskey. McRae stared at the ground.

"I know it's none of my business, Billy. You do whatever you want."

"I had another name before Billy Webb, for five years. That was false too. It was the name of the man who hid us at his ranch, my brother and me, when we deserted in '64. We called ourselves the Penders brothers."

McRae waited. It was up to Billy if he wanted to keep talking.

"When people don't know who you are, what does it matter what they call you? A name means nothing to strangers, only to ourselves. The man you met in Dodge was Billy Webb. Back in Carson City, I was Pete Penders. The guy who lent me that name had already borrowed it from a dead man. His real name was Arthur Bowman, but he preferred his false name. He didn't want to remember where he came from either."

Bob McRae put some coffee over the fire to heat up.

"Why did you leave that ranch?"

"I had to."

"But you wanted to stay?"

"I don't know."

McRae leaned back against his saddle. As Pete remained silent, he kept talking. "When I came to this country, we'd hardly crossed Missouri. Oregon belonged to the British, Texas and California were Mexican, and the plains were just a big reserve where we'd sent all the Indians, because nobody wanted this part of the land back then. Now, the country stretches from one ocean to the other. The West is almost entirely occupied, roads have been built. The pioneers aren't setting off in search of adventure; they're heading west because they believe in something that will happen to them there. Land, money, something that will belong to them. A real adventurer doesn't want any of that. The pioneers are weak; they're looking for certainties, and a woman to help them take off their boots in the evening. The women want kids, they want a church and a school. They want it to last. The adventurer, the hunter, they know things don't last. At my age, now, I don't even know who's right anymore. In fact, I've even started dreaming about that stupid damn house with a rocking-chair on the porch! But I don't have any regrets. Well, just one. I wish I'd taken another journey when I realised that this country was going to become the same as all the others. I knew it when they found gold in California, when I saw all those tens of thousands of guys travelling from the east to dig in rivers and try to make their fortune. A real adventure leaves you poor; it leaves you with nothing but memories and nobody to share them with. The hunter ends up alone, blind and mute. He dies in the mountains with nobody to mourn him. He freezes to death or gets torn apart by grizzlies. He marries an Indian girl. None of the hunters – apart from a few cunning ones – managed to save a dollar. Why? Because they didn't care. It was life that they wanted. After that, they became guides for pioneers and companies. The adventure is over."

Bob's jaws were locked shut for a moment. In the light of the flames, the lines on his face became a map of rivers, a multitude of tiny tributaries flowing into his mouth and his eyes.

"I don't know why you left that ranch, Billy, but it's clear as day that you've got a hole in your belly and that you'll ride a long way before you can fill it. Whiskey is often the first thing you want to swallow in order to fill that hole."

McRae had a bitter taste in his mouth. He spat on the ground and poured the rest of his coffee onto the fire.

"There's one thing you can't avoid as you get older, even when you don't have children, and that's to look at younger guys like you and to hope that they'll do better than you did. Hell, Billy, if only I could put everything I know inside your head and your legs, you could conquer the world. But nobody can put an old mind in a young body. They're too afraid."

The alcohol had shrunk Pete's eyes.

"What was that journey that you never took?"

"To the equator."

"The equator?"

"The line you pass when you go to the other side of the world, where everybody walks upside down. Down there, water flows upstream and wind blows from the ground. Pyramids rest on their point and the blood rushes to your head. Your feet barely touch the ground; you have to fill your pockets with rocks so you don't fly away. First you have to cross through Mexico and then a bunch of other countries before you get to Cape Horn, where the Atlantic and the Pacific meet, where boats go around the continent and back up to San Francisco. Cape Horn is at the edge of the equator, and that's why they have the worst storms down there, because just after that the ocean falls over the equator. A waterfall a hundred times higher than Niagara Falls."

Pete burst out laughing. "The earth is round. Doesn't matter where you go – if you jump in the air, gravity will you pull back to the ground. The equator isn't at Cape Horn and nothing changes when you pass it."

McRae laughed too, and rolled onto his side with a groan. He lay with one arm under his head and said: "Well, all the same, that's the journey I should have made when this country went crazy. Good night, Billy."

"My name is Pete."

Bob McRae lifted his head. "Try to get some sleep now, Pete."

For the next three days, despite exploring hundreds of square miles, spending sixteen hours straight in the saddle, from dawn till night, they did not encounter a single herd on the vast plain, with its horizon as flat as a calm sea. After the brief high of Rose Creek, the hunters' morale sank to rock-bottom again.

The second incident between Rusky and Pete took place one evening. Rusky was holding his mess tin with his broken arm, and Erdrich's nephew was serving the soup. Either because the kid was clumsy or because Rusky's mess tin fell from his stiff fingers, Erdrich's nephew poured the soup over Rusky's legs. In a rage, Rusky cursed and gave the kid a slap that sent him sprawling, half-conscious, to the ground. Erdrich froze and was perhaps about to say something, but Pete was faster and he threw himself at Rusky. The table collapsed under their weight. By the time they were separated, they had both landed some ferocious punches, and Rusky, despite his broken arm, was getting the upper hand. Both men were pouring with blood.

Vimy sent Pete away to wash his face, and Erdrich said that it was maybe time for the teams to separate again. McRae objected. That would mean Rusky's season was over and things would be more difficult for the other two bosses. Once again, they had to come to an arrangement.

"You'll have to promise us that things will settle down, Rusky. We'll all be screwed if you and Webb can't get along."

"He can apologise first. He started it."

"You want him to say sorry and that'll be it?"

"I can't promise that we'll be friends. He stabbed me in the back. But I'll wait until the season's over before I give him the lesson he deserves. You can tell him that, Bob, and make sure he does the same."

McRae went off to find Pete. "You've got a broken nose."

"It's not the first time."

"Still, I should put it back in place."

Pete stuck out his chin. With his thumb and index finger holding tight to Pete's nose, McRae paused.

"You have to apologise to Rusky. If not, we'll have to separate, and then the season will be over for all three teams."

"He can go fuck himself."

"You'll do what I say."

McRae yanked hard and the cartilage cracked. Pete bit the inside of his cheeks. Bob patted his shoulder.

"None of us liked seeing Erdrich's nephew getting smacked like that, but it's not the end of the world either."

Pete blocked one nostril and blew a wad of blood and snot from the other.

"You don't hit a kid. The strong should never beat the weak."

McRae laughed. "We can talk about that when Rusky gets his hands on you!"

Always armed, killing to live, spending whole days up to their elbows in blood, all of this made the bison hunters – survivors of the Civil War, and kin to no-one – calm men, on the verge of tears in the wind of the plains and prey to dark memories, men who were more fearful than dangerous around others of the same type. They were men who had seen more than their fair share of the world's evils, and all of them knew what was brewing that morning when Pete walked across the camp towards Rusky.

It was obvious that the young man was making a special effort when he started apologising for the fight the previous evening and promising that it wouldn't happen again. His head hanging just a bit too low to be sincere, Pete had just said: "So, yeah, I'm sorry, O.K.?" when Rusky took a long butcher's knife from under his fur and attacked him. Pete threw himself to the ground to escape the blade. Raising the dagger in both hands above his head, Rusky readied himself to impale his enemy to the ground. Pete whipped the Colt .45 from his shirt and put a hole in the black fur, the bullet entering Rusky's bulky chest and never exiting.

Rusky had waited for Webb with his hand on his knife. Pete had made his apology with his revolver, and no-one thought he had been entirely wrong to do so.

———ɯɯ———ɯɯ———ɯɯ———

My Brother.

Two brothers . . . almost nothing. And yet, when you think about it, so much. Our mythology. Brotherhood stronger than fate, brother-hood that turns the world upside down, plunges the universe into chaos when it goes to war against itself. Two brothers are stronger than the gods. There are brothers in the stars, brothers in books and old tales. Two brothers, each at the head of an army. Blood brothers. Brothers in arms. As if that connection were a danger, the threat of a total rupture. Two brothers without a mother or father.

I don't remember her, Pete. Only what you told me. That perfect mother who took me in her arms, I don't know if she existed but you told the story well and I like to imagine that she was the way you described her.

You never understood the fact that he was all I ever knew. That I could call him Papa when you always called him the Old Man. He was the only one. When he died, when we buried him in the garden, you didn't even want me to say a few words. I was afraid to make you angry by joining my hands so I held my hat instead to make a bridge between them. I remember the frozen earth, the pickaxe that echoed like it was ringing against solid rock, the sound the coffin made when it hit the bottom of the hole, like a boat banging against the riverbank. I also remember the sound his body made when you cut the rope and it fell to the floor of the barn, like an abandoned puppet. His hand that still gripped tight to the side of the ladder. I don't know how long I knelt there before you arrived, watching him hang from the beam with his fingers clinging to the ladder like he were holding somebody's hand. Maybe Mama's?

He was always thinking about her. I know you refuse to believe it, but he held on to that bit of wood as if he regretted his act. Or as if he'd wanted to cling to one last memory so he could leave with it filling his mind. It was because of his hand that I didn't dare take him down, that I waited for you to turn up. When I heard you enter the barn, I wiped away my tears so you wouldn't see them.

You always protected me, Pete, but you never let me be Papa's son. You only ever let me be your brother.

Why did you always pick fights with everyone you met in town? Provoking old Meeks who lost his son in the war, and you a deserter? You hate them all, Pete, all those fathers, because of ours. You climbed the ladder, you pulled his fingers off the wood and you cut the rope. He fell right in front of me. And he'd sworn so many times that you would end up on the gallows. He was afraid of you, Pete, ever since you aimed that rifle at his head. He knew that he wasn't strong enough anymore, that you'd grown up just like Mama asked you to so you could protect her.

Those winters that we spent, the two of us, at the farm, those winters were hard and long. They seemed to last half the year. Spring and summer went by too fast, but you were almost happy without him. You and I worked for the others, growing and harvesting what we needed to survive, and you sold our land, plot by plot. You became my father. You wanted to take his place. You wanted to make him disappear the way you made the farm disappear, piece by piece. When the soldiers came to take us to war, all we had left was the orchard around the house – those stunted trees that stood guard over us like ghosts. Once more you protected me. Our flight in the Sierra, the snow and the icy winds. Without eating, you carried me on your back to that cabin and that ranch. I'm still here and you are gone. All the efforts you made, to reach this point . . .

When it comes down to it, Pete, you're just like Papa. You have never known how to behave with anyone weaker than you. Except with me. Your brother.

You get mad at those who are stronger than you or who think they are, and you get mad at those who are weak and refuse to let it show. Like Papa, who kept thinking about Mama but preferred to beat us rather than admit it.

What kid are you protecting now? Without me, will you become like the Old Man? Because he's in you, Pete, and you know it. The Old Man is in you when you drink, when you look at a woman, when you ride a horse or shoot a gun. You're afraid and you can't show it because you were never able to be a child.

I miss you, but I know which one of us is suffering the most.

Take care of yourself. I hope you have enough to eat, that you're not cold, and that sometimes, out on the road, you find somebody who you can talk to.

6

A cold wind, the first breath of winter that autumn, blew through the camp. The hunters, as superstitious as old women, did not like that sensation on the backs of their necks. They raised their collars. Pete was readying his horse and the mustang – whom some suspected of being the cause of all this – was nervous, its ears back.

McRae wasn't sure how to behave. He felt uneasy doing this with all the others watching him. Pete put on his gloves. They were nicely made – too nicely made, like all his other things: his sable-collar jacket, his guns and his mustang, all those things that made him appear like a rich kid. When the other hunters thought about Billy Webb, they would remember a good shot and a guy who did not belong.

"We're like sailors here. What happens at sea stays at sea. That's how it works, self-defence or not. Except that you're not really one of us, Pete, and I can't guarantee that all these men will keep their mouths shut. I reckon you should forget the name Billy Webb. Anyway, Vimy and I found enough to pay you. You did your bit, so you deserve your money. When Rusky smacked Erdrich's nephew, I should have gone after him myself, then none of this would ever have happened."

Pete pocketed the cash. Bob McRae looked at the wolf furs wrapped inside the rolled-up blanket. "Most people in this country head east or west, but in your case, Pete, I would recommend heading north or south." Pete climbed into the saddle. McRae patted the mustang's neck. "Maybe we've become cold-blooded over time, but I don't reckon you should let your conscience bother you about all this. Rusky had killed two men before and it never stopped him sleeping at night. And

I'm not talking about Indians. Go south, kid – you'll meet fewer people down there."

Pete reined back the impatient mustang. "Towards the equator?"

McRae smiled. "Yeah."

"Where everything changes?"

"Everybody deserves to dream a little. Even if, after a while, those dreams become regrets."

"Is that the old wise man's advice to the young hothead?"

"Probably the only advice you'll take from guys like us."

Pete spurred Reunion and soon he was out of sight. He could have turned around to look at the camp, to see the covered wagons disappearing into the distance. He could have taken a moment to wonder what he'd expected.

That night he dreamed, half-awake, about the cloud of black dust that the bullet had torn from Rusky's fur, just like it had from the bison that they'd harvested. In the morning, the plain heard his thoughts: an immense confessional without priest or penitence, a wild, pagan church. Pete didn't dare even whisper his regrets, out of fear that an echo would carry them to someone's ears.

He advanced vaguely southwards, finding his way by the sun. The days passed slowly as he pursued a horizon that seemed to keep moving away from him. Sometimes he would stop just to stare at that distant line, trying to convince himself that it was motionless, that he would eventually reach it. But as soon as Reunion began trotting again, the horizon started creeping away.

There was no alcohol left, nothing in this plain to which his anger could cling. Nothing and nobody – except for the mustang. Pete would climb down occasionally and walk away from the animal to prevent himself hitting it. Or shooting it, so he would finally be alone. He also walked away out of fear that Reunion would hear him soliloquising and, through the mustang, so would his brother Oliver, Alexandra and Arthur Bowman, Aileen and the whole Fitzpatrick ranch, hundreds of miles from here. He wanted to sit where he was and wait for the horizon to come to him. He wanted to tear away the illusion and to see the vast plain for what it was: the four walls of a prison cell. He tried to convince himself that he'd been worthy. But worthy of what?

This Edenic pastureland met only the mustang's needs. Pete had to kill in order to eat. When he finished the bison meat, he began hunting. He caught a hare, and its smell as it cooked over the flames was like the echo of his thoughts, a signal of his presence. He was in Indian territory.

Imperceptibly the plain had risen. Without noticing, Pete had reached a clifftop, hidden beneath the convergence line that stretched for dozens of miles and formed part of an endless series of canyons. He didn't even know which State he was in. He stood at the edge for a moment, staring down into the void, to convince himself that he wasn't dreaming.

He rode along the clifftop until he reached a barranco, a dried-up stream going down a negotiable slope towards the bed of the main canyon, where grey water flowed. Legs tensed against the stirrups, he crossed the shadow line cast by the cliffs opposite and reached the river. He set up camp without eating or lighting a fire, and listened to the sound of the water.

At dawn he continued downstream, his belly hollow and his head empty, and watched the sun enter the canyon, illuminating new layers of earth and rock one by one. He tugged at the reins. At the intersection of a narrow barranco a few hundred yards ahead, there was an enclosure containing forty or fifty horses, and a building constructed against the rock in clay bricks the same colour as the canyon. A few figures were visible. He wanted to turn back, but he heard a rock rolling somewhere above him and glanced up. A lookout on a rocky outcrop was aiming a rifle at him. Pete dropped the reins and put his hands in the air. Two other men emerged from between the rocks and advanced towards him. He couldn't tell if they were white or Indian. Leather clothing, woven hats, coloured pearls, fringed knife sheaths, brown skin and dark eyes, dirty hands and faces, moving slowly, with American boots and guns, spurs at their ankles.

"*Qué haces aquí?*"

Mexicans.

"You speak English?"

"*Estás con el gobierno?* Ranger?"

"Ranger? No. Bison. Buffalo."

The two men exchanged a glance then observed the mustang, the bloody wolf furs, Pete's clothes; the one who had spoken first lowered his rifle.

"Business?"

"No. Just passing through."

Pete pointed vaguely southwards.

"Nobody comes here, except us, the Indians and the government men. What are you doing here?"

This one spoke good English.

"I'm going to Mexico."

That made the man smile.

"There are no bison in Mexico."

"And you, what are you doing here?"

The Mexican, his hair long under his hat, looked cunning and translated Pete's words into Spanish for his sidckick, who laughed. The two of them looked at Pete curiously.

"This is our home, *güero*."

More figures were appearing from around the enclosure and the brick house.

"You have something to trade?"

"Trade?"

"Business, *güero*. That's what we do here."

The Mexicans looked at the mustang.

"I have nothing to sell. I'm going to Mexico."

"The furs?"

Pete's legs were starting to cramp so he stretched them against the stirrups. The saddle creaked and Reunion snorted. The two men gripped their rifles.

"It's a custom, *güero*. Trading – it's a sign of goodwill."

"What would you have to trade for the furs?"

The long-haired one smiled again. "Anything you want, *güero*."

Ferguson glanced at the lookout just above him. "I don't understand what *güero* means. If it's an insult, you should tell me."

The Mexican raised his eyebrows and translated again for his colleague. They burst out laughing.

"It's only an insult if you are ashamed to be white. Paleface, gringo, yankee, *güero* . . . it all means the same thing."

"Do you have any flour? Coffee?"

"Anything you want, *güero*. And your mustang would fetch a good price."

Pete tried to speak in the same tone of voice. Making an effort to hide his fear was at least a sign of character.

"The mustang is not for sale."

There were about fifty men, women and children altogether; there were other houses concealed against the cliff wall, some of them no more than a simple brick wall with a door closing off the entrance to a cave. This was not a camp but a village. Some people wore plain white cotton, others were dressed like a mix of cowboys, Indians and flashy pistoleros. The more he looked at their faces, the less sure Pete felt that they were Mexicans. Most of them had darker faces than the first two he'd spoken with, and some of the women had the round faces of Indians. At the Eagle Saloon in Carson City, the men who talked about Mexico said it was a country where there were three races: the real Spanish, the mixed-blood immigrants, and the Indians. They said the immigrants grew moustaches so they would look like the Spanish, but above all so that no-one would think they were Indians. They said the Indians were too lazy to grow facial hair.

In this canyon village there were almost as many beards as men, and it was Pete Ferguson, with the sparse stubble on his chin, who felt like an Indian. They took his horse and escorted him to a brick hut in the shadow of a red rock overhang. A man sat there on top of a flat stone. His skin was darker than that of any of the others and he had a black moustache. His arm was in a cloth sling and his hand was swollen. He was sweating despite the shade, one leg bent and the other stretched out in front of him, smoking a small cigar. The four men around him posed as if for a newspaper photograph, two of them guarding their chief on each side. They looked tired, and the wounded chief no longer seemed to believe in the role he was playing. He flicked the stub of his cigar away and massaged his stiff leg.

"So, you said you hunt bison?"

A guard laughed and pinched his nose. Pete's clothes still stank of rotting flesh.

"I was working with a team, by the Platte River."

"The winter season has just begun. What are you doing here?"

"I worked three seasons with Bob McRae. Now I'm headed to Mexico."

The chief mused on this. He was sweating with fever and the whites of his eyes were yellow, but he could still think quickly and clearly.

"You were lucky you didn't meet Quanah Parker's Comanches. They'd give anything to add old McRae's scalp to their belt. What are you going to do in Mexico?"

"Travel."

The man coughed. "*Güero*, that's the most unbelievable thing I've heard in a long time. You're going to travel ... So you're an explorer, are you? A conquistador?"

He laughed and coughed again. He was maybe forty years old, with a smooth face. His skin was turning pale from the effort it cost him to think and talk.

"Not so long ago, you wouldn't have had to go any further. It was still Mexico here. So let's just say that you've kind of arrived already, *güero*, and that our laws of hospitality still exist. You can stay here if you want, trade something if you need. You'll have a bed and food, but tomorrow we're leaving."

Even the idea of this departure seemed to drain the man of strength. Pete's shoulders relaxed, his lungs finally started filling with air again.

"I need food. Why do you still stay here, now that it's no longer Mexico?"

The chief raised his head. The young explorer's curiosity amused him. He made a signal to the four guards and they walked slowly away, as if their roles too were now played out. The chief drank water from a jug, then handed it to Pete, who took a long mouthful while he wondered if the man's fever was contagious.

"You're rebels, aren't you? You're at war with the government?"

"Rebels? You have some strange ideas, *güero*. And for someone who worked three years with McRae, you don't seem to know much about this country. We're not rebels. Our ancestors came here long before yours, with the priests and soldiers of Catholic Spain. They learned to live and work with the Indians. We're Comancheros. That's the name they gave us."

He stood up and with one hand made a sweeping gesture that took in the canyon and the half-deserted village, the huts with their collapsed roofs, the skinny kids and the paths lined with animal and human excrement.

"I am Rafael, the chief of what remains of us."

7

An old woman cleaned out an abandoned house for him. It was set aside from the other buildings. Pete unloaded Reunion. Another woman, a young one this time, came and crouched outside his door. She unfolded a blanket, inside which she had brought bags of coffee, flour, black beans and lentils, a pound of lard and a bottle of alcohol. She arranged these goods on the ground and then waited, her head lowered. Pete spread out four wolf furs next to the food. The woman picked up the first one and he looked at her face with its fine features and long black lashes. She stroked the fur, turned it over, inspected the leather, held it up to the light to check what state it was in, rolled it up, placed it next to her and grabbed the flour, which she pushed towards Pete. After that, she checked all the furs, offering a measured quantity of food in return for each one. When the exchange had been completed, she stood up but Pete signalled to her that she should wait. He emerged from the hut with the fifth fur, the best of all, which McRae had given him. The hunter had told him that it was worth at least three times as much as the others. The young woman blinked, muttered something that he didn't understand, spun on her heels, making her poncho fly from her shoulders, and quickly walked away. Pete remained standing there, then turned to the long-haired man who spoke English, and who had overseen the entire trade. He was lying on a rock about ten feet away and pretending to sleep with his hat over his eyes.

The young woman came back, this time with a bottle of authentic bourbon, a box of ammunition for his Yellowboy, and a large polished turquoise. Pete spread out the fur and sat facing her. On his rock, the guard had lifted up his hat and was now keenly watching the negotiation. Even in this part of the world, at the foot of this canyon without food supplies, the young woman's merchandise was worth a lot more than the fur. Pete waited for her to push something towards him but she didn't move. In the end she became annoyed, and made him understand that it was up to him to choose. The bourbon, the bullets or the turquoise.

He reached his hand out to the stone, slid it towards him and looked at the young woman. She waited. She didn't touch the fur. Pete picked up the bottle of Kentucky bourbon, pulled it towards him and made a sign that that was enough, that he would not take the bullets. In a single movement the young woman rolled up her blanket, grabbed the fur and stood up. Her poncho swayed and stirred up dust behind her as she walked away.

Her guard came down from his rock.

"*Güero*, why did you treat Elena that way?"

Pete asked him what he was talking about.

"The first barter was fine, exactly the way it should have been. Your furs were not worth as much as the food, but the main thing was that she agreed to the trade. Why did you take out that other fur, which was worth so much more? That showed a lack of respect. She had no choice then; she went away to fetch all those things that are worth much more than you were offering. She had to satisfy her honour, so that she would still be worthy of appearing before you. And you, *güero*, you refuse to take it all! You leave the bullets! Elena is poor; she must have borrowed all of that from other people and it will be the worst shame imaginable to take back the bullets that she borrowed."

One hand on his hip, the other resting on his rifle, the Comanchero shook his head. "I don't know how Elena will be able to continue living here."

"But I didn't do anything. I wanted to trade the furs, that's all. I didn't mean to show her a lack of respect."

The guard stared in his eyes and burst out laughing. "I'm pulling your leg, *güero*! Elena is the prettiest girl in the village. It's not her you should worry about, but her husband, from whom she took the bullets, the bourbon and the turquoise!"

He left Pete alone and went to join the others. They had a funny story to tell about him now, the trade had been completed, and there was no further need for a guard.

Before joining them for the evening gathering, Pete went down to the river. He rubbed his skin with sand to get rid of the stink, and soaked and beat his dirty clothes. Then he put on a pair of trousers and a spare shirt that smelled of mildew.

The Comancheros were sitting around two big fires, over which they cooked meat and warmed up pans. Everyone was silent. Like their chief, they appeared saddened by the next day's planned departure. Rafael signalled to Pete to approach, but a man stood in his way.

"Are you the one who's got my turquoise?"

Pete took a step back, standing on the foot of another man, who sat behind him and prevented him retreating any further. Elena's husband put his face close to Pete's.

"It was nice of you to leave me the ammunition."

Laughter boomed around the campfires and Pete found himself with a bottle in his hand.

"*Dios!* My wife is so happy that I should at least have a few days of peace!"

Pete went back to his hut and returned with the bottle of bourbon, which he raised in the direction of the assembly and the husband, provoking a new burst of laughter. Elena, sitting apart with the other women, stalked off in a rage, her wolf fur over her shoulders. Pete sat next to Rafael.

"What happened to your leg?"

"It was a week ago. We were attacked by the governor's militia. I was hit by a bullet and I fell off my horse. Washington and Texas have decided to get rid of us."

"I thought you were just traders."

"And the army officers have done plenty of business with us. But it's politics, *güero*. Politics. During the war, we made raids on the Confederates. We stole horses and sold them to the Union. Washington was perfectly happy about that. After the war, we started trading with the Indians again. Only difference now is that they're at war with the Americans. So the government doesn't want us to sell them food, let alone guns or bullets. Without us, Quanah Parker and the last of his tribe wouldn't be able to survive. When we go to Mexico, he and his men will end up dead or they'll have to join the reserve at Fort Sill."

"The army gives free ammunition to hunters, so they can shoot bison."

"Politics, *güero*."

Pete lay back on the ground and placed the bottle of bourbon on his belly.

"So you're not Mexicans and you're not Americans either. What will you do on the other side of the border?"

Rafael took big gulps of his drink. For him, as for the other men around him, alcohol was a form of medicine tonight.

"Texas and California belong to you now, so our fate is sealed. The white men want us to disappear. Here and in California, Mexican families have had their land stolen from them. The government has passed laws that turn us into foreigners, like the Indians and the Chinese who built your railways and have been sent back home in boats. In Mexico, we'll be able to forget the English that you made us learn in your schools and we'll speak only our own language."

Seeking oblivion, Pete swallowed alcohol at the same speed as the Comancheros.

"What about you, *güero*? What are you looking for on the other side of the Rio Grande?"

Pete looked around him at these men swept aside by the advance of the Land Office's pioneers; he thought about the bison hunters pursuing the last of the prairie's herds; he watched Rafael, the wounded chief of this people, as he dissolved in regret. They were surrendering. They were giving up. The heat of the alcohol in his mouth made him want to spit. Drunkenness made him want to laugh.

"I want to know if I'm worthy."

Rafael turned to him and smiled. "Worthy of what?"

Pete did not respond.

"Are you looking for your destiny, *güero*?"

"My destiny?"

"The proof that you are stronger than yourself?"

The men around were speaking louder now. The alcohol had woken them, brought them back to life, but it was a joyless kind of life; their jokes sounded bitter and hard-edged. Pete could not understand what they were saying, but he sensed their aggression and felt himself sliding down the same slope.

"You can't be stronger than yourself. Only stronger than the others."

"You're looking for adventure. That's the sign of despair, *güero*. But you're brave."

"Braver than you!"

His voice had grown suddenly loud and, while not everyone understood his English, the tone had been clear enough to cut short all conversations. The Comancheros looked at one another. Rafael reacted calmly.

"There are too many of us here for us each to have a destiny, so we join together to share one. Sometimes men are strong enough to lead an entire people into an adventure. That's another form of destiny, a higher form. It is also more dangerous for the freedom of the people to follow such men. I am not the chief because I am an adventurer, but because I received an American education. I know that we have no destiny, that we can do nothing now but survive. You, *güero*, you want to act. You despise those who wait for something to happen, those who hope, just like you despise us tonight. But you don't know what despair is yet. Fighting against something when you know it won't change anything. Quanah Parker and his Comanches, they know. They are fighting against men like you."

Rafael stood up, supporting himself with his crutch, and advised Pete to get some rest and to leave them alone now.

Pete weaved his way between hostile faces. When he reached his little house, he leaned against the brick wall. His vision shrunk by drunkenness, he squinted at the lights of the campfires by the river.

By the time he woke, the families were already on their way, the mules and packhorses carrying the food reserves, barrels of water and personal belongings up the barranco then returning with their saddles empty to pick up what was left.

Pete filled his saddlebags, saddled Reunion and followed the last of the Comancheros. Higher up, on the plateau with its short grass, a dozen wagons were waiting. When they were fully loaded, they set off, moving away from the canyon like a colony of ants saving the eggs of a destroyed anthill. They followed the cliff southwards, the troop of horses bringing up the rear.

Incapable of riding in a saddle, Rafael was sitting on the back of a cart in the shade of a tarpaulin. Pete trotted beside him. The chief grimaced at every bump and jolt.

"We'll cross the Rio Grande in two weeks. You can come with us. The others agreed."

Pete doubted this, but clearly, for a reason he didn't understand, Rafael had used his influence to smooth Pete's acceptance by the convoy.

"Tonight we will meet with Quanah Parker's men. You should keep a low profile, *güero*, or it could cause problems."

Looking at the colour of Rafael's skin, Pete doubted he would make it to the border.

"What will happen if we meet the army during the trip?"

"Well sell them our merchandise. Then we'll leave. They'll let us go."

Rafael no longer had the strength to speak. He fell back onto the blankets that covered crates of guns.

They followed the canyon until afternoon and then headed east, descending from the plateau to the plain. The grass was increasingly yellow, the soil increasingly rocky. The wagons became covered with dust, and the wide river that flowed through the canyon kept branching out into ever-thinner streams that disappeared into the dry earth. Once again, the hills were far in the distance and the horizon was immobile. Two men on horseback rode off at a gallop, the convoy came to a halt in the middle of nowhere, and they quickly set up camp. The women began preparing dinner – the only meal of the day. The reserves must have been barely sufficient to reach the border. No fires.

When the two scouts returned, the horses and gun wagons were gathered together. Rafael divided the men into two groups: those who would stay to protect the camp and a larger number who would leave for the meeting. The chief's face turned pale as he strained to get into the saddle. Pete went over to speak with him.

"Will everything be O.K.?"

"Unless something unexpected happens, yes. If you stay at the camp, watch over our women and children until we return."

Pete nodded. "I can do that."

After the gun wagons and the group of Comancheros had vanished into the night, Pete stayed there with half a dozen men positioned around the camp to stand guard over about thirty people of various ages. He sat on the bench of a wagon, his Yellowboy between his legs. The women brought him corn tortillas and beans, as they did to all the guards. Everything was in order now, and the convoy was ready to go: animals fed, watered and harnessed. The man who had watched over Pete in the village came towards him and offered him some chewing tobacco.

"I prefer to smoke, but Rafael said no fires. My name is Ignacio."

They shook hands.

"Pete."

Pete slid a pinch of tobacco between his cheek and teeth.

"They left a long time ago. Is it always like this?"

Ignacio spat a jet of saliva and tobacco juice in the darkness. "It's been too long."

"What do we do if they don't come back?"

"They'll come back. There are too many men for the Comanches to attack them. But it's been too long. There must be a problem with the negotiations. Tomorrow we'll leave; they'll find us further on."

Ignacio returned to his post. Pete continued to slowly chew the tobacco while, somewhere, the last representatives of the Comancheros negotiated with the last Comanches of the southern plains, for one last cargo of arms. He remembered the wolf furs that the beautiful Elena had inspected, and thought that, if you held them up to the light, the skins of the Comancheros and Comanches must now be very thin. So thin you could see through them. The bison were disappearing, the Indians were disappearing, the Comancheros were disappearing. Furs and scalps. A nation of butchers.

At daybreak the convoy set off again without Rafael and the rest of the men. They had enough food for three days at most. Ignacio had told Pete that, in exchange for guns and horses, Rafael was supposed to return with more provisions.

"If the others haven't joined us in three days, we'll have to go to a fort and ask the soldiers for rations."

8

After three days without hearing from Rafael's group, Ignacio took over as the chief. The five armed men, the families left without fathers or husbands: they were all relying on him to lead them to Mexico.

On the evening of the fourth day, during which they had eaten almost nothing, the men lit a fire, despite the risks, and gathered around it. The women, the old people and the young white man sat in a wider second circle around them.

Pete was starting to understand a few words of Spanish. When he knew what the conversation was about, he could usually follow the gist of it. That night, there was no doubt about what the men were debating: how to reach the Rio Grande. Fort Sumner. Closer. The closest. A four-day trip. Ignacio shook his head. In addition to his reluctance to go near a military citadel, the four-day trip in itself was a problem. *Cazar*, to hunt. *Agua*, water. The same words kept recurring. And Rafael, the name of their chief.

But Ignacio no longer believed that Rafael would return. Too much time had passed. There were too many possible problems. Rangers. The army. Problems with Quanah Parker and his men, or with the Utes, the Comanches' enemies. We should wait for Rafael *al otro lado* – on the other side – said Ignacio. Cross the Rio Grande and wait for him in Mexico. That was the mission their chief had given him if he did not return. Ignacio's last sentence dropped into the silence: "*Y no volvió.*"

Behind him, Pete heard a voice, a whisper: "And he hasn't come back."

He turned. Elena, whose husband had left with Rafael's group, was sitting behind him. She had translated Ignacio's words for him. She drew back into the darkness as soon as she had finished speaking. Pete stood up.

"I can go and get food from the fort."

They all turned to face the *güero*, then those who did not understand English looked at Ignacio, who translated. Murmurs ran between the squatting figures.

"I'm white. The soldiers don't know me. If you give me a wagon, I can bring you back food."

Ignacio translated again, and men, women and old people all talked at once. When the hubbub had died down, half of the group stood up and walked towards the wagons. Ignacio approached Pete.

"Your idea is a good one, *güero*, but you won't go to Fort Sumner. Before the fort, on the Pecos river, there's the Chisum ranch. You'll be able to buy everything we need there. We'll keep going another two days together until we reach a river. There we can wait and hunt for the food we need until you return. We're collecting the money you'll need to pay for the provisions. One of us will go with you."

"You don't trust me?"

"We can't help being worried, *güero*, but it's also for your safety. Apart from me and Elena, Jorge is the best English speaker here. He'll go with you. You'll be part of a group of pioneers from Missouri. Nobody knows Jorge down there, so you can say he's your guide and that you need food for your families on your way to Santa Fe."

They put out the fire and the men stood guard with their rifles. Pete did not manage to sleep before it was his turn to stand guard. He stayed on a bench until daybreak, his eyes sore with fatigue. Their second day of fasting began. The last few rations of tortillas were distributed among the weakest. The convoy set off again and Pete volunteered to go hunting with Jorge – the man who would accompany him to the Chisum ranch – and another Comanchero, Esteban, a thin old man reputed to be the best hunter in the group.

The three horsemen headed west, tracking some barely visible footprints. A herd of buffalo or a stray male would have been their best chance, but Esteban was desperately hoping to come across a few pronghorns. If those American antelopes did not appear, then they would take anything they could find: prairie dogs, hares, rabbits.

The old hunter had a dented copper army telescope; on the first hill that they came to he stood up in his stirrups and scanned the land all around, then sat back in the saddle and shook his head. After a brief hesitation, he chose a direction – randomly, it seemed to Pete. They trotted straight ahead for about an hour, veered back to the west for another hour, then headed south without seeing a single animal, their arrival constantly heralded by the high-pitched chirping of prairie dogs. A few coyotes – inedible scavengers – scurried away and then followed them for a while before giving up, as if sensing that these hunters would have no luck.

Jorge did not appreciate the presence of the white man and was not at all happy that he was the one chosen to accompany this *güero* to the Chisum ranch. Pete kept an eye on him. Esteban pointed to a spot in the distance: a spiral of vultures and harriers a few miles to the north. They spurred their horses, and Reunion, who had not galloped for days, surged ahead, sharing with his rider a sudden desire to be alone.

The vultures were flying above a circle of grass that was thicker than the grass around it: the burrows of prairie dogs, whose tunnels and excrement fertilised the earth. Pete dismounted, crunched the lever of his rifle and bent forwards before slowly advancing.

In a small patch of squashed grass, an antelope was lying on its side, panting as heavily as a bellows. By its side, a fawn – no more than three days old – struggled to stand upright. The mother was dying and its flesh already smelled rotten. One of its eyes was opaque, covered with pus from a seeping wound.

Jorge pulled a dagger from his sheath, grabbed the fawn and slit its throat. Then he lifted it up by its hind legs to empty it of blood and, without waiting, sliced open its belly to gut it. The mother raised its head. Jorge dropped the fawn. He finished off the mother, then sliced it open and inspected its decomposing innards. He cut off a few still edible pieces of flesh and was suddenly surrounded by flies which, like the other scavengers in this apparently deserted plain, had appeared out of nowhere.

Meanwhile Esteban had followed some tracks and taken out his telescope. He came back quickly towards them after spotting the track taken by the herd that had abandoned these two animals. They put the twelve or fifteen pounds of meat – not nearly enough – into the saddle-bags and set off at a gallop. The tracks were clear and they spurred their horses to the point of exhaustion, then came to a halt at the foot of a low hill, not much more than a blister on the prairie's flat skin. Esteban picked up a handful of shit and smiled: the antelopes were close by. All three men turned at the same moment. A gunshot, then another . . . three or four rifles firing from the other side of the hill. Esteban stayed with the horses while Jorge and Pete ran off and climbed through the grass to the peak of the hill.

The herd, about thirty animals, was bounding fast towards them. Four soldiers in blue uniforms were riding behind them, firing rifles. A pronghorn was rolling in the dust. Sensing the presence of men on the hill, the antelopes suddenly changed direction and fled north-wards. The soldiers stopped when they saw this and looked up at the hill. Jorge and Pete flattened themselves against the ground.

Jorge began crawling backwards but Pete remained where he was. The Comanchero grabbed his boot heel and pulled on it. Pete did not react. His cheek was pressed to the butt of his rifle. Jorge pulled harder.

"They're scouts, *güero*, like us. If you shoot, the others will come."

The soldiers hesitated, unsure what kind of danger they faced. They were out in the open, at the foot of that small hill, and it would have been as easy to shoot them as ducks at a fair. Pete stared at the corpses of three pronghorns lying in the grass – enough to feed the Comancheros for two days – then put his eye to the viewfinder of his rifle and fired two shots above the soldiers. Their horses startled, and one of the riders turned and fled while the others searched for the origin of the shots. Pete snapped the lever on his Yellowboy and sent the earth flying just in front of their feet. He did not wound the horses. He let them go.

Esteban climbed the hill.

"*Qué pasa*, Jorge?"

Esteban saw the dust cloud and the four soldiers retreating, he saw the antelopes lying in the grass. Then he watched as Jorge lowered his head. Pete ran to his mustang.

"Hurry up!"

They rejoined the convoy late that afternoon. Pete untied the antelope from Reunion's rump and smiled at the women as they rushed towards it, crossing themselves. Ignacio patted Pete on the back and Jorge exploded: "*Maldito güero!*"

He yelled in Pete's face and as he explained what had happened the Comancheros fell silent, their smiles disappeared, and their faces turned towards the unfazed white man.

"It was that or starving to death. I'll go to the ranch on my own tomorrow. I don't need anybody with me."

Ignacio held back Jorge, who wanted to attack the *güero*. Pete grabbed the bridle of his horse and rode away from the wagons.

"*Güero*, you'll have to leave your mustang. The others don't want you to take it with you."

"The mustang stays with me. If I get into any trouble, he's my only chance of escape. I'm the one taking all the risk while you stay here."

Ignacio shook his head. "It's not courage we lack. Eleven men have already left with Rafael. These women are maybe already widows, these children fatherless. We can't leave them. After what you did yesterday, the soldiers will be looking for us. We don't have any choice now."

Pete repeated that his mustang would stay with him.

The Comancheros crowded around the wagon. Pete did not shake Ignacio's hand nor did he respond to the few waves offered by the gathered men and women. He urged the cattle up the track and the wagon lurched forwards. He would reach the outskirts of the Chisum ranch tomorrow. It extended over thousands of acres, so if he didn't come across any cowboys or herds, he would ride for another day until he reached the centre of the ranch. By then he would be close to the Rockies, and the passage to the west.

He heard a noise behind him, and, thinking that it must be Reunion, who was tethered to the back of the wagon, he turned. He saw a pair of ankle boots, a bare leg, a flash of fabric, a dress flying in a circle like a dancer in a saloon. He halted the carriage. Elena was holding onto the hoops. She crossed the floor of the wagon, heels tapping on the wood, and sat next to him on the bench.

"Go, before they notice I'm not there."

Pete did not move. "What are you doing?"

"That's a dumb question, *güero*. Now go. *Vámonos!*"

"Are you here to keep an eye on me?"

Elena snorted. "I'm here for the same reason you are."

Pete smiled. "What about your husband?"

"I have no children, *güero*. I'm not some *mamacita* with a fat horse's arse. My husband is a . . . a *mugroso*. He smells bad, he's poor, like all the others, and he's dead anyway. I can't believe they were stupid enough to give you a wagon and money! They are all going to die of hunger and I'm leaving with you, simple as that."

Pete looked at her. He whistled and the cattle shook themselves.

"You don't smell too great yourself, Elena. You need a bath."

She didn't blink. "Even if you had brought some food back, I would never have gone to Mexico, that peasant country, just to break my back digging in the fields."

"Whereas here you'll be a princess, right?"

She arched her back and puffed out her chest. "*Sí, güero*. A real woman."

"Oh, you're a woman, Elena, I don't have any doubts about that."

She laughed like a barmaid, as if she were about to burst into song.

"And you're a real man. Right?"

"We're a perfect match."

She was silent for a moment. She stretched out her legs, shook the dust from her clothes, and tied her hair in a bun. "You're not as dumb as I thought you were, *güero*. For a moment I actually believed that you wanted to save them."

Pete stared straight ahead. "They can hunt. They'll make it on their own, don't you think?"

Elena burst out laughing. "Find us some water. We need to wash tonight."

The green line of the stream glimmered before them. They approached as the sun set, coming to a halt under a mauve sky. Pete unharnessed the cattle and his mustang and let them graze by the riverbank. Their dirty clothes were sticking to their skin. Elena took off her poncho, unbuttoned her skirt, removed her ankle boots and woollen socks. Keeping her slip on, she took off her shirt and, bare breasts bouncing, pulled at Pete's boots. She unbuttoned his shirt and Pete grabbed the Colt from his belt and tossed it onto the grass. She pulled down his trousers. Pete slid into the cold water. Elena kneeled down behind him and, with her shirt rolled up in a ball, began to rub him, her belly and breasts pressed against his back. She may have been covered in dirt, but her gestures were as polished as a Carson City whore. Pete let her do it, his head leaning back on her shoulder. Elena's hand moved down to his erection. She dropped her shirt and caressed him before taking a firm grip. Pete put his hands on Elena's thighs, massaging her skin through the wet slip. When he held her more tightly, she stopped and put her lips to his ear. "*Güero*, we need to be further away from here for the next part."

She moved away from him and crouched down in the water, her back to him. She put her hands between her legs and washed herself. Pete rolled onto his belly, spread his arms and let the current pass over him.

She lit a fire and put the clothes out to dry. Then she took off her slip and, while she rolled it up in her poncho, Pete saw her naked, wet and brown-skinned. He smiled at how long it took her – a few seconds more than necessary – to cover herself. When night fell, she took some dried antelope meat from a bag she had brought with her. A good quantity, stolen from a family's share. Pete ate from his own reserves. They sat apart to eat, then she went into the wagon to sleep.

"*Buenas noches.*"

Pete lay down between the wheels. He tried to stay awake but he hadn't slept for two nights and he quickly slipped into sleep.

9

When he opened his eyes, Elena was standing in front of him, frowning. She was looking at him and probably wondering what she was doing here with this white man with no moustache, his wide body and his too-short limbs, his chest covered in ugly little curly black hairs. This white boy who slept like a child even with the sun high in the sky, who thought he was stronger than the men she had grown up with.

"Get up."

Pete stretched, smiling as he saw her turn away. He washed his face in the stream and put on his still-damp clothes while she harnessed the cattle.

They sat on the bench and set off again. Still groggy, his eyes gluey with sleep dust, Pete spoke without looking at her. "How far will I have to take you before I get the next part?"

"Out of sight of this plain."

Pete whistled. "We'll have time to get to know each other."

For two hours it remained cool, then at noon the breeze died and the sun began to beat down on the prairie, slowing down the thoughts in their heads. Elena had moved to the far end of the bench so as not to touch him. She pulled her poncho down to her hips and splashed her face with water from a flask.

"You want me to find another stream?"

She wasn't listening. She had sat up. Pete pulled on the reins. There were dark stains on the horizon, scattered across the pale yellow wash of the plain. He stood up, took off his hat and used his hand to shade his eyes. "It's a herd."

"I saw."

"This is the Chisum ranch."

"I know."

Pete checked that his Winchester was loaded.

"If we meet any ranch workers or soldiers, let me do the talking."

The cattle huffed and puffed for another hour under the hot sun before they came to the first cows: brown and white Herefords. There were several hundred of them in view. Pete waited, scanning the landscape from right to left. Elena became impatient.

"What are you waiting for?"

"Be quiet."

She gave a short, derisory laugh. "Are you feeling remorse? You can't save them, *güero*. It's too late. And if anyone could, it wouldn't be you. Just keep going."

She tried to snatch the reins from him. Pete slapped her.

"Stay here and don't make trouble. When I've caught two cows, you can leave and go find a job in a brothel."

He jumped off the wagon, grabbed his saddle and strapped it to Reunion. The coiled lasso dangled from the pommel. He took off his jacket, wrapped his Colt inside it, took out his knife and waited a little longer, searching the horizon to make sure that there were no cowboys around. Elena massaged her cheek. She looked at the cows and then at Pete. "What do you think you're going to do?"

At the Fitzpatrick ranch, Pete had taken part in the capture of several wild mustangs. He had never caught cows, but they were slower than horses and it wouldn't take him long to capture two or three of them. At worst, he could always take some weaned calves. He would take the meat back to the Comancheros and then go on his way. He could keep the money they had given him; he could tell them Elena had run off with it.

He rode forwards, remembering the bison and hoping that the cattle would be similarly stupid. He got as close as he could and spotted the first one he would try to capture. Reunion had been trained for this work; the mustang knew what he had to do, even if cattle were something new. Pete spurred the horse and set off at a gallop. The cow jumped and started to run. Pete kept his eyes on the target and began spinning the lasso above his head. He threw it. He thought he'd missed, but the rope slid over the beast's two horns and caught them. He let the slack out, coiling the other end of the rope around the pommel and riding alongside the cow. When it slowed down, he pulled hard on the reins and stopped, twisting the animal's neck backwards. It kicked out a couple of times then calmed down. Pete smiled. The cow spun round and yanked at the rope with its neck. Reunion lost his balance, the girth slipped, the saddle turned and Pete was flipped off the horse. Before he hit the ground, the cow managed to tear the saddle from the horse. His feet still in the stirrups, he was dragged over rocks. The saddle disappeared between his legs as the cow charged away. All the others fled too.

He rode bareback to the wagon. The left side of his face had been grazed and one sleeve of his torn shirt was hanging around his wrist. Elena was laughing. Pete grabbed the Yellowboy from the bench.

"What are you going to do, *güero*? Kill some cows so the cowboys can hear you for miles around? You don't know what the hell you're doing! You're going to get us into big trouble. Just take me to the ranch! You can buy some meat and leave me there."

Pete balled his fist, but at the last moment he opened his hand and slapped her face instead of punching her. Elena fell to the ground. Pete walked over to the mustang. He heard the hammer of a gun and remembered his Colt. He had time to turn around and wonder if that fury, lying on the ground was going to shoot or not. The answer came before he had finished asking the question. The detonation, the sudden shot of venom in his belly, his fingers trying to touch the wound, to grasp that electric shock, his head falling backwards, unprotected, and smashing against the wheel of the wagon.

Elena, presumably thinking that he might survive, was generous enough to leave him his horse, the reins tied to his wrist, before she fled. He untied the mustang and looked under his blood-soaked shirt. He decided to trust Elena: it was the first time he'd had a hole in his belly and he knew nothing about it, but evidently she had believed he would live and had quickly bandaged his wound. His belongings were there, his jacket under his head, its pockets empty. The rest of the Land Office money, the pay he'd received from McRae and Vimy, the Comancheros' money, the wagon and the cattle had all been stolen. His Colt and the turquoise had disappeared. All he had left was a handful of bullets and his Winchester.

Sitting up proved more difficult than reviewing his situation while flat on his back. He rolled onto his other side to spare his wound. Like a child learning to crawl, he fell flat on his face and bit dust. The blood started to flow again. The water in the flask – her final gift to him – was warm. The pain spread through all the organs in his abdomen, paralysing his hip and pelvis. Grimacing, Pete twisted his body so he could put his hand to his back. Elena had shot him from ten feet away and the .45's bullet had gone right through him. That meant it had not hit anything hard on its way – no bones, no vertebrae – but had found a passage through soft tissue. He managed to sit up at last but, incapable of holding himself upright, he bent over, lifted his legs and rested his forehead on his knees. He needed a better bandage to stop the bleeding, even though it seemed to free his stomach from a build-up of pain, like a burst abscess. He didn't like the idea of holding the blood inside him.

For a moment he stayed like that, curled in a ball, until his head started to spin and he thought he was going to faint. He slowly removed his shirt and tied it around his belly as tight as possible, so that he could hardly breathe, before putting on his jacket and buttoning it up to the collar. It felt reassuringly like he was wearing a narrow corset.

As he held onto the mustang's reins and pulled himself to his feet, it was as if he felt again, all at the same time, all the pains, blows, fractures and falls of his brief life. A cow's hoof on his leg, the plough falling on top of him, the recoil of his father's rifle the first time he fired it, which had dislocated his shoulder, the beatings the Old Man used to give him. Clinging to the horse's reins, he got to his feet. With his cheek to Reunion's thick, warm coat, he could smell all the miles they had ridden together, could feel the horse's reassuring presence, could breathe in his scent, the scent of the Fitzpatrick ranch.

Pete wrapped one arm around the horse's neck, the other around his head, and let himself fall, weighing down the animal until he bent his leg and kneeled down. Pete rolled onto his back and gripped his mane.

"O.K. Gently now."

The jolts the horse made as he stood up shook Pete's insides and he spat out bile, but at least he was on horseback now.

He urged Reunion back along the path they had taken to come here. On the way back he would find the stream where Elena had washed him. That was all he could think about now, the cold water on his wound. Each movement of the mustang's shoulders made Pete grit his teeth. Then the pain became a blanket in which he could wrap himself, a numbing heat. He found his place within it, and closed his eyes.

A distinct sound in the darkness. On his lips the salty taste of the horse's sweat. His arms were hanging either side of the animal's neck, the hair of his mane in his mouth. He patted the animal to check, then smelled something and lifted his head. The moon and the stars shone their light down on the whispering stream.

The mustang had faithfully followed the track. Now, head down, he was drinking. Pete tried to sit up. His skin was sticking to the bandage, the bandage to the fur of his jacket, the jacket to the horse's coat. He lost his balance, his arms and legs paralysed with cramps from clinging – a sleeper's reflex, just as it is a corpse's – to the horse's neck. His body remained stiff as it hit the ground. The gravel riverbank cushioned his fall. His head was in the water, which ran cold down his neck. He drank as much as he could, crawled away from the river and fell back asleep.

A fly tickled his lips. Pete opened his eyes. It was dawn.

The wound was mottled with blue and purple blood vessels around a scab that he carefully softened with water, gradually removing it from his skin. When the wound on his belly was clean, he did the best he could with his back.

Back when he was a kid in Basin, playing soldiers and Indians, he often heard the legend that, if you picked seven plants at random and mixed them together, you would obtain a medicine that healed the wounds caused by poison arrows. Pete crawled along the riverbank and collected a bouquet of about ten herbs, imagining that at least it wouldn't do any harm. He chewed them slowly until he had created a green paste. The plants had different tastes but the predominant one was bitterness; some wilted flowers with brown petals made him vomit. He turned one of the sweeter-tasting plants into a meal, first swallowing the juice then a few little mouthfuls. His stomach did not refuse the food: a good sign that the bullet had not done too much damage.

He waited until his shirt – which he had rubbed against some large flat pebbles – had finished drying, then he applied his child's remedy to the two wounds and tied the shirt around them, before filling his flask in the river.

Reunion kneeled down again, and he hoisted himself onto the horse's back. Most of the day had been spent resting and slowly, meticulously treating his painful wounds. Afternoon was melting into evening as they set off. Four days had passed since Pete had left the Comancheros. If they hadn't managed to hunt anything, they would have finished their reserves by now and would still be waiting in the same spot.

A day and a night; a journey filled with dreams of falls and jolts. The mustang stopped and amid the colours of the sunrise the smell of burned wood seemed like an olfactory hallucination, as if Pete's mind associated the blazing dawn with the odours of a fire. Then he saw the column of smoke drifting lazily up from the patch of greenery where the camp lay.

Some of the wagons were still burning: crumpled skeletons on circles of ash. Another one, still intact but with its cattle missing, had been abandoned in the middle of a small river after a vain attempt to flee. The people, like the animals, had disappeared. The grass was scattered with blankets and clothes, baskets and broken clay pots. Of the ten wagons they'd had before, half were missing.

Pete approached the devastation.

The blankets, he saw now, were covering bodies.

He slid off his horse, no longer aware of the pain, lifted up a corner of the wool and saw a grey face, eyes closed and lips drawn back. An old man. Pete recognised him but could not remember his name. There were four bodies: three of them old men, the other Jorge.

He found tracks of horses and wagons pulled by cattle heading eastwards: a troop of soldiers had taken the last of the Comancheros. A patrol sent this way after the skirmish with the scouts? Or just a squadron that had found them by chance?

Pete knew he ought to dig graves but he couldn't stand up. He crawled over to the water, sat in the grass and looked at the wagon with its wheels half-submerged, its torn tarp flapping in the breeze. He had been terrified that he would find children's bodies under those blankets.

He turned. A man was watching him, a ghost standing beside his horse, a rifle dangling from one hand. Esteban, the old hunter, stared at him empty-eyed, mouth half-open, as if wondering why he had been forgotten. Pete went over to him, holding his stomach.

"What happened?"

Esteban looked at the blood-soaked jacket then at the *güero*'s face.

"*Soldados.*" He didn't speak a word of English. He turned eastwards and raised his rifle. "*Los llevaron a Fort Dodge. Los soldados. Había salido a cazar. Habían desaparecido cuando volví.*"

Esteban had gone hunting; he hadn't seen; he wasn't there. They had gone. The old man stared at Pete's belly again.

"*Qué pasó?*"

"Elena."

Esteban blinked. "*La mataste?*"

No, Pete had not killed Elena. He shook his head and pointed towards the west. "She left, with the wagon and the cattle."

Esteban did not react. He stood there, motionless, watching the white man.

"Where will you go now, Esteban?"

Pete repeated the question, but the old man no longer seemed to hear him.

"Mexico?"

Esteban repeated the word: "Mexico." Then he walked into the river with his boots on and climbed onto the abandoned wagon. He returned with two flasks that he filled in the current. He emerged from the river with his boots full of water, which made sucking sounds as he walked, climbed into the saddle and waited.

Pete pushed Reunion onto his knees and clambered onto the horse's back.

IO

The blood had drained from old Esteban's face: his skin was grey and his lips and forehead were peeling like the bark of a dead tree. He was like a burned log that had preserved its outward shape but which would be reduced to ashes by a single breath of wind. He didn't eat, he offered his flasks to Pete, he didn't answer the *güero*'s questions about which way they should go or how far they were from the Rio Grande. Pete told him to go hunting – for anything, even rodents – or to dig up roots they could suck because they wouldn't last long in the saddle like this, but Esteban continued riding on in silence. Pete tried to shout but the pain in his belly was louder than his voice: "Go hunting! *Cazar* . . ."

Esteban looked at the blood on Pete's jacket, then at his face, which would soon be as pale as his own. "*Maldito.*"

In the evening, he treated Pete's wounds. He rinsed off the plaster of prairie herbs without saying anything, then took a sachet of yellow powder from a canvas bag and moistened it in his palm before carefully spreading it over the two wounds. After that, he got on his horse and rode away. Pete fell asleep, gripping his rifle in both hands, Reunion's reins tied to his ankle. At dawn, when he opened his eyes, Esteban was waiting in the saddle. They set off again, staring at the burning sun as it rose to their left.

His wound hurt less now, but he was weakened by the absence of food. His tongue was swollen and cracked, and the water bottles were empty. The ghost of the Comanchero rode twenty steps ahead of him, no longer even holding the reins of his horse, which was hunched up with fatigue and covered with dust. Pete squinted at his silhouette the way he would squint at the needle of a compass. His eyes closed and then opened again in a dazzle of white light. Esteban was no longer there. Pete looked behind. He had passed the old man while he was unconscious; Esteban had fallen from his saddle and his horse, unthinkingly, had stopped beside him. Pete turned around, slid off his horse and squatted next to the Comanchero. He lifted the old man's head and rested it on his leg. He shook a water flask but not a single drop came out.

"Where's the next river? The border? Esteban, the border? *Agua*?"

Esteban exhaled. His breath smelled of rotting meat. He'd bitten his tongue as he fell and a thread of blood had dried at the corner of his mouth. He lifted his hand towards Pete's face but stopped before touching it and pointed a bony index finger at his forehead. "*Maldito*."

Pete pushed the old man onto the grass and lay back with his hands on his wound. He stared at the blue sky and listened as the dying man muttered: "*Tu culpa, güero. Maldito. Elena putana. Maldita.*"

Pete kicked him. "Shut your mouth!"

Then he rolled onto his side to protect his face from the sun. Thinking of Rafael, he wondered if dying like this in the prairie was worthy of being considered a true destiny. What kind of life had old Esteban had lived? How many children, how many grandchildren? How many times had he already thought he was dying before he reached this age? Pete crawled over to him, put his hand on the old man's hollow chest and shook him, putting his face close to the stinking mouth. "Are you scared of dying, *viejo*?"

Pete had never imagined his own death before this day, not even in the Sierra Nevada with his brother after they ran away from the line of conscripts marched off to war like prisoners. That mad dash into the mountains, the cold that numbed their hands and feet, the endless winding paths. The deep snow that he dreamed about now: just a handful to put in his mouth, to feel it melt on his tongue. Not even when they were hiding in those holes in the rock had he believed they would die, not even when their breathing was so weak that it didn't steam beneath the frozen army blankets. Because he knew that they would eventually reach the end of the path, and that something was waiting for them on the other side. And then there had been the lake and the ranch nestling between the mountain peaks. Pete felt again the sensations he had felt during their ride through powder snow to the doors of that barn where they took refuge: the heat of the horses between their legs, beneath their bellies.

Pete looked at Reunion, who was dumbly waiting to die with him. He banged his fist against Esteban's chest. "I don't want to die! This is your fault! You and those bastards in your stinking tribe!"

The old man coughed and choked. He looked up at the young white man who was hitting him, and raised an arm. Pete saw the thin index finger tighten, trembling, in his direction, he saw Esteban's lips move. He kicked at the old man with all the strength that remained in his legs, rolling the inert body onto its front with his boot heels. Not another word came out of the old man's mouth, not another drop of saliva. Mummified, all that would remain of him was a skeleton cursed by another.

"Wake up."

Three dark figures loomed over him, blocking the sky and plunging him into shadow. The one who'd spoken squatted down and Pete recognised Elena's husband. He wanted to sit up, but his head fell back. The husband helped him into a seated position. He felt as if there were a ball of scrunched-up newspaper stuck in his throat. His eyelids were sticky with scabs. He grabbed a flask from someone's hands but it fell from his own. The husband raised it to his lips and poured a few drops into his mouth; they burned his gashed tongue. The man repeated his question in English: "What happened, *güero*? Where are the others?"

Pete managed to say: "Esteban?"

Elena's husband shook his head: "*Muerto*."

Pete reached out for the flask. He drank a few more drops and felt his mouth and throat relax. "*Soldados*. The army. Fort Dodge. Prisoners."

"What were you doing here with Esteban?"

Pete drank some more. "Went hunting. Came back too late."

There were five men around him now. The husband looked at his waistcoat.

"Why are you wounded?"

Rafael appeared, leaning on his crutch. "*Déjalo, Felipe. Póngalo en el carro, no podemos quedarnos aquí.*"

He had the impression that each of the four men who lifted him up were carrying away a piece of him, that his legs, his arms and his torso were separated, floating through the air yards apart. They laid him down in a wagon, in the shade of the tarp. Pete felt a presence all around him. Eyes watching, dark and shining. Children. A dozen perhaps, shoulder to shoulder, crammed together at the end of the wagon that had transported the crates of weapons and ammunition. He heard the reins snap and the wheels start to turn. Indian children, not mixed like the Comancheros, little savages of four or five, girls and boys, the oldest ones maybe ten years old.

For six hours they did not speak a word. The youngest ones slept, but when the wagon stopped they all woke up. Two men helped Pete to get down and supported him as he walked to the edge of a stream. Rafael's group had not suffered any losses. Pete asked what the children were doing there, but no-one answered him.

Four sentries were posted to the four cardinal points around the convoy. Rafael limped over to the white man, his arm still in a sling. The Comancheros' chief, whom Pete had thought close to death, was still hanging on.

"Tell me, *güero.*"

Pete cupped some water in his hands, he rubbed his face and neck. He said that the convoy had turned westwards when they started running out of food. That Jorge wanted to camp by the river and hunt while they waited for Rafael and his men to return. Ignacio had not agreed.

"He said you would meet us on the other side of the Rio Grande. Others said there was only one solution: go to Fort Sumner and surrender, ask for food to save the old people, the women and children. While they were trying to decide, I went hunting with Esteban."

Pete looked over at the wagon. Rafael's men had got the children down and were tying ropes around their waists. Rafael showed no interest in the Indians.

"You say the others were taken to Fort Dodge?"

There were yells trapped in Pete's throat; river pebbles that stopped him breathing while he watched the roped-up kids being given food rations.

"What are you doing with them?"

The Comanchero chief gave an irritated glance at the children. "They're the reason we lost so much time. Quanah Parker didn't have enough money to pay for the guns. The negotiations went on for a long time. Finally the Comanches told us to wait three days; they set off on an expedition and brought back the children in lieu of money. We can get a good price for them in Mexico. Did the soldiers come from Fort Dodge?"

Pete concentrated on his lies. "That's what Esteban said when he saw the tracks . . . You're going to sell them?"

"What happened?"

"There were a few dead. Three old guys and Jorge."

Rafael thought about this. He stared at Pete, who was watching the children. "The Fort Dodge troops had no reason to look for us here. I don't understand."

"You're selling children?"

"Who shot you?"

His belly tensed. Pete wanted to attack Rafael. Pain soaked his chest with sweat.

"Esteban."

"Old Esteban shot you?"

"He wanted go to after the soldiers and the prisoners. I tried to argue him out of it. He lost his head, he grabbed my pistol and fired. We walked for three days. He treated my wounds. I knew he was dying. That's when you found us."

Rafael stared out over the stream. He looked sad and resigned, the way he had been when Pete met him for the first time in the canyon. He looked as if he were searching this immense landscape, where nothing could be possessed cheaply anymore, for reasons to believe the white man's lies.

"I'm going to send someone to Fort Dodge to find out what happened to our families. We'll cross the Rio Grande in less than a week. In Mexico, you'll be under our protection."

Rafael did not need to say that it would be useless to attempt to flee.

"Where are the parents of those children? You think they're looking for them too?" Rafael limped away on his crutch. Pete yelled: "Or maybe the Comanches killed their parents before trading them for your rifles?"

Two Comancheros took his hunting knife and helped him walk to the wagon, where they threw him between the wheels with the sleeping children.

The fugitives lit no fires. The sky was overcast in the evening and the night was black, and as cold, it seemed to him, as all those nights he had spent in the plains after long, hot days.

The children, used to his presence by now, started whispering. Their smell filled the humid air: a musky mix of the leather they wore, the bison grease that smoothed their hair, their foul carnivores' sweat, the whole of it like the spray of a polecat. The odour of a butchering camp.

Pete leaned on the metal hoop of a wheel. In the darkness he could discern the children watching him, wondering what a white man was doing here with them.

"Good night."

Pete's voice made them jump. He curled up around his wound and closed his eyes, listening to the breathing.

—◇—◇—◇—

The Old Man.

By the end I was spending whole days in the living-room chair, suckling the bottles you brought, drinking as much as I could so I wouldn't be able to stand. Oliver still spoke to me but you hadn't said a word to me in two years – the time it had taken you to grow big enough. Two years of seeing your eyes reach the height of mine, your dark eyes looking into mine and then down on them. So I shrivelled up. Sitting in the chair I waited for the bottles and shrank back when you came close. You had gathered rage, anger and strength from sucking up mine.

I don't remember why I decided to get up that night rather than any other. Maybe I'd run out of alcohol. Maybe I was heading to the dresser to get more and instead of stopping in front of it I opened the door of your room. I don't know. But I was on my feet anyway, ready without knowing it.

You were sleeping on the floorboards rolled up in a blanket, keeping guard at the foot of Oliver's bed. Against the wall was the rifle that you had taken from me.

I stood there in silence, watching you. I was hoping you would wake up.

I thought about shaking you so I could talk to you but you wouldn't have listened.

I picked up my rifle; it wouldn't do me any good, but here men have rifles. Otherwise they're not really men, defending their land and their family.

Barefoot in the snow, I walked to the barn, my gun in one hand, a lamp in the other.

I didn't think I had the courage to make that walk on my own. My eyes were shining, Pete. And I said to myself that at least I was leaving you that, the courage of having done it. For most men it's a cowardly act, but for a father like me it seemed like my last chance. You'd take care of Oliver. You'd been doing it for a long time, in my place.

I didn't hear you following me. Were you only pretending to sleep? Did you know? How long did you hide in the barn, watching me do it? Watching me lean the ladder against the wall, climb up to the ceiling, tie the noose, attach the rope to the beam. My feet were blue with cold and they trembled on the ladder. My fingers were so numb they could hardly bend the stiff hemp. I was shaking all over, from my head to my feet, and I was crying because nobody could stop me. That was the saddest thing, Pete, thinking that nobody would even want to talk me out of it. Nobody except your little brother, who you'd left sleeping in the house. Putting my head through that noose was a duty and I was sad that this was the only way I could prove my worth.

Before I stepped off the ladder, before the rope tightened around my neck, I sucked up as much air as I could into my fear-crushed chest. It was instinct. I knew I should have emptied my lungs instead to shorten the suffocation and hasten death, but maybe I wanted to give myself one last chance? To give somebody time to arrive?

In a single contradictory urge for life and death, in a single show of fear and courage, I took a deep breath and stepped off the ladder. Would I regret that breath that would make me live a few seconds longer? Would I be alone, waiting for a witness?

The lamp was at the foot of the ladder where I left it – to illuminate what? – and I saw you approach my feet through the red and purple blurs of my bulging eyes.

You didn't climb the ladder to cut the rope, Pete.

You didn't think I was worth saving.

My legs kicked the air. I was scared.

What were you thinking about, my son, as you watched me shake? That I was responsible for the death of your mother? Your mother who was too beautiful, too gentle, too kind for me? That you and your brother had grown up in fear and it would finally be over?

I reached out to you with my hand. Do you remember, Pete, when you were a little boy and I used to hold your hand? It happened. Not many times, but I remember.

I was hanging from the rope and my hand touched the ladder. I didn't let it go after that.

You didn't shed a tear as you watched me die. You stood and in your balled fists you held the hands of your brother and mother. My other hand, the one hanging dead, fell into my father's – your grandfather's – who hit hard too, and he was holding hands with another old man, and him another, a line of old men on the other side of the ocean.

I was still holding your hand after I couldn't see you anymore and the blood had cooled in my temples. I held onto the memory of my family, the ladder, that ascendant power that lifted me up while gravity dragged me down towards the earth.

Did you see my lips move?

I didn't want you to climb the ladder, I only wanted you to listen to me. My eyes closed on you. I had poisoned your life. You poisoned my death.

But we weren't quits, for all that.

You had to make me talk, had to dig up my grave and make my jawbones move.

Silence poisons the words that it replaces.

We need to talk, just like one day you'll need to talk to your brother. Do you think he doesn't know?

Men shouldn't have their share of responsibility taken away from them. What would become of them without it? Mothers are not judged, fathers are: their value will be their children's too. I don't know what kind of man you've become, but are you sure you've really understood, Pete? Do you believe that the Fitzpatrick ranch has turned you into another man? Because that woman, Alexandra, taught you to read and write? Because that old soldier Bowman showed you how to scrawl out your anger on paper?

You wanted to run away; you brought this on yourself. The Old Man is in you. Under the rain of blows, you had no other choice than to become me to protect yourself.

Listen to those poor little children sleep. It's not a peaceful sleep. They have the rope of fear around their necks.

I can't help you – you and I can only fight each other – and yet I'm the one you called. You can't hang all the kidnappers on your own, Pete – the Comancheros and their chief.

You would have followed that Rafael a long way, wouldn't you? For a while there, you thought you were him, and you brought misfortune to his tribe. And on your shoulders now weigh the sins of the bad father that I made of you.

Tonight, Pete Ferguson, in your solitude, you want to believe in ghosts, just like those little Indians.

II

They broke camp after a quick ration of meat and water. One of Rafael's men, his saddlebags filled with food, set off at a gallop towards Fort Dodge. According to Pete's calculations, he would be there in two days. Four more to catch up with this little convoy – more or less as they would reach the Rio Grande. He had until then to regain the strength to ride a horse. Rafael had put a Mexican saddle on Reunion's back and the mustang walked slowly as he would have done for his owner.

Wedged against a railing, blankets around his back, Pete faced the crowd of children. Their silence and their expressionless faces made them seem stupid as they sat there, swaying from side to side. He wondered if they understood what would happen to them, then he realised that war and raids and kidnapping had been part of their lives for a long time. They were resigned, maybe, but not one of them had cried since the night before and you should always beware a child that holds back its tears. The Comancheros treated the little Utes like real prisoners, not only because of their value but because they knew these kids were dangerous.

They were intrigued by the white man. They watched as he untied his bandages, rinsed his wounds, wetted the yellow powder and rubbed it over his raw flesh. When he had finished, he put the flask down in front of him and used his foot to push it towards the children. The oldest girl opened it and passed it to the youngest ones. The oldest boy, when his turn came to drink, continued to stare at the white man as he poured the liquid down his throat.

"You speak English?"

There was no answer.

In the middle of the day, Felipe dropped some goatskins of water into the wagon, along with a jute bag full of grey pancakes so rancid that Pete couldn't swallow them. The Utes devoured them.

At night they set up camp in the middle of some shoulder-high bushes. The Comancheros rolled up the tarp and took down the hoops from the wagons so no-one would see them. No fire, no water. Soldiers, rangers, Apaches or Utes: Rafael and his men were in enemy territory. The sentries stayed close that night, the animals saddled and harnessed, the prisoners in the wagon – except for Pete, who was taken to see Rafael.

"How's your wound?"

"Better."

"You'll heal."

"And then?"

"Do you have something to tell me about what happened?"

Pete ignored the question. "I was wondering if killing a man meant having a destiny. You said there were too many of us for each of us to have a destiny, but there aren't so many of us who have killed someone."

Rafael looked at Pete curiously. "Have you killed a man?"

"Yes."

"I think that would depend on the reason that you killed him."

"Self-defence."

"Your life was in danger."

Pete laughed. "Oh yeah."

"Then that's not a destiny, *güero*, it's an accident. It's natural to want to live. You'd need other reasons for a death to change the course of a life."

Pete turned towards the children. Rafael followed his gaze.

"They don't understand what we're saying."

"They understand everything."

"Maybe."

"I killed my father."

Rafael took a step back, weighing Pete up, trying to get a better view of him in the darkness. "That's an unforgivable crime."

"And selling children?"

"They'll be treated well. In the Indian wars they're the spoils, but their new masters will respect them. The Indians took children and women long before we came here."

"So it's a tradition . . . What will you do with them, if nobody pays the price you're asking?"

"You should worry about yourself instead. You have a lot less value than they do."

As they headed south for the border, dark and pointed shapes appeared before them: they were moving towards the mountain sources of rivers that divided, weakened and shrank on the slab of desert from which they had just come. Pete's wound had scarred but it was still hard for him to move freely.

The Comancheros had stopped speaking to him. The horseman who'd been sent to Fort Dodge would return within three days at the most.

The convoy was now jolting along the green valley of Cienega Creek. The night before, Pete had heard the men talking about a town at the valley's end: Presidio, on the border. The vegetation was growing higher and higher here; they were riding in the shade of tall trees.

Pete turned his eyes away from the valley. The oldest of the boys was pulling at his sleeves. When he'd got Pete's attention, he elbowed the boy next to him, who thrust his hand under the leather of his tunic and handed him a roll of fabric. The older boy, glancing at the back of the wagon, unfolded the packet, which contained a large butcher's knife. The child placed it on the wooden base of the wagon and shoved it with his foot towards Pete, who hid it under the heels of his boots. The kid said softly: "*Mañana, Mexico.*"

The Utes knew as well as he did that, once they crossed the border, they had no chance of escape. They thought this man, from that power-ful white tribe, would be able to help them. Pete Ferguson, who could hardly stand, slid the wrapped knife inside his boot. The kid nodded, naively believing in his plan: that a wounded man and ten kids would escape from the Comancheros. With this knife, Pete might be able to get away. Alone. He nodded.

"*Esta noche.*"

At the confluence of another river, Cienega Creek opened out into a wider valley; in the middle of this valley ran a path covered with the tracks of wheels and hooves. The convoy turned east, away from this well-trodden path. The Comancheros urged their animals on until they had climbed the side of the valley, and came to a halt in the shade of a block of pale rock veined with purple lines, just like the clouds in the west as the sun went down. The prisoners were herded off the wagon and shackled. The dilated sun disappeared behind the mountains and night crept into the valley like a mist. At the end of this blackness, they saw the lights of a town glittering: the town they had all been nervously awaiting. They would reach the border tomorrow morning, within three hours.

Behind them were the desert and the plains. From east to west, the Rio Grande, Indian tribes and the army's border patrols. For Pete too, the town was the only way out. The Comancheros would not go there, with their cargo; they would take a more hidden passage along the river. They had set up camp in front of a big rock and were observing the town's lights as they worked out their own plan.

The children waited, bound together. Pete was tied to a wheel, his hands behind his back. The ten-year-old chief was there in the darkness, breathing fast. Pete could see his eyes shine.

"The knife."

The boy twisted himself and grabbed the knife from the white man's boot, then passed it to one of his better-placed comrades. Pete felt the blade rub in clumsy strokes against the rope that bound his wrists. The steel slid over his forearm and he felt the skin open, a little draft of cold air, then the warm blood flowing. The rope snapped. He freed the oldest Ute boy and the knife was quickly passed from one kid to the next until they were all free. Pete held the chief's arm.

"We can't flee together. You understand? It's impossible. You leave now, quick as you can. Head for the town."

He pointed at the lights.

"*Ciudad. Entiendes?* I can't go with you. Head for the mountain and hide. When the Comancheros have moved away, you can go to the town. You'll find help there."

The child nodded but didn't move. He tugged at the white man's sleeve. The sparkle in the boy's eyes reminded him of Oliver, clinging to him as the Old Man approached. Pete wanted to yell at them to run, to vanish while they had the chance. The little chief whispered: "*Con nosotros.*"

Pete seized him by the back of the neck and pushed his forehead against the kid's. "If we go together, they'll find us. I'm going to lead them away. Now go!"

He pushed him away and the boy fell onto his backside. The others froze.

"The knife."

The boy handed him the weapon then, looking anxious and murmuring, the children began to move, leaving their blankets behind in a heap. Pete listened, his eyes on the silhouettes of the Comancheros. He waited an hour for the children to get away, then started to crawl. With the knife handle between his teeth, he bit down into the wood whenever his wound rubbed against rocks. The cut in his wrist, deeper than he'd thought, left a trickle of blood behind.

The horses awoke at the approach of this strange, human-smelling snake. Pete cut the lead ropes of each one, then held onto Reunion's leg and stood up. The horses waited for the snake to tell them what to do. He saddled the mustang. He was nervous, and that nervousness spread through the horses. The snake was up to something. One of those things that horses helped men to do: tilling the earth, charging at cannons, setting fire to houses, pursuing and trampling on children.

The animals snorted and stamped the ground with their hooves. The creature that crawled and bled made a groaning sound as he climbed onto the mustang's back and the other humans stirred. The horses decided to flee with the man that was shouting: sounds of urgency and danger. Which direction? Follow the mustang, which was carrying his wounded master through the darkness, heading down to the coolness of the valley and the river. They saw the shining water and the path, the bushes and the rocks, as the men, blinded by the night, fired rifles behind them; the horses recognised the voices of those who fed and beat them and they continued to run from the whistling of the bullets.

The mustang and its rider who stank of fear were galloping ahead; they had reached the path and were heading nowhere, it seemed, but have the voyages of men ever meant anything to horses? They ran, breathing heavily, for three miles, until they came to another fork in the river. There, the snake-man stopped the mustang and started shouting again. What did he want this time? He whipped their rumps with his reins, yelling orders that said: *Go, run, scatter!*

The horses ran in circles. Reunion reared up and Pete clung tightly to the pommel of the Mexican saddle. The Comancheros' horses disappeared eastwards into the little valley. Pete spurred his mustang and followed the path towards the border town. By the time the Comancheros had found their horses, he would have reached the Rio Grande. Rafael and his men would search for the children first. They were worth more. With a bit of luck, the little Utes would also be out of reach by then.

12

Presidio del Norte at dawn was a dirty town, abandoned to the stray dogs that raced and yelped their way into the colonists' dreams. Pete Ferguson and his mustang crossed the town that led straight to the Rio Grande: a flow of turbid water rushing past the end of the only street. On the banks of a misty bend, Mexican ferrymen were sleeping on the floor of their boat. They startled awake when Reunion's horseshoes clanked against the wooden boat. They cried out as they saw the rider and his horse, both covered in dust. Still half in a dream, they quickly got off the ferry.

Pete swayed forwards, his chin on his chest. Reunion shifted his weight from one leg to the other and the movement threatened the rider's balance. The Mexicans turned towards the deserted street, wondering what army could be chasing this ghost. The man stared at the opposite bank. The ferrymen crossed themselves and sat close together so they could row in rhythm. The swirling water made the horse totter as its rider leaned forwards, arms dangling either side of the animal's neck.

The ferry hit the Mexican riverbank. The ropes were fastened and the ferrymen waited – not for money, but simply for the ghost to disembark. They were certain that this horseman was a soldier from the Guardia Blanca, the phantom army that attacked the poor and devoured the Indians, an assassin from the Guardia who'd got lost in the land of the gringos and was now going home. The horse stepped out of the boat and its worn shoes touched Mexican earth. The ferrymen immediately rowed back the other way, washing the large bloodstain from the floor of their boat with water from the Rio

Grande. They turned back to stare at the pale figures of the man and his horse, waiting immobile at the end of the straight main street of Ojinaga, opposite the straight main street of Presidio del Norte, as if they expected the country to wake at their arrival.

Pete, on the verge of unconsciousness, wondered vaguely if crossing a border almost dead from hunger and thirst, with a hole in his belly, was worthy of his destiny as a cursed son.

He came to in a room with rammed earth walls, lying on a wooden bed, wrapped up in a thick wool blanket that was soaked with sweat and stank of goat. An old woman, putting her hand into a jug, was watering the ground to clump the dust into balls. Rays of light filtered between the slats of the window blinds and the planks of the door. From a shadowy corner, sitting on a stool, one elbow on a table next to a hat, a white man was staring at Pete. The man turned to the old woman, said something in Spanish and stood up, leaving a coin on the table. The old woman bowed as she opened the door for him. The light burned Pete's eyes, so he lifted the blanket to cover them. The old woman cooled his forehead with wet flannel and he felt her rough fingertips and drops of water trickling down his temples. Words whistled between her toothless gums in a language that was not Spanish. She held a bowl of lukewarm, bitter liquid to Pete's mouth; the taste reminded him of the herbs he'd chewed in the plain.

A week passed in this room in sudden alternations of blackness and dazzle. He slept and woke streaming with sweat when his fever rose, then sank back into sleep as into a hot bath. He dreamed of old Meeks clinging to his leg in that alley behind the Eagle Saloon. He dreamed of his father's legs kicking the air like an animal caught in a trap. He dreamed of Rusky's face charging towards him, knife in hand, and of old Esteban with his grey lips whispering *maldito*. When he woke he was gasping for air and he pushed away the blankets until he trembled so hard that he had to cover up again.

The old woman brought him drinks and changed the bandages on his stomach, his back and his arm, where the Ute boy had caught him with the hunting knife. The man in the hat came to sit by the table every day. He asked the old woman questions and then went away, always leaving a coin on the table.

The fever receded and he was left with only pain. Pete's muscles were coming back to life: his neck began to move a little more freely and he started exercising – head forward and knees lifted – to make his stomach muscles work. After a few days he could sit on the edge of the bed and, by holding onto the wall, get to his feet. He lost balance and fell backwards and started over, repeating this until he could stand up without the support of the wall. He managed to walk over to the table and sit on the stool, and then he waited there for the old woman to return. She said nothing about it, sliding her shoulder under Pete's arm, and he held on tight to this thin old body that was, nevertheless, more solid than his own. The old woman's black wool clothes smelled of urine and grease. Pete was hungry. Lying on the bed, he put his hand to his mouth.

"*Hambre.*"

She brought him a bowl of black broth with beans floating in it. Pete's throat burned when he swallowed the first spoonful. The next day he walked to the table then turned around and went back the other way, before collapsing onto the bed. When he'd recovered enough strength, he got up again, went to the window, pried apart the blinds and, using his hand as a visor, looked outside. A courtyard, some chickens, a brown-brick bread oven, a pyramid of corncobs on a blanket, and a stone mill. He saw other houses and other bare gardens, without fences, and the dark figures of women under a white sun. He could hear a river flowing. Further off, beyond the wasteland surrounding the houses, he could see green fields and other figures, bent double, working. He closed the blinds when the sunlight started to give him a headache.

The man in the hat came in the evening and found Pete sitting at the table, wiping his plate with a tortilla.

"Is the food good?"

The man spoke English. His hair was grey at the sides and closely cropped. He was dressed in a suit that was startlingly clean for this dusty town. His skin was white – protected from the sun, just as his clothes were protected from dirt – except for his sharp cheekbones, which were red with rosacea. The señor must spend a lot of money to remain this white in Ojinaga. Pete put his plate down and nodded. The man smiled.

"I'm glad."

"Who are you?"

He held out his hand. "Javier Mendes."

Mendes had a weak hand, but he squeezed hard to make it clear he was an honest man, and placed his other hand on top of Pete's. Pete was wary of theatrical handshakes.

"You're looking a lot better."

"What do you want?"

Mendes shrank back slightly and opened his arms wide, palms open. His face tensed in a brief irritated grimace, but he changed his expression straight away, as if forgiving an old friend for his brusqueness.

"To help you."

"I don't need your help. I'll pay you back the money that you gave to the old woman."

Mendes inspected the bed and decided not to sit there.

"And how do you plan to pay me back? You don't even have a horse to sell now and you won't get much for that Mexican saddle. I think, on the contrary, that you do need me."

"Where is my mustang?"

Mendes looked sorrowful. "Your horse was hit by a bullet. It died on the quay, where we found you. It was a beautiful animal; I understand your disappointment. But that brings me back to the help that I am offering you. Many things have happened since you arrived here. Dramatic events."

Pete was no longer listening to Javier Mendes and his undertaker's voice. He was on the ranch with his brother, in the eastern fields, when he saw Reunion for the first time – a two-year-old colt. The son of

Trigger, Alexandra Desmond's mare, and Walden, Bowman's mustang.

The day Pete left the ranch, Alexandra had told him: "You'll need this horse. Reunion will always find his way back here."

Reunion, who had brought him all the way to the Rio Grande before falling. Now their tracks, from Lake Tahoe to Presidio del Norte, had been erased. He would never find his way back.

The Pete Ferguson of Carson City was dead, declared missing, swallowed up by a river along with his horse. A new Pete had appeared alone on the other side. Mendes kept talking, and his words brought Pete back to the little earthen room.

"What?"

"On the Mexican side."

"What did you say?"

"I said that bodies were found on the Mexican riverbank. The American authorities don't want to know about them. *Mierda Mexicana!* We must deal with them on our own."

Mendes wrinkled his nose. He looked as though he were about to spit.

"What are we supposed to do with them, huh? We're not the ones waging war on the Comancheros. The Americans blame us, but all this is their fault."

Pete's vision blurred. "What happened?"

Mendes opened his arms again. "The prisoners must have escaped; the Comancheros went after them. The children wanted to cross the river. There have been drownings before at this part of the river. The Rio Grande looks calm, but it's deeper than it appears and the currents are strong. We fished out seven corpses. There may be others that were swept further downstream. The same day, the Comancheros arrived in Ojinaga. I hope you will forgive me, young man, but I took the liberty of hiding your presence from them. That silence cost me a little, but tell me: did I do the right thing?"

"They're here?"

Javier Mendes picked up his hat and gave a satisfied smile. "I told you that you needed my help."

"What did you do with the children?"

"The bodies we found were buried in the cemetery."

Pete walked to the bed and put on his boots.

"What are you doing?" Mendes asked.

"I'm going to the cemetery."

"I don't think that's a good idea."

Like a leper led by a nun, Pete walked with his arm on the old woman's, a blanket over his head, as she guided him past gardens and courtyards to the edge of the town. They went past fields irrigated by water from a river that flowed from the south. Ojinaga had been built in the elbow of the Rio Grande and one of its Mexican tributaries, so while the town itself was sad and dusty, the countryside around it was a fertile paradise. The cemetery was surrounded by eucalyptus and fig trees that cast protective shadows onto the graves. There were wooden crosses, sculpted stone crosses, white-painted mausoleums designed to look like miniature steeples or palaces, and, at the back of the cemetery, below the dry-stone wall, the mass grave, its earth freshly turned. The old woman halted. Pete let go of her arm.

"Go away."

He pushed her and fell to his knees and she left the gringo there, with the blanket covering his head.

Pete returned to town at nightfall. He was feverish again. Javier Mendes was waiting for him in the old woman's house.

"How many are there?"

"Of whom are you speaking?"

"Comancheros. Is there an injured man with them named Rafael?"

"Rafael is here, yes. With eight of his men." Composing his face into a sad expression, the Mexican tried to find the right words. "Rafael is a trader who has . . . well, let's say a lot of influence on this side of the border."

"A competitor?"

Mendes applauded with his soft hands as if he had finally found the answer to an old problem. "Exactly!"

He sat at the table, chin on hand, and frowned, pretending to think.

"You seem very moved by the death of those Indian children. I understand: it's a tragedy, in a way. And I have no doubt that Rafael and his band, even if they didn't kill the children, are responsible for their deaths."

"Stop bullshitting me."

Javier Mendes feigned offence. "I beg your pardon?"

"You didn't pick me up in the street out of the goodness of your heart. You're a scavenger. You knew I was running from the Comancheros. What would you give to be rid of your competitor?"

Mendes dropped his act and smiled, happy that the negotiations had begun. "If you have grievances with these men, that is none of my business. Why would I offer you anything? That would make me an accomplice to your vengeance."

"I don't need an accomplice, or a commander either. All I need is a weapon and the chance to get out alive after it's done. You'll get what you want for almost nothing."

Javier Mendes took off his hat and looked inside it for a moment, as if checking one last point on a list that was written there.

"A horse for your Mexican saddle. New clothes. Thirty American dollars. And, as a gesture of goodwill, I will pay for the ferry that takes you back to your homeland."

"A horse, clothes, a revolver, money. No need for the ferry. I'm heading south."

Javier Mendes stood up. "Are you sure you're up to this task? If you fail or you are taken, can I rely on your silence?"

Pete snorted. "The police in this shithole must like you a lot. I doubt you have anything to worry about on that score."

Mendes held out his hand and smiled. "I knew my investment in your health was a good one. Once Rafael is dead, you'll have what you need to go all the way to the end of Mexico if that's what you want."

Pete ignored the proffered hand. "Where are they?"

Mendes slid his thumbs into the pockets of his waistcoat. "You've only been in Mexico two weeks and already you have made dangerous enemies. You should watch your manners. They're at the hotel."

"Bring it all tomorrow afternoon."

The old woman brought him the clothes, wrapped around a leather belt and a Remington double-action revolver. The clothes, like the gun, were second-hand. There was some underwear, a pair of cotton canvas cowboy trousers, a beige flannel shirt, and a waistcoat that was too small for Pete. He asked the old woman to clean and mend his own leather waistcoat. The green felt hat was round and wide-brimmed. When Pete put the clothes on, he looked like a Mexican peasant who'd won a small bet.

He dismantled the revolver and cleaned it piece by piece. It was a Civil War weapon, six bullets in the cylinder, a dozen more on the belt. He reassembled it, put it on the table and waited.

Javier Mendes returned as the churches of Ojinaga were calling the Indians, the mestizos and the Spanish to vespers. The horse he brought, a pony with a Spanish saddle, was grey.

"A *galiceno*. He'll take you wherever you want to go. Only ten years old and he's voice-trained. Obviously he doesn't understand English though."

Mendes was proud of his purchase. The horse appeared in good health, if a little heavy. Pete walked around it, patting its muscles, opening its mouth, checking the horseshoes.

"Alright. Tell me."

"Rafael and his men are on the second floor of the Rio Azul hotel. He's in room 21. There's a back entrance."

Lamps and Chinese lanterns shone from the buildings' facades. Waves of laughter rolled from swing doors out to the street, where kids played chase, imitating men by striking macho poses. The town of Ojinaga, a refuge for human debris from both sides of the Rio Grande, echoed to the sound of musical instruments and the high-pitched voice of a man recounting local folklore with the enthusiasm of a tired whore.

Mismatched couples emerged from cantinas arm in arm; shopkeepers and smugglers drank on balconies; from their little station, the policemen of the *guardia rural* waved to passers-by; the brothels were half-empty, and the girls in their windows looked worn out. It was a half-hearted sort of night, and it wouldn't last long.

Pete tied the grey horse to the stables behind the hotel, next to the horses of other clients. With the blanket draped over his head, he went to sit on the steps of a closed shop opposite the Rio Azul. In one hand he held a terracotta plate that he'd borrowed from the old woman. No-one threw a single coin in his begging bowl during the two hours that he spent there, drinking a bottle of whiskey.

The Comancheros sat at a table at the back of the hotel restaurant. Elena's husband and the others were there, a taciturn group, their faces distorted by the glass in the bay windows, but Rafael was absent. They quickly ate their meal, and the restaurant, like the others in the street, started to empty. A waiter went upstairs with a tray. Pete saw him appear at the lighted window of the first-floor landing, then the second.

Walking slowly, head covered by the blanket, he crossed the street and went behind the hotel. Next to the stables he found the door that Javier Mendes had described to him. He went in and walked through a corridor that was partly illuminated by the lights from the restaurant, then stopped next to an open door. He glanced in at the kitchen, where a woman or a girl was washing dishes. Pete waited until she turned away from him and then he advanced. He had reached the lit part of the corridor; the staircase was to his right. He lowered his head, and, for a fraction of second, before climbing the stairs, his silhouette passed through the light. He took the stairs two at a time and followed the candlesticks on the wall to the first-floor landing. The rooms were silent. He kept climbing until he reached the second floor and found room 21. He walked to the corridor's sash window and, before opening it, blew out the closest candles, then he stepped over the ledge. Below, he saw the lit-up street; on the pavement opposite, some policemen had opened a bottle. He crept along the cladding, in the shadow of the roof, until he reached Rafael's window.

The Comancheros' chief lay under blankets. His meal was on the bedside table, untouched. He was pale and glistening with fever.

A noise in the corridor. Pete crouched down. Someone knocked at the door of the room and he recognised Felipe's voice: "*Jefe? Necesitas algo?*"

Rafael made an effort to raise his voice: "*Me descanso. Mañana, Felipe.*"

"*Mañana, jefe.*"

Felipe moved away. Pete remained where he was, motionless. He was waiting for the other lights to go out, for the police to finish their bottle and go back inside the station. Ojinaga fell asleep and the light of the candles in the room flickered and dimmed. When his legs started hurting and the cramps in his stomach became unbearable, Pete stretched, cocked the Remington, and stood up. Rafael was in the same position, curled up even more than before. He was sleeping with his mouth open. Pete opened the window and put one leg inside. He carefully brought his foot down on the floorboards, then his other foot, listening to the wood creak. Eyes riveted to the bed, he pulled the curtain shut behind him and crossed the room. He went behind Rafael's back, picked up a pillow and raised his gun. The Comanchero slowly turned to face him.

"I didn't know if I'd ever see you again, *güero*."

His lips were dry and white. He stared straight into Pete's eyes. Pete didn't blink.

"The children drowned trying to escape you."

"If it wasn't for you, they'd have found new families and we would be with ours." He lay back in the bed. "Get on with it, *güero*, before this disease steals your little destiny."

He was still staring into Pete's eyes. Pete pressed the pillow to his face and buried the barrel of the revolver in the feathers, tightening his fingers around the butt to stop his hand trembling. Rafael yelled, his voice muffled: "What are you waiting for? You killed your own father! *Parricidio maldito!*"

The explosion deafened Pete and the recoil thrust his weak hand up towards the ceiling. The candle blew out. A smell like burned chicken and powder filled his nostrils. White flakes of down drifted slowly downwards in the darkness. He dropped the Remington, crashed over the windowsill and collapsed on the balcony. He hung from the railing and let go, landing heavily on the ground and rolling in the dirt street. There were yells from upstairs in the hotel. The grey horse was waiting for him.

Above the cemetery, the silver leaves of the eucalyptus trees danced in the moonlight. Javier Mendes was waiting, a man at his side, a wagon harnessed to mules hidden in the nightshade of the trees. The Mexican commander rushed over. "Is it done?"

Pete turned back to look at the town and nodded. "I lost the Remington. Do you have a gun? I need to leave now."

In the silence that followed, he looked away from the lights of the town and saw Mendes' pale suit, just visible in the darkness.

"What's wrong?"

"I am afraid that going south will not be enough."

"What?"

"I told you Rafael was an important man on this side of the border. Maybe I didn't make clear just how important . . ."

"What are you talking about? Give me the money!"

"You won't get far. Rafael was in business with the police and the army from here to Chihuahua."

"Give me the money!"

"Go with this man. He works for me. You have no choice."

Mendes took two letters from his pocket and stuffed them in Pete's hand, then he whistled. Behind the low cemetery wall, a small figure appeared. It jumped over the wall and joined them: a kid, his head barely reaching Pete's shoulder. Mendes pushed him forwards and the boy put his foot in the stirrup of the *galiceno* and galloped away.

"Rafael's men will waste time following him. Get in this wagon with my employee. Tomorrow at daybreak, read the letter that is addressed to you. The second one is a letter of recommendation to one of my partners. It would be a shame to lose the services of a young man with your abilities."

Remembering their previous encounter, Mendes did not offer his hand. His employee was already sitting behind the mules and calling anxiously: *"Venga! Venga!"*

"Some day, Mendes, someone will find another loser in the street and he will come for you. And he'll be even cheaper than me."

"Venga!"

Pete jumped into the back of the wagon.

13

Pete Ferguson sat on the sand of the riverbank. The sand was clumped together with a clay mud where stubborn shoots of green reeds struggled from the briny water. It was low tide and this sandy tongue shone with potholes of water where trapped fish waited for the sea to return. The crocodiles had left their hidden nests in the tall vegetation to gather food. They slid into the fish-filled puddles while, in the still wet bed of the Panuco river, the heads of otters nervously appeared and disappeared. While the reptiles binged, the otters were safe. Tails flickered, jaws snapped, and fish spurted out of the pools in jets of silvered water to land on the mud. The crocodiles swallowed them in a single mouthful then returned to the pool until they had eaten everything that moved.

Pete turned when he heard branches crack. A male, fifteen feet long, emerged from the reeds, its skin covered with dried mud, and headed towards the other crocodiles; the smaller ones moved out of its way, leaving the fish as tribute. The male passed about thirty feet from Pete without even looking at him. When crocodiles have fish, they don't bother attacking bigger prey; or so said the inhabitants of Tampico, who did not come out to watch the monsters eat, only occasionally with rifles so they could shoot them in the head and sell their skins.

The boat would leave the next morning. Pete had come here one last time to see the crocodiles. Daylight was fading and the pools would soon be empty. He stood up, and the reptiles, beginning their digestion, watched him with their small eyes, the points of their scales shining in the sun. Pete threw the bottle of tequila in the mud. The sea was back and the otters had vanished. He followed the path that led from the lagoon to the town.

Javier Mendes' man had driven him to Monclova, in the State of Coahuila, hidden in his wagon under Indian blankets, stinking leather bags, jewellery made from bones and pearls, and traditional clothes traded for food or alcohol by starving Indians; an innocent-looking cargo for a tradesman like Mendes. Pete had suspected that there was something else hiding under those piles of trinkets. Mendes' man – Benito Juan Alfonso Guerera, as he introduced himself – had given Pete a rifle, which he kept close to hand during the six-day trip to Monclova. Benito was probably relying on his passenger to protect the goods, but Pete continued to keep an eye on the Mexican. While he looked like a simple-minded muleteer, it was possible had been ordered to deal with the gringo. Pete had killed for money. Mendes might have decided to rid himself of this burdensome witness. But Benito was what he appeared to be: a simple man who transported Indian junk (and an American fugitive) along discreet paths and didn't ask questions.

Pete had read the letter in the envelope that had also contained the promised thirty dollars. Javier Mendes had a ship-owning partner in Tampico who did some shady business in Central America and was always on the lookout for "solid men". Pete had grimaced when he read the word "solid": he had felt weak since leaving Ojinaga and was worried that he had caught Rafael's sickness. He was sore, frail and trembling, just as he had been before carrying out the murder.

The second letter was for the ship-owner, whose name was written on the envelope: Aznar.

For a week he had lain on the blankets at the back of the wagon as it travelled through Mexico. His wounds had healed but he couldn't sleep. He had improved his Spanish vocabulary, quickly memorising this new language. He paid careful attention to pronunciation and accent, learning it like a child, imitating sounds first without even trying to understand what they meant. Imitation was a survival strategy he had developed during his years with the Old Man. The more words he learned, the safer he felt.

In Monclova, Benito had given him a leather bag taken from the wagon and had told him to keep the rifle. Then the two men had shaken hands outside a coaching inn.

For one American dollar, Pete had travelled on a stagecoach pulled by ten horses that was headed towards Saltillo. The journey to Tampico was supposed to take twelve days. He wore his Mexican hat as the coach bumped along the San Luis Potosí track. In Matehuala he had changed to a different stagecoach company and headed in a different direction – to Ciudad Victoria, the last stage of the trip before the coast.

Pete had travelled a thousand miles through Mexico, watching the country unfold through the windows of stagecoaches: arid land scattered with cactuses, edged with bare mountains. This was the dry season, he'd been told, but he doubted that a drop of rain had ever fallen on this land. The paths followed the flattest route through the hills, cutting villages in two as they baked in the sun, as if the American deserts continued on forever on this side of the border.

And then, as the path approached the sea, the landscape had started to change. Fields, rivers, green mountains: a fertile land. The clothes changed too, as did buildings and faces, and Pete realised that the deserts they had crossed were only one part of this country whose size was unknown to him; that the rest of the world must be much bigger than he had ever imagined. He'd been told that it would take weeks to reach the country's southern border from Tampico, and that most Mexicans had no idea what it was like down there: the immense mountains and tropical forests, those evergreen lands inhabited by Indians, descendants of the Mayans, whom no white man had ever yet encountered. This country was so vast that it was a mystery to its own people.

It was early December when he arrived in Tampico: a medium-sized town with a mild climate, the air humid and salty, with its wrought-iron balconies and its stone buildings, its port on the Rio

Panuco, one mile from the estuary. Pete had slept in a shabby little inn, imagining that this was where he belonged as a fugitive. The managers had been apologetic, embarrassed to have a white client in their unworthy hotel. The next morning he'd rented a horse to take him to the ocean. He'd spent the day sitting on a beach, watching the sea for the first time in his life. Pete sat in the shade of some trees, his head spinning. The immensity of the world seemed to make his flight infinite and he felt he would never learn enough words to say all this.

He went into town, to the port where he'd been told that Captain Aznar's ship was moored.

It was a two-mast sailing ship, about a hundred feet long. The captain introduced himself. Javier Mendes' partner wasn't much older than Pete: a rich kid, he thought, playing at trade with his family's money. Like all businessmen in this country, he spoke English. Aznar read the letter.

"You've got the wrong Aznar. My father is dead and I've never heard of Javier Mendes."

Pete walked away.

"Hang on." Aznar's son caught up with him. "I don't work with my father's former partners. All that's left of him is this boat. I transport merchandise and sometimes passengers. Are you looking to go to sea?"

Pete looked at the boat. "Yes."

"We'll be leaving in a week for Puerto Barrios, in Guatemala. There'll be stopovers at Veracruz and Cancún."

"Guatemala?"

"The trip to Puerto Barrios lasts a week. Bed and board is eighteen dollars, and you'd have your own cabin."

Aznar paused. Pete waited.

"In the letter, this Mr Mendes writes that you could be useful. He says you did him a service and we can trust you. What's your line of work?"

"I can train horses and kill bison."

Aznar smiled and held out his hand. "Call me Segundo. Come back tomorrow. I'll show you the boat. Have you ever sailed before?"

Pete looked at the boat again. Impressed, he decided there was no point in lying.

That evening, he started drinking in the inn. Then in other bars around town, cantinas that grew smaller and dimmer as he went. An American dollar laid flat on the table ensured a good welcome from the bar owners and the curiosity of the other drinkers: toothless men who spoke no English, to whom Pete told the stories of the three men he'd killed. The first one in a barn, when all he did was watch; the second out of fear and to save his own life on the vast American plains; the third in a hotel room to wipe out his sins – three men who gnawed away at him, who made him feel hollow inside, an emptiness that he filled with alcohol. The Mexicans banged their fists on the table, laughed as they listened and refilled their glasses.

He spent his second night in Tampico sleeping on the streets, a few feet away from the last tavern he'd visited. There, he had shoved some men who didn't answer his questions.

Early that morning he walked to the port and stood on the quay next to the *Santo Cristo*. Aznar said nothing about the state he was in and invited him to have a coffee on board.

The young captain showed him around the boat. Pete stared wide-eyed. A schooner. He tried to remember a few words. Topsail, fore-mast, topgallant sail, shrouds, bowsprit. An American boat, built using French designs for a fishing boat. The *Santo Cristo* had participated in the 1848 war against Mexico and had then been disarmed and sold by the U.S. Navy. Segundo Aznar had inherited nothing but debts and a bad reputation from his father; all he had left was this schooner.

The ship smelled of varnished wood, hemp rope, sailcloth. Aznar showed him the holds and the cargo being loaded on board: dismantled printing machines, crates of ink and paper. He was going to Guatemala to deliver equipment, bought second-hand from Mexico, for a newspaper. During the stopover in Veracruz another passenger would come aboard, Aznar told him: the founder of this newspaper and a well-known Guatemalan poet.

Pete hung around the port and then, following the riverbank back to the town, saw for the first time an enormous scaly lizard, ten feet long. He had leaped backwards, thinking that he must be hallucinating. Someone explained to him that it was a crocodile, like the ones that lived in Africa, which Arthur Bowman had told him about one time.

He spent the rest of the week watching these monstrous creatures during the day, finding a semblance of calm in their company as they ate fish and basked in the river mud. At night he drank in the cantinas and drunkenly picked fights with equally drunk Mexicans. One night he took a prostitute of indeterminate age back to his inn and slept with his nose close to her sour-smelling armpit. Each day, too, he went to visit Segundo Aznar, who continued to welcome him without asking questions.

The cargo was soon loaded onto the ship. They were just waiting for the last pieces of the large rotary press.

The day of the departure, he went to see the crocodiles one last time. He drank tequila while he waited for them to eat every fish in the pothole pools. In his nostrils he could still smell the scent of eucalyptus trees, the odour of the dug earth in the Ojinaga cemetery, the stink of those red-stained feathers floating in the air.

The water was so transparent that in the shallows Pete could see the schooner's shadow moving along the seabed. This water seemed no denser than air; sailing through it was like a dream of flying, vertiginous, from which you woke by falling. The ship slipped away from the coast and the sea became darker and more turbulent. Pete's stomach shrank, his head grew heavy. It hurt to move his eyes and his tongue was dry.

"Stay on deck," Aznar advised him. "The boat doesn't move so much in the middle. Stare at the horizon. By tomorrow you won't be seasick anymore."

He sat against the wall of the wheelhouse and breathed through his nose, keeping his mouth shut to stop all the alcohol he'd drunk in Tampico surging back up and out.

There were seven crew members on the *Santo Cristo*, in addition to the captain. Another passenger had come on board the night before their departure, a man that Aznar had not mentioned to him. This man stayed locked in his cabin. Once they had safely left the shore, some sailors began cleaning and tidying the ship while others went down into the hold or the kitchen, painted varnish onto wood or mended the sails while glancing at the trolling lines thrown over the rails. They were discreet, obeying the orders of their young captain without a hint of rebellion. Pete ended up getting used to the ship's movement and the weight in his belly lightened. They were due to arrive in Veracruz at night: a quick stopover, said Aznar, just enough time to pick up their new passenger. The other man already aboard made his first appearance on deck late that afternoon. He was a middle-aged man, well-dressed, who smoked a pipe and greeted Pete with a slight nod. He looked at ease on the boat. Aznar went over to him and the two of them chatted for a moment.

Pete was served dinner in his cabin. He ate a little, then finally fell asleep, waking a few hours later when he heard sounds of agitation up on the deck. Through the porthole he could see the lights of Veracruz and he rushed upstairs to watch. The *Santo Cristo* sailed past the giant black walls of a fort, which seemed to emerge straight from the water. After the discovery of this country's vast size, the first sight of the Veracruz citadel proved another shock. He thought about the adobe and wood forts of the American army, then of the little low houses in Carson City and of its ignorant inhabitants, for whom the world ended at the county line; he thought of Arthur Bowman, who had travelled the world when he was younger and who avoided the people of Carson like the plague because they had seen nothing and yet believed that their hometown was the only place in the world worth seeing. The fortifications in Veracruz – with its stones older than the United States – would have scared the life out of those regulars at the Eagle Saloon.

The schooner entered the harbour and they moored it to the deserted quay. Pete could make out the dotted lines of warehouses, cocooned in sea mist, by the milky-white light of the lanterns that hung from their walls. There were no curious bystanders at that time of night, only two port officials in uniform who talked with Aznar for a few minutes in the faint halo of a storm lamp. Pete saw him hand a few banknotes to the men, then he raised his lamp and swung it from side to side several times. The sounds of metal and wheels clanked along the cobbles of the quay and a horse-drawn carriage came to a halt in front of the *Santo Cristo*. A man in a long overcoat – the Guatemalan poet – shook Aznar's hand and two sailors helped him to climb the gangway ladder. As soon as he was aboard, the mooring ropes were loosed. The ship passed in front of the high walls and Pete stayed on deck until dawn, breathing in the pure sea air until the last remnants of alcohol had been purged from his blood.

At breakfast time he went down to the saloon, the biggest room on the ship. Eight people could sit around the red wood table, but the only ones there now were Captain Aznar, the passenger with the pipe, and the one who had secretly boarded in Veracruz. The three men watched Pete come in and greeted him. He walked around the table. The first passenger introduced himself:

"I'm pleased to meet you, Mr Ferguson. My name is Alberto Guzman."

Then the poet, who was at least ten years older than Guzman, gave a broad smile. "Eduardo Manterola."

Aznar, Guzman and Manterola were all white in complexion. They all spoke English, and other languages too perhaps. When the sailor who was serving them left the saloon, a silence fell around the table. The three men ate quickly, as if to get this repetitive necessity over and done with. The poet wiped his moustache and tossed his napkin on the table.

"So you are a traveller, Mr Ferguson. Do you know Paris?"

"Paris?"

"In France."

Alexandra Desmond was from France. She used to mention it sometimes, nostalgically, the way Bowman would mention Asia or England.

"No."

"But perhaps you heard about the events that took place there last spring?"

Pete put down his cup of coffee; it was made of porcelain and he found it hard to get a grip on the too-small handle. The question had not been asked in the usual tone of travellers getting to know one another. Pete looked at Captain Aznar, who lowered his eyes. The poet, Manterola, started cleaning his glasses, and it was the man with the pipe, Guzman, who took over from him:

"The revolt of the Parisian people, the brief establishment of the Commune and its pitiless repression, Mr Ferguson."

Aznar broke the tense atmosphere by saying with a smile: "I don't think Mr Ferguson has had much opportunity to read newspapers recently. Isn't that right?"

Guzman did not leave the question unanswered for very long.

"Unlike Captain Aznar," he said, "I know Javier Mendes. I wonder what service you could have performed for that blackguard, Mr Ferguson."

So, Aznar had told the other two about the letter; Pete watched each of them in turn.

"What are you going to do in Guatemala?"

The poet put his glasses back on. Apparently he couldn't see a thing without them.

"Things."

Guzman: "Are you a man of action, Mr Ferguson?"

Aznar locked the door of the saloon.

The poet: "Or a man of principle?"

Pete smiled. "Are the two things mutually exclusive?"

"One or the other is enough for us."

Pete sat back in his seat. Glancing through a porthole, he caught sight of the swell of the sea and noticed the movements of the *Santo Cristo*, which had slipped from his awareness.

"Why do you need a man of action? Or a man of principle?"

The three men had already weighed the pros and cons; this

conversation was merely the final step before their decision. It was the poet who spoke next. "While our Communard comrades in Paris were fighting, the liberal revolution took place in Guatemala." He paused, and smiled scornfully. "It put an end to the reign of Carrera, that uneducated swineherd, and of his successor Sandoval. Granados, that *philosophe éclairé*, was elected."

The three men all smiled.

"Granados the liberal . . . The people believed his words, all his promises of reform. But the country is run by the same men as it was under Carrera's tyranny. The people are starving to death and all the land is in the possession of a few men. Granados is the puppet of masters whom the liberal revolution has neither stopped nor changed. This tyranny is even more pernicious than the last one, because it is flying the flag of the people."

The poet's eyes were shining, while Gruzman tried to find even stronger words and the captain looked as though he wanted to laugh. Pete rolled a cigarette, scraped a match on the exotic wood and took a drag. His hand was trembling slightly and he put it on the table to hide this fact.

"A man of action is paid for his acts. Why do you need me?"

Guzman looked at Aznar, then at Manterola, who nodded.

"We have money, Mr Ferguson."

II

I

Guatemala, April 1872

The *Santo Cristo* approached the coast by night again, this time the coast of Guatemala. Puerto Barrios, the country's only port, was squeezed between British Honduras – a Victorian enclave – and Honduras. Each border was about twenty miles from the port, which was the Guatemalans' only access to the Caribbean. Segundo Aznar negotiated with the customs officers for a discreet landing for his passengers and his merchandise. Wagons arrived quickly, and twenty-odd porters immediately got to work, unloading the pieces of the printing press. Pete got into a stagecoach with Manterola and Guzman. Drawn by the horses, they left the port and the town before dawn, cantering along a black earth track that led into the country's interior.

Daybreak was monochrome and flat, a line of orange above the hills, and the temperature instantly grew stifling.

There they were: the forests Pete had heard about in Mexico, those mountains covered by giant trees, exhaling grey and blue wreaths of mist into the floors of the valleys. Log bridges spanned the whitewater streams that poured from the mountains in torrential veins, carrying broken branches. They passed Indians – on foot, or on donkeys or mules – as they made their way along the track, but nowhere did they see any cultivation, as if this land were good for nothing, the forests too dense, the ground invaded by clumps of parasite plants or creepers. Their stagecoach passed successive waves of mountains and forests. The carriage was obviously not a form of public transport: the drivers did not pick up any other passengers and they changed horses twice, buying food at the coaching inns, which they then brought to their passengers.

Pete was not allowed to get out of the stagecoach and walk, except for those times, always at night, when he could take a few steps towards the inn. Each time, standing on the path, facing the forest, he listened to the incredible chorus of insects and frogs that drowned out the voices of men.

Their destination was Antigua, a town about an hour west of the country's capital, Ciudad de Guatemala, which they took great care to avoid. They arrived after six days of travelling.

Antigua was a hill town surrounded by volcanoes, where the air was cooler and fresher than it had been on the track. They had spent the past two days climbing steadily to this altitude.

At the entrance to the town, Guzman left the carriage and shook the old poet's hand. They arranged to meet one week later, when the *Santo Cristo*'s cargo had reached Antigua. Manterola and Pete were dropped off outside a small, two-storey building on avenida Norte: a yellow facade with white-painted corbels, on this wide street with its loose polished cobblestones. A woman, almost as old as the poet, opened the wrought-iron gate. She greeted Manterola, calling him Maestro and rejoicing in his return after months away. Manterola introduced her to Pete.

"Señor Ferguson, my new secretary. Mr Ferguson, may I introduce you to Faustina, without whom this house and I myself would have long ago been in ruins."

The old servant greeted the young American without bothering to conceal her hostility or her irritation that the return of the Maestro should be spoiled by his presence.

His fingers wrapped around a small glass of rum, the poet stared out at the Plaza de Armas with its crowd of merchants, beggars and people strolling around outside the cathedral square and the arcades of the Palacio del Ayuntamiento. Manterola did not drink much, and the glasses that he would sometimes swallow as impatiently as a child tended to make him sombre and anxious. Like most of his fellow citizens, he was a sad drunk. But in the absence of Aznar, Pete preferred his company to Guzman's. Behind his spectacles, Manterola's eyes shrank as they scanned the square below.

"He who has never seen a crowd turn on one of his comrades does not truly know men."

His lyricism grew bitter after a few drinks. In the final stage of his sadness, his anxiety would turn to disgust for his own kind. He waited for Pete Ferguson to react. But the young American, dressed in a new suit, was busy watching women walk by.

"A few years ago," the poet went on, "in this very square, a mob of poor people stoned and burned an Indian girl, about fifteen years old, whom they accused, with her husband, of having kidnapped a muleteer from rue Insurgente. The palace guards did not intervene. She shielded her face from the stones. You could see the bones of her arms through the skin. She fought like a fury under the bales of flaming straw. Her hair . . ."

A man stopped by their table and put a hand to his hat. "*Buenos días*, Maestro."

Manterola ignored this uninvited guest, who moved away without protest. Pete ordered two more rums. He liked to listen to the poet spew out his contempt for the world.

"This mire is the reason we fight. All these ignorant people . . . it is our duty to help them become something better."

Pete smiled and Manterola turned back to the square, his teeth bared.

"When the mob burned that girl, Carrera was still the ruler of Guatemala. But does anyone really believe that under the reign of men like Granados, crowds of honest people will no longer stone women? A chief does not change his subjects. Sometimes I still harbour the hope that the subjects will change when they have no chiefs at all and they are free. But the revolution also feeds on this violence. It is a dream of new men, but it exploits their old flaws. It wasn't Carrera who set fire to those straw bales, it was the future heroes of our revolution. There are some who hide so they don't have to see such spectacles, hoping that their conscience will leave them in peace, like that man you told me about, Bowman, who has retreated from the world. There are cynics – like you, Señor Ferguson – who take advantage of any situation. And then there are the genuine nihilists, those who laugh at stagings of the great Shakespearean theatre, sitting in the front row so they can set fire to the decor. But the suffering is real, Señor Ferguson; real people inflict it and real people are its victims. It is our duty, as poet and revolutionary, to sing the song of suffering and resistance, come what may."

Drops of rum trickled from the corner of Manterola's mouth. Pete finished his glass.

"You've had too much to drink, Maestro."

"It is easy to judge politicians corrupted by power when knowledge makes men pretentious and cowardly. That is what you are saying, is it not, Señor Ferguson?"

Manterola stood up, leaning on his walking stick. Pete buttoned up his waistcoat and paid for the drinks.

"I'm not sure Guzman would appreciate hearing you talk like that."

The Maestro gave a tired laugh. "Guzman does not believe in doubt. He is like Robespierre."

They left the Plaza de Armas and walked down a perpendicular street. Other bourgeois men and women greeted Manterola, but it was Pete, grinning under his hat, who nodded in response. The old poet ignored them and they took this as an eccentricity of genius when the truth was it took all the self-control he had not to spit in their faces. Eduardo Manterola was an official poet of the liberal revolution, acclaimed by the government, dashing off romantic verses on progress and peace between peoples. He was published and discussed. He also wrote for clandestine Latin American newspapers under other names: polemical tracts exalting the land and its men, excoriating those in power and the injustices they perpetrated, denouncing the liberals as the puppets of Europe. Perhaps the doubts that the Maestro nursed about human nature were based on his own hypocrisy. The poet did not always pretend to enjoy his life in society, nor in the past – or so it was whispered in Antigua – the young women, young men and money he'd possessed. After a few drinks, Manterola hated his court of toadies, but most of all he hated himself for having succumbed to its temptations.

They disappeared down alleyways further and further away from the centre of town until they reached a guarded building. Here, they went through a door and down a staircase to a vast cellar where the roar of the printing presses shook the demijohns of ink on the shelves. Guzman, fingertips stained black, his face pale in the lamplight, was revising the next issue of *Grito del Pueblo*.

The poet slumped down on a bench, hands crossed on his walking stick, and watched the energetic little man in glasses, his pipe no longer lit but still in his mouth, as he made notes and gave orders, pacing from one end of the cellar to the other to adjust a press, leaning over the shoulder of someone composing a page, taking the paper back to the light so he could read it. He only left the print room for a few hours every night: he was a busy little mole, always with a speech in his mouth, while Manterola paraded up on the surface, hung around on café terraces, mute in his role of public poet.

Guzman signalled to them and the three men went into a small meeting room. Away from the roar of the presses, they sat around a table. Guzman quenched his thirst with large glasses of red wine, which he poured from a bottle kept in a bucket of cold water.

"Aznar will soon be coming back with her. Is everything arranged for the reception at the palace?"

Manterola nodded. "We have received our invitations and Señor Ferguson has taken care of the transaction with the young servant."

They were speaking Spanish. Guzman turned to Pete and addressed him in English. He didn't want to admit that the American now understood his language without hesitation.

"So the money we are paying you will finally be put to some use."

Pete poured himself a glass of wine and stood up. He smiled. Guzman started speaking Spanish again, because the cause sounded wrong in the language of the Yankees.

"The special edition of *Grito del Pueblo* will be ready to distribute all over town. I'm printing five thousand copies. I'm going to flood the streets with it."

The printer looked as though he were carved from oak; the old poet, with his ulcers and imaginary illnesses, gently nodded his head.

"Granados' police are on our scent."

Guzman waved such fears away with a gesture of his hand. "In two days they can destroy our press again, but it won't matter. Nothing will ever be the same after this. Is everything arranged for your departure?"

Manterola nodded. "On the day of the reception I will send word to the palace that I don't feel well. My secretary will go in my place."

For the next and almost certainly the last issue of the clandestine newspaper, the Maestro had written an article signed with his real name.

"I do not want to die without those pigs knowing the truth," he had said to Pete one evening, his fingers gripping a glass of rum. "Let them know what I was!"

This article was his testament. He worried that Granados's police would discover the plot before it could be carried out, that he would be thrown in prison before his name could appear below the text, and that the people, who loved their poet so much, would not weep for Eduardo Manterola on the day of his execution.

Aboard the *Santo Cristo*, and in Guatemala since they had arrived here, Manterola, Guzman and Aznar had told Pete Ferguson all about their country and their cause. The conquistadors, the kings, the conservatives and the liberals, the wars of independence in Central America, the false fratricidal battles between politicians and industrialists, the wars – as in Yucatán – where the victims were the people and the Indians, the latifundia, the evangelism, the prisons, the economy run by Europe and the United States, the social struggle. They had showered him with theories and names: Bakunin, Proudhon, Reclus, Owen, Fourier. Names that Pete had already heard in the mouth of Alexandra Desmond at the Fitzpatrick ranch. Back then he had imagined those revolutionaries as bandits or pirates, charging into battle on horseback followed by jubilant armies of the people; what he had discovered instead were cellar rats patting one another on the back when they read their pompous articles, feverish intellectuals stifled by secrecy. What a transformation – from darkness into light – the revolution would be for these men in their basements.

Pete couldn't have cared less about their cause; he had negotiated his price – a thousand American dollars to enter the Palacio del Ayuntamiento with a gun, hand it to a woman and create a diversion. The woman was the passenger who would soon arrive with the captain of the *Santo Cristo*.

"The essential thing is that you give her the revolver. Aznar and Manterola will wait for you at the meeting place, then take you back as agreed to Puerto Barrios."

The plotters had other matters to discuss, so Pete left the cellar and then the building on his own. He was a free man again now, a bourgeois strolling around the streets of Antigua as he wished.

Night fell. He was a regular on avenida Norte these days. He went there to drink under the Santa Catalina Arch, to watch the last rays of sunlight cling to the peak of the Agua volcano, its grey smoke turning pink in the sunset. When the wind blew from the south, above the great volcanic lake, the town was covered with a film of ash; the inhabitants closed their doors and shutters; the shopkeepers shut up shop. The poverty and violence that Guzman and Manterola talked about were nowhere to be seen in Antigua; the only threat seemed to come from that volcano. Twice already the town had been devastated by its eruptions. The government had then built the new Ciudad de Guatemala, further east, to protect them from the volcano's anger. Antigua had become an outdated double of the new capital, home to the aristocracy, the old banking families and the more recent fortunes of modern commerce. It was here that President Granados came to celebrate the arts: in the old palace, the old city, the past.

At the terrace where he sat, people greeted him as Señor Ferguson. Since his arrival he had attended the Maestro's public readings, he had been invited to meals on shaded patios where fountains gently splashed, and everywhere he went he had been introduced as the Maestro's secretary, graduate of an American university and connoisseur of Spanish literature come to help Manterola in his work and research. The curiosity of Antigua's leading citizens regarding this erudite American gave rise to endless toasts praising the union of North America and Central America, in the name of the peaceful entente of poets, the abolition of borders and the greatness of culture. He was asked about his country and the books he'd read until at last this taciturn man, his stocky body deforming the suits he wore, partial to a drink, with his rudimentary Spanish, became the subject of increasingly scandalous speculation. The poet's reputation – for mixing with commoners and street boys whom he ordered his old servant to clean up – fed the gossip about his American secretary: perhaps an *amigo especial* rather than an employee.

Pete drank, and, like Manterola when he was drunk, ignored the looks and the greetings. He would go to bed late, get up early, and wait for the appointed time.

The Gallo Blanco cantina was a safe place: not a cellar but one of those back rooms filled with merchandise where Manterola, Guzman, Aznar and their associates liked to meet up. Pete enjoyed this game of clandestine meetings and spies' signals. How could men like this be dangerous, with their big ideas and their underground newspaper that hardly anyone read? Who would even bother keeping them under surveillance?

Aznar had returned. He was there, tired from his voyage, surrounded by the smell of spices and poultry, accompanied by two men of mixed race. Pete shook the young captain's hand, then turned to the tiny woman who stood beside him, a blanket over her head, drinking water from a jug. All he could see was her throat tightening as she swallowed. Her trachea moved like a little thoracic cage under her dark copper skin. She was, he realised, an Indian woman.

2

The Indian did not speak. She sat on a crate in the corner of the storeroom while the men talked in low voices; head thrown back, concentrated on the jug she was emptying, she seemed to pay no attention to the discussion. One of Aznar's men brought her another jug, which she drank at the same speed. This tiny woman had a mighty thirst, and Pete felt a desire to drink water too. Was she the killer hired by Guzman and Manterola? Her eyes were big and motionless and her moonlike face looked as if someone had tried to squeeze it into a square. With her filthy blanket, she resembled a pauper. Pete doubted she could understand anything of what the revolutionaries were saying, let alone that she might have any grasp of what anarchism was or any knowledge of these white men's theories.

The meeting ended and the men went their separate ways, disappearing into the backyard or leaving through the lounge of the inn. The two men who had arrived with Aznar left with the Indian woman. Pete led Segundo aside.

"I have to talk to you."

They sat at a table in the restaurant, and the owner, a friend of the cause, brought them food and drinks. It was late; the candles had been blown out on the other tables and the last customers were leaving.

"What is all this bullshit?"

The tone of Pete's question was an abrupt change from that of the meeting.

"What do you mean?"

"You hired a half-wit to do the job?"

"Lower your voice."

Pete pushed away his plate and poured himself a glass of rum.

"No way am I going into the palace to give her a revolver. She'll get us all thrown in prison. You can tell Guzman to stop printing his newspaper – it's going to end in a massacre."

Aznar smiled. He wrapped a tortilla around a green chilli pepper and bit into it. Pete waited for him to chew and swallow.

"Why are you smiling?"

"Maria is not some uneducated Indian woman. She's been with us for a long time and she's walked halfway across the country to be here. If you give her the gun, she won't fail. You can't understand why she is sacrificing herself."

Pete stared at him.

"If she's dumb enough to walk into your trap, that's her problem. But you shouldn't get your hopes up on my account, captain. Not you or Guzman or Manterola. You can keep your sermons on the poverty of the people for the others. I'm sure I have more in common with that girl than I do with you. There's only one thing I want to know: can I rely on her?"

Aznar smiled.

"Your Spanish is good now, gringo, and you're looking more and more like the man we needed to hire." There was a hint of disappointment in his voice. He slowly raised his glass to eye level, a gesture of farewell rather than celebration. "You can rely on Maria. She's a real fighter."

"Where will you hide her?"

"At the printing press, with Guzman."

Pete thought about this. "The servant I gave the money to, she worked at the palacio and she was an Indian. Is that why you chose her?"

"So that Maria could take her place."

"And that servant . . . if Granados' men get their hands on her, what will she say?"

Aznar shook his head. "You don't understand, Pete. With the sum you gave her, she went back to her family lands and she'll be able to feed them for years. Nobody will find her where she is now."

Pete whistled. "With two hundred dollars?"

"The money we are going to pay you is a fortune in this country."

Pete refused to be impressed. "The risks I'm taking can't be measured in the local currency. Your Maria needs a good bath if she's going to pass for a palacio employee."

Aznar pretended to ignore the poor taste of this remark. The two men finished their bottle, and the gringo ordered another. Pete went home drunk to his apartment on avenida Norte and could not fall asleep. He thought about Aznar, wondering if the captain truly believed his own words: that Maria had chosen to sacrifice herself, that it was not the cause that was sacrificing an Indian. Aznar would doubtless reply that there was no difference, that Pete could not understand.

On the balcony of his room he sat with his back to the railing, shirt open, and rolled cigarettes. The town was already celebrating; pedlars had come here from the mountains and the capital and were sleeping on the streets under their stalls or their carts full of homemade trinkets. Garlands hung over the streets and the echo of firecrackers ricocheted between buildings; children, having escaped from home, ran past, while women spun around in their long dresses to the music of guitars and tambourines, as if they were truly Spanish. Pete Ferguson, the only white man still awake on his balcony, closed his eyes and listened to the shouting and the singing, the populace of Antigua enjoying a night to itself before the arrival of the president and his court. He stood up, put on his jacket and left the poet's apartment building.

The carved stone steps were damp and slippery; the spiral worsened the dizziness brought on by alcohol, and the printing press, having been stopped for the night, could not guide him with its noise. Leaning a hand and a shoulder against the wall, Pete descended to the door and stopped to catch his breath. Then he knocked five times and waited. The door was opened by one of the men who had arrived with Aznar, his skin pockmarked from an old illness. The heat, the smell of ink and engine grease and pulp made him feel sick. The copies of *Grito del Pueblo* were piled up around the compositor's table. The printing presses squatted silently in the darkness. At the far end of the cellar, Aznar's other man stood guard outside the door of the meeting room. Lying fully dressed on a bed on the tiles, Guzman was reading. His round glasses made him look even more like a mole.

"What are you doing here?"

The pockmarked man joined his colleague. Pete watched as he entered the room at the back and closed the door behind him.

"I want to talk to her."

Guzman stood up and barred the way. "No way. Go home. You're drunk." The mole could not stifle a smile. "Besides, Maria wants nothing to do with you."

"With me?"

"With whites."

Pete looked at Guzman, his face as pale as a mushroom, without a single ounce of indigenous blood, a pure Spanish descendant. So not only did he consider himself the voice of the people, but he imagined he was half-Indian too. If Manterola was an incestuous father to his people, Guzman saw himself as their virtuous patriarch.

"Let me pass or you'll have to find someone else to go to the palace tomorrow."

Guzman did not move straight away. He puffed his chest out, before exhaling and giving way. "No more than a minute."

He made a sign to the man who was guarding the door.

The Indian woman was sitting at the table, her blanket still on her shoulders: a coloured fabric from the mountains, darkened by the dust of her journey. The pockmarked guard left the room; Pete closed and bolted the door. From the other side, he heard Guzman protesting and banging his fist against the wood.

She looked at him. Her eyes were dark, and slanted at the corners like the Chinese, but rounder so he could see the whites around the iris when she stared at something, the way she was staring at Pete now. Her hair was tied in a long plait, her nose was slender and straight, her nostrils flattened. Her lips were very thin, but the shape of her mouth was supple; her expressionless face could come to life at any moment. She looked even smaller than he remembered: an adolescent in the shape of a woman. Her posture, hands crossed on the table, resembled a child imitating an adult's patience.

The assassination plot; the guards on the other side of the door; this woman-child bewitched by her own thoughts and watched like a treasure chest: it was a virgin sacrifice, thought Pete. As if Manterola, Aznar and Guzman had gone into a forest to seek out a pure symbol to be burned, offered to the cause by an illiterate tribe. A girl who must believe she has supernatural powers, like those Indians in the plains who believed their amulets would protect them from the American cavalry's bullets.

Pete spoke to her in Spanish, despite not knowing if she understood that language. "I'm the one who will be with you at the palacio tomorrow."

"I heard about you. The gringo who came from Mexico on Segundo's boat."

She had replied in English and called Aznar by his first name. Pete felt ridiculous in his worn bourgeois suit, stinking of alcohol. He was scared and the Indian girl could see it.

"I wanted to be sure that everything was clear, that you aren't going to make any trouble for me."

Maria's nostrils dilated and her mouth tensed. Pete thought she was going to spit.

"You have nothing to worry about, *mercenario*."

She was not ugly; it was just that Pete could not understand a face like that. Did this little woman have a husband and children somewhere?

"You've seen me. You will recognise me tomorrow. You can go now."

Her clear voice had a deep bass throb to it, a huskier sound like a dry throat. This was not just irritation at being faced with a white, it was real anger. Pete swayed. In a dizzy spell he saw his father again, on the doorstep of their house the day that Billy Webb died. Pete saw himself, sitting at the table next to Oliver, staring steadily, ready to rip into the Old Man. Then he looked at this dark-eyed, ferocious little woman, ready to rip into him. She drew back when he grabbed a chair and sat facing her.

"They're going to kill you."

She quickly recovered from her surprise. She frowned. Pete could smell her now: a scent of fresh butter and musk. He had a sudden memory of some newborn kittens, the sickening warmth of the delivery, the wet fur coated with grease. He saw the grain of the skin on her neck: human silk. He wondered what his own smell made her think about, what memories the Indian would find to describe the scent of this white man.

"The people will rise up."

"The people aren't going to save you."

"Nor are you. Just give me the gun, and then you can run away."

Pete spoke more quietly, suddenly despairing of the possibility that she could understand him. "Guzman and the others are using you."

Her expression did not change. "We are using them. It's our cause, not theirs. You know nothing, *mercenario*."

He didn't know what else to say.

"And . . . your family?"

She stood up to open the door and Aznar's men immediately went to her side. Pete walked past them, shoulders hunched. He had a sudden desire to roll in the sawdust on a saloon floor, to punch and be punched. The two men looked ready for this too.

He left the cellar. It was daybreak by the time he got home. The celebrations were over and avenida Norte was deserted. On the balcony he watched the sun rise over the town and the great Agua volcano.

—w—w—w—

My Mother.

My firstborn. The folly of mothers, no longer being whole. Giving birth to solitary beings. Flesh of my flesh, what remains of me. Patchwork myths invented for your brother.

You are the child without tears by my graveside, who wanted to throw himself in.

I would have pushed you out again, you know.

You thought: Who do we have left, now that she's abandoned us?

A husband and two brothers, together.

And now you are reduced to making the two of us talk – the man and the woman who made you.

It was early when you came to the room that day.

I was waiting for someone to come; that light that you hope for. I had only a few minutes to be done with it all. And it was you who came, my firstborn, my last.

You wanted me to live, or to die before he *came. You wanted it to be just the two of us. You didn't want Oliver to wake up. Your brother was two years old and you swore to me you would look after him.*

You never wanted your brother to wake up after that.

You told him about before – my memory – to send him to sleep, and about what there would be after – dreams of California – so he would keep his eyes closed.

How your tears hurt me. I held you tight in my arms and then I went.

You felt my hands release you.

What an emptiness. What a fall.

Quickly, tell me about that woman who took care of you on the ranch, that Alexandra. Do you think we could have been friends, the two of us? Her the reader and me the farmer, the peasant?

Is she as beautiful as your memories of me?

Did you love that woman, my full-grown firstborn?

Is it because of her or because of me that you left that place? That you made other women suffer? That you fought? For her, who took care of your brother and you, without seeing that you were strong?

I wish I could have met that man who took you in, straight-backed and solid, so much stronger than your father. Do you think I could have been friends with your new family?

The ranch is so beautiful.

Do you think that if I loved you enough – more – I wouldn't be dead? Do you think nobody dies if they truly love?

These questions would have no meaning as long as you, my son, were not loved. You who have killed in this world where we die.

What do you want to say to your mother tonight?

You are far away, further and further away, and you don't know anymore if I was really that beautiful.

If I really loved you that much.

If I am just your invention.

Do you have something to tell me, my firstborn?

Have you found it?

What?

Another child sacrificed?

A square moon?

The sun has risen. I imagine you in a distant country, in a beautiful town carved from volcanic rock.

It is a bright day and you are alone. You will go outside and walk in the cobbled streets. You are always running away and you still haven't found anyone to talk to, in this world where we die.

3

A row of soldiers, rifles across their chests, separated the onlookers from the illuminated arches of the palacio. The crowd peered over their shoulders and the soldiers stood up straight, chests puffed out, at the approach of the presidential convoy.

Miguel García Granados was a slender man, a hidalgo with a friendly smile below the high forehead of a schoolteacher. A friend to Cuban and South American poets that old Manterola despised, he was the heir to a military family who encouraged him to learn not only about books but about the art of war. A skilled strategist, he had won the elections against Sandoval the previous year. A liberal, moderate in his views and chosen by the people, he could get out of his carriage without fearing the whistles of the crowd or gunshots from the Plaza de Armas.

On the steps of the Palacio del Ayuntamiento, between two rows of valets in livery, Granados turned to wave, his wife beside him smiling at the crowd. The envious mob acclaimed this handsome couple who were so unlike them. The fantasies of the crowd were untroubled by any moral concerns: elected president or bloodthirsty dictator, the public wanted to take the ruler's place on those steps. They applauded and they cheered for more. After the president, it was the turn of the provincial governors, the representatives of the great families and the influential property owners who were given an ovation; after all, they were allies, however remorsefully, of Miguel García Granados.

The only restriction on their dreams of entering the palace: the crowd had to imagine themselves as white.

That was the essential contradiction of these recent years. Guatemala had been ruled by a president with Indian blood, but Rafael Carrera was an uneducated pig-keeper and a dangerous madman who had ended his days locked in a church, surrounded by armed men, drinking like a fish in his medal-strewn suit, receiving foreign envoys and ordering executions. Granados and his friend General Barrios were not mad. They confiscated the possessions of the bishops – who had owned half of Ciudad de Guatemala and a good portion of the country itself – and redistributed them among more competitive investors, friends from here or elsewhere. First there were the Belgians, then the Germans. More and more Germans, to whom the liberals gave land – a lot of land – so that they could cultivate coffee with more success than the representatives of Léopold I. To provide these new liberal plantations with a labour force, while also putting an end to the national scandal of vagrancy, the new government passed a law: the *ley de vagancia*. Any Indian who walked along a street – any vagabond – would be picked up by the police or the army and forced to work on the haciendas.

It was perplexing for the people. They missed Carrera's Indian blood, but at the same time they were reassured that someone reasonable had taken the country's destiny in hand.

Ovation after ovation . . . then the guests entered the palacio and the doors were closed. The last guest had arrived unnoticed, alone and on foot: that young American, Ferguson, secretary to Maestro Manterola, who could not attend because he had the flu. Everyone would miss the delightful presence of the poet and his spiritual conversation. The poets were friends with the president, everyone knew that. Just as people said that any man who was kind to animals could not be a bad man . . . well, a president who was friends with poets could hardly be a bad president, could he? The American wore a pale suit. He climbed the stairs like a cowboy and showed his invitation.

An orchestra composed of about twenty musicians was playing some pleasant music: a slow rhythm, a complex melody, and instruments that Pete Ferguson had never seen before; a music full of little flourishes and embellishments, reminiscent of birdsong filling a forest one spring morning, when the horses are calm and the night has been peaceful. Pete remained standing in the entrance to the main hall, impressed by the music that seemed to make the chandeliers shine brighter, the jewellery of the women, the smiles of the men. Waiters slalomed through the crowd, carrying trays of champagne flutes. Not daring to stop one of these servants, Pete headed for the buffet and stealthily grabbed a glass. He didn't like this pale, stinging drink, which he had tasted with Manterola; he drank a second glass to get rid of the taste of the first. The music stopped and heads turned towards the small stage: the mayor of the town was about to speak. Pete looked around, scanning the crowd for a short dark figure.

The mayor greeted everyone, thanked the assembled guests and artists, then bowed low and moved aside for the governor, who thanked the mayor for this magnificent welcome in this magnificent palace in the heart of this magnificent city. Antigua, the architectural pearl of Hispanic culture, built by the ancestors of this wonderful audience, on this South American land which had been transformed into a jewel of civilisation by patriotism, hard work and art. This was a country that was now independent but would never forget what it owed to its origins, nor the duty that was theirs now – the governor looked at the two hundred people in front of him – to help carry Guatemala into an even more glorious future. He would now leave the stage for a man under whom the nation would become a political, economic and artistic force in the world. The man who had brought change and prosperity to Guatemala: President Miguel García Granados. As the crowd applauded, Granados took a piece of paper from his pocket and unfolded it.

Pete saw her behind the buffet, carrying a tray of food. The reason for her presence instantly sobered him up, and he passed a nervous hand under his waistcoat, where he felt the revolver wedged into the belt of his trousers.

He was probably the only one to spot Maria, hair tied in a bun, dressed in the same black uniform as the other servants. The Indian woman looked at Pete, but her face betrayed no emotion. He picked up a glass of champagne and had drunk three more before Granados had finished his speech. The president invited all his guests to enjoy themselves and, above all, he humbly insisted, to converse with all the artists, painters, poets and sculptors who were present tonight, without whom the beauty of Guatemala would be incomplete.

"Listen to them, not to sad servants of the State like us, whose thankless work can never rival the creative genius of such men."

The burst of applause and laughter startled Pete. An elderly couple, whose faces he vaguely remembered, came over to ask him how Maestro Manterola was feeling. Pete began to speak to them in English, tried to slip back into Spanish, but after stammering a few words gave up and left the couple there, looking surprised.

The orchestra had started playing again, and the music was more lively this time. The president and his wife opened the ball and Pete watched them dance, Granados slim and dignified, one hand resting on his wife's back, their arms straight and their hands joined as they cut wide circles on the marbled tiles. Other couples began to dance too, officers in ceremonial uniform, the women in dresses that rose as they spun around. The music and the champagne were making Pete dizzy and he peered through the flow of dancers for the little Indian woman. The waiters brought drinks and food. Granados had vacated the dance floor and a small group had formed around him: men in black tuxedos and bow ties. Maria had vanished, and Pete smiled. The Indian had obviously fled: she must have realised that Guzman's plan was insane, that the dance of the rich could not be stopped by a handful of idealists, that the ball would go on. She had run away, and Pete Ferguson, the old Maestro's secretary, wanted to laugh in the midst of this crowd drunk on self-regard, with their perfectly executed dance steps and their orchestrated whirls. When a man with a waxed moustache unsmilingly approached the American and asked him for the latest news of the poet, Pete bent down in a grotesque bow and felt the revolver beneath his shirt dig into his ribs. In a loud voice he declared that the Maestro had been laid low by an intestinal complaint while he was working on a poem about the liberal revolution. The man turned on his heels. The people around him were staring at Pete and he bowed to them all before going to the buffet and asking for a glass of whiskey. Women, chins raised and noses wrinkled, shook their heads: one could not be surprised that a poet with questionable morals such as Manterola should have sought the services of a Yankee with such uncouth manners.

The orchestra was playing more upbeat numbers now. A line of men advanced upon a line of women, crossed through them, took their arms, turned, changed partner and reformed the lines, bowed and curtsied, began again. Guzman must be biting his nails in his cellar as he counted the piled-up copies of *Grito del Pueblo*. Aznar and Manterola, waiting in a horse-drawn carriage on the outskirts of the city, were waiting for Pete to bring them the news. But their chosen assassin, that infallible Indian, had deserted, and the party at the palacio was in full swing. No assassination. No revolution. And he wouldn't get his money. Pete raised his glass towards the dancers, saved – without knowing it – from parliamentary democracy.

"*Quiere otra cosa de beber, Señor Secretario?*"

The signal. Pete turned.

She had approached him from behind, a white napkin folded over her arm, a tray resting on her palm.

"What are you doing here?"

She didn't blink. "*Quiere otra cosa de be . . .*"

"Go away."

She looked up at him, frowning tensely. Between her teeth she hissed: "Give me the gun."

"Get out of here."

He had spoken loudly. Faces turned towards them. Maria blinked and tried to compose herself. She whispered: "*Dame el arma.*"

"Go away."

Pete grabbed the tray from her and threw it on the buffet table. Glasses broke, porcelain plates shattered into pieces on the tiles. The guests who had been splashed drew backwards; the dancers froze. Around President Granados, the circle of businessmen bristled; the mayor signalled to a subordinate, who clove his way through the crowd. Maria crouched down to pick up the debris. The mayor's henchman looked at her, then at the drunk American.

"Is there a problem, señor? Is she bothering you?"

"What?"

"Is there a problem with this Indian, señor?"

Two other waiters rushed over to clean up the mess.

"This Indian?" Pete grabbed Maria by the arm and forced her to her feet. He yelled into the employee's face: "This Indian here?"

The mayor's man shrank back and some officers came over. Pete led Maria through the dancers, holding her close to him, one hand on her back. He turned to the buffet and the stunned guests. "There's no problem with the Indian!"

He started dancing with her. Maria, still in shock, felt as light as a feather. Sweat was beading on her clay-coloured forehead. Her legs could no longer hold her up. He squeezed her harder and turned her faster, stumbling and bumping into the other guests until they had cleared a circle around them. The American in his pale suit, like a cowboy dressed for church, lifted the Indian servant's feet off the floor. The revolver rubbed between their bodies. Maria felt sick; her head fell back each time she was spun around. Pete went one way, then another, slamming the heel of his shoe on the floor like a farmer from Basin dancing to a banjo tune. The orchestra had stopped playing. Pete banged into a wall of shoulders. Three young officers grabbed hold of him. He clung to Maria, who was swept into the melee. The officers tore his hands off her and threw him outside. The high doors banged shut.

At the foot of the steps, on the Plaza de Armas, the people of Antigua were also dancing. Maria was still inside the palace. Pete crossed the street and disappeared among the workers in search of a place where he could keep drinking.

Swaying and half-blind, Pete got lost on the way to avenida Norte and collapsed against a wall to catch his breath. He heard footsteps behind him, but was too slow to turn around. He took a blow to the head. He was vomiting as he lost conscience.

4

Pete felt as if he could still hear the palacio orchestra: the painful, distorted echo of a waltz. He wanted to bring his hand to his forehead to stop the whirlwind but was unable to lift his arm. He was lying in a room with the blinds closed, his ankles and wrists tied to a bed. He tested the resistance of the ropes, but they were too solid for him to free himself. His suit was soaked with the stink of vomit, tobacco and alcohol; when he breathed this in, he felt his stomach turn. Needles of sunlight shone through the gaps between the blinds, illuminating motes of dust as they hovered in the air. He told himself he had finally arrived in Guatemala, in the style of his arrival in Mexico. Filthy, stinking, but with a bump on his head instead of a bullet in the belly. He was making slow progress in the art of crossing borders.

The door opened and the pockmarked man entered. He stood guard at the room's entrance, as he had in the cellar.

"Where is Maria?" Pete asked.

The man stared straight ahead.

"Guzman? Manterola? Were they arrested?"

The pockmarked man said nothing, a silent guardian of the talkative white men's cause. Pete heard a floorboard creak in the corridor. Someone had stopped outside the door and was waiting to come in. The music continued to drone through his head and he could still feel the Indian girl's body against his, still see her terrified expression; she had looked the way Oliver had looked when the Old Man raised his fist. The door opened and she crossed the room to the window. Pete sat up to see her back. He imagined her against a wall, her neck defying the firing squad.

"Guzman is on the run, Manterola too. His testament won't be published. The newspapers – and all the machines – have been destroyed. Aznar has vanished. He must be trying to get back to Puerto Barrios and his boat. The police are after them."

Her shoulders moved in a way he couldn't interpret: a silent snort or a painful inhalation.

"I was counting on your greed, *mercenario*. But you weren't up to it."

She half-opened the blinds and leaned forwards to look outside. Her black hair caught the light. Children's voices, carried on a warm gust of air, reached the room.

"You owe us."

"What do I owe you?"

"A battle."

He smiled.

"What's the pay?"

"Your life. This will be a real battle."

She left the room. The pockmarked man took a knife from his belt and cut the ropes around his ankles. As he did the same thing for his wrists, the man whispered: "*Gracias para Maria*, Señor Ferguson."

Then he left without bolting the door. Pete rubbed his hands and feet. He walked over to the window, swaying slightly. Cob houses, dirt streets, broken tile roofs . . . below this, the old, calm Antigua and, behind it, the smoking volcano. He was in the suburbs of the city, on the mountainside.

He slept almost all day. The other half-Indian man returned at nightfall, threw some clothes on the bed, and put a candle and Pete's travel bag on the floor.

"We found your things at Manterola's place. You shouldn't keep a personal diary; if Granados' police had found it, the situation would have been even worse."

"Who read my notebook?"

"Get changed now."

The man stood there watching while Pete took off his suit and put on the clothes he'd brought. Sandals, cotton trousers with a braided wool belt, a cotton shirt and a red wool poncho, a black hat, all of it already worn, with the sour sweat smell of another man. Pete left his dirty secretary's suit on the floorboards. When he was dressed, the man gave a sort of disgusted nod at seeing the gringo disguised as a Guatemalan peasant. Next, he brought an enamel bowl, a sliver of soap, a razor and a mirror.

With his short legs, his broad shoulders and his brown hair, in the dim lamplight, with his face shaved, Pete could pass for an Indian – as long as he pulled the hat down over his forehead and walked like one, back bent. He went through his belongings, keeping only a few changes of clothing and his notebook, which he packed in the canvas bag.

The street that led down into town was deserted at this time of day. Perhaps the neighbours were hiding. Pete was impressed by the silence; he felt as if it had been arranged specially for their little group: Maria, the two guards, and him. They sneaked out of the house, left the neighbourhood, and then the suburbs. Pete's legs were heavy and his breath was short and he found it hard to keep up. They reached the forest that covered the mountainside. The air was cooler there. For three hours he followed Maria, with one of the men at the head of their group and the other one bringing up the rear. They walked until the path ended at the grey bank and black expanse of the volcanic lake of Amatitlan. Then they hid and waited until a light, reflected by the waves, flashed twice and then went out. One of the men responded with the same signal, and a few moments later a small boat came ashore and they climbed into it. Two strangers were in the boat, rowing silently through the dark water.

The first rays of dawn appeared as they reached the opposite bank, where they got out of the boat without exchanging a single word with the strangers. Well-rested, they walked quickly under the cover of trees until they came to a sun-bleached track. There, they had to wait again; the flasks were empty and the heat was stifling at the foot of the Agua volcano.

A cart drawn by a mule stopped in front of them. Maria and one of the guards jumped up. Pete stayed with the pockmarked man.

"One more hour, señor."

"My name is Pete."

The man nodded. "Gustavio."

Pete could not guess his age. His unlined face looked youthful, but the traces of his illness seemed to age him. He was tall and strong for a Guatemalan.

"Where are we going?"

Gustavio walked away, scanned the track, and came back to sit down next to Pete. "Jutiapa."

"Where's that?"

"In the south."

"What will we do there?"

The man smiled and shook his head, embarrassed that he could not respond. He had orders.

"Never mind, I'll find out soon enough."

Gustavio lowered his head. "It's her place, Señor Pete. We're going to Maria's home."

A wagon drawn by two cattle and driven by an old Indian man picked them up sometime later. There were crates of potatoes and bags of flour on the floor of the wagon. They were given a bundle containing some cornbread and a flask of water. Pete watched as the volcano and its black plume shrank into the distance. Then he lay down on the hemp bags, rocked gently by the wagon's movements.

"Where did you learn to speak English, Gustavio?"

"With Maria. But I don't speak it very good."

"We can speak Spanish if you prefer."

"No, no! I like to speak English."

"Was it really Maria who taught you?"

"To read and write too, Señor Pete."

Pete took off his hat; the thick wool was scratching his head.

"You must keep wearing the hat, señor."

Pete looked around, at the empty track, the mountains and the forest. "There's nobody here to see us."

Gustavio translated this into Spanish and the old man turned around and laughed in Pete's face. His mouth was toothless. Gustavio raised his legs against his chest and covered them with his poncho.

"These mountains are full of people. For miles ahead, they already know that there is a wagon with three men on the path."

Pete stared incredulously at the green slopes where not a single roof or column of smoke betrayed any human presence. Gustavio's face darkened. "Well, that's not completely true. The old man laughs, but there are fewer and fewer Indians here now."

Pete tried to imagine a number. He tried to work out what it meant, to say that the mountains were full of Indians, and that now there were fewer and fewer.

"In my country too the government is at war with the Indians. The army is herding them onto reservations. Are there reservations here?"

Gustavio, who did not understand and began to doubt his English, replied in Spanish: "I don't know what you're talking about, Señor Pete. There are no reservations for the Indians in Guatemala. It is sickness and slavery, from the time of the *conquista*, that has killed them. Hundreds of thousands, Señor Pete. Now slavery no longer exists, but the Indians die in the haciendas. They die because they can no longer live their way of life. The fate of half-bloods like me isn't much better. We have grown closer to the cities and many of us treat the Indians like dogs, to be in the white men's good books. We join the army and run small shops. A few become rich and try to marry white women so that their children will have lighter skin. There is no war against the Indians in Guatemala, señor. They are the poorest of the poor and they have no rights: that is what is killing them."

The old man nodded in agreement.

"Why don't they fight?"

"There were a few battles at first. The Xincas, Maria's people, were warriors, and they tried to resist. But the Spanish had horses and the strongest swords in the world. But most importantly, the Indians did not realise that the conquistadors wanted everything. By the time they understood this, it was too late: they had been decimated and uprooted. Today, the whites have guns and battalions of soldiers to wage war. For the Indians, paying a man to be a warrior is as absurd as those thousands of acres of coffee plants that do not feed anybody. Pedro de Alvarado, the first Spaniard to come here, won a battle against the Xincas and then made them his soldiers so he could conquer El Salvador. It is said that the Xincas abandoned their weapons out of shame and let themselves be killed by Alvarado's enemies. Forgive me, Señor Pete . . . I know that you were with Señor Guzman for the money. But Maria says that's how it is, that we must use you and learn from you. That it helps our cause to employ soldiers who know how to fight."

"I'm not a soldier. In my country, I ran away so I wouldn't have to go to war."

The old man burst out laughing. Gustavio swallowed. "What are you saying?"

Pete replied in English: "That I didn't come here to fight with you. Manterola and Guzman recruited me because I was white and I could get into the palace to give Maria a gun. That's all. I don't know what she's told you, but you're wrong about me."

Pete lay back and put the poncho over his head to protect his face from the sun. He was sleeping when Gustavio shook his shoulder. They had arrived at a crossroads. Gustavio jumped down from the wagon and Pete followed him. The old man continued along the path without a word or a wave.

They followed the other track. It was smaller and potholed, its wheel ruts filled with water. The plants were still dripping from the recent rain. After they had walked for an hour, it started to rain again, and they moved between trees by the side of the track to avoid the mud.

It was still raining at sunset and Pete shivered with cold. Gustavio turned onto another path. Pete could no longer see where he was putting his feet. He tripped over tree roots, twisted his ankles in holes. The path kept dividing but Gustavio never hesitated. At last they saw a light: a fire and two silhouettes beneath a tree whose branches looked like arms held out over the flames. Maria was drying her long, plaited hair above the fire. Gustavio greeted the second half-Indian man and squatted down to warm his hands. Since they had descended from the wagon, he had not spoken a single word to the American. Pete wrung out his poncho, put it back on, still wet, and leaned against the trunk of the tree.

"Do you have anything to eat?"

The man whose name he didn't know brought him some tortillas then disappeared. Gustavio stood up and followed him, and so did Maria, leaving Pete alone beside the fire. After an hour, they still hadn't returned. Pete had burned their reserves of wood and all that remained were the embers, which crackled in the rain. He rolled up in a ball inside his poncho, as close to the heat as he could get. Amid the noises of insects, the creaking of the trees and the whisper of rain, he thought he could hear, carried on the wind at intervals, a sort of moaning.

5

When he woke, he felt as if he'd been drinking bad alcohol in bad company, as if he were emerging from a mute drinking binge with his throat full of words.

He stayed rolled up in his poncho, his hands between his thighs, while he waited to hear the hiss of wet earth beneath the feet of the Indian woman and the two men.

Gustavio shook him awake. "*Vámonos, mercenario.*" He did not react and the man shook him again. "*Ándale.*"

Maria and the other one were waiting for him. Pete stood up, his back stiff, his joints numb. Gustavio raised his voice. "We must leave now."

"You don't give me orders."

Maria interjected coldly: "*Ya basta.*"

For twelve hours, with the occasional brief pause, they followed the craggy track, which by evening was no more than a mule path. They climbed mountains, descended into valleys and passed silent Indians who did not even look up at them. Where were they coming from and where were they headed? They walked in silence in search of something that was fleeing from them. As if Carrera, Granados and all their predecessors had cut the tongue out of Guatemala, and its inhabitants, heads down, were roaming all over to find it again. Maria, the two men and these ghosts shared a secret from which Pete, in a thousand ways and for a thousand reasons, was excluded.

They stopped beside the track, beneath a tree that looked identical to the one from the previous night, and gathered dead branches that concealed food. Since their departure from Antigua, an invisible army had been watching over their journey, ensuring Maria's survival. The rain had ceased, the air was warmer. They stretched out their ponchos to dry. Pete's leather sandals had torn his skin. Maria spoke to the other man, and that was how Pete finally learned his name.

"Santos, *hierbas para sus pies*."

The man returned with a handful of stalks, which he ground between two stones to produce a thick sap. He placed one of the sticky rocks in front of the Yankee and motioned him to spread the mixture over his injury. The paste quickly soothed the burning and, as it dried, transformed into an elastic film, like a second skin.

That evening, Maria and Gustavio went off together to sleep, leaving Santos with the American. The two men did not speak to each other. Pete, lying on a bed of branches, heard Gustavio's moans from somewhere. Santos put more wood on the fire. He, too, was listening. He turned his head towards the place where his companion was groaning rhythmically, slowly making love to the Indian woman. His brief orgasm – two hoarse cries – was swallowed up by the sounds of the forest: the insects, the frogs and the whistling of mosquitoes.

"We'll be in Cuilapa tonight." The two men no longer spoke to Pete; it was Maria who said this to him when he woke. "We'll get information on what happened in Antigua." She didn't look at him. She chewed a mouthful of tortilla. "We'll spend the night in town." Santos and Gustavio extinguished the fire and covered the traces of their presence. "Tomorrow we will go in two groups to Jutiapa. On horseback." She stood up and wiped her mouth. "Santos and Gustavio will ride together. You'll come with me."

Santos pointed at the wide, grey, foaming river. "Los Esclavos."

This was the strange name of the river that they crossed at dusk over an uneven arched bridge made of half-eroded stones that led into Cuilapa. Had Pete already seen this town or was it just that it so closely resembled the idea of it that he'd formed in his mind? The town was like a smaller, poorer version of Antigua; it must once have been magnificent, but it had become abandoned for reasons – drought, war, disease? – that were both mysterious and disturbing. The grass grew between cobbles on the streets, and Pete thought of those abandoned mining towns, those nests of ghosts in which he had slept more than once as he fled across America.

The men were excited now, and he realised that they were going home. Maria, on the other hand, had appeared sombre ever since morning when she announced the last stage of the journey to Jutiapa. He tried to imagine going back to Carson City or Basin and, like her, without his even being aware of it, he got an ominous feeling in his chest.

A kid ran off from the corner of a street, and they followed him to a crumbling, three-storey house; a woman waved to them from the doorway and they all rushed inside.

The woman hugged Gustavio, shook hands with Santos and with the gringo in Indian clothing, and quickly introduced herself – Amalia, Gustavio's wife – before hugging Maria too.

She told them to sit down at the table and, by the light of a candle, she brought them food. They quickly swallowed the bean soup, and Maria gestured at Pete to follow her. On the first floor they went into a bedroom where Amalia was waiting for them, candlestick in hand. The two women spoke in a language that Pete did not recognise. The only words he heard were the names of Manterola and Guzman. Amalia put the candlestick on the floor and, with Maria's help, moved a wardrobe out of the way, revealing a secret passage in the brick wall. Maria and Pete went in there and found themselves in a dark room; behind them, the wardrobe creaked and the hole in the wall closed up again. Pete waited, without moving, listening to Maria's breathing close by. A door opened and another candle lit up a storeroom cluttered with dusty furniture. Another woman led them into the next room. She lifted up a curtain and they passed through another wall with a hole in it, which came out on a roof terrace. A ladder at the end of the terrace led to another flat roof, strung with drying laundry, and yet another ladder that led down to another roof where Maria stopped, taking two blankets from a clothesline. She threw one of them at Pete and sat leaning against the low wall that surrounded the terrace; he sat against the opposite wall. Dogs yelped and cats fought. The black line of mountains stood out against the paler sky. She looked at him, her eyes round and wide and staring in the darkness.

"Manterola has been arrested, Aznar is on the run, and nobody knows what has happened to Guzman." Her voice was numb with anger – and disgust at having to speak to Pete. "The government is searching for a gringo who took part in the plot, the young American who pretended to be the poet's secretary. You have no choice now, *mercenario* – Manterola has talked."

She lay on the floor and pulled the blanket over her head.

"What will happen to him?"

From under the blanket she answered: "If he survived the interrogations, he'll be shot. Or maybe Granados will pardon him because he's a poet. He's bound to be in a terrible state, anyway."

Her muffled voice accentuated the detachment of her response. Pete thought again of old Manterola, swallowing rum and cursing the uneducated mob for whom he was fighting from his writer's desk.

"You don't seem too bothered about that."

"The only weapon we have is our life. If you're not ready to risk it, you're unarmed. It's our last freedom."

"Like whoring with Gustavio and Santos."

He was angry with himself, not for the words he had spoken but for the emotions betrayed by the way they rushed out. She must have spotted that, because she replied as slowly as possible: "*Una putana, sí.* Like those girls in the Antigua brothels you used to visit. But I don't sell my body, I give it – but only to fighters. You fucked Guatemala and left a coin on the table, but you weren't capable of doing what you were paid to do."

"What difference would it have made to kill Granados?" Pete asked, in the Maestro's disillusioned voice. He interpreted her silence as a victory and tried to rub salt in the wounds. "What really upsets you is that I saved your life. That I stole your revolution for a dance."

She threw off the blanket and sat up. "You were scared and you saved your own skin. And that's all! Manterola will die pointlessly because of you."

He savoured her anger, letting it stew while he rolled a cigarette.

"I lived on a ranch where there was a woman like you. She read books and she was always talking about revolution and socialism. One day she told me that if I was lost in a town, I should find a writer and knock on his door. I think Manterola would have opened his door if I'd knocked on it. I can't say the same for you and your fighters."

Maria was pretending not to listen to him anymore.

"I danced with this woman once. There was a party at the ranch – just some old guy playing a fiddle, not like that big orchestra at the palacio . . ."

"Stop talking about that!" she interrupted.

She walked across the terrace and lay down farther away, where he couldn't see her.

Pete finished his cigarette and took his notebook from the canvas bag. Sometimes he needed a pencil and the slowness of his fingers for the words to come. Sometimes he found it easier to imagine them without having to look at the letters traced on the paper. He opened the notebook at the last page and looked up at the moon.

———— ᔥ ᔥ ᔥ ————

My Brother.

I never had a nickname for you, and you never had one for me either. In Basin, we were just the Ferguson brothers, indistinguishable, the progeny of Hubert Ferguson; his discards; what was seen of him in town. Little brother: that was all you said.

Here, it's winter. There's been a lot of snow and we're running low on feed. Or maybe it's been a mild winter and the foals are in good health. I don't know anymore. Maybe I'm getting it mixed up with the year that you went away. My memory is starting to play tricks on me; the time when you were with us seems more and more distant. It's like grief, Pete, and the moment is coming when I will live without you. Find a way to not be alone anymore. I always thought I had to grow to catch up with my big brother. Soon I will be as old as you were when you left. Because, like dead people, you aren't getting older anymore. Mama never aged, and nor did Papa. Now I watch Alexandra and Arthur wearing themselves out, and Aileen growing up. So fast, Pete . . . If only you could see her.

I go into town more often now. Girls are getting interested in me. I'm a partner in the Fitzpatrick ranch.

All these things that I didn't used to dare do without you.

It's late, big brother, and my eyes are closing. Is it summer or winter where you are? How distant would we have to be before we weren't looking up at the same sky?

I'm sorry, I don't have many words tonight. I'm intimidated by the stars and I'm no longer really sure that I'm talking to someone.

———ﬔ—ﬔ—ﬔ———

At dawn a man came to fetch them from the terrace. They followed him from roof to roof, from house to staircase to alleyway, moving silently through a silent town, to a stable. Two tired horses, old saddles on their back, snorting hay dust. Two badly rested, sour-tempered horses. Maria wanted to give the man some coins, but he refused her money; he balled his hands into fists and wished her good luck.

They crossed the bridge over Los Esclavos again. Patches of mist drifted along the riverbed. It was Maria who spoke first.

"What were you doing in Tampico, when you met Aznar?"

Perhaps it was the solitude of their journey, the bad night's sleep on the roof, tiredness, but there was in her question a sort of peace offering that Pete felt relieved to accept.

"I was looking for a boat."

"A boat?"

"A way out."

"You were on the run?"

"I killed a man in Mexico."

They suddenly stopped talking. Maria stood up in her stirrups and looked behind. She pulled on the reins, twisting her horse's neck. "Get under cover!"

The low branches whipped their faces. The horses snorted in the long grass. They jumped down from their saddles and forced the animals to go down into a ditch where a stream ran. On the path above them, a dozen soldiers in green and white uniforms, rifles on their backs, sped past on horseback. The ground shook and clumps of earth raised by the horses' hooves rained down on top of them. Maria held a revolver up by her face, an old Colt Root that looked enormous in her hand. They waited for silence.

"Are they looking for us?"

"Who else? You still think this is all just a game? If they catch us, your white skin won't be enough to save you."

She slid the Colt under her poncho, then lifted up her skirt, and Pete looked at her dripping legs. Grimacing, she pulled a leech from her calf. Pete pulled up his trouser legs and found two of the black creatures moving up his thigh. He crushed them in his fingers and they got back in the saddle.

"Gustavio and Santos?"

"They left before us, during the night. If all goes well, they'll get to Jutiapa before the soldiers." She gestured with her head towards the direction the soldiers had taken. "Those ones work for the government. But in Jutiapa, we'll have to deal with Ortiz's men. He pays them well and they do everything he asks. They're the ones we need to hide from."

"Who's Ortiz?"

"The governor. Santiago Ribeiro Ortiz."

That name plunged Maria into silence. For an hour they said nothing more. They remained vigilant.

"In America, I worked with bison hunters. The oldest of them was a good man and he told me about a voyage he wanted to make. When I got to Tampico, I was looking for a boat that could take me on that voyage."

"What voyage?"

"To the equator."

"Why, what's there?"

"The middle of the earth."

"I know what the equator is."

He smiled.

"The old hunter said that everything was upside down at the equator. That pyramids stood on their points, that water went up to the sky, that birds walked instead of flying, and that you had to fill your pockets with stones to keep your feet on the ground. He said the earth spins backwards there, that dreams are real and truths so solid that you find nuggets of them in sand mines. The air there is so light that you can see for miles and miles. Once you've crossed the equator, nobody works anymore because effort is impossible with gravity reversed. Strength doesn't exist there either. Anybody who's violent becomes exhausted and they can't move anymore. Feelings take shape when you speak their name and time flows more slowly so you have the time to say them."

"You're making this up. The old hunter didn't say all that."

Maria glanced at the canvas bag swinging against the American's hip.

"Is that what you write in your notebook?"

"No."

"What do you write?"

"Letters from people who aren't there anymore."

"Dead people?"

Pete pulled on the reins and both horses came to a halt at the same time. The afternoon was ending and in the long shadows it was hard to be sure what he could see. They got off their horses and Maria cocked her revolver.

The mule had been shot in the middle of the path and left there to rot. Pete squatted down to read the tracks in the earth: horseshoes, deep-dug bootheels – the soldiers they'd been following for half the day. The gun trembled in Maria's hand. She bit her lip.

"It's Gustavio's mule."

6

The first person they met was a woman carrying a baby on her back, but Maria did not ask her anything. Then they saw a boy with a piglet on a lead. Maria didn't speak to him either. Then a peasant leading a cow, accompanied by a little girl of four or five. Maria greeted them, but did not question them. Finally they saw an Indian, a man walking with a stick, one of his feet horribly swollen, the flesh cut by the straps of his sandals. He and Maria exchanged a few words in Xinca, their language, which would soon be dead. Then she put a coin in the old man's hand and went off with the gringo. On a hill in the setting sun, the shadows of trees planted in rows were the first geometric forms that Pete had seen in a long time; the first signs of human activity. After one last bend in the road, the forest came to an end; the mountains plunged down to a cultivated plain where four paths converged on a town. Maria left the road and took the path that ran alongside the plantation, under slender-trunked trees with large dark leaves, their branches hung with yellow fruit in the shape of ribbed mortar bombs.

"Governor Ortiz's land. These are his cacao plantations."

The path started to rise and the old horses struggled up the slope. Maria stopped in front of some moss-covered granite rocks.

"We can spend the night here. Make a fire."

The scent of resin rose from the wood as it burned. Pete had tried to get Maria to talk, to find out what the old Indian man had told her, but she had not uttered a single word. He was about to lie down and try to get some sleep when she got up, a finger to her lips, and took the Colt Root from its holster. She moved away from the firelight. Pete pulled apart the flaming branches and kicked the embers so that they hissed like snakes in the damp grass. Maria had vanished like a cat in the woods. He rolled over to the trees, crawled through the brambles and froze when he heard a voice:

"Maria?"

It was a whisper, fifteen or twenty feet away.

"Maria?"

"Paul?"

Pete jumped. Maria was just behind him.

"Is that you, Paul?"

The man spoke in a louder voice. "I've been looking for you everywhere! Show yourself, Maria!"

She stepped over Pete and rushed away. Pete stood up and saw her moving towards the silhouette of a man, who took her in his arms amid the stars of the still incandescent embers. He held Maria's face in his hands and kissed her forehead.

"You're alive!" The man spoke Spanish with an English accent. "I heard what happened in Antigua. But there was no word of you."

He gently pushed Maria away from his body and lifted her face to the sky, trying to frame it in the moonlight.

"A message arrived today, saying that Gustavio and Santos had been locked in the Casa Negra and that you'd gone the same way as them with the American."

He kissed the Indian woman on her mouth and held her tight to his chest.

"You shouldn't stay here. Ortiz will send his dogs after your scent."

"He doesn't know I've come back."

"Maria . . . the Casa Negra. They'll talk. You know they will."

All Pete could see of the man were the angles of his face and shadows, the pale hair on his head and his long, slim outline. He picked up his belongings that were scattered around the fire. "I'll go fetch the horses."

The man had left his horse a few hundred yards further down the path. Maria and Pete's animals had not had time to recover and they were breathing heavily as they climbed this endless slope. For hours on end, eyes half-closed with sleepiness, struggling not to collapse, they inched their way up the mountainside.

Finally the man raised his hand and Pete heard a whistle in a tree above their heads. Two more times after that, the man signalled to lookouts in the branches and Pete glimpsed the lights of fires in the hollow of a valley, between two steep mountains, that disappeared into the misty and still-dark distance. In huts without walls, women, men and children awoke and watched the three riders pass. An old woman, held up by two younger women, was led over to Maria, who jumped down from the saddle. The old woman, taking the last few steps unaided, opened her arms wide.

The tall white man who had kissed Maria also got down from his horse. Immediately his horse was led away. Pete could see the man now in the grey light of early morning. His tall, thin figure, lost in the black of his clothes; his hair, which Pete had thought blond but which was actually white; and the large wooden cross that hung from his neck, around which was a priest's white collar. When he stood up straight, he walked like someone who'd taken a bad fall: spine and neck fused, pelvis creaking with every step. He was not as old as his prematurely white hair would suggest, but he struggled to move. Two Indian women helped him to sit down in a large seat carved from a tree trunk.

The old woman and Maria were still holding each other, talking softly, forehead to forehead. The entire tribe surrounded them. There were about fifty of them altogether, dressed in long coloured robes, round hats with flat brims, baggy trousers in faded colours . . . their clothes were woven and patched, and they were all barefoot. Maria was led into a hut and given food. The circle of villagers reformed around her. The priest signalled to Pete, who wished he was wearing his old clothes – his leather waistcoat and his gun, solid boots to walk in the mud of the village, if you could even call this a village. The men glared at him and women spat on the ground as he passed, covering their mouths with their hands and whispering in Xinca. The priest invited him to sit on a mat, but Pete remained standing. Remnants of food were burning in the fires. The place stank of damp, rotten meat.

"They didn't think they'd ever see her again."

The priest's eyelids fell slowly over his eyes, as if being closed by invisible hands. Pete thought about Rafael, about the hope you must give up if you want to live without surrendering: the sight of this gathering of peasants pressing around Maria made Pete think that the Comanchero had been right.

"Who are you?"

"My name is Paul Hagert."

"They haven't built a church for you yet?"

"I'm not a missionary. I live with the Xincas."

"You're not here to convert them?"

"They converted me, Mr . . .?"

Pete stared at Hagert's chest. "You're still wearing a cross."

Paul Hagert turned the wooden cross in his hands. It was covered with a layer of grime.

"I don't keep it for the same reasons as before."

Maria, the old woman beside her, was speaking to each of the other inhabitants in turn; they placed gifts and food at her feet.

"What are they doing?"

"They are honouring and celebrating her return."

"Are these people the reason she wants a revolution?"

"You seem annoyed. Aren't you a comrade of Maria's?"

Pete turned to face the priest. "What I want to know is if there's anything to drink in this place."

"There's pulque. That's all I can offer you."

"What is it?"

"Fermented cactus sap. They call it honey water."

Paul Hagert spoke to one of the women who was looking after his hut – the only building in the village with anything resembling walls. Pete wondered if the priest had wanted the walls so he could enjoy his Indian women in peace. The woman brought him a bottle of opaque liquid and cleaned two dubious-looking glasses with her fingers.

"It's not much stronger than wine. Maria banned distilled alcohol from the village."

The drink was horribly sweet and syrupy, but Pete made do with it. He had decided not to move from here, and to remain as far away as possible from the Indians.

The sun, having risen above the valley, had now dissolved the mist. The Xincas had left Maria there with the old woman, who was preparing an infusion in a saucepan over a fire, throwing in handfuls of leaves. Then she undressed Maria in the shrouds of light that illuminated the smoke and threw a blanket over her shoulders. Pete looked away.

"How did you get here?"

"Like all white men: on a trading ship that I thought was the representative of civilisation."

The bottle was placed on a chopping block darkened by dried blood. A sort of white down was stuck to the side of Pete's glass.

"I came here on a boat that was transporting a printing press."

Hagert smiled. His rotten teeth were proof of his liking for this sugary drink.

"Another ill-fated mix-up, that. My ship belonged to the Society of Jesus. I was a Jesuit priest."

Pete looked at the witch. She was waving a small, flaming branch above Maria's head.

"What's she doing?"

"She is using sage to wash her journey off her."

The witch walked on her twisted legs across the space that separated her hut from the priest's. Still holding aloft her incandescent branch, she stood in front of the young American, enveloping him in smoke and talking very fast. Pete waved his hand to disperse the smell of burned sage.

"What does she want with me?"

Hagert sent her back to her own hut, still muttering.

"She says that the vision must not come here. She says you must not cross the path of the Xincas and that you are not a prince."

"What does that mean?"

"Hard to be sure . . . Are you ever going to tell me your name?"

"Pete Ferguson. She spoke of a vision?"

"The old woman has visions more and more often these days. The more senile she becomes, the more the Xincas believe that she has divine powers."

"What did it say, this vision?"

"It spoke of a white prince with whom Maria was waiting to dance."

Pete almost choked on a mouthful of honey water. "To dance?"

"That's what the old woman said. It's a very old prediction."

Pete thought about Maria's frightened face when he had held her in his arms on the dance floor of the Palacio del Ayuntamiento. In Cuilapa, on the terrace, she had grown angry when he mentioned the ball. His thoughts were interrupted by Hagert, who continued speaking.

"It was the year we arrived here. We had walked from the north of the country. A dozen Indians had died during the trip and I had a fever myself. The former owner of this land – an old Belgian by the name of Van Dorp – went to Governor Ortiz, who came here with his troops to chase us away."

Pete blinked. The alcohol was starting to flow through his body, giving him that familiar numb sensation, when his voice started to echo inside his head. He felt simultaneously lighter – happy to talk – and heavier – sprawled on the mat.

"Ortiz?"

"The governor took advantage of the situation to expel the old Belgian at the same time and take possession of the lands himself. He became one of the biggest landowners in the south of the country and now he no longer needs elections to remain in power. The Xincas fled into the mountains with Maria."

"So this vision – about the dance – goes back to that period?"

"Why are you so interested in these superstitions, Mr Ferguson?"

"Just curious."

Hagert gave a brief smile and got to his feet. One of his women rushed over to help him.

"You'll excuse me, but tonight's ride has tired me out too much to continue this conversation. Tomorrow morning, if you're still curious to learn more about the Xincas, I'll take you to see a wonder very near here."

Pete raised his glass in acknowledgment. Hagert said something to his Indian woman. After she had accompanied the priest to his hut, she returned with another bottle of pulque, which she placed on the chopping board, eyes lowered before this white man who had emerged from one of the old witch's visions.

Maria had disappeared and the sun was high. The heat was rising from the damp earth. There was nobody left on the little mud street but a few kids and some chickens. Pete leaned against the priest's wooden seat, took off his stinking poncho and finished the bottle of pulque to wash his journey off him. He opened the second bottle and imagined himself a bandit, living like a king among the Xincas, on the old priest's throne. Well, his arrival had been announced in a vision, hadn't it?

He finished the honey water and slept for the rest of the afternoon, his mouth sticky with sugar and his belly swollen. One of Hagert's women brought him some food, then told him in Spanish to follow her to another hut next to the priest's. A bed had been made for him. He asked for another bottle. When she brought it to him, Pete thanked her by smacking her bottom and burst out laughing.

He was sleeping, drunk on pulque and fatigue, when the Xincas came back from the fields at the end of the day and gathered around Maria to eat dinner.

7

In a cup next to his bed was a decoction of roots the colour of coffee. He gargled some and spat the bitter liquid between his bare feet.

The priest sat on his humble throne and gazed wisely at the village's inhabitants. The Indians greeted him respectfully but distantly. Hagert had found a place for himself here, but he was still not one of them. Perhaps, even after all these years, they still mistrusted the white man. Around Pete, they lowered their eyes, pretending to ignore his presence.

Hagert took long draughts of the root decoction, probably as a way of punishing himself for overindulging in the pulque.

"Did you sleep well?"

"I needed it."

Until now, Pete had not seen a single weapon in the village. In truth, there was a tranquillity among these people that he had not experienced in a long time.

"Come and eat something before we leave."

"Where are we going?"

"I told you yesterday: a place I would like you to see."

Hagert smiled, pleased with the surprise he had in store for Pete.

"Where's Maria?"

"Come and eat."

The horse he had ridden from Cuilapa seemed to recognise him and bit his sleeve, a gesture that Pete wasn't sure how to interpret.

"On horseback we'll be there in an hour. It'll give us time to get to know each other better."

"What if I don't want you to know me?"

"Well, you listen and I'll talk then."

Hagert grimaced with pain as he bent his stiff knees and stretched his aching back to get on the horse.

"I think it is high time you learned more about this country and this continent, Mr Ferguson. You see, I have grown weary of discovering truths that help me to live but not really to understand. Knowledge is a more complicated but subtler guide. Do you have the faintest idea what I am talking about?"

"My father was a believer in discovering truths with his fists, if that's what you're alluding to."

Hagert grinned, exposing his grey molars. "Don't worry, I won't call you my son. And my forgiveness, which probably doesn't interest you anyway, does not have the importance it used to have. It no longer guarantees heaven, only my trust, which I now bestow on men whom I have learned to distinguish from bastards."

Pete followed Hagert's horse up a steep path, lowering his head under branches that clawed at his hat. He turned around and saw the huts of the village below, nestled between the trees.

"You don't hear confession from the Indians?"

Hagert laughed and Pete had the impression that the priest's lungs were expelling dust.

"They carried me on their backs, healed and fed me. Do you think it would be charitable of me, once I was back on my feet, to make them kneel before me and confess to sins that they haven't committed?"

"But you haven't abandoned your cross."

"They gave this to me after I lost the one I was wearing when I arrived. They were afraid that I would feel lonely, that I would miss my gods."

At the bottom of the next valley, there was a wooded plateau surrounded by mountain peaks, a deep triangle of four or five miles where huge trees grew. Some of them, ten or twenty feet higher than the others, were covered with red and yellow flowers that stood out against the green of the leaves. Pete saw, emerging above this canopy, the rectangular summit of a pyramid, its grey stones, and the last steps of a staircase half-covered in vegetation. Large birds of prey circled slowly above the stone peak. The songs of birds and insects rose from the forest guarded by this gigantic abandoned monument.

Pete got off his horse and took a few steps towards it. The entire plateau looked as if it were suspended between the surrounding mountains.

"Is this . . . is this the equator?"

Hagert had joined him now. "No, we're still a long way from the equator, Mr Ferguson, but this place is magical in every respect, I'll give you that. Follow me. From here, we must continue on foot."

They followed a path that snaked between the colossal trunks, supported by large hanging roots that billowed like curtains and were high enough to hide men and their horses. No rays of sunlight reached the earth, blocked by the leaves sixty feet above their heads, and the ground was a carpet of undergrowth, attempting to live in the shadow of those giants which were, themselves, covered with creepers. Mosquitoes whined; spiders as big as hands scattered down holes. It was cool, almost cold, in this fertile humidity. Pete followed Hagert as closely as he could. The vegetation grew increasingly dense and the path was starting to disappear. Without slowing down, the Jesuit pointed at a strange mound. Pete saw carved stones under the pile of plants. Now he knew what to look for, he spotted other domes like that one and understood that the whole plateau was a field of ruins, an abandoned city buried under the knotty arms of roots. He tried to imagine streets between these mounds; they would have been avenues, in fact, fifty or a hundred feet wide. They were walking down the middle of the biggest one, leading straight to the pyramid. Who? When? Why? The questions were crowding his mind when Hagert held up his hand to warn him to stop. Pulling him by the arm, the priest dragged him down to a crouching position in the vegetation.

A procession of Xincas was moving along the path. The old woman, decked out in bone and glass jewellery, was at the head of the line, carried on a chair by two men. Behind her, in a long dress, wearing a profusion of necklaces and bracelets, was Maria. Her face and hair covered with green paint, her eyes and lips circled with red, she could barely stand; two women helped her walk. Next came a dozen villagers, all wearing feathers and face paint. None of them saw the white men. Maria looked drunk, her head swaying from side to side, as if the big gold earrings she wore were weighing her down.

Hagert slowly stood up, a finger on his lips, and they waited for the Xincas to move out of sight before returning to the path.

"What was that?"

"An ancient ceremony. This is only the second time it's happened in the ten years I've been living with them. It's a sacrifice."

"A sacrifice?"

Hagert, the old defrocked priest, pointed up at the sky. "Didn't you notice the vultures?"

They arrived at the foot of the great pyramid. Its carved rocks, three feet high and six feet long, were covered with moss but inch-perfect in their alignment. Three sides of the monument were vertical; only the side with the steps had a slope, though even that was almost vertical. The staircase was like a ladder, the steps two feet apart, which had to be climbed up on all fours. Hagert sat on the first step.

"I will wait for you here, Mr Ferguson. If I made it to the top, I would be incapable of getting back down. It's a funny idea, isn't it? A priest who refuses ascension out of fear that he will not be able to descend again."

Pete started climbing the outsize steps, his muscles tenser than was necessary, checking every place he put his sandals and hands, following the vertical movement of the roots that led to the peak as if they were the pyramid's veins.

Approaching the summit, he turned around. At this height he had the impression that he was clinging to a wall. He could see Hagert far below. He felt a surge of vertigo and flattened himself against the rock, sliding his fingers into a crack and looking at the tree branches around him. The closeness of the vegetation calmed him down. He took a moment to breathe, relaxed his grip, and started climbing again. When he had risen above the canopy, the sunlight blinded him and he had to blink until his eyes adjusted. He was pouring with sweat by the time he reached the top and lay down on the little esplanade: a tiled area of about thirty square feet that ended in a blind wall. There was a bench carved into the wall and, at either side of it, two rows of terraced seating. The vultures circled above him. He dragged himself over to the bench and leaned against it.

At the end of the esplanade, just before the staircase that plunged down into the void, was what looked like a blood-stained millstone. It was only then that Pete saw the carcass, its belly slit open and its innards spilled all around. This was the sacrifice the priest had mentioned: a poor little goat, at the summit of this massive monument.

Bent double, he went over to the sacrificial table. A bowl filled with blood had been left next to the intestines, which were stretched out into a sort of hideous map. The smell was sickening. The animal's eyes were closed, its eyelids buzzing with flies. Pete moved away from the corpse and sat in the sunlight for a moment, delaying the feast of the vultures that circled ever lower. Then he climbed up to the last row of seating, at the angle of the wall. He pressed himself against the stone and contemplated the vast triangle of the valley.

It was a lost world – a dead world – that, apart from the Xincas of the village, hardly anyone had visited in centuries. Older than Veracruz, more ancient than the conquistadors, a hundred times older than Carson City, as big as the city of Antigua, where thousands of Indians had lived. That the Spanish should have rid themselves of poor tribes like Maria's, he could understand, but for them to have conquered cities as great as this one was beyond his comprehension. Pete thought about New York and Chicago, those metropolises described to him by Alexandra Desmond and Arthur Bowman, those cities so big that no enemy could dream of taking them, and tried to compare them to this vanished world.

He approached the staircase, looking again at the valley and the mountains around, the trees in flower that he could almost touch if he reached out his hand, and then he kneeled down to descend the steps backwards.

Step after step, going back into the shade of the branches, he found himself in the stale, cool air of the forest, amid the sounds of the fauna and the relentless, parasitic flora. His breathing grew calmer as he drew closer to the ground. Hagert encouraged him. "You're almost there, Mr Ferguson!"

The priest was still pale: the rest he'd taken did not seem to have done him any good.

"I call this place the Valley of Vanities. The Xincas still believe this pyramid has special powers, that it's an altar between heaven and earth where they can make their offerings to the gods. There are no priests left who really understand their religion; the old woman is losing her memory and a lot of the time she just makes it up as she goes along. She uses Maria as a prop to impress the others, but none of it has much meaning anymore. These rituals are not only useful in keeping their community united, it's also a form of reassurance. There are only a few of them left and they come to this place, where an empire was wiped off the map, because they believe that slitting a goat's throat will save them."

"Who destroyed this city?"

"Time. When the Spanish came, the valley was already in ruins. The Xincas lived in small communities in the region and spoke a language that was not the same as the one spoken by the Mayans. It was thought that they were the last representatives of that civilisation, but in truth nobody really knows. Maybe they were just a caste of warriors in that empire, who have now forgotten the art of war just as they have forgotten their religion. Maria is the only thing left that they believe in that is not a distorted memory: the daughter of a legendary chief; their last link with the past."

Hagert looked mysterious, as he always did when speaking of Maria.

"The Indians of this continent made offerings to the Sun God so that his light wouldn't go out. They lived in terror of the end of the world. Their gods were *partners*, with whom they'd learned to negotiate in order to be less frightened. The sacrifices were the quickest means of resolving conflicts with them. Debts were paid in full every season, never any longer than that. When the Spanish declared that there was only one, omnipotent god, the Indians imagined that it would be advantageous to trade it for their pantheon of thin-skinned deities. Buying favours from one god would be much simpler and more efficient. They discovered too late that the white men's god had withdrawn from the world and did not negotiate with anyone. That the debts owed to him were eternal and that no sacrifice would mollify his judgment. The whites reduced these superstitious tribes to the state of slaves: proof positive that their god was the strongest. As the Indians feared, the world ended, but it was not their Sun God who was responsible for it – it was the god of the men who wore crosses around their necks. When I look at these ruins, I wonder about the empires we have built in Europe and America. Do you think they have more chance of surviving than this one had, or do you think all our plans for the future are mere vanity?"

Pete had drunk all the water in his flask but his throat was still dry and he found it hard to speak.

"I've never seen anything as big and incomprehensible as this."

Hagert slowly stood up, one hand supported by the American's arm.

"It took me a long time to understand what I saw from the top of that pyramid. It will take you time too, Mr Ferguson, but you are younger than me. Perhaps you will get there quicker than I did."

The Jesuit began walking back along the path and Pete stayed for a moment at the foot of the steps. He looked up through the gap in the trees at the peak, from which he felt he still hadn't truly descended.

The Xincas had lit fires and the men, bare-chested – their bodies small but muscular – were doing some kind of warrior dance. They waved bows and lances around an Indian man dressed in city clothes, with fake military stripes made from bones on his shoulders and scraps of coloured fabric on his chest designed to look like medals. On his head was a ridiculous fringed hat with stag's horns tied to it. He was wearing a painted terracotta mask, the mouth open in a smile filled with dog's teeth under a black moustache. Governor Ortiz. An Indian woman armed with a branch carved to look like a rifle was dancing in front of this carnival governor, her face painted green and red. Tambourines were pounded and shaken in rhythm and the Xincas sang. Hagert, sitting on his infidel's throne, pointed to one of the dancers.

"That one is you."

Pete sat up. "What?"

The pulque, the pounding and the singing had gone to his head. He blinked and in the light of the flames saw a Xinca dancing hunched over like a monkey, bow-legged, arms dangling to the ground, dressed as a soldier, armed with a wooden pistol, his face painted white. The carnival Pete Ferguson was also dancing around the governor.

"What are they doing?"

The Jesuit contemplated his glass of honey water for a moment. "The ceremony that you are witnessing today is a warrior rite. The Xincas practise it when they send one of their people on a dangerous mission."

Hagert's voice choked on the last two words.

"What mission?"

"Governor Ortiz is a political enemy of the liberals and President Granados. He makes agreements with the conservatives of El Salvador and ignores the orders sent from Ciudad de Guatemala. But faced with the threat of a revolt and after the attempted assassination in Antigua, Ortiz has the same aim as Granados: to crush the rebellion. His men will soon find us here."

Pete watched the Indians dancing. "So . . . what are you saying? They want to kill the governor?"

The priest dropped his head forwards and did not answer. Pete burst out laughing.

"It didn't work with Granados so they're doing the same thing with Ortiz?"

"They still believe that, by killing the chief of their enemies, they will end the war. They don't know that princes have been replaced by politicians, Mr Ferguson."

"But she knows!"

Maria was sitting under the roof of the old witch, who – face painted – was circling around her like a fly. Suddenly Pete understood and he turned to face Hagert.

"They're sending her?"

The priest was crying.

"Are you going to let her do it?"

The Jesuit lifted his head. "I can't change her mind and I can't protect her. Only you can do that, Mr Ferguson."

Pete jumped to his feet. "What are you talking about?"

Hagert grabbed hold of him. "She won't give up. Gustavio and Santos will be hanged in two days, she will leave tomorrow . . ." he groaned. "The Xincas will go deeper into the mountains to hide, but Maria doesn't want to flee anymore. I can't stop her. You must go with her, Mr Ferguson."

Pete turned to the witch's hut. Maria was staring at him. She kept staring until he turned to look at the dancers, and then at Hagert slumped on his throne, at the village, the valley behind it sunk in night and, above them, the plateau of the pyramid. The Xinca warriors continued gesticulating around the fake governor. The green warrior woman and the American monkey were dancing together, just as the old witch's prophecy had said they would.

Pete went to his hut and stuffed his belongings into his bag. He sneaked behind the huts, through the darkness, to the horses. His old horse was sleeping on its feet. No-one was guarding the animals, no-one was watching him, this fugitive among fugitives. Everyone was fleeing except for her. Pete saddled the horse, listened to the tambourines and sat on the ground under the star-scattered sky.

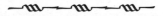

Arthur Bowman.

I know war. I know that men, when armed, are indistinguishable. That if you give them a rifle, there are no more farmers, fathers, craftsmen or engineers; there are only soldiers, and the great lie: borders no longer exist, war passes through them. They don't protect us, they just lock us in our own little war against ourselves. Even here, in the Fitzpatrick ranch, because I am here and because the war arrived here with me. Sergeant Arthur Bowman of the British East India Company. The war was in your father's house. In the snowy Sierra when you had to escape the army. In your brawls in Carson and in Lylia's bed. In old Meeks' balled fists. Among the Comancheros and the bison hunters, all those veterans unwanted now that railways and cities must be built, now that we must conquer and prosper and forget the five hundred thousand soldiers who have fallen on their backs and on their bellies in the last five years.

You have run away as far as you could. You have nowhere else to go and the war is still there.

Your little Indian woman would like to get out too, but sacrifice is her only weapon.

I wish I could have commanded armies of warrior women like her. And I hope I never have to fight against them.

On the eve of a battle, everyone writes letters. Suddenly you can summon a past that shines brightly in all its details. You cling to every particle of the present but it slips through your fingers like water even as you widen your eyes and dilate your nostrils. And the first thing you smell is the other soldiers' fear.

What irresistible, repugnant solidarity, knowing that you will not be the only one to die. And then you do the maths, you estimate: One in two? One in three? *You look at your friends. You feel ashamed and you weep that it has come to this:* Him, not me. All of them, not me. *On the eve of a battle, the reasons for our existence are more solid than those for the existence of others.*

But look at her, Pete: she is not asking for anyone to go with her. Your Indian woman will go to fight alone while you stay there counting your army: Me, me and me.

You don't understand that you have to save her, Pete, because the two of you are in the same trench. On the eve of a battle, when you look at her, what calculation will you dare to make?

You think all men are like your Old Man, the race of men from whose stupidity you must flee, whose malice you must combat. But there are also beings with whom you can choose to take your place. There is a place beside that woman.

Every day would have to be the eve of a battle, Pete, to calculate those who will live, work out how to save the greatest number of them and share their fate.

Your solitude has become impossible to fool. You are approaching your goal.

8

The empty huts were not really different from the huts when full, because the Indians had nothing to take with them. They disappeared towards the Valley of Vanities, the men taking the tools they would need to plant vegetables, the women carrying bundles on their heads, the children lagging behind, the old witch transported on a stretcher. All that was left were Hagert and his servants, the American, two readied horses, and Maria, who was already in the saddle.

The Jesuit played with his cross. "Make her give this up, Mr Ferguson, I beg you."

Pete turned his back to the priest and spoke to himself, but loud enough for the Indian to hear. "I have no intention of dying in this damned country."

Hagert watched them ride away. Maria, frowning, did not say goodbye, so Pete raised his hand. He had to do something.

She led the way, following abandoned paths between neglected plantations, descending towards the valley of Jutiapa, the lair of Governor Ortiz.

An Indian girl determined to kill a rich, corrupt landowner who was also a killer: Pete couldn't help feeling sympathetic towards this plan. But without weapons, riding on two old, rheumatic horses, without even a respectable pair of boots on their feet to be buried in, the heroism – that sickness of nations – did not speak to him at all.

"What do you plan to do once we're in town?"

"*Una arma, una bala.*"

The hangings were due to take place the next day at dawn. Half of Ortiz's soldiers and half of the city would be there. Maria didn't care, as long as the governor himself was there too.

"What about Gustavio and Santos?"

She did not answer any more of his questions until they had reached the last of the hills covered with kapok trees overlooking the city. She observed the plain. Along the paths that converged on the city, horses and stagecoaches raised clouds of dust. Hangings were as popular in Guatemala as they were in Nevada.

"You can leave whenever you want, *mercenario*. I was wrong about you – you won't be any use to me."

Maria gathered wood and built a fire with three stones. Pete wanted to slap her. He stared at the trunk of the kapok tree below which she was making camp. Its smooth bark was covered with thorns, as on a rose bush, but each one was as big as a thumb. The tree was armed to the teeth, completely paranoid. Rodents and birds were unfazed by those spikes. Lynxes and pumas used them to help them climb. Insects weren't bothered by them either. Man took as much cotton as he wanted from kapok trees and, when he needed to, cut them down just as easily as he did any other tree. The tree was armed for a war that had ended long ago. Maria, on the other hand, was going into battle unarmed. And she was right: the gringo was as useless as that thorn-covered tree.

Pete chose a bit of root that was not bristling with spikes and leaned his back against it. He took off his hat and tossed it on the ground. "Shit!"

The Indian, with her high forehead, her high cheekbones and her severe teacher's mouth, looked at him as scornfully as if it were the tree that had spoken.

"What are you doing? Hagert isn't here. You don't need to pretend anymore."

"Pretend?"

"To stay. You don't have to pretend that you want to do something. Go away. Leave me alone."

Pete burst out laughing.

"You can stop pretending too, Maria. You know perfectly well that killing Ortiz won't change anything."

Pete realised that he had called her by her name for the first time, and the memory of those leeches stuck to her legs came back to him. Maria stood up, her lips trembling. God knows it wasn't easy for an emotion to find its way to her face. She threw her head back and stared at the kapok tree, trying to stop the tears from falling, to make her eyes swallow them back. But these tears were too big.

"I have to do something for Gustavio and Santos."

Pete lowered his head.

"You can't save them."

He bit his cheek until he tasted blood.

"We'll go to Jutiapa. They'll see that you're there. Just like you showed the others that you weren't running away. Often, the only things we can do are to be there and to bear witness. That takes courage too. Sometimes . . ."

Maria went off to cry. Pete fed the fire and waited. She didn't come back, and he slept for a few hours in the arms of the tree roots. When she woke him, the sky was still black.

"Get up, gringo."

He rekindled the fire and they forced themselves to eat something, shoving the food down into their knotted stomachs. In the firelight Maria's face looked drawn and Pete had a fleeting vision of the old woman she might one day become, her future face revealed by the fatigue and despondency of the present. When their meal was over, they kicked dust over the embers, got back in the saddle and rode away from the hillside.

Perhaps the thorns on kapok trees had no use but to prevent men climbing them so they could tie ropes to their branches. You needed a ladder if you wanted to hang someone from a kapok.

Poor people travel on foot, so at the entrance to the town they left their horses in the stable of a cantina. Poor people cover their heads so as not to offend the rich with their ugliness. The poor people of

Guatemala are not white, so Pete hid his face. The rich cannot bear people who have less, but have more to say for themselves, so they walked in silence to the main square of Jutiapa, which was named after the governor, Santiago Ribeiro Ortiz, to watch two of their friends be hanged.

When she saw the gallows and the ropes tied in nooses, Maria felt dizzy and she grabbed Pete's arm.

They had to get closer so that Gustavio and Santos could see their faces. They moved through the crowd and stopped in front of the cordon of soldiers surrounding the platform. The executioner was up there now, his face uncovered, a functionary in black suit and top hat. Outside the gates of the governmental palace, in the shade of that building, four rows of seats had been set up for the town's worthies. The sun was peeking over the rooftops now, shining down on the square and the public. The sky was cloudless. It was a sharp, cutting dawn, in tune with the city's mood.

Ortiz emerged from his palace. He was tall, fat and dressed in black. He wore a hat and he walked with short, quick footsteps, escorted by ten soldiers. He took his seat on the terrace. There was a smattering of applause among the worthies, some of whom nodded as he passed, but the crowd did not cheer his arrival. Barely had he raised his hand in a general greeting before faces turned to the palace gates. A cloud of dust rose from the crowd's stamping feet.

The Casa Negra, Hagert had said, was not the government prison. It was an annex of the palace, Ortiz's private prison where his faithful henchman – known as the Secretary – interrogated those from whom the governor wanted information, or upon whom he wanted to take his revenge. The only prisoners who ever returned from those damp cellars were the ones whose execution served the public interest. The others were never seen again.

Gustavio and Santos emerged from the gates under escort, their faces swollen and bruised, their arms supported by soldiers, incapable of walking a single step on their own. Ortiz and the worthies removed their hats and the crowd imitated them. Maria put her hand to her mouth so as not to cry out. She took a step forwards and the soldier in front of them nervously barred her way.

"Stay where you are!"

The murmuring grew louder as the condemned prisoners neared the gallows. The executioner, a short, plump man, put his new hat between his feet when the two men arrived at the top of the steps. The soldiers who were holding them gripped them even tighter, perhaps anticipating a vain escape attempt or readying themselves to lift the prisoners up if their legs gave way completely.

Gustavio and Santos were thirsty. That was all Pete could think: that the two men were dying of thirst. They opened and closed their mouths like fish on sand. Pete wanted to yell at someone to give them a drink of water. The wood of the gallows, warmed by the sun, was dry; the fabric of their clothing was rough; the dust covered their skin and blocked their pores; the fibres of the ropes that caressed their necks were bristly like cacti; the Adam's apples of the two prisoners slid up and down in their throats; their eyes were burning. They did not dare look at each other. They looked at the crowd, a swell of anger, sadness and expectation. Pete, too, felt suddenly dizzy and his mouth filled with saliva, so much of it that he had to spit. Mouth open, he was drooling like a dog as he saw, once again, his father, throat crushed by the rope, face turning blue, lips moving. Hubert Ferguson, asking his son for something to drink.

The judge who had expedited the trial stood up from his place among the town's worthies and his voice, suddenly bursting forth in the incredible silence of the square, made Maria jump. A sheet of paper in hand, he read out the list of crimes for which the men had been found guilty: plotting against the State and the democratically elected President of the Republic, Miguel García Granados; criminal association with foreign agents; high treason; and vagrancy. The sentence was death by hanging. The absurd accusation of vagrancy – the reminder of that contemptible law – took the crowd to the edge of anger, though they remained silent.

Gustavio and Santos were losing what strength remained to

them. They were trembling more and more. Santos was the first to lower his head and look into Maria's eyes. She let the poncho fall to her shoulders so he could see her face. Santos silently spoke the name of the little Indian woman. Gustavio in turn saw her, and the two men had tears in their eyes. Water, at last. Salted. Gustavio fell to his knees and the soldiers lifted him up. Maria threw herself forwards and Pete pulled her back. He hissed: "What are you doing?"

He wanted to put the blanket back over her head but she pushed him away.

"Gustavio!"

The woman's cry petrified the crowd, even the executioner.

Faces turned to the gates of the palace, where Ortiz's secretary was dragging Amalia by her arm.

On the platform, Gustavio blinked, his gaze, like that of the entire city, turning to his wife, who was screaming. Amalia cried out his name and planted her heels in the dust while the Secretary kept forcing her to advance.

Gustavio yelled: "Leave her alone! She didn't do anything! Leave her alone!"

Amalia stumbled up the steps. The Secretary pulled her up to the platform. He put his hand on the back of her neck and turned her head to face the crowd. The man's voice drew shudders from all those who had encountered him before or knew of his reputation.

"The two accused refused to give the names of their accomplices. For this reason, Governor Santiago Ribeiro Ortiz does not pardon them. But your government has decided to pardon this woman, this wife and mother. On the condition that she talks!"

The Secretary shouted into Amalia's ear, so that everyone would hear his words: "Give me the names of their accomplices!"

Gustavio, desperately weak, begged his wife: "Amalia, *por favor*, don't do that! *No digas nada!*"

Pete threw the poncho over Maria's hair and led her back through the crowd. But Amalia had already followed Gustavio's gaze and she pointed in their direction. The Secretary stared at where she was pointing. Gustavio yelled: "Amalia, no!"

Santos reacted at the same time. The executioner had not yet shackled their feet. They shoved past their guards and charged at the Secretary, knocking him to the floor. Guards swarmed over the gallows and immobilised the two prisoners. The Secretary shouted: "They're here! They're getting away!"

The crowd, which had come to see two of their kind be hanged, responded with one vast voice: "Let them live! Death to the Governor! Free Jutiapa!"

Pete had put his arm around Maria and was leading her away as fast as he could. They pushed against the tide of men and women swarming towards the gallows. She turned around to see. The surge forwards, the executioner, the soldiers holding Gustavio and Santos on the trapdoors. Amalia scratching the guards' faces. The executioner pulling the lever, the soldiers jumping backwards to avoid falling with the hanged men. The crowd attacking the gallows and the worthies who were fleeing from their seats . . . Maria screamed like an animal. Pete dragged her on with one last effort and they were expelled from the crush of the mob. The soldiers who were pursuing them had been stopped or knocked out.

They were in an alleyway. They passed a small crossroads where a fountain bubbled. Maria had lost her poncho and her dress was torn, exposing a shoulder and a breast. She was staggering, just behind Pete, wishing she could stop at the fountain to quench her unbearable thirst. Gunshots echoed between the walls of the streets. The stable was just ahead, the horses saddled. The American took the reins in one hand and Maria's lead rope in the other. They left the city at a gallop. Towards the green mountain, with its springs and its rivers. To escape . . . and to drink water.

9

The riot in Jutiapa had held back the pursuing soldiers, but the dust must have settled on the square by now and the Secretary have sent more troops after them. If they joined the Xincas, they would be handing the tribe to Ortiz. That left the north, Antigua and the ghosts of the resistance network. Pete's horse died first, its heart giving way on the ride up the mountain. Maria's carried them a few miles further and met its end just as they reached the forest. The gringo carried the Indian on his back, grabbing onto roots as he climbed the steep slope, away from the beaten track. With Maria's inert little body on his shoulders, her limp legs beating against his, the air in his lungs felt as heavy as sand. He crawled, fell down, got up again, hoisting her up his back, again and again until evening, when he collapsed with his face to the ground. Maria was lying on top of him like a lead blanket. His clothes were in tatters, his feet bare, and he had no idea where they were. Maria's head was pressing against the back of his neck and he could feel the blood pulsing in her temple, a lock of her hair tickling his eyes and nose. Pete inhaled her smell and they began breathing in sync. He took the woman's hands in his own and put them against his ribs. Maria, unconscious or incapable of resisting, hugged the American in her arms and the night rolled over them.

She wasn't there when he opened his eyes. The spiderwebs were beaded with dew, which had accumulated in tiny puddles within the hollows of dead leaves, like reservoirs for insects. His hands and face were swollen from bites and stings. Pete had slept all night, without moving a muscle, and he had not felt it when the Indian moved away from him. He licked drops of water from the grass, stretched his body, and began to walk towards the top of the mountain, hoping to find a clearing so he could estimate their position. The surface of the ground became rocky – those lace-like volcanic rocks, full of little air holes – and he had to climb over them, scraping his hands in the process. Cactuses grew in this rugged landscape, birds nested in the holes, and lizards skittered around looking for eggs to swallow. It took him half an hour to reach the promontory; Maria was there, sitting looking out over the plain at Jutiapa. They were only about ten miles from the city, on the steepest side of the mountain. Governor Ortiz's city was not in flames; no plume of black smoke announced a battle or a revolt. The soldiers must have suppressed the uprising. What had happened to Amalia? Maria stared at the pale stain of buildings as if she could still see the gallows on the square. Pete sat next to her. She breathed out slowly.

"We came back in 1860 from the northern plantations. Not to take back our land, just to live there and grow enough vegetables to survive. Old Van Dorp was not a bad man, but he got scared and he fled to the city to warn the governor, who gathered his troops. They killed five of us and took Father Hagert to the Casa Negra. He came out weeks later, white-haired and broken-backed. Four of Ortiz's men dragged me into some dried-out coffee bushes. I was fourteen. I learned many things that day. I learned about desire and its satisfaction. Possession. Self-sacrifice. In those bushes, I managed to abandon my body. The governor's soldiers weren't fucking me, but themselves. They were turned on watching one another rape me, yelling that I was so ugly that they were doing me a favour by taking my virginity. But it's not them I remember really, it's Ortiz: sitting on his horse and watching. What turned him on was seeing his men obey him. When he felt like it, he said that was enough. They left me there, searching for some scraps of clothing to cover myself. They thought they'd given me a lesson I would never forget. They wanted to shut my mouth forever. Later, I learned that there was nothing wrong with giving your body to a man when you wanted to, and I learned other languages so I could speak with all the inhabitants of this country."

She paused, still staring at the distant city. She gave Pete enough time to say something, but he stayed silent.

"It's true that Ortiz forgot about me a long time ago, but he knows that there are Indians on this mountain that he hunted before and who haven't disappeared. I am not a metaphor: the Indian woman raped and dispossessed of her land, like the inhabitants of this country. And my tribe – or what's left of it – is not Governor Ortiz's bad conscience. We are just the excuse he needs to have an army around him and to continue getting turned on by their obedience."

"The right to do what he wants in his own home."

Maria smiled. "You know why condemned prisoners spit in the face of their executioner? It's not to insult them, but to prove that they are not afraid. With the rope around your neck, getting enough saliva in your mouth to spit is quite a feat."

She stood up.

"I'm done with this place, gringo. What do you plan to do?"

Pete looked at his bare feet. "Leave this country before I end up on the gallows. Find Aznar, if he's still in Guatemala. And a pair of boots."

"I can help you find Aznar."

Pete glimpsed Maria's skin beneath the torn fabric of her dress. She caught him looking and he blushed. The Indian shook her head.

"You could try to take me, gringo, but you wouldn't manage it. It takes a courage you don't have to sleep with a woman like me while looking her in the eyes. A bit like finding enough saliva when you're on the scaffold."

Pete stayed to look at the city where Maria had gone to see her lovers hang, his head filled with the repulsive image of a dangling corpse with an erection. He felt uneasy, refusing to remember whether his father had been erect while he was dying, while Pete looked him in the eyes.

The Cuilapa track was the only one that led to Antigua, but they could not take it. They followed it from a distance, beating their own path through a mass of vegetation. Maria picked what food she could find, and there was plenty of water. In the remote shacks of a few peasants they were given hospitality and some food to add to what they had found as they were walking. At night, Pete set snares. Rodents and lizards: enough meat to keep them going each day. One starless night they passed through Cuilapa and crossed the bridge over Los Esclavos, that cold, misty river.

The return to the old capital inverted and corrupted time, whereas before this Pete had been content to push it ahead of him. Since leaving the ranch, he had never retraced his footsteps. Now his journey was turning back on itself, a backwards step that proved the definitive impossibility of fleeing. He had entered the Indian's time: of eternal return, of a combat that could only be carried out here, now and always. When she stopped walking that evening, Pete sat closer to her.

"What will you do in Antigua?"

"Are you worried about me, gringo?"

"You said you were done with this place. Where will you go?"

"What about you?"

"Do you just not want to reply, or do you really want to know where I'm going?"

Maria lay on the ground and turned away from him. "When you have left, I will go to live the life of an Indian woman. What else do you think I can do?"

In front of them, the Agua volcano was belching smoke. For two days the black plume had guided them towards Antigua and they reached the great lake of Amatitlán in the evening. They drank their fill and then went back through the undergrowth to find a sheltered spot to sleep. In the morning sunlight, they looked at each other, surprised by this luminous volcanic land. When they came out of the forest, they were black with filth and they stank, their clothes had lost all vestige of colour, their hair was tangled, and Pete's beard was a nest for vermin. He walked away and Maria took off her clothes. She dived into the water and rubbed her clothes clean. Out of sight, he did the same.

Dressed in the still-damp wool and cotton, staring at the reflections on the lake, they waited until the time seemed right for them to go on their way. A pause for breath before continuing, and soon they would reach the city, where they would have to hide.

"Are you going to see the equator, gringo?"

Pete looked at her. He no longer saw her as small; the proportions of the world had changed and were now matched to those of her body.

"How old are you, Maria?"

Her face went blank. In a country where surviving childhood was a notable feat, nobody asked people their age. Here, once you were past thirty, you had lived.

"I was born in 1847."

"Do you think you'll live much longer?"

"Nobody can know that."

"I think you can know if you still have enough time or not. The time to do something else. The desire to go on. Real time. There are people who tell themselves that they've had what they could, that this life was enough, and they're already a little bit dead. If I don't find Aznar, I'll find another boat."

She gave a little laugh. "I'll be an Indian wherever I go, gringo. Even at the equator."

"But you can't see it from here."

Maria stood up.

"We have to go."

"There's nobody left in Antigua. Where do you want to go?"

"To the Gallo Blanco cantina, where . . ."

Pete thought: *Where I saw you for the first time.*

"I remember that place. But there's nothing left in Antigua, and you know it."

In the darkness, they sought out the paths less taken. She talked to him of spies, said that the city was full of them, that half of the people were working against the other half. Pete thought the world couldn't care less about them.

At the Gallo Blanco, the owner's wife went into a panic when she saw them. Her husband had been arrested, she didn't know what had happened to Aznar, but Guzman was still hiding in Antigua. They would have to talk to Manterola's housekeeper; she might know something. She begged them to leave before they were discovered.

Pete found his way back to avenida Norte and pushed open the wrought-iron gate. They walked across the patio and knocked at the poet's door. Faustina opened it and almost cried out, but Pete pushed her inside and closed the door behind them.

"We're going to spend the night here and you will bring us food for as long as it takes us to find Guzman."

Pete opened the sideboard where Faustina kept the alcohol and pulled the cork from a bottle of brandy. The old servant was more shocked by the presence of the Indian girl in the poet's house than by the return of the brutish American.

They ate dinner without candles on the table in the large living room. Since the Maestro's arrest, Faustina explained to Pete, the situation had been difficult. Only the poet's reputation kept the mayor from expelling him, but his fate would soon be decided after the trial. Pete asked how Manterola was and Faustina had to hold back her tears.

"I don't know if he'll live long enough to go to the courtroom, Señor Ferguson. They wouldn't let me take him any food, and he was so weak..."

Maria wiped her mouth with the back of her hand. "Do you know where Guzman and Aznar are?"

Faustina listened to the question then turned to Pete before she gave the answer. "I have not heard from Señor Aznar, but Señor Guzman came to bring me a message that I took to him in prison. There is also a place where I can leave messages from the Maestro for him."

The old woman cleared away the table, happy to serve, even for the American.

"I warmed up some water and prepared a bath, Señor Ferguson. You still have some clothes here. Your room is ready." She deigned to glance at the Indian. "I also prepared the storeroom."

When she had left the room, Maria leaned towards him. "She'll denounce us to save the poet. We have to get out of here."

"She won't do anything tonight. We can leave when we know how to contact Guzman."

"Ask her now and then let's go."

"I'm going to wash myself and get some sleep. You can have the bedroom, I'll take the storeroom."

He took the bottle of brandy upstairs. The bathroom adjoined the Maestro's bedroom. Faustina had put a candlestick on a sideboard, in front of the mirror, with a towel and one of Pete's suits carefully folded next to it. Pete threw his Indian rags on the floor and slid into the hot bath, putting the bottle on the tiles below.

He woke up shivering. The water was cold, the candles almost burned down. He dried himself and went into Manterola's bedroom. In the desk drawer, the pistol was still there: the little double-barrelled pistol engraved with arabesques and inlaid with mother-of-pearl. He put the candlestick and the gun on the desk blotter, took out a sheet of paper, dipped a quill in the inkwell.

Once the letter was finished, he went down to the ground floor. In the candlelight he looked at Maria, who was sleeping fully dressed on a wool mattress in the storeroom.

He went up to his old bedroom and lay down, arms crossed behind his head, to await the dawn.

10

"Where do you leave messages for Guzman?"

"Plaza de Independencia. There's a bench near the fountain and a crack between two stones."

"When does he pick them up?"

"Every other day. He'll come today."

"You can go shopping for me, and leave this message at the same time."

Pete gave her a page folded in two. Faustina had tied a black scarf around her head. Maria watched them from the living room. Pete put a hand on the housekeeper's shoulder.

"The Maestro would not trade his life for ours. Don't do anything stupid or he'll be angry with you for the rest of your life."

The old woman blushed with shame, as if the American had read her thoughts, and bowed before leaving.

Barefoot in a suit, he went into the living room and sat down. Maria was pacing around the house, keeping to the shelter of doorways. Pete poured himself a glass of port.

"She'll come back."

"You only know how to trust whites, gringo. You never imagined that Indians could help you; you only thought about Aznar and Guzman. The old woman would do anything to be the poet's slave again."

"Your Indians don't have a boat."

"I'm leaving."

Pete smiled. "Granados is more interested in Guzman than in you, but Faustina hasn't denounced him. She won't do anything. You should calm down and take a bath – you smell bad."

She stared at him contemptuously for an instant, wiped her damp palms on her dirty skirt and hesitated; her nostrils narrowed as she lowered her head. She disappeared into the kitchen. Pete heard the stove door open, then the sound of logs thrown into the firebox. She was going to warm up some water. He moved his chair around so he could keep an eye on the front gates. He put the little Derringer on the pedestal table beside him, next to the bottle of port. It was a gentleman's pistol that made no more noise than a popping champagne cork.

When Faustina returned, she put a pair of new boots and a wrapped parcel on the dining-room table.

"I also delivered your message, Señor Ferguson."

"As soon as we get a response from Guzman, we'll go. Are you supposed to visit the Maestro today?"

Faustina replied that she went to the prison every afternoon.

"Can you give him a letter?"

"There's a guard, but I can pass him papers. Sometimes we can speak without being heard too."

"Good. I'll give you a message for him too. Take the parcel to Maria." The housekeeper was about to take offence, but Pete smiled, his mouth sweetened by the port. "She's still in the bathtub, so I can't go. Just leave the parcel in her room."

Faustina had chosen a grey cotton maid's uniform and a pair of flat leather shoes. Maria swelled with anger before realising that the old servant had chosen wisely. An Indian woman in a nice dress was either a whore or a source of great curiosity. Next to the gringo, this servant's outfit was the only plausible one she could wear. Her feet, widened by the walk and the sandals she'd worn, barely fit into the tight leather shoes. Wearing the grey dress in front of a mirror, she was assailed by memories of the orphanage. The Xinca children in uniform, hair neatly combed, fringes straight, standing to attention in the canteen, hands held out for the hygiene inspection. Rage roared in her chest again.

When she went into the living room, the American was drunk, but he looked handsome in his pale suit, despite or perhaps because of his bare feet. There was a pair of new boots on the table. Maria pretended she didn't care about her dress, although she was irritated that she hadn't made a better entrance.

"So she delivered the message to Guzman?"

"We'll have the response tonight."

Before he could make a comment about her outfit, she walked over to the pedestal table, drank all the port in Pete's glass and went out to the patio. Through the window he saw her take off her shoes, which were hurting her feet. The Indian frowned at the sun. She was crying. She came back into the living room and filled another glass.

The smell of food wafted through from the kitchen. Faustina was making the meal that she would take to the Maestro. Soon she would leave for the Antigua prison, the message for the poet sewn into a clean shirt.

Maria drank glass after glass, without a word, and fell asleep in a chair. Pete watched her deaden her senses. He too would eventually be too drunk to think, but he continued to keep guard while slowly sipping his port, observing Maria's calves, the hem of the maid's dress on her skin, her squarish feet with their callused heels.

———— ⁄⁄⁄— ⁄⁄⁄— ⁄⁄⁄—

Dear Maestro,

If Faustina delivers this letter, it will be the first I have written in two years to someone who will actually read it.

I am at your house with Maria the Indian and I wanted to talk to you about that other woman who told me, once, that if I was ever lost in a city, I should find a writer. You are the first writer I ever met, and I set off on a political adventure with you. I think that was also something that this other woman wanted me to understand: that literature and politics go together. I hope you will die free to write again, or honourably in front of a firing squad of soldiers impressed by your face, not in that cell where Faustina goes to visit you. You deserve a writer's death, even if I don't have the faintest idea what that would be – certainly something noble and spiritual.

I am going to leave this country to which you introduced me. I hope you won't mind if I take a volume of your poems with me, chosen from your library, and your Derringer. I am going to find another boat, with the hope that I will meet another poet and go on a new adventure.

Maria doesn't know where she will go. To be honest, I don't think she knows where she is anymore. Along with you, she was the one who helped me to know this country. Maybe she should go to sea too, but changing the mind of this woman would be a job for a man like you, someone good with words, not a Yankee like me. But listen, Maestro Manterola, there is now a new problem. I don't know if I can leave Guatemala without her. That is the story I am writing to you, Maestro Manterola: of an adventurer with no destiny and an Indian woman with no land. I hope you will like it and that it will warm you a little bit in your cell, that you will have the desire to keep going.

Despite the circumstances, the secrecy and the lies, we were friends. That is the memory I will keep of you, along with your poetry that I am taking with me. This message is not that of a traitor asking for forgiveness, Maestro. I didn't want to be your misfortune, I just wanted to save Maria.

Perhaps I will see you again soon, in a cell or in front of that firing squad. It is for her to decide that now. Guatemala or the sea. Let us leave our fate to the women. Isn't that, Maestro, an ending worthy of a poet?

Hasta luego.

Your faithful secretary

Faustina returned late that afternoon and disappeared into her room, her eyes red from crying on the way back. Maria was woken by the housekeeper's arrival. Her eyelids drooped over her round eyes and she washed her face in the kitchen.

"I'm not used to drinking."

"I could tell."

"It's better than being used to it, don't you think?"

Pete pulled a red chilli pepper from a bunch that was hanging from a ceiling beam. He chopped it up with an onion and put a frying pan on top of the stove. He broke half a dozen eggs into the pan, sprinkled them with pieces of chilli and mixed them together. He put the plates on the small kitchen table and divided the contents of the pan between the two of them. They pushed the pieces of omelette onto their spoons with pieces of bread and ate quickly, both leaning forwards. The chilli stung their eyes and made their foreheads sweat.

"A good hangover recipe." Pete said as he wiped his plate with the bread. "This is the only meal I know how to make."

Maria laughed and wiped her hands on the grey dress.

Faustina returned from the fountain at ten o'clock. She brought a message from Guzman, which Pete read and then passed to Maria.

"We're leaving."

The housekeeper trotted to the kitchen and came back with a bag of provisions, which she handed to the American.

"I'll carry that," Maria said, sarcastically. "I'm the servant."

Faustina rummaged in her apron pocket and took out three carefully folded banknotes.

"This is from the Maestro." The housekeeper lowered her eyes. "He told me to tell you that you can take the book."

"What else did he say?"

"The Maestro told me to say to you, Señor Ferguson, that your skill with words was enough to . . . to decide to take the next step of your voyage together."

Pete pocketed the money.

"Don't worry, Faustina, I'm sure that Granados will pardon the Maestro."

They left the house and were crossing the patio when the old woman called them back. "Wait!"

She gave Pete a leather waistcoat that came halfway down his thighs, and an American hat that he remembered once seeing on Manterola's head. To Maria, she gave a soft wool shawl and a headscarf. She quickly wished them good luck and padlocked the gate behind them.

The meeting with Guzman was at midnight, on the Ciudad de Guatemala road, on the outskirts of town. They walked confidently like two people who know where they are going. With the shawl and scarf for Maria, the waistcoat and hat for Pete, they looked like a wealthy couple going home late at night. They took backstreets, made detours, retraced their footsteps and then headed east again.

"Guzman said he knows where Aznar is. That means his boat is still there."

"The boat may be there, gringo, but Guzman and Aznar will not be as sentimental as Manterola. They'll make you pay for your betrayal."

She said all this quite naturally. A traitor must die.

"I'm not naive."

"So you know what to expect from this meeting with Guzman?"

"That's why you're going to do the talking."

Maria smiled. "Is that why you carried me on your back? So I'd negotiate for you?"

The street grew dark as they approached the edge of town and the houses became increasingly few and far between. They sneaked between two buildings and followed a drainage ditch that ran behind, in order to avoid any sentries. After that, they returned to the black path and quickened their pace. Further on they saw the glow of lanterns outside the coaching inn where Guzman had arranged to meet them. Four or five shacks, about a mile from the city. They recognised the one mentioned in the message: a former restaurant converted into a feed barn, and squatted down in the darkness, waiting in silence. The lights of the inn were there to guide any travellers, but the place was closed for the night. Maria stood up.

"Wait here."

Pete grabbed her arm. "You needed to see Guzman too. That's why we stayed together. And you need to leave this country too, you said it yourself."

"I know what I said. I'll find you your boat, gringo, if you want to take it."

The American was going to say something else. She felt his fingers tighten around her arm.

"What?"

"That boat . . . If you don't go . . ."

He didn't finish his sentence. He let go of her arm, jumped over the ditch and disappeared between the trees. Maria stayed there for a moment, listening to him run away, the dead branches cracking under his feet. Then she hissed between her teeth that the gringo was a madman.

II

Maria walked towards the inn, disturbed by Ferguson's hesitation. Her mind was following paths that she did not want to go down. She thought again about those tranquil hours spent in the poet's house, about how she had felt, being close to the American, behind those walls and the padlocked gate. She remembered his looks and his gestures. What had the housekeeper said when she passed on the poet's message? *To take the next step of your voyage together* . . . Maria tried to concentrate. She was walking alongside the windowless wall of the inn now, approaching the former restaurant. She paused, waiting for her head to stop spinning. She was back on the dance floor in the Palacio del Ayuntamiento, the orchestra was playing, and then the old woman was placing embers on her belly after Ortiz's soldiers had raped her. The old woman was in a trance – this was twelve years ago – rolling in the dirt, eyes rolled back in her head, repeating that Maria the Baptised would dance with a white prince. She put her hands on her knees, bent over double and took deep breaths. *The next step of your voyage* . . . She walked around the building and found the back door, which opened without difficulty. *Together.* The gringo was crazy.

"Guzman, *estás allí?*"

Ferguson was crazy, but he was right. She should leave this place. Guzman was dangerous. A paranoid intellectual, backed into a corner.

"Alberto Guzman?"

The interior of the building had been taken apart, the walls and staircases knocked down to store heaps of feed; she could make out the patterns of old wallpaper, the ceiling stripped of its floorboards and, ten feet from the ground, the windows with smashed panes. The moonlight illuminated bales of hay.

"Guzman, *dónde estás*?"

"Here."

Guzman's voice hissed behind her back. He was standing against the wall next to the door, motionless, trying to blend into the faded floral motif of the wallpaper, his glasses reflecting the latticework of the windows for an instant. He wore a small straw hat on his head and a poncho over his arm. He dropped the poncho and in a circular movement he aimed the barrel of his gun at the Indian woman, the feed and the door.

"Where is Ferguson?"

"He got scared. He didn't trust you. He left on horseback for Puerto Barrios. He wants to find a boat so he can leave the country."

Guzman pointed the gun at her again. "On horseback?"

"Manterola left him some money. The American bought a horse."

"What?"

"Manterola helped him to escape."

Guzman moved closer to her. "The American betrayed us and Manterola is helping him to get away, is that what you're telling me? You're the one who hid him after his betrayal at the palacio. You came back to Antigua with him. He leaves me a message, then he disappears and you come here in his place. What the hell is going on?"

Maria took a step forwards and the intellectual shrank back, surprised that she was not intimidated by his size and his weapon.

"The American realised he couldn't rely on the network any-more. Gustavio and Santos were hanged in Jutiapa, Governor Ortiz is searching for me, and the Xincas are on the run. I have to leave this country too. I need to find Aznar. Where is he?"

Guzman calculated quickly. What this Indian girl was saying was plausible. "I have to leave too," he said.

But something wasn't right. He shook his head and raised his gun again.

"Why did you help Ferguson after what happened in the palace? What happened in Jutiapa?"

"Tell me where Aznar is."

Guzman raised his voice. "Manterola betrayed me. Ferguson is on his side, and so are you. What are you doing here?"

This time, Maria stepped back. "Calm down, Guzman."

"You all betrayed me. They destroyed my newspaper!"

Seeing Maria jump into the hay, he fired at her. The detonation made the shack's walls tremble. The bullet whistled through the air and buried itself in horse feed. Guzman, shocked by the noise and violence of the gunshot, yelled as he moved towards her: "Tell me where Ferguson is! I will punish him for what he did. And you, too, must pay for your crimes!"

He cocked his pistol again. In comparison, the small click of the Derringer sounded ridiculous.

"Drop your gun, Guzman."

It sounded so ridiculous, in fact, that Guzman barely reacted when he turned and saw it.

"I never trusted you, Ferguson. Or Manterola. You're both deviants. Decadents. The Indian was a mistake too, I always said that."

Pete squeezed the Derringer's trigger. Guzman put his hand to his neck and was motionless for a second. He looked at his palm covered with shining blood and raised his gun towards Pete, who fired again. Guzman stared incredulously at his belly. The American had fired from too far away, and he had not hit any vital organ or artery; it would take him an hour to bleed to death. Pete threw himself at Guzman, who reacted with surprising speed, his too-slow thought processes overtaken by animal instinct. He hit Pete in the forehead with the pistol and the force of the blow sent him flying onto the floorboards. Guzman aimed at Pete's head. The three tines of the pitchfork pierced the flesh between his ribs and his vertebrae, and sank into his lungs. With one hand grasping at the back of his neck and the other at his lower back, the anarchist tried to reach the source of the pain. Maria let go of the handle and Guzman collapsed without realising who had killed him.

Maria swayed on her feet. They could see lamps moving outside, could hear voices coming from the coaching inn. Smoke was rising from the hay bale where Guzman's bullet had landed and was drifting towards the windows. Pete picked up the dead man's pistol, grabbed Maria's hand and pushed open the door.

They had been running for an hour and the flames were still lighting up the sky. First they had gone straight along the path, as fast as they could, then they had turned into the forest, seeking to disappear. The entire country was burning behind them. Soon the earth would give way beneath their feet. They rushed towards the ocean, not knowing whether Aznar's boat would be there waiting for them.

Once Faustina's provisions had been exhausted, they went back to their fugitives' diet: kneeling by streams to drink water from their cupped hands, chewing on seeds and plants they found on their way. Pete Ferguson planted his boot heels in the loose earth, dragging Maria, refusing to let go of her hand. In the evenings he wrapped himself in the leather waistcoat and Maria wrapped herself in the shawl, their backs touching as they slept. At night she spoke Xinca and her dreams woke her. The only words he could understand were the names of Guzman, Gustavio and Santos.

Skirting Ciudad de Guatemala on the northern path, they approached the small town of Mixco at night. They crossed the peak of a hill overlooking the village and Pete lingered between the great black silhouettes of pyramids that stood out against the paler sky. Now it was Maria who dragged him by the hand.

"Come on, we can't stay here."

She was afraid, so close to these vast sacrificial altars. Pete looked up at the monuments, lower and squarer than the great pyramid in the Valley of Vanities; he wanted to stay here, to climb up to one of those celestial tables to wait for the sunrise.

They left the ancient Indian city and headed towards a few lights, halfway to Mixco.

"We're not going fast enough, gringo. We need a horse."

She looked at the fences, a stone house with lighted windows, some other buildings around it – a farm.

"They must have horses in the barns."

Pete obeyed the implicit order. He leaped over the fence and disappeared. She heard a door creak open, then a whinny. She saw a light flash suddenly beside the house: a man with a lamp, standing on the front steps. The American fired and the bullet ricocheted from the stone wall. The farmer threw himself to the ground. Pete fired twice more into the air before reaching down to Maria. She grabbed his hand and jumped up onto the horse. They rode it bareback, and Maria held onto the American as tightly as she could. The earth vanished fast now under the galloping hooves. The horse could run but it was used to working the fields too; it was solid enough to carry them both.

By the early morning they were well past the capital and they rejoined the track they had taken four months earlier, going the other way, when Pete had just been appointed Maestro Manterola's new secretary. He continued going back in time, rediscovering a Pete Ferguson that no longer existed, that other Pete who now appeared to him helpless and lost, whereas now, although starving, he was riding with Maria and he had found his place.

When they kneeled down to drink in the morning, the horse bent down next to them to swallow its share of water. When they slept through the day like fugitives, it remained standing above them.

No-one could connect them to Guzman's death. Who would even know that the charred body in the coaching inn was his? He was just one more ghost on Pete's trail. Basin, old Meeks, Rusky, Rafael and the seven little graves in the Ojinaga cemetery. Ortiz, Granados, Gustavio, Santos and Guzman.

The horse was their ally. The Caribbean sea, with its cannibal islands, was close. They could feel its warm breath a little nearer every day. Their faces grew gaunt. Ten days riding at night and sleeping in the humid folds of tree roots. Waking up and going to sleep with the mist, hands cut from the grass stalks they ripped up to feed their horse.

On the morning of the eleventh day, climbing up the last hillside in the slate-grey dawn, they discovered the vast blue tongue of the gulf. That day they slept without keeping guard, amid silent snakes and the yowling of wild cats.

After that, it was all downhill. They slept for a day and a night close to Puerto Barrios, on a grey sand beach. The sound of the waves infiltrated their dreams. In the early morning Pete undressed and walked into the slack water up to his shoulders. He let the tide take him and opened his eyes, head back in the water. Above the moving surface he could see the first colours of sunrise. The salt cleaned his cuts and grazes.

He smashed coconuts on the edge of a rock and put them on the ground next to Maria. They drank the milk and scratched out the white flesh. The sugar tasted good. Their gums bled as they bit into the flesh.

Pete lay on his back, his belly aching.

"If you find Aznar, don't trust him."

Maria traced lines in the sand. "If Segundo is here, there won't be any problems with him."

"What about what happened with Guzman?"

Maria's fingers came to a halt. "He doesn't need to know about that for the moment."

She went on her own. An Indian would be more discreet than an American, and Maria remembered a place in Puerto Barrios where the captain used to hang out when he was ashore. She knew Aznar well; he was the one who had recruited her, she explained, just as he had recruited Pete. He watched her move away and for a few moments he walked behind her, pulling the horse along by its bridle, then he turned back to the beach. Fishermen were throwing nets into the water. Eastward, in the direction of the town, a few small boats were coming back from a night at sea. Pete walked over to the fishermen and sat next to them, turning to face the dark shapes of buildings at the end of the long beach, the pier and the skyline of Puerto Barrios.

—ɯ—

She waited outside the church near the cantina. The port was slowly coming to life. The long wooden pier stretching out into the water was an extension of the peninsula on which the village was built. Wooden huts ran alongside the beach; in the centre were villas, shops and the mansions belonging to traders, shipowners and landowners. The church was in the middle, its square close to avenida Central and the pier, like an arm enclosing the bay of Santo Tomás de Castilla. Maria was startled by the sound of a coin, tossed onto the ground between her feet by an old man. She stood up without picking up the money, and walked along the avenida towards the cantina. This was where she had met Aznar the first time, three years ago, and where the young captain had introduced her to Guzman.

Since she looked like a beggar, she remained at a distance from the restaurant. The waitress appeared, setting the tables and arranging the chairs on the terrace; she was politely greeted by the first customers. Maria walked over to her.

"Excuse me . . ." Maria stopped in the doorway and spoke quickly in a low voice. "Aznar, the captain of the *Santo Cristo*, is he here?"

The waitress glanced at the customers on the terrace. She too spoke quietly. "What do you want?"

"I'm looking for Segundo. Where is he?"

"I don't know him. Go away."

"I'm a friend of his. I need him."

Maria stood in front of the woman and pulled the scarf from her head, exposing her face. "Maybe you remember me? I've been here before with Aznar."

"Aznar has gone. Nobody here speaks his name anymore. Go away, *indígena*!"

Maria moved away as fast as she could. Several times she became lost in the identical-looking streets before finding the shop she remembered: a place that sold sailing equipment, where Aznar often came. Another network rendezvous had taken place here. A wagon stopped outside the warehouse and some half-Indian men unloaded coils of rope. The door to the office next door was open and in the doorway, a cup of coffee in one hand, stood the owner, whom she recognised: a pot-bellied white man with a neat beard. She waited until he went back in and followed close behind.

"*Buenos días, señor.*"

The owner recoiled. "*Dios!* What are you doing here? Get out!"

"I'm looking for Captain Aznar. It's urgent. Is he in Puerto Barrios?"

The owner narrowed his eyes. "Are you the Indian?"

He ran behind her and locked the door, then grabbed her shoulders and shook her. "Where is the American?"

Maria returned to the beach that evening. They lit a small fire and grilled the fish that the fishermen had given to Pete. Two days later, early in the morning, the owner of the shop in Puerto Barrios found them there. He came in a tilbury and they left together.

The *Santo Cristo* was anchored in the creek, floating on water as clear as glass. On the beach were abandoned palapas, scraps of torn fishing nets, the skeleton of a boat washed up on the shore, its wooden ribcage open to the sky. Two palm trees, branches heavy with coconuts, leaned down over the water, their hairy roots stripped by the waves. A rowing boat sent by the *Santo Cristo* was moving towards them, two men working the oars and Captain Aznar standing at the bow, a cigarette between his lips, the smoke disappearing into the white air. It was noon, the sun beating down from above and the land breeze as warm as a hotel bath. Maria slid down from the horse. The shopowner waited in his tilbury, his belly hanging over his thighs, his face shaded by a hat. Pete stayed on horseback. Aznar looked north at the coast, towards Puerto Barrios, and then south towards the nearby border of Honduras. He jumped from the boat onto the sand and Maria walked out to meet him. They exchanged a few words. After that, the captain spoke to the fat merchant. Loading was complete, he said; all they were waiting for was the last passenger. The shop-owner confirmed that the passenger would arrive the next morning, then the two men wandered off so that the rest of their conversation would not be overheard. The merchant got back in his carriage and left without a word to Pete or the Indian.

Aznar came over to him.

"*Buenos días.*"

Pete got down from his horse. Segundo stood on the sloping beach, one leg behind the other to keep his balance, and looked as though he were on his guard, ready to run or attack. The two sailors in the rowing boat were armed, with revolvers in their belts. Maria, sitting in the sand, lowered her head. Pete opened his waistcoat to show off Guzman's gun.

"Hello."

Segundo gave a little smile. With one arm he made a gesture that took in the surrounding landscape, the creek, the boat and all of them. His smile vanished and was replaced by an expression of disappointment. He was unhappy with the situation. The roles had been badly assigned. The actors had had enough. He regretted it, and he wanted to know how to make things better.

Pete took the pistol from his belt and gave it to Aznar, then walked over to the Indian. She looked at Aznar's schooner the way her ancestors might have looked at the first Spanish boats to reach their shores. As if they were inconceivable, perhaps even invisible, so hard was it for these wooden monsters to find a place in their imagination.

"What are you going to do, Maria?"

She turned her eyes away from the boat.

"You have made me a foreigner in my own country, gringo." She stood up. "I'll follow Segundo."

III

I

French Guiana, the dry season, October 1872

At anchorage, the pitching of the *Santo Cristo* made Maria sick. Her face was grey in the lights of the storm lanterns hanging from the ceiling of the saloon. Aznar ordered the rowing boat back in the water and two of his sailors took her to the beach.

"Indians are sometimes so ill that they can't eat or stay hydrated. They die during long voyages. If she can't stand the sea, we'll have to drop her off in Honduras."

Segundo was leaning next to Pete. The two men watched the rowing boat and the beach.

"Maybe it's the idea of leaving her country that's making her weak. She'll sleep on land tonight and come back tomorrow morning with the Frenchman."

"What Frenchman?"

They sat in the rear saloon with a bottle of rum. Pete noticed the American flag waving above the stern.

"You're not flying Mexican colours anymore?"

Segundo raised his glass. "To your new life as a pirate, Americano!"

Pete clinked glasses with him. "So the Frenchman's a pirate?"

"A friend of the cause."

Pete finished his rum. "Where are we going?"

"Where do you want to go?"

"To the equator."

"What will you do there?"

"No idea."

Segundo threw his head back. "The *Santo Cristo* is headed in the right direction, Pete. But before we arrive at the equator, we need to make one stop."

"Where?"

"In America's biggest rubbish dump. French Guiana, my friend. A prison as big as Guatemala."

He lifted his head again to look at Pete.

"I'll take you to see the equator, but first we must visit the penal colony."

Aznar was getting drunk, and his tone had changed. He stared at Pete, and Pete stared back.

"You have something to tell me, Aznar?"

"Nothing at all, gringo. You're imagining things."

Evening fell and Captain Aznar got into the rowing boat. The sailors took him to the shore. Pete saw him walk to the palapa where Maria had taken refuge.

He was on deck the next morning, long before dawn, waiting to see the semi-circle of the beach appear, then the rowing boat returning with its passengers. He counted them: the two sailors, Segundo, the Frenchman and Maria's slumped figure.

The captain offered Maria the use of his cabin. The Frenchman, in his forties, was slightly taller than Pete, with pale eyes, thick dark hair and solid hands – a friend of the cause, but more a man of action than an intellectual of Guzman's stripe. He introduced himself to the American, speaking with the same accent as Alexandra Desmond.

"Sébastien Ledoux. So you're the American?"

"Pete Ferguson."

"Welcome aboard."

Ledoux laughed and followed Segundo.

Pete stayed on deck to watch the sailors work and the ship start to move. It was a pleasure to be back on the schooner. The sails snapped. A sailor whistled at Pete, who was standing in the middle of the deck, and threw him a rope. He pulled it as hard as he could before tying it around a cleat. The *Santo Cristo* listed, American flag flying, and its bow cut through the first wave.

—⟋⟍—

Maria did not leave Aznar's cabin for three days.

Pete got up in the night with the sailors on watch. He smoked and drank, stared at nautical charts, interpreted currents and winds. During the day, he memorised the names of sails and decks, observed the clouds and the swell, learned how to handle the sextant. At the same time, he discovered a new way of navigating: he learned how to use the sun or stars to pinpoint his position on a map.

The Frenchman showed an interest in Pete and asked him questions about the United States. Then, after he'd got enough answers, he started holding forth himself. His opinion of the United States of America apparently counted for more than Pete's experience of the country.

Sébastien laughed a lot. He liked to drink and he enjoyed fighting for his cause, he insisted. Otherwise why bother? He was by far the craziest of all the revolutionaries Pete had met. He was also the most dangerous.

"The United States is the biggest farce the world has ever seen, Pete. In real time, the construction of a new nation based on the principles of modern democracy! The old empires began by dividing the American cake, thinking that there would be plenty for everyone – between civilised trading partners! – then they went to war so they could possess it all. But something else happened. Because the idea came to the envoys of those old empires that they could make their own fortune there instead of fighting on behalf of Europe. So they proclaimed their independence. After that, they needed armies to defend their new country, right? So they recruited . . . who? *Us, the poor and the needy!* During your Civil War, ten times more men arrived at America's ports than died on the battlefields. Those who didn't go straight to war were hired to work in factories or to build railways. But be careful! They were promised the earth. Imagine, Pete, promising the world to the slaves of the Old World, where every last scrap of garden and pavement has belonged to the same families for over a thousand years?"

Sébastien Ledoux refused to identify himself as an idealist, claiming that he was just a fanatical criminal, and that this was more than enough for him to be effective.

"And beyond all that, my American friend, the *pièce de résistance*: the Constitution! Tailored to the needs of the American people, to protect them from the tyrants of the Old World who wanted to pursue them all the way to their paradise across the ocean! Meanwhile, the new bosses of America were comfortably settling into the shelter of this document that was written especially for them by a few of their philosopher friends!"

The Frenchman made all the crew laugh. He would holler at people and buy them drinks. He had everyone in his pocket and it was with Pete that he tried hardest to become friends.

"Eat with me tonight! I'm bored shitless on this boat!"

Ever since he had first heard that raucous laugh, Pete had been suspicious of him.

Aznar had left the deck to Sébastien and spent all his time in his cabin with Maria, avoiding Pete's company.

"She's still sick. She can't come out."

Pete still didn't know what they would do in French Guiana. He brooded over this while he was stuck with Ledoux.

"Tell me more about that ranch. You said it was about two and a half thousand acres? Tell me your life story – there's nothing else to do here!"

Pete lied, inventing places and names, because he didn't want to open himself up to this man.

"Tell me about Paris, Sébastien."

The Frenchman lied too. In the end, Pete managed to sift through his bullshit and discover the bare bones of the truth. The son of a Parisian brothel owner, an orphan, raised by an aunt, a messenger for criminals in his neighbourhood, then an enforcer and a burglar, he said, stealing only from the rich. More likely, he had been a pimp. Thrown in prison, he must have helped some anarchists to escape and, in the process, become their friend. Sébastien had needed to leave France and they had helped him get away. Now he was here to return the favour. Either that, or to pay off a debt. Everything even vaguely heroic in his account of his life struck Pete as having been borrowed from other people's lives. Some acts of violence and a few dirty tricks were probably as close as he had come to a war or a revolution. More intelligent than he appeared, he spoke English fluently with Pete and Spanish with Segundo and the crew.

Pete played along and lied. One evening, Segundo summoned him to the saloon.

The Frenchman had unfolded a map on the large table.

"There are four of them."

Sébastien Ledoux pointed to a small black dot on the paper: a town situated on a riverbank.

"Saint-Laurent. The other side of the Maroni is Surinam. The Dutch colony has come to an arrangement with France: any fugitives who get that far are sent to a labour camp. At the mouth of the river, the currents and tides make it hard to cross in small boats. There's a risk that you'll wash up on the shore and be arrested. Not to mention the sharks."

He pointed at a small archipelago a few nautical miles from the coast. "At the Îles du Salut, the prison guards throw convicts' corpses into the water. One third of the prisoners on those islands do not survive the first year, and there are two thousand of them spread over the three islands. The sharks in those waters must be the fattest in all of South America. There are even sharks thirty or forty miles up the rivers, where the water is still briny. They fight over the best catches with the crocodiles."

Ledoux burst out laughing, but Pete and Aznar remained silent.

"There are many more prisoners who end up dead in the forest camps. The insects only get to eat some of them, the rest goes to the jungle vermin."

Aznar stood up, moving out of the lamp's halo of light.

"You need a good reason to go ashore in French Guiana. France has a monopoly on trade with its colony, and that's without even mentioning the temptation foreign ships represent to convicts. We'll moor at

Saint-Laurent to deliver parts for a steam pump in the Îles du Salut. The equipment is from New Orleans, from a network under contract with Fawcett & Preston in Liverpool. Once the cargo has been unloaded, we'll have to hide in the Maroni estuary that night and wait for our comrades' signal."

Pete tried to concentrate, but he couldn't stop thinking about Maria, who had left her cabin for the first time and was now sitting in a corner of the saloon.

"How long before we reach French Guiana?"

Segundo replied in French while continuing to observe Pete. "If the wind and the weather stay as they are now, we'll reach Trinidad and Tobago in ten days. From there, it's a five-day trip to Saint-Laurent-du-Maroni."

"I'll send them a message from Trinidad so they know to expect us."

Pete asked the Frenchman: "Who are the four?"

"Two comrades who were imprisoned four years ago and two others who were deported only a year ago: Communards who arrived with enough money to bribe bureaucrats and buy equipment for the escape. There, too, you must be rich to get out. With every passing year, you become weaker and your chances of survival grow slimmer. Anyone convicted for less than eight years has to stay in French Guiana for the same time again once he's been freed. It's called doubling. But if he's been sentenced to more than eight years, he must spend the rest of his life there. Those four had sentences of twenty-five years. The judges might easily have sentenced them to just nine years – that would have been enough to get rid of them – but they like nice big numbers. Anyway, as I said, most of them don't last longer than a year."

Sébastien laughed again.

"You know what the prison authorities give to the men who have to stay there? A small plot of land. They're offered the chance to become French Guiana's new colonists and property owners."

He was choking on his laughter.

"That's even better than in your country, Pete! In French Guiana, private property is a reward for prisoners!"

When Pete turned around, Maria had left the cabin. He went out without saying a word. She was on deck, holding onto the rail, her head leaning overboard.

"Still sick?"

Her copper-coloured skin was dull and there were deep lines on her forehead and around her eyes. Maria did not reply. She bent over again towards the black water that rushed past the hull.

"You shouldn't have left Guatemala," he added. "When we get to Trinidad, we'll find another boat to take you home."

He walked away, then came back towards her.

"I'll sleep outside tonight. You can take my cabin. That way, you won't have to go in his."

"Leave me alone."

2

They spoke English in Trinidad and Tobago, Sébastien told him.

"It's Victoria's doormat, my friend. So she can wipe her feet on it before stepping into South America. There are no more slaves here, American, just like in your country, only Negroes. Same thing in French Guiana, since 1848. The penal colony was created in 1854 and nowadays the prisoners work for the colonists who lost their slaves. Don't look at me like that – it's just a historical coincidence!"

Trinidad was green, with beaches as white as pearl oysters, surrounded by the turquoise Caribbean sea. Pete could not imagine that the cold, black water near the seabed could really be the same water that looked like this on its surface. The island must be floating. And yet the continent was right there, as unpleasant as ever, separated from the island by only a few miles of water. As the schooner headed for the Port of Spain, he wondered if the prison islands of French Guiana were as beautiful as this.

The port authorities – two British soldiers – came aboard. The false papers for the *Santo Cristo* and Sébastien Ledoux were approved without difficulty. When Captain Aznar implied to the British officers that the trip to French Guiana was not really to his taste, they nodded enthusiastically. "That place is a source of shame for the civilised world. The Queen has made Trinidad a sanctuary for escapees from that hell."

French convicts who managed to reach Trinidad and Tobago were brought under the protection of the British Empire and sometimes even given material aid so they could continue their voyage. Sébastien sniggered once the Englishmen had left the boat.

"The politicians who made French Guiana into a penal colony were inspired by Victoria's example in Australia! The British are only doing that to annoy the French. They're the ones who gave France its taste for a penitentiary utopia. Sending your criminals to the distant, scummy ends of the Empire so that they can become colonists, cleansed of their crimes by exile and imprisonment! You think the English have any more love than the French do for their thieves and anarchists?"

Maria stayed on board while Pete walked around the port. They all looked the same to him, from Tampico to this one, with their warehouses and their louvered shutters. Boats and cargos, humid heat, Indians or Negroes working, urged on by whips or low wages, white men keeping lists, women under parasols. Trade as the sole occupation and sole link with the homeland, which was talked about constantly, mentioned in the names of wharfs and streets, restaurant menus, clothes and architecture, anything that might remind people of their native country. Boredom was a gangrene in these places, the only forms of entertainment being cock-fighting or dog-fighting for the men, plaintive letters from cousins in London or Madrid for the women.

Maria had been right to stay on the boat. This paradisiacal port would have made her even sicker.

The Frenchman, who had gone into town, returned to the *Santo Cristo* that evening. The sunset, brief and colourful, was accompanied by some singing and the sound of musical instruments coming from the labourers' and fishermen's neighbourhoods. Sébastien Ledoux watched a sailing boat move past the pier.

"My message for Saint-Laurent is on that boat. In twelve hours we'll be on our way to French Guiana and they'll be ready for us."

"How long has all this been planned?"

"Months."

"Segundo will be paid, but what will you get out of this business?"

Sébastien Ledoux smiled to himself. "I'll free my comrades."

Pete leaned on the rail and watched the sailing boat vanish into the distance.

"The two prisoners – not the Communards but the other two – those are the ones you want to free. Are they old friends from Paris?"

The Frenchman slapped him on the back. Not hard enough to hurt, but too hard to be friendly. As if, swept along by his good mood, he had accidentally demonstrated his strength.

"It's funny, you look like a cowboy, but you're not stupid, are you?"

Aznar was ashore. Pete went down to the lower deck and hammered on his cabin door. He kept knocking until Maria opened it. She smelled of alcohol. The entire island smelled of rum and homesickness. She moved to one side, like a whore answering the door to one of her clients. In her dishevelled servant's dress, she bowed to the American. "Come for your share, gringo?"

"The Frenchman's up to something. I don't know what, but we should get off the boat."

"What he's up to is something courageous, gringo. That's what scares you. That's what makes you want to run away."

"We have to leave the boat."

She slammed the door in his face.

Pete went back up to the main deck, walked along the gangway, and headed towards the voices and music coming from the port's taverns. The blacks drank bad raffia wine and spoke a strange sort of English that he barely understood. They did not speak a word to the American when he entered a bar, and he was left to drink alone, the tables around his pushed further away.

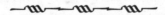

Alexandra Desmond.

You were ridiculous, in love with the woman you couldn't have. That mother you dreamed would be yours alone, without having to share him with Oliver, your little brother with his naive love. A child's love, you thought, considering yourself a man. With me, you were ridiculous; with Lylia, you were a coarse brute.

You humiliated her and beat her. She told you she loved you and you spat in her mouth. You thought a man like you should have a woman like me, not some scatterbrained kid from Carson City. A woman like Arthur Bowman's wife. You think he didn't know?

Do you think Lylia was wrong to accuse you? That you were innocent of everything she said you'd done?

You hated it when people called you that: young man.

You grew up like a tree on the seaside, Pete, pushing against a wind that always tried to bend you in the same direction. You became incapable of standing up straight, of understanding what I had to give. The wind pressed you to the ground, and you fled with it at your back. You were not yet a man, in this world where children are given guns.

The tree of freedom is not watered by the blood of tyrants; it's a gallows to which we tie our children and slit their throats. A tree whose branches flower with the hanged bodies of patriots.

Arthur and I saved two children. The sons of a beautiful woman who died too young and a man whose touch killed plants. A lumberjack, Pete. Oliver was still young enough to accept our offer, but you were too hardened, you had grown up too early, you were too bent over. A strength formed in reaction; an arc in tension.

You didn't kill old Meeks, not in the way they said. But you did kill him, in this world where sometimes you can kill like that, just by being an angry young man.

And now this one . . .

Do you think a woman like her could love someone like you?

The men who hurt her looked like you, Pete Ferguson. She knows it. You know them, those men. You are your father's son. They have different faces in which you recognise your own. Rusky. The Frenchman. Aznar too. Those of your blood.

You have to change – or change the world, as she wants to do. Well, making a woman who doesn't love us love us – that's changing the world, isn't it? Will you have to seduce the world, Pete Ferguson, to make it love us?

You don't change for other people, Pete. Why would you need to, except to be someone different? Changing the world just means learning to see it differently. Through other eyes.

Calm down, young man, the Indian will spit in your mouth when you talk to her.

Swallow it. Swallow your anger. Why should she agree to see the world like you, Pete Ferguson, if you keep looking at it in this way?

Begin by no longer thinking about those old women, young man. Your mother, a worn-out memory; me, too old. We bow out and leave you with the young woman. It's up to you to do the rest.

One day, you'll have to read me the book of that poet, the Maestro Manterola, who is going to die in prison.

———❦———❦———❦———

Along the coastline, the sea took on the colour of the rivers. The mud of the forest dissolved in the blue and the currents carried it south-wards. The continent was flat, a green slab without end, the brown blood flowing from the rivers, and above it all the low clouds. The heat grew ever higher along the coastline of Venezuela, of England's little Guyana, of Holland's Surinam, and at last in front of the Maroni and French Guiana.

"In Saint-Laurent, my friend, the guillotine stands ready all year round. Apparently, it has to be used regularly so it doesn't rust."

"The guillotine?"

The Frenchman looked at Pete and smiled. "It's true: all you know is bullets and the rope. There are no hangings in the land of human rights, Pete. Here, we cut off heads with a machine invented by a humanist, a friend of the French Revolution. It's amazing how much you still have to learn about this world!"

The estuary was three or four miles wide, open like a fish's mouth on the guts of the continent.

"No hangings?"

Aznar was on the deck, telescope to his eye, observing the shore and the little tree-covered islands in the middle of the river. Ledoux gestured to these green islets with his chin.

"If there are no problems, that is where they will wait for us tonight."

"Are there any guns on the boat?"

"Relax, Pete. In two days, you'll be in Brazil. End of story."

No boat was moored at the pontoon of the port of Saint-Laurent: two quays that ran perpendicular to the riverbank. Outside the customs building were a square shaded by flame trees in flower, a green lawn and the main street, carved from the red earth, that ran towards the centre of the city. After the customs building, there was a wall, fifteen feet high and three hundred feet long, and a gate through which six men could walk side by side. Above this was painted a single word that Pete assumed meant the same thing in French as it did in English: *Transportation*. The arrival of the *Santo Cristo* provoked a certain agitation in the moribund port. There was no trade in Saint-Laurent other than the importing of criminals. Soldiers armed with rifles patrolled the streets. Some white colonists stood around, curious, and on the pontoon a group of men waved to the boat.

Aznar and his sailors carried out the manoeuvre, and then customs officers and some prison officers came aboard and the captain presented them with the manifest. The officers were in a rush to get the formalities over with so they could talk about the merchandise in the hold with Ledoux, the French engineer.

"The pump on Île Royale has been broken for six months. It's the dry season now and the reservoir is dry. The hospital is running low on water, and that's without even mentioning the members of staff, their families and the prisoners."

The customs officer declared that everything was in order, the main hatch was opened, and the Frenchman, amused by his role as a specialist, went down into the hold with the prison officers. He showed them the parts and explained how to assemble them. Prisoners in filthy white uniforms, with red-striped trousers and shirts, came onto the deck and the unloading began. They kept glancing at the boat and the crew as they worked under the close watch of half a dozen soldiers posted on the pontoon.

The prison officers invited the engineer, Captain Aznar and his deputy, Mr Ferguson, to have a drink with them under the arches of the customs building. Two prisoners brought out a table and some chairs, and set the table with carafes of water, wine and rum. They filled glasses while the Frenchman translated their hosts' remarks for Segundo and Pete.

"There are lots of soldiers around because there was an escape last night. Four prisoners got away."

The officers laughed as they explained, "Escape attempts are commonplace. The prisoners can move around relatively freely. From time to time they get the urge to try their luck. Most of them are recaptured after a couple of days. Starving, dehydrated, captured by the Surinam military, or dead. For those who are not found straight away, we send headhunters – former prisoners, with dogs – who know the country well."

In the port they could see a great crowd of people of all colours.

"The Chinese run the shops from here to the forest camps and on the Surinam shore. They either help the escapees or hand them over to the authorities, depending on the size of the bribe they're offered."

Pete interrupted this conversation to ask about the prisoners with brown skin. They were Arabs, the prison officers explained: criminals from France's North African colonies. As they were the most hated of all the prisoners, their detention was the harshest of all. The officers could do with them whatever they wanted. In return for an improvement in their living conditions, the Arabs became deputy guards. Turnkeys. That way, they became even more hated, but they were untouchable. If the prisoners behaved well, after a few years they left the camps and cells to take up employment in the city. Here or in Cayenne they would work as servants for colonists or members of the administration. They slept in prison, but moved around freely during the day. That was the aim for most of these prisoners: becoming first-class so they could get a job, improving their lot or putting some money aside, like the four who escaped last night, so they could try to find freedom.

Without asking, Pete could guess the identity of those foul tramps who hung around the port. They were the freed convicts mentioned by the Frenchman, doomed to stay there without work because everyone could obtain the services of the real prisoners for nothing. Why pay a free man's wage to these pathetic wrecks?

Pete chased down the rum with two large glasses of water. Having satisfied their guests' curiosity, the officers returned to the more pressing subject of the steam pump. Aznar and Pete excused themselves and left the table.

They walked past the transportation gate, open onto the large courtyard, which was formed of the same rust-coloured earth as the main street. There were about twenty buildings, situated either side of a central aisle. The grey and pink figures of prisoners and armed guards moved around under the dry season's boiling sun. They walked in the shadow of the wall, passed the prison and found themselves at a large crossroads where a breeze was raising a cloud of red dust. All the buildings in the town were organised around the vast prison. Before becoming a penal colony, Saint-Laurent had been nothing. Pete slowed down as he saw a group of unescorted convicts coming towards them – six men and six straw hats. Aznar slowed down too. The men lowered their heads and passed them in complete silence, their feet bare on the burning ground, carrying spades and shovels over their shoulders. The houses and enclosed gardens here were all perfectly maintained.

They went past a school where the guards' children were reciting a lesson in unison. The town was already coming to an end; they had crossed it in a few minutes and, at its exit, the street separated into two tracks – one heading east, the other south. At this fork in the road was the cemetery, its entrance flanked by two large mango trees, the fruit still green. The two men sat in the shade for a moment.

"This place makes me sick, gringo. I've never seen anything like it. It's so false and so real at the same time."

Pete took off his hat and wiped his forehead. He watched a troop of ants, transporting scraps of a leaf. They were coming down a tree trunk and moving towards the gravestones, thousands of them, leaving a perfectly clean path behind them. Apparently they had decided to strip the entire tree of all its leaves.

"It's not the place you should be wary of, Segundo. The Frenchman is up to something. You should keep your eye on him."

"I have my eye on him, gringo. I don't need your advice."

"And Maria?"

"What about Maria?"

"Are you going to take care of her?"

"Maria will die, as all Indians do when you tear them away from their land."

"If you don't protect her, I will."

"She doesn't want your help, Pete."

Segundo smiled, not at Pete but at certain memories that he was trying to coax from his mind.

"I'm going back to the port. The sooner we get this over with, the sooner I'll be rid of you lot."

Pete continued to watch the ants, with their little green sail aloft in the air. They reached the bottom of the mango tree. Pete walked back through the town, passing its inhabitants, guards and prisoners, walking like convalescents in the hospital's crimson park, their progress slowed by the heat.

3

Night came too soon, the day ending like a shutter closing. The lights in the penal colony went out, gates were padlocked, chains tightened, and the guards' shifts assigned. The prison officers had stayed under the arches until sunset; utterly drunk, they clung to the Frenchman, who went back on board the boat.

"Stay here tonight, Monsieur Ledoux! You can go back in the morning!"

"We should take advantage of the tide, gentlemen. It was a pleasure to make your acquaintance!"

"Say hello to Paris for us, Monsieur Ledoux!"

"I certainly will!"

The two officers would not let go of the rail.

"Say hello to France, Monsieur Ledoux!"

"If you happen to be in Belleville, give the old neighbourhood my best wishes!"

"Farewell, gentlemen."

Aznar's sailors moved quickly and in silence, eager to get away from Saint-Laurent and the prison's long black silhouette. They did not hoist the sails. Aznar stood at the wheel and guided the *Santo Cristo* into the river's current and the ebbing tide. If they took too long, the mud banks would be exposed, rendering the shore inaccessible. The sky was cleared by a sea wind and the stars made the sky appear vast once again. Aznar steered the schooner between the islands and the shore, following the path of shining water. They passed the first island and the Frenchman at the bow lit a signalling lamp, repeating the same code at regular intervals. Another, dimmer light answered him from the shore, casting shadows from the mangrove roots. The trees' spidery legs crept over the mud, which shone in the lamps' beams. Aznar moved as close as possible to the bank before changing tack.

"Ready the anchor!"

The schooner turned around and stabilised itself against the current.

"Drop anchor!"

A sailor freed the winch and the steel links made a racket as they spun. The anchor hit the surface of the water and the chain unspooled until its descent began to slow. The boat shook several times. The anchor dragged along the riverbed, then the chain tensed and the schooner came to a halt. The lamp on the shore started to move, and the agitations of light and shade transformed the mangrove into a fantastical centipede. They heard anxious voices. Nobody except the Frenchman understood what they were saying. The four men held onto roots as they advanced, pushing a dugout canoe ahead of them over the mud. Their lamp sat on the canoe and they pushed with their bellies flat on the boat, up to their hips in mud. Whenever one of them let go, he would disappear up to his neck and groan as he pulled himself out, helped by his nearest comrade. They reached the water thirty feet from the *Santo Cristo* and climbed panting into the canoe. The sailors threw them ropes, then leaned down, arms outstretched, to lift them up to the deck. The canoe was taken by the current and vanished in the night. Aznar shouted: "Weigh anchor!"

Two sailors stood at the winch and raised the sail, so the wind could help them with the manoeuvre. All lights off, the *Santo Cristo* tacked back into the current. The four escapees took off their mud-covered prison uniforms. The Frenchman picked up these jettisoned clothes and threw them overboard. With the abandoned dugout and those scraps of fabric floating in the estuary, the four men's escape would perhaps be recorded as death by misadventure in the prison's registers. Dressed as sailors, shivering, the escapees went down into the hold to hide.

"Rip current!"

When the tide was going out, the two currents met. The water from the river and the ebb crashed into each other, thrusting up like ocean waves and raising a white line of foam in the night. Aznar headed straight towards these thirty-foot rollers. The prow of the *Santo Cristo* stabbed into them, lifted up, slowed violently, then swayed like a swing. It hung there for an instant, before plunging downwards, the stern flying up like a kicking horse. A few men banged their heads and some crockery was smashed, but they had passed through the rip current. Aznar set an eastward course. The Îles du Salut were passed that night and by tomorrow morning they would be in sight of the Brazilian coast. Another five days to reach the delta of the Amazon, the biggest river in the world according to Aznar, and Macapá, in the estuary, the city that straddled the equator.

The Frenchman was in the hold with the escapees. Pete guessed that half – maybe more – of the crew were with Sébastien. Segundo knew it too, but remained obstinately clinging to the helm of his ship.

"What are you going to do, captain?"

Aznar watched the night through the open windows of the wheelhouse, checked his compass, and listened to the sound of the sails to estimate their tension and the strength of the wind.

"They need me to pilot this boat. But you and Maria are useless to them."

Pete went down to the cabins.

"Open up, Maria."

The cabin stank of vomit and excrement. Aznar had ended up moving out and he now slept in the wheelhouse. The Indian had transformed this cabin into a foul cave. They were forbidden to light any lamps. Pete opened the porthole window and sat on the bunk, as close as possible to the draft of air. Maria was somewhere in the darkness, where he couldn't see her.

"They won't let us land. It will all end tomorrow. Do you want to die here?"

He heard her stirring somewhere. An empty bottle rolled along the floor and banged into the bunk. Then he heard a pistol being cocked.

Pete stiffened and moved along the interior of the hull to get away from the faint light coming through the porthole.

"What are you doing? Where did you find a gun?"

He smelled her odour and felt the barrel touching his throat.

"You stole my country from me, gringo. My village, my mountains and my men."

"I saved your life."

"Guzman should have killed you."

"You'd be dead too."

"This sea is my death. We are waiting to drown, that's all."

"The Frenchman's going to get rid of us."

He felt the pressure of the barrel diminish and heard Maria step away from him.

"I explored the boat. I went everywhere. I slept against the wood, listening to the water on the hull."

"What are you talking about?"

She left another silence. The sea whistled through the porthole.

"There are guns on board, hidden in the hold."

"We have to get off the *Santo Cristo*."

She laughed.

"How? To go where?"

"The lifeboat. When we've passed the prison archipelago, when the boat moves closer to the coastline again, the sea wind will push us. We have nothing to fear in French Guiana; we're not criminals here."

They fell silent, both of them petrified by the noises coming through the cabin wall – from the hold. A struggle. The cries of a slaughtered beast.

"I'm going to lower the lifeboat into the water. We don't have a choice anymore."

The noises were above them now: footsteps, running along the gangways towards the wheelhouse. The *Santo Cristo* changed tack. Pete looked up at the black ceiling. Voices, barked orders, the sound of a body hitting the surface of the water. He felt Maria's hand grab his. He thought she wanted his protection, but she stood up and led him away. They went out into the corridor, advancing towards the blank wall that separated them from the hold. She let go of his hand, and he heard wood creaking and sliding. A passage hidden in the wall. She pulled him and he followed her. The main hatch was open; they saw white sails in the night, the stars, the movement of the mainmast sweeping the sky. Lying on the damp wood, she rummaged through secret compartments.

"The guns aren't there."

She covered her mouth with a hand and moved back against him. Two bodies were crammed together, like crumpled bags, between two ribs of the wooden framework. The two Communards. The representatives of the cause, murdered by their allies, Parisian criminals. Maria got to her knees: head thrown back towards the bright square of the main hatch, the pistol resting in her lap, the grip held tightly in both hands. She took deep, jerky breaths. Above them, the mutiny went on, the voice of the Frenchman giving orders, a gunshot that made them jump. Maria turned to face the American. She was crying, her tears white in the starlight.

"I don't want to die at sea. Take me back to the land, Pete, please."

"Stay here. Shoot anyone who comes into the hold. When you hear my signal, run to the back of the boat and jump. Don't think, just jump. I'll be there."

Maria moved as far away from the corpses as she could. Pete crawled back to the passage in the wall. He went down the corridor and into the saloon. The table was set, so he grabbed a steak knife. Someone was coming down the steps. Pete hid under the table, between the chair legs. A lamp lit up the saloon, then the light disappeared into the corridor and he heard the sound of wood cracking: a cabin door being kicked in. He threw himself into the corridor and up the stairs. The lifeboat was there, hanging over the phosphorescent groove created by the schooner. He turned back and crawled along the gangway, towards the brightly lit wheelhouse and the silhouette of the wheel, never taking his eyes off it. Perhaps there was still a chance to convince Aznar.

He froze. His hands touched a warm liquid. Segundo was lying on

235

his back, sprawled across the gangway, arms suspended over the water, his throat slit. The Frenchman was steering the boat. Pete crawled backwards.

He attached the end of the lifeboat to a mooring cleat and cut the falls. The lifeboat fell, bounced, and let in some water before stabilising, carried along in the *Santo Cristo*'s wake. There was a gunshot, then another, up ahead near the hold. Pete stood up: men were running on the deck. He jumped into the water and held onto the lifeboat. He sank down into the black, warm water, which covered and choked him as he fought against the current. He dragged himself to the surface, coughed, and sucked in enough air to yell: "Maria!"

Lamps converged on the stern and the saloon. He heard the Frenchman bellow into the wind: "The lifeboat!"

A small shape, like a cat, leaped out of the saloon. In two bounds Maria had hurtled over the rail, and he saw her, dress swelling as she fell, fly down into the water. His feet wedged under a bench, Pete reached out his arms and plunged underwater. He felt something and tightened his grip. Maria came to the surface; he was pulling her by the hair. She grabbed the gunwale and he hurriedly cut the rope connecting them to the schooner. The lifeboat made a nosedive and then stopped; the lights of the ship receded in a few seconds, the white triangles of the sails changing direction. Pete put his fingers in his ears. Above his head, Maria emptied the cylinder of her pistol, aiming at the lamps. One of them went out and they heard a cry. There was the sound of gunfire in response, but the mutineers were firing randomly – the lifeboat was invisible against the dark water. The wind was with them; the schooner would have to tack endlessly to come back after them.

Guessing at the direction of the coast, Pete started rowing with all his strength. The lifeboat was equipped with a mast, disassembled and lashed to the gunwale. The lamps of the *Santo Cristo* quickly faded; the two craft were headed in opposite directions, and the points of light now appeared only intermittently when the boat was lifted up on the waves. Maria and Pete suddenly became aware of the sounds surrounding them: the howl of the wind and the hiss of the sea spray that whipped their clothes and the lifeboat's hull. But it was not the sea that was splashing them: it was raining, a heavy downpour as warm as the sea, which crackled on the wood and their heads. Pete raised the mast, stretched out the shrouds, hoisted the sail and hauled in the sheet. Maria curled up in a ball at the bottom of the lifeboat. For two hours, three hours, he clung to the handle of the tiller, searching the darkness for the dark mass of the continent. He thought he had lost his way, that they were headed out to sea, eastwards towards the horizon where it was starting to change colour. A faint white line. But it was not the rising sun, it was the foam from the waves in the rip current. He could hear them panting now, like an animal.

"Maria!"

He pulled her towards him and she wrapped her body around his leg. He held the tiller to his ribs and they were swallowed up by the white mouth, the wood of the lifeboat cracking before they were spat out by the current, water up to their knees, frantically trying to breathe. Swept along by the backwash, they drifted.

When she opened her eyes, the sail was beating in the wind, the sheet whipping against the air. The gringo was asleep and the lifeboat had washed up on a mud bank where dozens of crabs ran. The creatures were asymmetrical, with one claw small and red and the other purple, half the size of their body. They were still about a hundred feet from terra firma. The sea was calm, barely even lapping the shore, and the lifeboat was lying on its side. The sun was high in the sky and from the ground came the vibration of thousands of insects. Maria lowered the sail and covered them with it for protection from the burning sun. She lay down next to Pete under the damp, salty canvas.

A few hours later, he woke her. Squinting, she sat at the tiller and he started to row. The tide had taken them and lifted them up towards a brown river about ten feet wide. The mud and the mangrove trees gave way to the forest and its brushy shores, the branches meeting above the water, forming a cool green tunnel. Pete took down the mast, which was getting tangled in the trees. A few pulls on the oars was all it took to keep them moving with the saltwater that headed for land, redirecting the river from its bed and into the depths of the forest. They left the mainstream behind and found themselves floating in the middle of drowned roots, gliding over a mirror that showed each tree trunk twice its real length. They came out into a vast swamp, covered with tall, half-submerged grass. Snakes with black scales swam out of their way, and everywhere they could see birds nesting, white waders taking off, invisible creatures making the shining surface of the water undulate as they fled. The sun made them thirsty. They found the line of the stream, which was shrinking as it penetrated the solid, shady ground between the trees. Their boat came to a halt; the sea current was no longer pushing them forwards. Pete tasted the water: it was fresh. Finally, they could drink it from their hands, and when the ebbing tide started dragging them back towards the ocean, they moored the lifeboat to a tree root. Maria stood up, rocking the boat as she tried to get her balance.

"What are you doing?"

Nose in the air, she shushed him. "Can't you smell it?"

"What?"

"Fire."

The Indian sat back down and suddenly grabbed the unloaded pistol, which lay in several inches of water. Just as suddenly, she held the gun away from her body and dropped it back in the water. She and Pete put their hands in the air. Leaning against a tree trunk on the bank above them, a woman was aiming a double-barrelled shotgun at them. It was another woman, unarmed, her face shaded by a man's hat, who spoke. In French.

Pete articulated as clearly as he could. "*Pas français* . . . Not French. English? *Español?*"

"Spanish?"

He nodded, and the two women looked at each other.

"You speak English or Spanish?"

"No. We should take them to Mama."

The one with the shotgun shook it to indicate the direction they had to take. "Get out of the boat."

4

The track led straight from the river to the village, located five minutes from there in a one-acre clearing. Houses on stilts, built between the stumps of trees that had been felled with axes. Another plot of land was being cleared now: trunks lying on the ground, branches and stubble burning, the air hot and dusty. The village was growing.

But there were no men here. The women chopped down trees, sawed planks and beams, cut branches with machetes, cooked, hammered nails, fed the chickens. They smoked pipes, carried rifles on their shoulders, hoed vegetable gardens; they looked like those female pioneers leading convoys, like those girl soldiers who ran farms and villages during wars, like those indefatigable widows of the West. The children were silent; they, too, worked. The boys were the only males here; none had yet reached puberty. Some of the women were toothless, some dirty and lame, others clean and well-dressed. There were about forty in all.

The Indian and the man who did not speak French were watched by the woman with the rifle while the other one climbed the staircase of a house. She came back out, accompanied by a matronly woman who was taller than Pete. In Spanish, she asked him: "Where are you from?"

"America."

"America? And what are you doing here?"

"Our boat had an accident."

"And her?"

Maria cut in before Pete could speak. "Where are the men?"

The woman with a wrestler's shoulders raised her eyebrows when she heard the Indian speak. Then she turned to the American. "Where did you find an Indian who speaks Spanish?"

She stood in front of the tiny Maria.

"What tribe? Palikur? Arawak? Galibi?"

Maria spat at her feet. "Xinca."

The white woman recoiled, though she didn't really look offended. "Xinca? Never heard of it."

Maria stood tall. "I am from Guatemala."

The crowd around them was growing bigger all the time.

"Where?"

She put a question in French to the assembled women, and a woman replied; Pete heard the words "Mexico" and "Guatemala". There followed an intense debate, cut short by the tall woman, who raised her hand and addressed the American. "You can't stay here. We'll give you some food, but you have to leave the Women's Village. She can stay."

Pete was not sure he'd understood correctly. "The women's village?"

"You go with the men, she stays here."

"I'm not going without her."

Maria did not react. The Frenchwoman smiled. "She can visit you when she wants to."

Maria was led through the crowd of women. Pete tried to grab her, but the shotgun was pressed into his belly. The tall woman moved the gun's barrel out of the way.

"Calm down. The men's camp is just over there. You won't be far away, but you can't come to the Women's Village without authorisation. It's a rule. Understand, Americano?"

Pete nodded, although he didn't fully understand what was happening.

"Stay here, Maria. Don't leave this place!"

The white women, with the little Indian woman among them, watched him leave the Women's Village. He waved to Maria.

The woman with the rifle stopped before the entrance to the men's camp and pushed him forwards. Pete went on alone towards the tents and the shelters, where he saw four men in hammocks around a fire that had been lit to repel insects. One of the men got to his feet and walked over to the woman with the rifle who had escorted Pete. He called out to her, and froze with his hands up when she aimed her gun at him and barked something. Pete greeted the men in English. One of them, under a palm roof, sat up in his hammock.

"Damn it! British?"

"American."

"What are you doing here?"

"I have no idea."

Pete looked at them, sprawled there, waiting for the women to authorise them to visit the Women's Village. He guessed that the colony's whores had gathered together and created a brothel in the middle of the forest, receiving clients only when they wanted to. The man who spoke English was covered in tattoos from head to foot. Under his nose was a drawing of a moustache; on his temples, going up to his shaved head, interlaced thorns, like Christ's crown; on his chest, an anchor and some ships. A sailor. He grabbed a bottle from his hammock.

"They don't like it when we drink, but nobody will be going there until tomorrow, so we can knock back a few."

Each of the men had a bottle stashed away. The sailor looked in relatively good health, but the others were emaciated, like convicts. The man handed him his bottle and Pete sat down in the shade of the palms.

"Is the town far from here? So there are no whores there – they're all here in the Women's Village?"

"Whores?"

The sailor said something to his companions and their faces darkened.

"Those women are our wives, mate. We're trying to get them back. The other men go to the harlots in Cayenne, and blow all their earnings on them."

"You're not ex-convicts?"

"Not all of us, mate. Some of us are genuine morons who came here of our own free will."

"Your own free will?"

"Exactly. Unless you think gold takes away a man's free will."

"There's gold here?"

"Ha! Where have you come from?"

This time when the sailor translated for the others, they grinned – and Pete saw their rotten teeth.

"Not only is this country a giant penal colony, it's a giant gold-mine too. Even our wives are panning for gold!"

Here the names were simple. To hear them was to listen to the history of the penal colony and its inhabitants. The rivers were *criques* and the houses – from the hammocks to more elaborate constructions with roofs – were *carbets*. A goldmine was a *placer*. There were Women's Villages and Men's Camps. The *placers* had evocative names: Free Women, At Last, Thanks Be to God, Paris, Lyon. And so did the *criques*: Thirst Quenched, Little Creek, Big Creek, Green Creek, Blue Creek – and the *carbets*: Saved, Hope, Return. There was a Generous Creek, a Beautiful View House, a Good Luck Mine . . . and also a Drowned Creek, a Snake House, a Pity Mine.

The tracks were named after the places to which they led. The Men's Camp of cast-off gold-panners was on the Women's Village track. On the banks of Gabriel Creek, the women used rifles to defend the Free Women's Mine. They didn't find much gold – just a few grams each month – but it was enough to keep them alive. And sometimes they unearthed a bigger nugget.

"The women don't catch gold fever like we do," the sailor said. "They're born with a stronger resistance to that madness."

"How did they come here?"

"We brought them over from France."

There were wives who had joined their fortune-seeking husbands, former prostitutes (Pete had not been completely wrong), former convicts, guards' widows . . .

"How did we end up here, waiting for them to let us see them? We deserved it, mate!"

And then there was Mama, the tall one, the chief.

"Is Mama your wife?"

Pete thought the sailor was going to make the sign of the cross. Instead he put his hand over his heart, where a three-master was tattooed.

"Good God, no! Mama has widowed more men than you could count. I'm not saying she killed them, but she survived everything that finished them off. You have to wonder if she maybe gave them a bit of a shove into their graves. In any case, don't worry about your wife, American. She couldn't be any safer than she is there."

"She's not my wife."

The sailor winked at him. "Don't worry about it, mate. I'm not going to criticise you for it. I've seen couples of every colour on my travels: yellows and whites, reds and whites, blacks and whites . . . Good God, I've even seen reds and browns, and blacks and yellows! In this damned country and this rotten forest, I've seen every kind of marriage and children who are a bit of everything. Being alone soon rids people of their bourgeois, religious prejudices. Look at me – I'm French, and I married an Englishwoman! You and your Indian . . . nobody will give you any shit about that here."

The sailor patted him on the shoulder and Pete decided to drop the subject.

The inhabitants of the Women's Village were the most tenacious colonists in French Guiana. They had decided that the forest, with its climate and its diseases, was not an excuse to lie down on a pavement in Cayenne and slowly drink themselves to death. When they'd had enough of seeing their housekeeping money disappear in brothels and bars, they had kicked their men out. They had organised themselves around the angriest and cleverest of them all – the one called Mama – and they had bought some land and a gold concession that no-one else wanted. Washerwomen, dressmakers, gold-panners and market gardeners, the inhabitants of the Women's Village traded with the Chinese, colonists, hunters and sailors. They bartered with the Indians and the Bushinengues, the Saramaccas, Paramacas and Ndjukas, descendants of escaped or freed slaves who had gone off to live in the forest and who still spoke their African languages. They owned land and they were determined. They worked with everyone, and no-one tried to pick a fight with them. Their most powerful weapon? They had put their husbands on a starvation diet. Penniless, the men had come crawling back to find themselves with a pickaxe in hand, the bars and brothels out of reach, and a kid in their arms. Most of them had gone away again and never returned.

The Women's Village was perhaps the sole success in the history of prison utopias: purging French society, through exile and brutality, of its criminals and deviants, and remaking them, after a period of penitence, into French Guiana's virtuous new colonists. Except that the men were excluded from this success, and that the women of the village hated France. For them, France was a prison bureaucracy in itself.

At the Men's Camp, four poor fellows awaited an audience with their spouses and swore by all their gods that they would never touch another drink – or another woman – ever again.

"What about you, sailor?" Pete asked.

"I came off a boat. I followed a pavement until I came to this dive. Some guy was buying rounds of drinks and two days later I was in the forest, digging at the bottom of a creek. That was five years ago. I met my Englishwoman in town: the widow of a freed prisoner. She wasn't really a whore, she just did what she had to survive after her hubby snuffed it. She's a great girl. But I loved my rum too much. And anyway, a sailor far from the sea . . . that's not going to work, is it?"

Work, fidelity, sobriety: these were the demands made on the men in the camp. If they could meet them, the couples would be brought back together in houses outside the Women's Village, in town or on a *placer* in the forest. The sailor was sceptical about this next step. In his opinion, the women were better off in their village, without their husbands.

"It's not like they don't have needs like we do, eh? But it will end up with our village next to theirs, and we'll just see each other when everyone wants it. And why not? We'll share what we need to share."

244

The sailor had grown melancholic, and he seemed weary of the palm liquor.

"She's a great girl, my Englishwoman, and I miss my daughter . . . you have no idea. In this giant shithole, our kid will grow up like no other kid in the world, playing and laughing, and that's the best thing I've done in my life. I'll do what her mother wants me to. I'm going to stay here and see my little girl grow up and take care of her. She already speaks two languages. She's the new world!"

The sailor lifted up his chin and stretched back his neck, and in the light of the fire Pete saw a necklace made of fine lettering. *Marinette*, his daughter's name, was tattooed from one collarbone to the other.

The bottles were empty and they had found Pete a hammock, hanging under a *carbet* of palm leaves that had been quickly rebuilt and even more quickly renamed House America. The four men in the camp, though slightly drunk, had gone to bed as soon as darkness fell, accustomed as they were to the country's short days.

Pete, rocked by the swaying of the hammock, fell asleep thinking of little Aileen, who would soon turn eleven, up there on the Fitzpatrick ranch. Then he thought about Maria, who would never want to leave the Women's Village.

5

A woman came to fetch them. They needed help on the logging site. The five men followed her.

The women did not abuse their power. They treated the men like probationary employees: cautiously and attentively. They wanted to bring some order back to their union, so they would have at least a chance of surviving in this country that ate everything in its path: trees, houses and hopes. Confronted with the density, the luxuriance, the proliferation, the parasitic nature, the horizontal and vertical competition, the speed and the ambition of the forest, the Europeans who ended up in French Guiana really needed to know what they were doing. Nature had a good head start on them, but at the Women's Village they believed in rolling up their sleeves and getting on with it.

Pete looked for the Indian, but could not find her. When the men sat at their table to eat lunch, under the large central *carbet*, a four-year-old girl came and sat next to the sailor. Maria did not come to eat with them and they started work again. Pete asked Mama about her. She did the best she could in Spanish to explain that Maria was in a dark hole and that no-one could go down there with her. Pete, she said, should stay at the Men's Camp and wait, if he wanted to see her again. She asked him if he really did want to wait.

"What?"

"She might die."

"Of what?"

"Nothing, everything, how should I know?"

Pete went back to the Men's Camp with rations of food as his wages and bathed in the cool water of Gabriel Creek. That felt good, but he didn't linger in the water. The sailor had warned him that there were stingrays hiding in the sand at the bottom of the creek; under the rocks and roots there were eels that stung so strongly that they made sparks of fire in the water and you lost consciousness and drowned.

The men ate a sad dinner together, and Pete divided his ration in two: half was for him to eat now; the other half he would take to Maria tomorrow, if she agreed to eat.

The Indian refused to swallow anything. She had lines around her eyes and her skin was pale like dried earth, burned by the sun and the salt of the sea. She is fasting, Pete thought, to purge her body of all it no longer needs. The exile's diet. Lying under a mosquito net, Maria had no old witch now to help her, to hypnotise her with chants and prayers while awaiting a vision, that elegant arrangement between the gods and the world of humans. She had to do it alone, so Pete just told her that he was there, that he would wait for her.

"I won't move from here until you're better," he assured her before leaving the shelter.

He continued working at the Women's Village and dropped by to visit her every day to prove to her that he was not a hallucination. He placed one hand on her forehead and repeated that he was not going to leave.

The women paid him in money now. When the logging was finished, the men helped construct three new shelters, then they were hired to work on the mine and pan for gold in Gabriel Creek. When he had enough money, Pete made the sailor a proposal.

For several days they thought about the drawing, then about the letters and words that would accompany the tattoo. It was a plant that would grow all along his body, from his feet to his head.

"A root," Pete had explained to the sailor. "I want a root that holds me to the ground everywhere I go, because I don't have a home anymore. And I want it to go all the way to my head so that I never forget that I am going somewhere on earth, even if all I do is walk."

The sailor had drawn pictures since he was a child. Everywhere, all the time, he had covered sheets of paper, wooden planks, pieces of fabric.

"Nobody ever explained to me what use it was to have this eye for drawing, to be able to imagine something or copy and trace it. And then one day, when I was ten years old, I saw a show at a fair in Alfortville. There was a guy who supposedly came from the islands, a cannibal captured by explorers during a voyage in the Pacific. He was white like you and me, mate, but he was covered with tattoos and he had earrings in his ears and wooden jewellery all over his body. It took me days to get over that vision. Then I made two decisions: I would be a sailor so I could see the Pacific islands, and when I was there I would learn to draw on skin."

Among the people who lived at sea, he had a reputation. Men would arrange meetings months in advance in various ports so that, during shore leave, he could tattoo them with a picture of their dreams, or their worst nightmares, which they would confront by covering their body with them – storms, shipwrecks, a woman's face or name. The sailor was a sort of witch doctor who could ward off bad luck, his needles tracing charms into the skin. Convicts, just like sailors, were mad about tattoos. The pain was part of it – the price of the exorcism, the proof that you could withstand it for hours, teeth gritted – but it was not the most important aspect. The essential thing was to prove – bare-chested under the sun that beat down on prisons in Africa, New Caledonia or French Guiana – that you had a story. That you were not merely a lump of flesh doomed to rot.

"A destiny?" Pete asked.

The sailor nodded. "A miserable destiny! The real verdict: the one that judges and juries and good people do not understand. For convicts, it's something that makes them grow, protects them. I've tattooed some real tough bastards and they asked me to tattoo their childhood home, the way they remembered it. I've tattooed cowards whose pasts made me feel ashamed; if I'd gone through half of what they went through, I'd have given up long before. You know what they say: there's the dead, there's the living, and there's sailors. Sailors and prisoners are tattooed with life and death. When I used to scribble stuff on bits of paper as a kid, I never would have imagined that I'd end up here, doing that for men like them . . . But you, Pete, your skin is still virgin, you've got nothing written on your back. What story do you want to tell?"

Pete thought about this. "The story of a bad seed."

The sailor laughed and took a nut from his pocket. He held it between his thumb and index finger, turned it around and lifted it up to the sky.

"Mate, I'm going to do your tattoo with this – a good seed! I brought it back from the Pacific islands. Candlenut trees grow as if they were at home here, in this damned country of convicts. One seed, just one, that I brought with me! I planted it, and in two years I had a tree that was producing fruit. A big enough harvest that I could replant them and have enough nuts for an armada of tattooists. I use their burned shells to make the best charcoal in the world. A bit of coconut oil and you have the best ink imaginable. For the combs that we use to do the tattooing, a few teeth from those sharks that swim up the rivers work perfectly. You'll have a tattoo just like the old men in Polynesia taught me to make."

He looked at Pete.

"It's a sacred art."

"Where is Polynesia?"

"I'll tell you about it when I'm working. If you want to know more, you'll have to get tattooed."

Pete went into the little chapel in the Women's Village, a hut with walls made from branches and a cross engraved on the door. Inside, there were two benches in front of a picture – a crucified Christ drawn in the sailor's inimitable style.

Maria was sitting on one of the benches and looking at this convict-like Jesus, thin and muscular, proudly nailed to the cross. Instead of the white loincloth, the Son of God was wearing prisoner's trousers torn above the knees, making him look like a pirate. And, since the sailor was the sailor, he had added a tattoo to the dying Christ's chest: a sacred heart with its crown of thorns. And on the two bumps of this organ of mystical intimacy, between the thorns, he had written two letters: A and p. *Administration pénitentiaire*. The prison bureaucracy, the enemy of pirates and free men, employer of authentic brutes and genuine bastards.

Mama had told Pete that Maria had got out of bed during the night. Candle in hand, she had walked through the Women's Village and had closed the chapel door behind her. For days she had stayed there, locked in. The women began to whisper when they spoke about Maria. Her low masses stirred up a wind of mystery, a superstitious breeze that blew through the village. The former convicts and whores, who had so often been threatened with the flames of hell, were suspicious of this Indian with her saintly ambitions.

Pete sat next to her on the bench. Frowning deeply, Maria silently questioned the Christ in his stripy trousers. The god of the Christians did not answer. Maria the Baptised settled her accounts and Pete merely observed her, before telling her again, as he was leaving, that he was there if she needed him. He left part of his food ration at Mama's house.

One Sunday, he showed Maria some sheets of paper. "This is what the sailor is going to draw on my skin. It's a climbing plant. It starts at my feet, with my toes as the roots, and it will climb up my leg, all the way to my head. There will be words too. Or names, rather. The names of the people I think about and who I imagine writing to me in my letters."

With his fingertip he followed the lines of leaves and stems on the picture of his naked body drawn by the sailor. The plant stopped at the base of his back; the rest of the tattoo had not yet been designed. Maria looked down and watched the movement of Pete's index finger, then she looked up at the Christ on the wall. Pete smiled. She had looked; for an instant, she had come back to him. The next day she ate some of the food he had brought her.

The following Sunday – a day of rest for women and men – Pete and the sailor finished the sketch of the tattoo and he went to show it to Maria. She was sleeping. She had gone to bed the previous evening, but not with her eyes open, staring at the ceiling, as she had on the days before this; this time she had closed her eyes and lain on her side.

"She went to bed to sleep," Mama told him. "To rest."

Pete went over to her.

"The drawing is finished," he whispered. "We're going to start the tattoo next week. The sailor says it'll take eight days. So that means eight Sundays. Two months. After that, you and I will talk. You can tell me if you want to leave or to stay here."

The price of the tattoo included the sailor's work, the manufacturing of the ink, and the purchase of pencils, paper and laudanum in Cayenne.

"You're a tough guy, Pete, but after two hours under the hammer nobody can take it anymore, apart from the Maoris, who are warriors, three times bigger than us, and even they end up in a trance because the pain drains all their strength. In fact, what you need to bear this is not a solid body but a soul of stone."

The sailor did not add to Pete's bill the cost of patching up his hut. Because the sailor wanted to do things properly, he said; he wanted to be fully prepared for the biggest tattoo he had ever created. First, a plank bed big enough for a family, raised on feet twelve inches from the ground. The palms on the roof were changed, and he built half-walls too, to shelter them from the wind but let in the light. Panels made from branches and palms could fill these gaps if it started raining outside. Two other men from the camp gave them a hand with the work. The third had disappeared, having grown weary of waiting for his wife to let him return, and realising that he was incapable of giving up drink. Eaten away by the parasites of too much time spent in the tropics – gold fever and dreams of returning to France – he had gone back to Cayenne. His imprint would fade, just as it had for all the others who had given up. But his surrender had galvanised those who remained, united around Pete's tattoo and the idea of destiny.

"Ink House!" the sailor proudly named his hut, once all the work had been completed.

—ᵚ—

After waking at dawn, Pete and the sailor went to Gabriel Creek to wash themselves. The air and the water were still cool at that time of day. The sunlight and the mist drew cathedrals in the branches; the forest was a vast window of luminous, translucent greens. The nocturnal birds had returned to their roosts and the birds of day were singing; cicadas rubbed their forewings together, while the giant stag beetles, exhausted by a long night of sex and fighting, thrummed into hiding in cracks in the tree bark. Upstream, the first clouds of smoke from the Women's Village drifted with the mist along the river. Over there, they were waking up and washing themselves in the same water; bubbles and white smears of soap flowed between the two men's legs.

For the past two weeks the sailor had been gradually reducing his daily alcohol consumption in order to be on top form. Since the previous day he had forbidden himself and Pete to drink coffee.

"No tremors. What we need is calm if we're going to make it through this."

And yet, in spite of these preparations and all his experience, the sailor was like a cat on a hot tin roof. This worried Pete.

"What's wrong?"

"What do you mean?"

"Why are you in this state?"

The sailor replied without looking at him, staring up the track to the Women's Village. "I need two hands to do the tattooing. Someone else has to hold you down and pull your skin flat while I work."

The sailor swallowed his saliva.

"My assistant is Harriet."

"I'm going to strip off in front of your wife?"

"And here she is!"

She was walking along the path in the morning light, wearing a clean dress, her hair nicely done. She, too, looked nervous. So this was Harriet – Marinette's mother – the whore that made the sailor's heart pound.

6

With the loincloth tied around his waist, Pete drank two mouthfuls of laudanum.

"I've never taken opium before."

"You'll sleep like a baby, mate, and you'll have wild dreams. You know, those dreams that get mixed up with reality and become part of your memories."

The sailor thought for a moment and then smiled.

"The problem is that, afterwards, you'll wonder about your memories, because you won't be sure if they're real or not."

Pete lay on his back, his clothes rolled up in a ball under his head, his naked skin touching the planks. His gaze wandered from the sailor to Harriet, from Harriet to the sailor.

The sailor, scrubbed clean and smelling of soap, bare-chested, his skin like old parchment telling the story of his long, errant life, looked simultaneously as sober as a priest and, in the presence of his wife, as giddy as a lovesick adolescent. He didn't dare glance at her as he prepared his equipment.

On a white sheet, the sailor placed three slender bamboo stalks, each about eighteen inches long, with the tattoo combs tied to their ends. There were three different widths of shark tooth, each of them carved into a straight line, the smallest no more than a fine point. Alongside these three combs was a fourth bamboo stalk, thicker than the others and weighed down with a stone: this was the hammer. Into half a coconut shell the sailor poured a few drops from his ink bottle. He kneeled at Pete's feet, wedged a cushion on his thigh and waited, looking at his wife.

Next to Harriet were some clean cloths, a bowl of water, a bar of soap and a razor. She rolled up her sleeves and kneeled down facing her husband.

The tattoo design was on the wall, separated into several sheets of paper showing the climbing plant section by section, with its flowers and its letters.

"The most painful part will be when I go over your bones and tendons. And also where the skin is thickest, because I'll have to hammer harder so the ink goes through your epidermis. And also where the skin is thin . . ."

While the sailor explained all this to Pete, Harriet slid the razor blade over his calf. Pete got shivers in his belly and he felt embarrassed. The sailor smiled.

"Yeah, you'll see. There are certain places where it doesn't hurt quite as much. How do you feel?"

The sailor's voice sounded low and unnaturally slow and Pete felt his body flatten against the wooden bed, drawn down by gravity; the laudanum was starting to take effect, and the erotic frissons from the touch of the razor and Harriet's hand were diminishing. When he spoke, there seemed to be long gaps of silence between the words. "I . . . feel . . . good. I'm . . . fine."

Harriet wiped the razor blade on a sheet, rinsed the shaved skin, and placed a cloth soaked in alcohol on Pete's leg, covering it from his knee to the top of his thigh under the lifted loincloth. She massaged his right foot to relax it. Pete watched her do it. The sailor stared longingly at his wife. With the cushion under his elbow, he held the hammer in his right hand. On his thigh he placed the thinnest of the combs, the one with the fine point, whose tooth was suspended over Pete's foot.

Harriet was one of the prettiest women in the village. Round, and not very tall, she was twenty-five or twenty-six but there was something sincere in her look – a touch of virginity that must have made her very popular in the brothels of the Caribbean colonies. Her teeth were solid, which was good because she smiled a lot, proving that strength and sweetness are not opposites: plenty of tough men had died here long before she would. Pete turned to look at the sailor, and for the first time saw a remnant of that innocence in him, a hint of youth, preserved by the salt of the sea perhaps, the way brine pickles food. Despite all the exhaustion and deprivations and little deaths of their journeys, these two had put enough aside for each other.

The sun was above the treetops now and its rays shone on the palm roof. In a few minutes, the temperature would reach its peak, and it would stay that way until sunset, the hour of snakes. Pete watched the couple as they leaned over him, their hair almost touching, Harriet's in a bun, the sailor's standing up in tufts. He thought about Maria's hair and remembered the way it had smelled when she slept next to him on the bed of leaves in the forest in Guatemala. One of Harriet's hands held his ankle and gently squeezed it, while the other held his toes and pushed them down, stretching his foot. He was in the Guatemalan jungle, holding Maria's hand. He was pulling her behind him. Guzman was dead and they were fleeing together. They panted as they ran towards the blue Caribbean sea. Someone was calling them . . . the distant voice of the sailor.

"The blue, my love, in the lagoons and islands of Polynesia, is the most incredible blue I've ever seen. A colour you think could only belong in a painting. A blue that does not really exist, so transparent that you don't dare jump in the water, for fear that you'll smash into the ground."

The tattoo island. As the sailor worked, he told Harriet about his travels in the Pacific. He hadn't been to her bedroom in weeks, because the sailor had started drinking again. The rules of the Women's Village demanded abstinence. Bad habits are parasites that feed on our wounds; persistent creatures that live hidden in our bellies. So, the sailor had weaned himself off alcohol, starving those creatures whose death sometimes feels like our own. He had starved himself in order to have a steady hand, in order to make the perfect tattoo, and in order to lure Harriet here – his assistant, whose heat Pete could sense radiating from under her dress – so he could tell her about the southern seas. In the hope that his tales would melt his nomadic whore, his genius daughter's mother. Pete half-opened his eyes to look at them. Harriet was smiling. Her hand around his ankle was burning hot.

"What a feeling it is, my Harriet, to jump into that blue! Those islands, too, barely exist. Imagine, my love, spits of land so thin that in certain places you can leap from one side to the other in a single bound. Imagine those lines, white with sand and green with trees, that make circles in the ocean, like the craters of a volcano enclosing the blue within. The sharks can enter those lagoons through subterranean passages. Those creatures from the deep black go into transparent waters to copulate and bask in the sun. We hunt them so we can eat their fins and carve their teeth into sacred combs."

Pete stared at Harriet. A shiver stung his foot, a shot of venom, a needle of heat that touched a nerve under his skin. The pain ran all the way up to his temples. The first ink root of the plant had just entered a bone. The silence between the two warning shots was long, and during that time the sailor and Harriet looked at each other, bathed in the Polynesian blue. The shark bit Pete for a second time and another shot of venom sped through his body. There was a world parallel to this one that existed in the silence between words, the void between acts and thoughts: spaces big enough to take some rest between the hammer blows. A hollow substance. The transparency of lagoons opening on the void. Pete could see clearly now that we too are parasites living in that hollow belly, imagining that our death is the world's.

He wanted to smile but he was already laughing without his body, which he had abandoned to the sailor and Harriet. The hornet was back, stabbing his foot with its stinger. He closed his eyes. He wished he could join Maria, asleep in the Women's Village.

"The inhabitants of the islands are always naked, my Harriet. There, you see through everything, and the women smile like you do, with teeth as white as pearls."

Harriet's hand moved up to Pete's calf. She held him down here, pulling the skin taut while the sailor engraved his drawing. Soon he would write the first name. Pete's hand grasped for the bottle of laudanum, but the world at the end of his hand was too enormous for him to be able to find anything. Harriet leaned over him and lifted the cool glass bottle to his lips.

"Drink."

Pete couldn't manage to thank her. Harriet undressed above him, facing her husband. She was naked to the waist; beads of sweat ran from her throat, down between her white breasts. They must be happy, these lovers, what with the size of the tattoo and all the days it would take them to finish it. The hornet hammered his leg and his skin tore like the hymen of a rediscovered memory. The new wave of poppy milk swept him away and Pete finally vacated the bed, leaving his body there behind him. He went along the track to the Women's Village and the hut where Maria was sleeping. He walked with one leg burning: the carnivorous plant kept climbing up his flesh. He was thirsty.

Harriet poured another drop of syrup into his mouth.

Maria was lying with her eyes open. She lifted up the blanket and Pete slid in next to her. She mounted him, or perhaps it was Harriet moaning on top of the sailor, the two of them lying next to him. Maria's big eyes shrank as she leaned over him, until they became two black pearls. He dived into them, became lost, disappeared.

When he awoke he was alone on the bed, a sheet pulled over his body. The Ink House was empty, his dream and the tattoo-lovers vanished. He lifted up the sheet so he could understand where that burning was coming from. The black flowering plant, the skin around it red, grew from his foot, twisted around his ankle, entwined his knee and sent a stem creeping up his lower thigh, its growth temporarily stopped. By twisting his body, he was able to see the muscle of his calf, enveloped by lines of vegetation, the names wrapped around the plant stems.

The first Sunday was over. Night fell.

In the Women's Village, Maria went from her bed to the chapel, from the convict Christ to sleep, the same every day. She ate only the food that Pete brought, refusing everything else she was offered. She had reduced the possibility of a new world, having lost her own to the American and the chapel.

Every Sunday, Pete lay on the wooden bed and the island lovers found each other above him. The plant grew, he drank opium and went to join Maria, while beside him Harriet gave her pale flesh to the sailor's dark dragons, ships, storms and sirens.

At the hour of snakes, when he woke alone, Pete lit a candle and took a pencil and paper.

Letter to Maria.

On my foot a thistle takes root. It is the emblem of our country, the land that my parents left. According to the legend, the Vikings of Norway, who had come to attack the Scottish village of Largs, crossed a field of thistles; one of them, barefoot, was pricked and cried out; woken, the Scots won the battle.

I walk on the thistles of that country that I have never known, or across the stories that my mother used to tell me, stories that I told to my brother Oliver; I no longer know which parts are real and which parts I invented. Scotland, for us, is an imaginary country. On my ankle I told the sailor to write its old Gaelic name, Alba. The ankles follow our nose, which sniffs the wind and points where we're headed; they turn the feet in the direction that we walk. I think about my mother when I was a newborn in her arms – with her dead in mine – her fine nose in the wind of the Scottish sea, her eyes scanning the horizon, her feet itching from stinging dreams. She is on a pebble beach and thinking about America. With our ankles, we stand on tiptoes to see a long way and guess the future. She moves to take a step that way and the thistle climbs up my calf, it becomes a light, floating aquatic plant. Along those leaves like hair, the sailor wrote her name with his sharks' teeth. The calf carries me forwards, the way my mother travelled the world to arrive on these shores. Coira Ferguson. In Gaelic, Coira means boiling pond, she told me. With her volcanic character, like hot bubbling water, Coira Ferguson travelled to the town of Basin, Oregon, buried under snow during its long winters. It was Coira who gave me that desperate desire to flee. She didn't make her trip alone though. He was already with her. The man who, after that, only ever wanted to stay in the same place and rot. This was the Old Man, Maria, and I have to tell you about him and his death. But before that, he made that trip with Coira – a love too delicate for her husband's – and that was probably an act of courage on his part: she had dreams, he offered to help her make them come true. And so began the path of thorns that made the Vikings cry out and presaged their defeat. Around the knee, hammered into my bones and tendons, grazed by sea algae, is the Old Man's name: Hubert Ferguson. The knee bends and straightens; it is the joint of courage and humiliation. Perhaps we forgive in the same way we pay tribute: knees bent. When it touches the Old Man, the algae becomes a hawthorn branch on my thigh, with its thorns and its little flowers, on the muscles that carry the world. The thighs are to the shoulders what the ankles are to the nose. What is held aloft on our shoulders is supported by our thighs: the world and the past. Atlas, knees bent and thighs tensed, bears the weight that crushes men who wish to live without gods. On the thorns, some scattered letters that can be arranged at will to compose all the words and all the sentences we can imagine. One of them, among all those possible phrases, could be: the night of the barn. *But the sailor didn't know that, and he tattooed the letters that I gave him in a random order. It is a message that can be read only if you already know it, hidden in the thorny bushes of guilt. I'll tell you about that too. About the raw dawns that follow my long nightmares. In my thighs, the weight of the secret, perched like a bird of prey on my shoulders. The lie is a sea urchin, which the sailor tattooed in the palm of my right hand with red ink made from madder, bought specially from a Chinaman in Cayenne. The*

259

lie is a red sea urchin. It stings and poisons anyone to whom I reach out, and it wounds me when I ball my fist in anger.

Hawthorn trees flower around my waist, around my pelvis, that crenelated tower at my core, the summit of my legs. The hawthorns become a trumpet vine, a fast-growing and persistent creeper, with its flowers that look like they're heralding a celebration and a birth. It is there, too, at the hips, that I asked the sailor to draw a straight line, all around me, going through the door of the navel. This is my equator, Maria. On this line, after the sailor and his wife made love next to me, Harriet rested her face. When I awoke, the sailor had left us and Harriet was sleeping on that freshly tattooed line.

The trumpet vine climbs up to my heart and between the lines of my ribs there are four names, in four flowers shaped like megaphones: Alexandra, Arthur, Aileen and Oliver. I'll tell you about them too. About the family that I left behind. The Fitzpatrick ranch is named after a young Irish couple who were travelling with Arthur Bowman. Jonathan, the husband, died while out hunting; he fell into a mountain crevasse. His wife was pregnant and she died. Her name was Aileen. Bowman buried them together under a giant redwood and decided that this was the end of his journey: on Lake Tahoe, beside the graves of these two parents he'd found during his travels, like ancestors younger than he was.

Oliver, my brother, is the only other Ferguson alive on this side of the world, born from the womb, of Coira Ferguson the dreamer. Oliver owns half of my heart. Often I risked my life to save his, to protect him from the Old Man, from the war, and from the snow-covered mountains that wanted to devour us. That is why my heart is half his. It beats for both of us; I saved some of it for him. What emptiness and heat there is inside this ribcage! This is where we try to be a part of the world, by filling ourselves with its air. It is here that adventure, fear and our taste for the abstract come together; here our destiny is blended. Did you know, Maria, that destiny begins when we escape what we ought to be? We wait for ourselves here on earth. Parents, a country, a language, a story . . . there is a *place already prepared for us. A nose in the wind, a wandering ankle, an impetuous calf, a proud knee and solid thighs, a sidestep and we are no longer what we were supposed to be. Our destiny: nothing, if not a story worth telling, a letter that demands to be written, life as an adventure, however modest it may be, containing a large element of risk, of the unknown.*

The trumpet vine climbs over my ribs and around to my back: it's a tree now, an apple tree in blossom, like the ones that the Old Man planted around the farm, which never bore any fruit. The sailor says that in Japan, at the far end of Asia, the men's bodies are tattooed all over with these blossoming trees. The apple tree spreads its branches and its leaves diagonally towards my shoulders. This is the part of the tattoo that I cannot see. In the forks of those branches the sailor has drawn memories, like birds' nests. Little drawings made with the finest of the sharks' teeth. A mountain and a lake, the house on the Fitzpatrick ranch as I described it to him, a rifle barrel, a mustang named Reunion, a bison, a book, a schooner named the Santo Cristo, a pyramid. Two branches rise up to my neck, growing thinner, and the two points become letters hidden behind my ear. The tree is whispering to me the names of Maria and Pete.

Two months have passed, the rainy season has begun, and as the plant has grown you have recovered: ankles, calves, knees and thighs, you are standing now, the tower of your abdomen strong again. You are ready. I am going to ask you for your dreams and, if you want me to, I will help you to make them come true. You are waiting for me at the Women's Village. I will go down on one knee, Maria, I will hammer the tattooed name of the Old Man like a nail into a coffin. I am a destiny in paper, ink and scars. Kneeling for forgiveness, promises, pleas, my arms open wide.

7

Going to see Maria, with only a few lines of ink to defend himself, scared Pete Ferguson more than throwing himself under a barrage of the Old Man's fists, jumping onto a wild mustang or walking across a few yards of tall grass to shake Rusky's hand. It frightened him as if it were something that no man had ever faced before, whereas in truth the whole history of humanity was of making those few awkward steps to find your other.

He thought he was ready. He thought it impossible to be readier, except by being older than he was. On the track to the Women's Village, Pete blinked and scratched at his palm, crushing the still-warm sea urchin. Maria might laugh in his face, or slap him, or squat on the ground, skirt lifted up, and stare at him while she took a piss. It didn't matter. She might refuse, but she had to see what had changed, this woman who had fought all her life for change.

He saw the shelters and the smoke clouds of the Women's Village, which men besieged on their knees. Pete felt like a messenger, a diplomat carrying a white flag, an envoy sent by those who were still waiting. He felt brave too, because he was going to face the toughest of all the women: Maria, waging war against the god of her masters and his Book, in which – an uneducated, instinctive revolutionary – she had found the unbearable idea of a better world, the discovery of a hope nurtured and instantly annihilated by those who followed the cross. Maria was in a fever because she was purging herself of the germs caught from Hagert the Jesuit, the poets with their soft hands, the Guzmans in glasses and the Aznars with their predatory ideals. And he had to convince her that he – this white child, bullied and then spoiled, on his path of mercy – was worth hearing, that she could still dream that a thing might change, even the most ludicrous thing: this gringo, with no feeling for revolution, with nothing but a bit of courage for death.

He stood outside Mama's shelter, and, on the back of his neck, behind his ear, the letters of their two names still burned with the last bites of the sharks' teeth. On her porch, this restful Sunday, Mama was soaking her feet in a bowl of salted water, killing the parasites embedded under her nails and in her skin.

With his fingertips, he touched his lips, dry from laudanum and the long walk here. The colours were strange: the red wood of the shelter, Mama's dress, the enamelled bowl, the earth beneath their feet. The lines separating objects were not clear. He wanted to speak but he had long ago forgotten how to articulate. Mama slid her wrinkled feet into her leather sandals, walked past him without a word and left him standing there like a shrub in the wind.

He went through the main room, its floorboards striped by the light slanting through the blinds, and knocked at the bedroom door. Maria never answered. He waited for a moment before going in. Lying on her side under the mosquito net, she watched him move towards the bed.

Pete unbuttoned his shirt, unfastened the hemp string holding up his trousers, and dropped his clothes on the floor. He sat on the wooden floor and stretched out his right leg.

"It's a thistle, the emblem of our country, Scotland. There are several legends about this thistle . . ."

Maria moved her hands under her cheek, lifted her head and opened her eyes wider.

Pete told her about the tattoo. He introduced her to his mother, Coira the dreamer, Hubert the strong man with no courage, Oliver the brother whom Pete had protected so that he could grow up without wounds, keeping all of the pain and the scars for himself. The alcohol and the madness on the dilapidated farm. The night of the barn, when the Old Man climbed the ladder and his eldest son watched him do it, knees trembling but refusing to bend. He told her about crossing the Sierra Nevada and discovering the Fitzpatrick ranch: the Ferguson brothers' first equator. Standing in front of Maria, Pete turned around so that she could follow the line that encircled his hips. He explained what happened in Carson City and why he had fled, the atavistic fatalism that had come to America on the boat with Hubert Ferguson that ran through his own veins. He talked about the names engraved in the trumpet vine flowers.

There was this man, Arthur Bowman, who fascinated her and scared him. A rock transformed into a man, or maybe the other way round, who found love and protection and wanted to become a child again. There was this man whom the gringo admired and feared, and then there was what she sensed beneath his story: that Pete and Bowman were very much alike, which is what made them wary of each other. Finally she decided that she liked this violent, broken man who had built a wonderful ranch so he could hide there. He, too, Pete said, in this world where everyone dies, is a man who has killed.

There was this red-headed woman, the woman with the books, Bowman's outspoken wife, the intellectual pioneer who wrote for newspapers, who stood up to men, who spoke of love and equality, of community and peace. A woman at war, and the gringo had fallen in love with her. If Bowman resembled Pete, Maria hoped, listening to his description of Alexandra Desmond, that she bore some resemblance to this powerful woman.

Aileen was the angel who illuminated the lake in the morning and made the sun set on the ranch when she fell asleep. Uncle Pete used to take Aileen for horse rides in the mountains. Aileen had turned eleven since he left the ranch. Maria thought she could hear the little girl laugh as she listened to Pete rekindle his memory of her.

Night fell and Pete lit three candles, which he placed on the floor. Then, on his knees, turning his back to Maria, he told her the rest of his story: the tree growing from the Scottish thistle, its branches reaching out to the sea, the pyramids, Mexico and Guatemala, the schooner and its captain. The last branch and its two names, which

Pete presented to her, head lowered, like a samurai offering his head to his lord.

The effects of the opium milk had worn off. He felt fine.

Maria looked at the vast tattoo, those successive plants that hugged the curves of this stocky little white body, that gave him a more vertical thrust, a new lightness in spite of the dense blackness of the ink. She touched her fingertip to the thorns on his thigh, followed the plant up to his hip, kneeled behind Pete and pressed her cheek to the blossoming apple tree, put her arms around his belly, encircling the equator.

Pete put his hands on Maria's.

The sighs, groans and cries of Maria and Pete were heard that night in all the houses of the Women's Village, in those wooden shelters without windows or walls. The lovers set off a wave of solitary caresses. Women came out of their shelters so they could hear more clearly. Harriet and two other wives disappeared down the track to the men's camp, and many other women regretted that night that there weren't more men to go around.

Candles were blown out and night fell on the Women's Village. Lovers fell asleep together.

The next morning, they began the construction of a new shelter, away from the village, named Nuptial House. Pete and Maria decided they would move there after they had found a permanent roof. The distance between the village and this new home was big enough that the lovers could not be heard all the time, but small enough that a great cry of pleasure could still be perceived.

The hut was crudely built. Maria and Pete hung a large hammock there and slept in it together, pulling the fabric over themselves, enclosed for the night in a cotton cocoon, their sweat mingling.

They started working at the Free Women's mine, shovelling the banks of sand and silt in the meanders of Gabriel Creek, sifting for flakes of gold with a pan. They received their share (the rest went to the village) effectively earning labourers' wages, without having to pay for their roof or their food.

Harriet and the sailor moved in together in March, during a brief pause in the rainy season. The "little March summer", they called this twenty-day respite before the start of the great downpours. Before the floods came, the entire village – helped by new men come to redeem themselves and new women here to take refuge from them – searched the creek for every last scrap of gold. Harriet and the sailor now had their own Nuptial House, close to Pete and Maria's, where they lived with little Marinette.

Maria spoke only with Pete. They communicated in Spanish so the others wouldn't understand them. Pete spoke increasingly good French, discovering the Latin roots that linked it to Spanish. He wanted to speak to everyone in their own language. Maria started to teach him Xinca.

In May they watched in fascination as the rain poured down in torrents. The earth could not absorb that much water, and the sky could not contain that much when there were deserts full of rocks and dust elsewhere. The rivers swelled to the point where Pete wondered how much land would be left in French Guiana. He and Maria walked along Gabriel Creek to the great Mahury river, surrounded by vast swathes of marshland where wading birds hunted for fish and crocodiles lurked.

One day in June they set off for Cayenne, aboard a small sailing boat that provided the only transportation, however irregular, to the town. Maria hid their pistol under her clothes. They arrived, shivering, in the capital of the French colony after four hours of stormy waters and whipping rain. The Indian was not allowed to sit on the benches of the covered deck, so Pete stayed with her in the open. The cold that entered their bodies, on this generally warm island, was deep and disturbing, like the shivers of a fever or a weakness that could not be permitted in French Guiana.

The rain stopped as they stepped onto the landing stage covered with water from the street, which poured off the edge of the dock in a long, salty waterfall. A park of avocado and mango trees, surrounded by soaked lawns, ran alongside the beach of black rocks. The shutters were closed in the low houses with their four-sided roofs; the wind rose from the sea and buffeted the empty porches. Maria walked one step behind Pete, her head lowered. He wanted to hold her hand, but she pulled it away from him and in a cold voice told him to walk ahead of her.

"You'll get us into trouble."

Pete looked around them at the lifeless houses.

"There's nobody here."

"Keep going."

They entered the city along a street that ran perpendicular to the coastline. On this street there were brick pavements more than a foot high and they walked on them to escape the mud. A ray of sunlight appeared. During this temporary lull, Cayenne looked more appealing, and a few figures braved the outdoors: some convicts sent to clean the square, an immense park planted with royal palms, their trunks smooth and straight. Some white people appeared on the walkways. There was a café at the end of the square, with music from a pianola coming through its windows and the sound of voices singing. They saw pale suits, the glimmers of clean linen in the sunlight. *Café-restaurant Les Palmistes* was painted in fine lettering on the facade.

The shipping company's offices were a little further along on the left, and they followed the pavement without going through the square, keeping as far as possible from the laughter and conversations of the colonists.

Maria did not want to go inside. She squatted on the pavement, making herself as small as possible. Pete went alone into the offices of the General Transatlantic Company, but they did not offer transportation to the city of Macapá, in the Amazon estuary. They advised Pete to make enquiries with other local shipowners whose boats went along the coast to Brazil. They went from office to office without success. They could go to Belém in Brazil, but from there it would be as far to Macapá as it was from Cayenne. They traversed the city in vain.

Unlike Saint-Laurent, Cayenne was not merely a penal colony. There were inhabitants who were not guards, shops that did not sell chains and restaurants that were not canteens for prisoners; there were mansions and official buildings: the mayor's office, the naval court, the governor's house, buildings with signs for mining and trading companies. In the streets there were soldiers and bourgeois couples; the city looked wealthier than Saint-Laurent, but it had the same sad feel. If Saint-Laurent had been a convict town, Cayenne was a city of masters and slaves who had been replaced by prisoners. An atmosphere of failure reigned in this port, once regarded as France's entry point to Eldorado, now its human dumping ground.

They took refuge in the room of an inn recommended by Mama, run by a former inhabitant of the Women's Village.

This woman, curious for news of her old comrades, bombarded them with questions as she prepared supper. They went to bed when the sun set and listened to the sounds of the city. Maria pressed her back against Pete's belly.

"This place is not for us. We can only live in the forest now. That's the only place they'll leave us in peace. I don't believe in your equator."

"Many things have already changed."

"Yes, I have no home."

Stung by her criticisms, Pete wanted to push her away. For Maria, he was nothing more than a piece of driftwood to which she clung in order not to drown. He pulled his arms away from her, jolted by a shudder of self-loathing. She took hold of his hands and pressed herself even more tightly against him.

"I'll go with you. You'll need me down there, when your pyramids fall from their point and crush you. You don't know anything about pyramids."

She wished him good night in Xinca and he replied in her language; this brief exchange, in a language that soon nobody else would speak, reassured them both. She turned around and kissed him, her square moon face with its large shining eyes and its boiling lips breathing out air as hot and humid as the air in the penal colony.

The next day, Pete went alone to the port and finally found a boat – a small commercial steamer, owned by French and Brazilian traders –

which would take a few passengers and was going through the Amazon estuary. It was scheduled to leave in early September. At the company's offices, he paid an advance fee for two passengers.

After a second night in the city, they took the rowing boat to the landing stage at Mahury and, relieved to be back, walked from there to the Women's Village.

A month passed. The rain fell less hard. Maria started having stomach pains. She stopped working in the gardens and stayed in their shelter, lying in the hammock. One evening, coming back from the mine, Pete found her kneeling on the floorboards, crying, her skirt sticky with blood, her cupped hands holding little black and purple clots of viscous blood. Mama took her to the creek to get washed.

Pete lay on the floor next to the hammock. Maria let her hand dangle towards him.

"It's not the first time. It's because I was raped by Governor Ortiz's soldiers. Babies just fall out of me. Nothing can stay in there."

Maria had tried to have a child with her comrades Gustavio, Santos and even Segundo Aznar. After sacrificing herself for the cause, she had wanted some form of compensation.

Pete gently rocked his little revolutionary and wondered whether he wanted a child. And, if he did, what it would mean to choose a woman who could never give birth.

8

Head covered by an ochre-red cloth to protect her from the sun, a canvas bundle slung across her shoulders, Maria shook hands with all the women who had taken care of her. Pete had a rifle, which he held by its barrel, butt to the ground, like a walking stick. His hair and beard had grown long. He put his hand on the sailor's shoulder; the sailor was sad to see his favourite tattoo leave. Mama was frowning, her jaws tensed. She was anxious on behalf of the Indian who was leaving with this American, a naive kid who thought a few lines of ink had transformed him into an indestructible pilgrim. She had insisted on the couple taking a gun with them. You'll need to hunt, she told them.

But what did Maria and Pete think? They had come here at the same time, but not really together; they were leaving united by something that was hard to explain. They accepted the comfort of being a pair, but remained as mistrustful as beaten animals or old cynics. There was a monklike silence between them, as if they were incapable of putting words to their feelings. And if no word could express something, did that something actually exist? Leaving was their response to this menacing silence.

Marinette, sitting on the sailor's shoulders, waved longer than anyone else, until the boat was nothing more than a tiny dot on the river. On deck, the other passengers had edged away from the couple.

In Cayenne, they waited in the port until the little sailing steamer had been loaded with its cargo, its reserves of water, coal and food replenished. On the sea front, the manicured green lawns, the trees and the lively terraces made the capital look more welcoming than it had on their first visit. The prisoners slipped silently from shadow to shadow. They watched as the prison boat that came from the Îles du Salut and Saint-Laurent moved into the port. Three guards in uniform were escorting a prisoner – a thin white man not much taller than Maria, with no teeth and big round eyes. A recaptured escapee. The man was bare-chested. Around his neck were woven leather necklaces hung with little white bird bones, superstitious charms that jingled together on his jutting chest. He looked at the Indian woman with her bearded man, and his smile grew wider. A guard pushed him forwards.

"Get a move on, Belbenoît! We don't have all bloody day!"

Pete nodded in response. The short man's smile faded as he concentrated. He was already making plans for his next escape.

Pete stood up and took Maria's hand. He presented their tickets to the captain, an old Brazilian who spoke French with a strong accent. The sailors had crude tattoos and the discretion of men who raised families on low wages. A ship's boy showed them to their cabin at the end of a corridor: no porthole, two bunks, one above the other. Another cell, for the five-day coastal trip to Macapá. The company's owners had agreed, for a supplementary fee, to waive the formalities of a customs check for Pete and Maria.

As long as the steamer remained in the port, they stayed in their cabin, its metal walls rusted by the salt and the heat. Compared to the easy glide of the *Santo Cristo*, Pete felt as if he were travelling in the belly of a galloping horse. Maria soon got sick and curled up in a ball, as she had done aboard the schooner.

They went up to the gangway that led to the wheelhouse to take some air. At last, the sea and the sky were all they could see. Rays of sunlight were filtered by the clouds, turning the colours of the boat and the water a uniform grey. Behind them, the continent was no more than a black line. Maria looked down so she wouldn't have to see the coast swaying up and down. She clung to Pete, who suddenly felt weak.

The captain – a small, thin man with a face that was all wrinkles – had worked as a child in sugar cane plantations near Belém. This first part of his life could be summarised in two words: teeth and dogs. The sugar had rotted his teeth, he told them, clacking his dentures – a monstrous set of yellowed donkey teeth, held together by springs that creaked like a fairground ride. As for the dogs, they were Cane Corsos, massive black watchdogs that came up to his navel and guarded the plantations against anything that tried to enter or escape. These beasts had come from Italy, where they had killed bears in Apulia; here, they killed jaguars, and loved to feast on the flesh of fleeing slaves or farm labourers. The captain, his dentures grinding sinisterly, banged on the hollow-sounding metal hull of his boat and declared that sugar cane did not grow on water and that dogs could not run on it. The captain told them his life story without asking for theirs in return.

That evening they stopped off in Ouanary, the last French village at the mouth of the Oyapock river, the border between French Guiana and Brazil. There were no French customs guards here. They saw a Chinese shop, two houses on stilts, some dugout canoes, and three men who boarded the steamer: Arab ex-cons, who either helped prisoners to escape or hunted them down, depending who paid them the highest fee. These three men were armed and did not speak to anyone. As night was falling, a few cable lengths from Brazil, the three men jumped into a long canoe with six black rowers in it. With this cargo unloaded, the captain clacked together his donkey teeth and held his nose. Turning to the French coast, he said: "That country, my friend, was invented for the glory of our worst nature. But you are in my country now. Good riddance to France, and welcome to Brazil!"

Pete went down to the cabin to give Maria this news. She had fallen asleep as they crossed this invisible border.

The steamer went from estuary to estuary. People waited hours for the boat to arrive, bringing their post from abroad. The captain knew the men who came out to meet the boat; he exchanged news with them, each time asking his two passengers to remain hidden. Waterways led to villages and plantations all over the place, and news travelled quickly along the coast. Everyone knew that an American had participated in the escape of the four convicts the previous winter. The captain had made the connection between that event and Pete, who wished to pass secretly into Brazil. But he had received his share of the money paid to the company to ensure their safety. And anyway, he enjoyed the American's conversation.

"At our next stop, I'll have a small favour to ask you, captain."

"We'll stop this evening at a large plantation called Jerusalem. The day after tomorrow, we'll be at the Río Amazonas. There'll be something waiting for you and the Indian there."

The steamer travelled for an hour upriver and moored at a rudimentary pontoon where a cart and two farm labourers were waiting. Some goods were exchanged along with a few coins, then a sailor, following his captain's orders, bent to the ground and rummaged around for an instant before getting back on board.

Pete went down to their cabin and sat next to Maria, who rested her cheek on his thigh. He stroked her hair, then the palm of her hand, and dropped four smooth little stones into it. These were what the sailor had picked up from the ground. Maria rolled the little stones between her fingers, weighing them in her hand.

"Thank you."

With two stones in each hand, she lay down and caressed these pieces of land.

Islands as big as green lakes. The brown lines of the river like the tracks left on the plain by charging bison. Land and water were inverted in the reflections of leaves and ripples. In this dizzying vision of curved lines, solid and liquid fought over paternity of the delta. The continent was not yet real, floating on the water in gigantic pieces, a drifting land. The change of direction, the calmness of the water and the duel between these two elements drew Maria out of the cabin. While the steamer weaved its way between the islands, the captain joined them on the gangway. He signalled to the sailor at the helm, pointing towards a shore where vast mud banks showed on the surface. On one of these spits of land, hundreds of yards long, a pale stain lay on the mud shore.

The closer they drew, the surer they felt. It was a beached ship. They soon recognised it: the *Santo Cristo*. Aznar's schooner lay on its side, the starboard row of portholes peering out of the mud. The sails, still hoisted, torn and green with mould, fluttered in the warm wind. At the sound of the steamer's engine, birds took off from the masts and monkeys leaped from the bow to hide in the forest. Navigating slowly amid the mud banks, the steamer moved as close as it could, the engine revving noisily as it struggled against the current.

Rain, wind and dead leaves had left the *Santo Cristo* looking like a ghost ship. Creepers from the branches overhanging it had wrapped around the handrails and the shrouds, and the hull was covered with algae and dried earth. The captain and the crew all crossed themselves.

"The schooner has been there since last winter, two weeks after the French anarchists escaped from Saint-Laurent-du-Maroni."

Maria balled her fist. Pete pinched his nostrils, fighting against an urge to vomit as he pictured Segundo Aznar that night on the *Santo Cristo*, lying on his back, his throat slit. Without its captain, the schooner had ended up wrecked in the biggest delta in the Americas.

"And the passengers?"

The captain spat his false teeth into his hand; he could speak more clearly without the wood rubbing against his gums. "You have to know the delta to navigate on this canal, particularly in the winter. When they ran aground on this island, the river was in flood; there were no mud banks here. If they'd made it to land, they'd have stayed close to the boat and someone would have seen them. There's freshwater on this island, and enough game to hunt. If they'd followed the river, either swimming or in a small boat, they'd have been swept out to sea and died. In truth, nobody knows what happened on board this ship. There are guns on the deck and signs of a struggle."

"You've been on board?"

The Brazilian captain rubbed his gums together and shook his head. "No. The smugglers and river pirates have come close to it too, but in all the months the schooner has been here nobody has taken anything from it. *Maldição*. I hope that during the next rainy season the

Amazon will carry this boat out to sea and sink it. Then nobody will ever speak of it again."

The captain signalled to the man at the wheel to take them away from this place. The engine roared and the steamer reversed before heading eastwards towards the city and port of Macapá.

So the mutineers, the two Parisian crooks and the Frenchman had met their end here, lost, terrified, angry, guns in hand. They had killed one another, devoured one another, fugitives who had been free for no more than a few days. Which one of those madmen had steered the *Santo Cristo* into this mud? Who was to blame for all those deaths?

On deck, Pete drank a bottle of rum he'd bought from the captain, who sometimes joined him for a few mouthfuls.

In the cabin, Maria played with the stones in her hands, smiling as she dreamed of Pete's equator, where stones did not fall and where water, freed from gravity, rose up to the sky. Nobody would ever drown in that water.

An immense stone fort on a peninsula on the river heralded the city of Macapá and welcomed boats coming from the delta. The captain broke into a smile.

"The Irish and the English came here first, three or four centuries ago, to trade with the Indians. They were kicked out by the Portuguese, who were themselves expelled by the French, who wanted the Amazon to be the border with French Guiana. The Portuguese retook the city, the delta and the river. They had just been ousted from Morocco by the Arabs, and the colonists who came here decided to deal with the situation permanently. This was in 1764. They drew up plans for a fort like the ones they had on the African coast: star-shaped, with no blind spots."

There was not a single tree around Fort São José, just a vast swathe of low-cut grass, like the manicured lawns in Saint-Laurent and Cayenne that Pete now associated with the presence of convicts or slaves. The captain pointed to the turrets and arrow slits.

"The fort is still armed, and the cannons can fire on the Amazon in every direction. Your equator is upriver, where the water goes crazy, a few miles from the city."

Maria felt Pete's arm weigh more heavily on her shoulders. Soon he wouldn't be able to stand up straight. He was about to reach the end of his voyage and discover the void that would follow this accomplishment. She had rested during her long convalescence in the Women's Village and she knew that it was now her turn to carry him.

They left Macapá the next morning at dawn, on foot, guided by the captain's nephew, a young man who spoke only Portuguese. They had taken a cheap room near the docks and had not slept well. If they walked quickly, they could reach the imaginary line of the equator before nightfall. An odour of fish and damp wool rose up from the river. The forest, even hotter and more humid than in French Guiana, smelled of rotten fruit and fermented grapes; the humus distilled its own alcohol from dead leaves and wood.

It soon became apparent that they had no need for a guide. The track that followed the Amazon was wide and well-worn; they gave the nephew his wage for the day and sent him back to Macapá. He grumbled something: a warning, accompanied by arm gestures that seemed to incorporate the river and the forest. They turned their backs on him and continued down the track. The captain's nephew remained where he was, watching them, torn between his duty not to leave them and the order he had received to go back.

Part of Pete Ferguson's journal, written in Macapá, was found much later in the archives of the Fitzpatrick ranch, along with a letter sent from Brazil, written by a certain Maria Bautizada in March 1874, seven months after the couple's arrival in the Brazilian city.

9

I left Basin nearly ten years ago now, with the barrels of the soldiers' rifles in my back, and I left the Fitzpatrick ranch nearly three years ago, at night, driven out by anger and hatred.

In the alley behind the Eagle Saloon in Carson City I laughed in the face of old Meeks, who stood there with his fists balled. He was drunk too, yelling insults at me and weeping for his son. When he threw himself at me, I sidestepped him. Carried away by his rage, he collapsed without me having to touch him.

Sometimes alcohol transforms men into something else, sometimes only into what they truly are, deep down. The Old Man was cowardly, his son was a nasty piece of work.

Meek died at my feet. Suddenly it was as if I was holding the Old Man against me, after I'd cut him down, and I yelled and yelled.

Meeks was one of the worst men in town. When his son went off to war, he told him to come back dead or covered with medals; his son even bought a round of drinks in the saloon. The Meeks are brutes from generation to generation. I was the one they picked on in the evenings when they'd had too much to drink. And they always had too much to drink.

Old Meeks did not receive a coffin with his son inside, nor even a box with a medal, nothing but a letter saying that he died on a battlefield down south.

I hit his chest until I heard his ribs breaking. We were covered in mud. His heart stopped beating, and Lylia, who said hers was broken, found us at that very moment. I don't know what she saw. A murder, an opportunity to get revenge, or a young man so repugnant that her love turned suddenly to disgust, her disgust to the hatred that drove me out of town.

. . .

The equator did not exist.

For a few coins, a man showed us a leaf on the water inside a saucepan with a hole in it, and the leaf turned one way and then – a few steps away – the other. But I didn't believe him. What did that prove? I couldn't even cry. My tears would have been ridiculous next to all that water in the Amazon. We went back to Macapá and I started wasting away.

. . .

I write a few lines whenever I have enough strength. I've been bedridden for weeks. Whole days pass without seeing Maria. I don't know where she goes. She comes back, sees me, and goes away again while I sleep. I feel as if I'm having opium nightmares.

I no longer have the strength to keep the ghosts away from me. The dead who used to scratch at the doors have come in, dripping from the river, stinking of rotten fish and whores' foul vaginas.

The equator did not exist.

Just the leaf spinning backwards in that improvised siphon. The man said he was showing us a miracle. He begged for a coin for that con trick he pulled on honest travellers. I would have killed him for that lie. Trying to make us believe that the world can change. Look! The leaf is spinning the other way. Follow me onto the battlefields, you will die for the leaf. To war! We will build a new country, plant the tree of liberty, write a new chapter, build a bigger dream in a new dawn, we will forge a new path, smash down walls, push the limits, rewrite history, we will establish a new order and walk on uncharted land. We will invent a new world. To war!

The man on the track of the equator, with his saucepan and his magnetism trick, was the officer who came to fetch Oliver and me from the farm. He was the man from the Santa Fe Railway, with his freight train that would transform the prairie. The owner of the saloon, serving alcohol to desperate drunkards. The banker who loaned money to the Old Man. The men who sold ladders and ropes. The men who bought bison skeletons, the fertiliser of the future. Look, it's spinning in the other direction! The conquistador's cross.

He kept going back and forth, either side of the imaginary equator, showing me the leaf inside his saucepan. Each time, I felt more and more panic, watching this and knowing that nothing was happening, that the man was crazy.

Maria didn't look at the leaf. She took those little smooth stones that the sailor on the steamer picked up for her and threw them in the Amazon. She didn't want that earth anymore.

The creepers scratch at the doors of the house.

. . .

I haven't written anything for a long time. I don't know what happened during all that time. Maria comes. She talks about fever. I am mummified.

They have to throw away the sheets I slept on. Maria washes me. Are we magnetic? Do the acids and the fluids in our bellies spin the other way on the equator? We are siphons.

Maria is afraid that I won't survive. I understand her anxiety.

The end of the year is approaching, the time of wishes and resolutions. I laughed on my stinking bed.

It is hard to end things well. We are too scared of the end to give it the respect it deserves. What we do matters only to those who remain. We often lack the courage and generosity to end things well. My end here will not be a good one. I lack strength. Perhaps I could manage to say a few words, but words too require strength.

I am struggling without the brute that I used to be; I lack his strength. The brute who thinks his death is mine.

. . .

Fewer words. I have to save them.

"Don't try to speak," Maria tells me.

This Indian knows death better than I do. She knows what has to be done, just like she would know how to look after a child, although she never will.

. . .

I wanted to introduce Maria to Oliver. Show her the ranch. Most of my thoughts, when I remember them, drift towards the ranch, towards the graves of Aileen and Jonathan Fitzpatrick with their unborn child, under the big tree. I ask Maria to lay her cheek on my ravaged stomach. I confuse comings and goings.

...

There are agents of destruction in my veins, malign fevers that soften my bones. I have aged a lifetime in only a few months. I am older than the Old Man.

...

Between each entry in my journal, entire days disappear in silence. The blue lagoon, the space between things. And then I write, terrified, the announcement of my return, my death delayed yet again, not knowing if I have been resurrected or if I am merely dreaming.

...

I will leave without knowing. What will be the last sentence I write or speak? Perhaps this one, which means nothing. Often I just repeat Maria's name while the pencil falls between my fingers and I try to grab it, panicked as I see myself die.

...

All year, the same days: the sun rising each morning at the same time, the same sunset. Nothing happens. At the equator, all is identical and permanent. The leaf in the saucepan, on the exact line of the equator, does not move at all above the siphon. The water is not freed from gravity, it is gravity; it falls straight, without the elegance of a twist, without the slightest resistance.

...

There are no seasons here. Nobody could say: When winter ends, Pete Ferguson will start to recover. No seasons. The breath of the Amazon and the screech of the forest. Pete Ferguson is not getting better. He has written his last words.

...

Oliver, Maria. Maria, my brother. The Fitzpatrick ranch, where the winter is so long. On the banks of the lake, when they need to drink, the horses crack the ice with their hooves.

...

Where is Maria? My last word?
How will I die without her?
She is my ladder. I will hold Maria's hand.
  . . .
The Old Man sometimes said that I would end up being hanged. He
hanged himself to prove it. But I had a destiny, far away from my father's
rut. I am dying of a fever in Brazil. Did the Old Man even know that this
country existed?
  . . .
Hold my hand.
  . . .
My empty belly hurts. I curl up around the equator tattooed by the
sailor. My exhausted core, no longer strong enough to hold me upright.
  . . .
Hold my hand.

——— ⁕ ——— ⁕ ——— ⁕ ———

March 1874, Macapá, Brazil

To Mr Bowman, Alexandra, Oliver and Aileen
Fitzpatrick ranch, Carson City, Nevada, United States of America

My name is Maria Bautizada. I was born in Guatemala and I am
writing to you from the city of Macapá in Brazil, where I am today
with Pete. If by chance this letter reaches you, I doubt there will
still be enough time. And even if there were, the distance between
you and us is so great that you would not be able to do anything.
  I almost want to stop writing now. But if, one day, you read this
letter, at least you will know what happened to Pete.
  I met him in Guatemala in April 1872, in the backroom of a
restaurant in the city of Antigua. It was a secret meeting, which
would lead a few months later to us fleeing my country together
on a boat headed south. For months, Pete looked after me. Now I am

looking after him. He is sick and it is on his behalf that I am writing to ask for your help, because we have exhausted all our resources. I told him that I was writing a letter to the ranch. I don't know if he understood. When he is conscious, he talks about the lake as his home.

In the great plains of your country, Pete met a hunter who told him about the equator. Macapá, in Brazil, is very close to this line that separates north from south. That was the aim of his voyage, of which you know the beginning and I the end.

Pete and I are lovers. We are not married. I am a Xinca Indian.

In French Guiana, a sailor tattooed the story of his life on his body; your names are engraved in his skin and he told me all about you.

He is no longer the same person he was when he left Carson City. I have to introduce you to the man I am caring for, the other Pete Ferguson, whom you don't know.

In Antigua, when I met him, he was fleeing Mexico, where he had killed a man. All I know is that this man was responsible for the deaths of several children – Indian children. Pete had gone to Mexico because he had also killed a bison hunter in America, to save his own life. That is all I know. When he arrived in Guatemala, I thought that Pete Ferguson was a killer and a mercenary. We paid for his services, so he would fight alongside us against the corrupt government of my country. He drank and we were suspicious of him. By saving my life, he caused the collapse of our organisation. I hated him for that. I did not believe I was worth more than those with whom I fought. Pete had calculated things differently. A few weeks later, I killed one of my former comrades to save Pete's life. We fled across the sea to French Guiana, where we were welcomed by the women of a village, situated in a jungle. There, with Pete's help, I fought against dejection and fevers.

We were happy in that community, but we couldn't stay there. Pete had begun this voyage and it couldn't end there.

We had to keep going to the end. There was no other possibility. We made it.

Oliver, you are the one to whom he wrote and about whom he thought the most. He said that part of his heart beat for you. In the letters he wrote to you, he imagined you happy at the ranch, grown into a man who was calm, strong and honest.

Mr Bowman, the words that Pete spoke about you were more disturbing. But little by little I saw the darkness leave his face when he talked about you. He wrote to you too.

Mrs Desmond, you and Mr Bowman were the parents that Pete dreamed of having. When he wrote (he is too weak now to continue his journal), he imagined that you would be proud of him. You gave him this freedom, the last freedom for which he still fights: words.

Aileen, you must know how to read by now. Your Uncle Pete's brightest smiles came when he thought of you.

I work in the city – any work I can find – to pay for our rent and food. Brazil is no more welcoming of Indians than any other country in the world. I earn what I can to keep us alive. But we will only survive if we are in good health. The weak and the sick always die. My efforts are for nothing. Each day that passes is not a remission but a weakening. I have come to believe that he will not recover unless he wants to, that nobody else can help him. His immense energy will soon be exhausted. I will try to keep him alive until we receive a reply from you. Having something to look forward to will help us.

The man you knew was transformed by a voyage that saved him but killed him at the same time. He was only able to make that voyage because of what he learned from you. I am happy to have known him. His homesickness for the ranch has become my own.

We are in Macapá, state capital of Amapá, in Brazil. We are staying on Porto Rio Street, with Senhora Cardeal.

Macapá is a big trading city. Boats come here every day from other big cities in Brazil. I guard the hope that your reply will reach us here.

With all my respect,

Maria Bautizada

10

The little steamer struggled up the delta. Everyone in Macapá knew that the thick black smoke pouring from its chimney meant that the engine was at full throttle, the men on the boat working flat out.

Somewhere on the continent, deep inland, a hard rain had fallen and the flow of the Amazon had swelled without warning. On the dock, the crowd watched the steamer drag itself towards the port at a worryingly slow speed. When the hawsers were finally secured, the captain drank greedily from the bottle of rum that someone handed him. "My God, one minute longer and we'd have had to smash the boat apart to feed the boilers!"

The next man off the boat was a tall, thin, pale man in a crumpled suit who asked how to get to Porto Rio Street. The captain scowled. The pale man was looking for the gringo and his landlady, Senhora Cardeal, the captain's sister. But, well, here was the thing: Senhora Cardeal, her husband and he, the captain, had thrown out the American and his Indian a long time ago. You can't go on giving people credit forever. Nobody knew what had become of them since then. Even more troubling, the pale man worked for the Banco do Brasil. He became impatient and in the end the captain showed him the way to Senhora Cardeal's house.

The landlady pointed the banker towards the track that ran alongside the river and told him that the American and the Indian had gone that way when they left. This was four or five months ago now. The man asked where he could hire a cart and a guide, preferably not somebody in the senhora's family. It was embarrassing, dealing with these bankers: you hardly ever saw them and then, when they came to Macapá, they treated you like shit.

The banker became anxious. He had been chosen for his calmness under pressure, but what could he do faced with the reality of a place like this? The people in charge of this mission, Americans, were completely naive. If the couple had left Macapá, he would not be able to find them. At best, he would stumble upon two makeshift graves with anthills heaped above them.

The cart owner remembered the American and the Indian speaking Spanish, but he had no idea what had become of them. Did it really matter?

The small community of Indians beside the river was a pathetic little trading outpost. No lights, neglected palm shelters, refuse everywhere. Sheets of newspaper used as packaging were rustling in the wind, like giant leaves on the branches of trees. The camp's occupants woke in the middle of the day, their heads heavy with alcohol, eyes puffy, scratching their bellies. Dugout canoes drew towards the shore. There were about fifteen people here, including women, sleeping off their hangovers. The banker arrived the day after his talks with the city's merchants. When he saw the empty bottles scattered all over the ground, he understood where the Indians' wages went.

He asked them questions and they replied with gestures: further, higher, over there, one day on foot. If he paid them, they could take him there in a canoe in five hours.

The Indians washed their faces, pushed their boats into the water and grabbed their paddles. They rowed in silence, digging into the river at a steady rhythm, inching their way upriver against the current until they reached a small beach of pale sand in a bend of the river, at the mouth of a small creek. The day was ending; the banker, soaked through, paid for one of the oarsmen to accompany him while the canoe waited there.

The track was well-worn. His barefoot guide advanced in silence. After walking for an hour, they smelled woodsmoke. The banker did not really believe it was them, but he patted the inside pocket of his jacket all the same, checking that the letter was still there in its waterproof case. The letter that he had to deliver personally, if his mission was successful, to a certain Mr Ferguson.

An Indian woman stood in front of a shabby-looking hut. She watched as they approached. The guide crouched down next to the fire without a word, while the banker stood in front of the woman.

"Maria Bautizada?"

There were dark rings around her eyes. Her arms were thin, her hands swollen. She was dirty and she stank. She was dressed in the same way as the river tribe.

"Yes."

"Is Mr Ferguson with you?"

He reached into his pocket and pulled out the letter.

"I've brought this letter for him. I am supposed to bring both of you back to Belem. Is he here?"

Maria looked at the letter, then at the banker. In Spanish, she replied: "I don't know if he'll be able to make the journey."

She led him into the hut and lit a candle stump. The Banco do Brasil employee put his hand to his mouth. It took him a moment to understand that the man lying on the ground was still breathing. It was impossible to believe that a body with so little flesh on it could really be alive.

The banker fled the hut before he vomited, leaving Maria kneeling next to Pete, reading to him the letter from the Fitzpatrick ranch.

The banker offered the Indians a good sum of money and they rowed through the night to wake a doctor in Macapa.

When the doctor arrived the next morning, Pete Ferguson opened his eyes.

It took three weeks before Pete was considered strong enough to make the journey, three weeks and an impressive number of trips between the couple's camp and the city. The expenditure of money, time and skills required to bring these people out of the forest was beyond all comprehension. It was not as if he had discovered a goldmine there, after all, just an Indian woman and a white man.

While Pete was clearly in a worse state, Maria too required medical attention. Their bodies were inhabited by every imaginable forest parasite. The doctor joked that creepers and orchids would soon start growing out of their flesh. Quinine soothed their fevers; alcohol cured their infected wounds; purgatives cleaned their systems; food revitalised their muscles.

As the doctor nursed them back to health, he was surprised to note that neither Ferguson nor the Indian seemed very pleased to be leaving the forest. The American kept rereading the letter.

They left Macapa in early August on the same steamer that had brought them there. The captain with the false teeth bent over backwards to make sure they were treated like princes, and the boat strayed from its usual route to take them to Belem without any stop-overs.

The manager of the Banco do Brasil was there in person, on the dock, to welcome them. They were taken to the closest good hotel, Pete on a stretcher, Maria holding his hand.

Their room overlooked the seafront and the large Ver-o-Peso market; they barricaded themselves inside, frightened by the incessant activity and swarming crowds on the avenue below. A new doctor was taking care of them. The bank manager came to visit them in the first week, then the man who had found them in the forest, and after that they were forgotten. All charges were paid by the bank. As soon as they were discovered, a telegram had been sent to the United States and the bank was hoping for a quick response.

Maria started going out. She would walk in the shade of the palm trees along the avenue that bordered the port and the sea. Once Pete was steady on his feet, the two of them went out together. He gripped Maria's arm with one hand, his other hand leaning on a walking stick. His bones had been decalcified by months of malnutrition. The doctor told Pete that his balance would return and his muscles grow back if he exercised regularly, but that he would always walk with a limp. They rested in the shade of the market, its wooden cladding faded by the sea wind and the rain. Pete stared at the blue sky, Maria at the blue paint of the building.

"In the forest, I used to catch morpho butterflies. I would sell them to the Indians, who sold them to white people. Their wings were an astonishing blue colour, like the blue in the sailor's Polynesian islands."

The bank manager paid them a final visit in September. He said he was delighted to see them in such good health, though in truth he was embarrassed by the presence of the Indian woman, who was benefiting as much as the American from the money sent from the United States. The Ferguson family had spared no expense. But it was intended only for Pete Ferguson.

"Everything is arranged. A General Transatlantic Company steamboat will take you to the port of Colón, in Panama. The voyage will last ten days. From there, it is a two-day river journey to the Pacific coast. At the port in Panama City, you will board an American steamboat to San Francisco, where you will land on 6 October. Your brother will be awaiting you there."

The manager handed him the sealed transcript of a telegram. The terse message terrified Pete. He read it out to Maria: *Awaiting your return to ranch. Voyage arranged. Situation sorted in Carson City. No danger. See you in SF on 6 October. Oliver.*

After that last visit, they were left on their own. Pete would take baths and Maria would climb into the tub with him, soaping his tattoo with a sea sponge.

"How do you feel?"

"I don't know if I can go back there, after this . . . failure."

"What failure?"

"Not finding anything. Not bringing anything back."

Maria tensed. Pete pressed his body against hers.

"That's not what I meant. Of course, I found you. But nothing else."

Maria pushed him away. "You died trying. What more could you do, *pendejo*?"

She got out of the bath and Pete watched her walk through the bathroom and the bedroom – all this foul luxury, this end to his struggle – leaving a trail of water on the waxed floorboards. He whispered: "I didn't die the way I should have. Hanged."

He looked at Maria sitting naked on the bed, the vexed expression on her moonlike face, her small breasts, her brown skin, still miraculously soft after all those months of hardship. He got out of the bath and walked over to her, feeling the blood harden his penis. She lay on her side, her back to him, and guided him inside her, then twisted her body up so she was on all fours. They had sex like animals from the forest, making the hotel bed creak, hoping that it would break apart beneath them. They rolled on the floor, grabbed hold of the vanity table. The mirror shook as the Indian woman pulled him harder into her, this thin white man with black tattoos on his prematurely aged skin. They looked into each other's eyes through the mirror. Maria's belly kept banging into the table until it became painful. She pushed Pete onto the bed and he fell backwards. She straddled him, eyes closed. Rolling on top of him, her legs gripping the ink equator, she let loose cries of orgasm and war that she imagined could be heard even in the Women's Village.

II

The air was cold and clear. The sea wind entered the bay, effortlessly pushing ships as big as houses. Hundreds of chimneys spread a grey fog above the city's rooftops. The smoke of San Francisco, in the blue California sky, made Pete want to go down into the hold, to smash the hull open with an axe, and to sink the boat here. He envied Maria, who had been sick and bedridden since they left Panama, because she had seen almost nothing of their voyage.

He had been here once before, with Bowman, who had come to sell several stallions. Pete had grown bored with the negotiations and Bowman had found him dead drunk in a saloon on Market Street. Apparently, the city had since swapped its low wooden houses for three-storey brick buildings. Every warehouse was big enough for a locomotive train to enter with all its carriages.

The port was an inextricable forest of sails. The steamboat made its way through the other ships in anchorage, finally reaching the company's dock.

Pete went down to their cabin. Maria was waiting on the bunk, the suitcases next to her, her skin whitened by seasickness. She refused to stand up until the ship was moored and had stopped moving. Pete was just as pale as she was. They stayed there, not speaking, not daring to leave, like poor immigrants in a first-class cabin, until the sounds above them on the ship had faded almost to silence and a fist banged on their door.

"Pete?"

He shuddered. His hand crushed Maria's.

"Oliver?"

His brother opened the door. He was out of breath, dressed in a banker's suit, moustache gleaming, eyes blinking. Pete grabbed his walking stick. His body trembled as he leaned on Maria's shoulder. Oliver, arms open wide, had stopped dead. Pete saw the shock in his brother's eyes. Pete Ferguson, the big brother, was now a small skeleton, hollow-eyed, grey-bearded, his suit hanging from his shoulders, able to walk only with the help of a stick; even his anxious smile was ruined by rotten teeth. Both brothers needed great courage to carry on believing that their reunion was not impossible. They hugged, clumsily.

Maria looked at Oliver's face, the tears in his eyes, as he nestled his head in Pete's neck. This man reminded her of the Pete Ferguson she had known in Antigua. The two of them looked more alike than Pete had told her. After Pete's voyage, however, a stranger might well have guessed that Oliver was his son. Holding his brother's arm to prevent himself falling, Pete turned to face Maria.

"Oliver, Maria. Maria, Oliver."

Oliver held the woman's hand in his and leaned forwards, a rough-edged young gentleman.

"Thank you. Thank you for writing that letter. And welcome."

He stood up, controlling his enthusiasm.

"There's a carriage waiting on the dock. Come on, don't stay here, I've booked us rooms in a nice hotel."

Pete's fingers squeezed Oliver's arm. "The city . . . It's too noisy. Too many people . . ."

Oliver looked at the two of them, disconcerted.

"We can leave right away if that's what you want. We'll be at the ranch in three days."

Pete gave a little smile.

"Three days? It's a week's journey to the lake."

"The Central Pacific trains go from San Francisco to Truckee in two days. After that, it's just one day on horseback to the ranch."

Oliver turned to the Indian. "Do you ride, Maria?"

He followed her gaze to his brother's hunched back and walking stick and his cheeks turned red. He rolled his shoulders under his itchy new suit.

"Well, we can rent a carriage in Truckee."

He rushed out into the corridor, came back to take the suitcases from Maria's hands, then moved forwards again at the same speed as Pete, walking behind him and trying not to look at his twisted legs. Oliver bit his lips as he saw the two of them on the dock, keeping a wide berth from the porters and other passengers; he walked past them, carrying the luggage, and cleared a path for them through the crowds to the carriage. He helped Pete up to the seat, then held out his hand for Maria, who did not even see it. Oliver ordered the driver to take them to the Oakland ferry.

The carriage boarded directly onto a steam barge, with its passengers and horses. Pete and Maria refused to get down. The barge was passing the small island of Yerba Buena in the middle of the bay when Oliver broke the silence. "Arthur and Alexandra will be at the ranch when we arrive."

He lowered his head.

"They didn't come because I'm in charge of all Fitzpatrick business in San Francisco. Arthur has aged a lot since you left. Both of them have."

He looked up. Pete was watching the uninhabited island as they went past it.

"Aileen wanted to come welcome you. She got mad when I told her it wasn't possible. Knowing her, she'll probably still be sulking about it when we get back! She asked if you were a princess, Maria."

Maria pressed herself against Pete, her face turning even paler.

"Maria suffers from seasickness."

His brother's attentiveness and tenderness towards the Indian were inconceivable to Pete. Oliver smiled in response, but that was one of the last smiles of that journey, because none of them could bear to pretend anymore.

The carriage dropped them outside the brand new brick building of Oakland train station. A train was leaving that night. Oliver reserved an entire first-class compartment for the three of them. The noise in the departure hall was too much for the couple, so they went to wait on the platform. Pete had not felt this cold for two years; he was almost curious about these new sensations. He and Maria ended up walking closer to the slow-moving locomotive and standing in the warmth of its steamy breath. Oliver brought cups of coffee to these people who looked so old, though one of them was exactly his age. He began to notice the way the other travellers were looking at them. The tiny Indian woman, too well-dressed, in the arms of a white man returned from some distant war, and the man in the suit who was looking after them. The passers-by stared disapprovingly at Maria. Oliver pushed the couple towards their train carriage.

Maria had never been on a train before. It made her just as sick as the boat had done. Without a word, she curled up in a ball on the upper bunk, leaving the two brothers in the light of an oil lamp. The train moved, creaking, up the first slopes of the mountains. A steward brought them bottles of liquor and wine, and served them dinner; Maria's remained under its silver lid until Pete started to eat it. There were vegetables and steaks, and crusty bread that made his gums bleed. The two brothers sat in silence as the train shook and jolted. Pete ate noisily, downing glasses of whiskey and red wine, while Oliver sipped and chewed quietly like a solid member of the middle classes.

"You said in your telegram that there were no problems for me in Carson now. What happened?"

Oliver wiped his mouth. He recognised his brother's true voice: cold and authoritative. Was the Indian listening? He sat back in his seat.

"There were some changes. The ranch is much bigger now – you won't recognise it," Oliver said excitedly. "We're on the same level as Eagle Ranch now." Pete stared at him, and Oliver made himself calm down. It came back to him suddenly, like a cold flash: his own passion for the Fitzpatrick ranch, and Pete's mistrust; this was the issue that had driven them apart, leading inevitably to his big brother's departure.

"The Fitzpatricks have more influence than they did before too." Oliver glanced up at Maria's bunk. "But what really changed is Lylia."

Pete gritted his teeth. "What's she done now?"

"She changed her testimony," Oliver stammered. "She said you didn't kill old Meeks that night."

He hesitated, and Pete leaned towards him. "What else?"

Oliver sat up, but his voice sounded weaker. "We got married. Lylia is my wife now. And we're expecting a child."

Pete burst out laughing. "You married that snake? She always went after money, but I never would have guessed she was capable of that! Straight from big brother to little brother!"

Oliver stood up, knocking over plates and glasses, opened the compartment's sliding door and violently banged it shut. Maria started awake.

"*Qué pasa?*"

"Nothing. Go back to sleep."

He drank more booze and waited. His brother did not return. Pete lay down on his bench seat and let the movements and sounds of the train rock him to sleep.

They awoke to the smell of coffee. Oliver was there, silent in front of their breakfast; he had changed his clothes, and was now dressed in the more comfortable suit of a wealthy rancher. Pete rubbed his hand over his stubbly chin and his dry lips. He poured himself some coffee and rinsed away the foul taste in his mouth.

"I shouldn't have said what I said last night. It was the alcohol talking. I'm not used to it anymore. I'm in no position to judge anyone, let alone you and Lylia."

Oliver did not know how to react. He had long ago learned to forgive his brother, but he had never heard him apologise before. He looked up at Maria, perched on the edge of the bunk, her nose pressed to the window; she wiped away the condensation, fascinated by the spectacle of the passing snowy mountains. Pete, too, turned and squinted at the white landscape.

"In Guatemala there are mountains as tall as these, but it's so warm at the summit that it never snows."

Oliver addressed her. "At the ranch, we've already had three feet of snow, and parts of the lake have started to freeze."

"To freeze?"

"The water turns to ice."

She looked at Oliver, then at Pete. There were, she realised, words that Pete had never used when speaking with her, an entire English vocabulary to describe this world that the Indian did not know.

The train station in Truckee was a pile of planks as badly constructed as its platform. By the Central Pacific office, with its frosted windows, three passengers boarded the train and three others disembarked. The carriage was waiting for them. The telegraph wires followed the route of the railway; Oliver had sent a message from the station in Oakland.

Once the suitcases had been loaded into the back of the carriage, they sat on the bench under thick woollen blankets. The driver handed out scarfs and hats, politely greeting Oliver as "Mr Ferguson". The six horses, breathing out huge clouds of steam, set off along the frozen track, rapidly passing the silent houses of this growing village.

"Last time I was in Truckee, there was nothing here but a coaching inn and a brothel for the railway workers."

Pete brought his head back inside and closed the curtain of their private carriage.

"When you say that the ranch has grown, I get the feeling you're not kidding. The Fitzpatricks must be rolling in money."

Oliver was proud to explain that he hardly ever looked after the horses anymore; that was Arthur and Alexandra's domain now. He and Lylia were in charge of the cattle. The two and a half thousand acres had become ten thousand and the Fitzpatricks now bred cows – a breed imported from Europe, crossed with the Angus, which was adapting perfectly to the local seasons. Oliver said with a hint of regret that he no longer lived on the ranch, but in Carson City with Lylia, in the building where the Fitzpatrick Ranch had its headquarters. To hear him talk, the breeding of horses had become a secondary activity.

It took Oliver a few attempts to be able to pronounce Lylia's name without choking on its syllables. Pete glanced at Maria, whose approval he seemed always to be seeking, before leaning forwards and patting Oliver's knee.

"You've done a great job. I'm happy for you."

Oliver smiled – a smile that remained hanging in the cold air. Pete had not been able to conceal his discomfort at any mention of the ranch's success. The younger Ferguson stopped talking about it; his brother was too fragile – this idea dismayed him – to bear all the changes that had occurred in his absence. Perhaps he had hoped to find things the way they were when he left so he could start over. But his past had not waited for him; it, too, had changed. That was what Oliver, ever since their reunion in San Francisco, had been telling Pete without meaning to.

Only one mountain peak separated Truckee from Lake Tahoe. After the ascent, with the driver yelling and cracking his whip, the horses drew breath as they walked slowly across the brief plateau, then the carriage began its descent. Pete lifted the curtain and stared out at the Sierra Nevada, the summits sharp and white, like the spine of a gigantic dragon lying asleep, where he and Oliver had almost died ten years earlier. The brothers were thinking the same thing. Maria, her face half-buried under wool, observed them. Oliver found it hard to withstand the Indian's gaze. Back when Pete had fled Carson, he used to kick the Indian beggars who hung around the city's streets. Maria's voice, with its Mexican accent, made him feel like a guilty child.

"How long do the winter and the snow last at the ranch?"

"In tough years, from September to March. In good years . . . from September to March."

Maria did not understand this joke. She frowned. Oliver cleared his throat. "We'll be there before nightfall."

12

It was like a celebration to welcome back a deserter from the war. Night fell too quickly for the faces to get used to one another. In the lakeside house on stilts, the long lamp chimneys made it difficult to look at anything directly. They cast shadows around the eyes and the brighter they burned, the more you realised that it did not change anything. Maria ate without appetite, an opportunistic little animal. Pete, though starving, did not touch his food, as wary as a creature confronted by a snare.

Bowman and Alexandra were tired. Lylia was no longer a young woman; her neck, cheeks and bust had all been swollen by pregnancy. The table was long and the gaps between the chairs were too big. Whenever anyone spoke, they always sounded too loud or were inaudible. Maria understood English perfectly well, but the others spoke to her with exaggerated slowness, articulating every syllable, asking the most naive questions.

They had not read Pete's journal, only the letter from Maria. They knew nothing, so he had to explain everything. Pete's fatigue turned to feverishness and the pointlessly burning oil gave him a headache. The food was too rich, the wine too expensive. Bowman could barely conceal his disgust for this bourgeois extravagance, and only Lylia, poorly seconded by Oliver, seemed keen to play her role – Lylia who had wanted to send Pete to the hangman. Alexandra, sitting next to Maria, ate too quickly, and swore to herself that tomorrow – outside, in daylight, on the real Fitzpatrick ranch – they would be able to talk properly.

The only one whose presence made Pete happy was Aileen. Her

parents had not been able to tame this wild girl, with her dishevelled hair and rumpled clothes, whom Bowman said spent more time on horseback than in her mother's books. When she saw her Uncle Pete, Aileen had not been frightened or torn between joy and shame, like the others, she had been disappointed. How could he ride a horse in that state? She kept glancing at him during the meal, her eyes darting back to her plate whenever he looked at her. This limping ghost was not her uncle; he had been replaced by an old, tired man. Aileen came up almost to the height of his shoulders, and her hair was redder than her mother's, though Alexandra's hair was no longer the colour that he remembered. The same was true for Aileen's blue eyes, which seemed to have stolen the sparkle from her father's.

Pete rubbed his ribs, where the sailor had tattooed the names of all these people. He stood up, searched angrily for his walking stick, announced that he was too tired, and excused himself. Alexandra hurriedly cut short the silence.

"We've prepared the guest room, but if you'd prefer your old hut, I've made a fire in there too."

She was talking about the hut where Arthur and Alexandra had hidden the Ferguson brothers – kids who had deserted the army – when they first arrived at the ranch. It was next to the barn, built against the rocks, a hundred feet from the house. Pete could not imagine sleeping anywhere else. He nodded, and said something in Xinca to Maria, who stood up in turn and said goodnight to these hosts who were so different from the people described in Pete's letters. Nothing here was as she had imagined it would be. She felt ashamed of the letter she had written, the feelings she had expressed. These people reminded her of the bourgeois couples who came to the orphanage to choose children. None of them had ever chosen her, the little Indian girl with the big head, not until the visit of Hagert the Jesuit, when she was as old as the red-headed girl who kept staring at her out of the corner of her eye.

Alexandra walked with them along the path of packed snow to the hut.

"Get some rest. Tomorrow we'll have lots of time, and we'll be able to show you the ranch."

Maria was already sick of this ranch, around which everything seemed to revolve. They closed the door and went over to the stove, the two of them observing the decor, new to Maria, but so old and familiar to him. Pete approached the window. On the porch of the main house, in the light of a lamp hanging from the ceiling, stood Arthur Bowman. He was smoking, leaning against a post, and staring at the hut. Maria stood next to Pete.

"What is he doing?"

"The day Oliver and I arrived here, he stood there and kept guard over us for days and nights on end. I've never been so afraid of anyone in my life."

Maria lay on the bed. The hut was the first thing that did not appear to have changed, and she felt at ease here.

"They don't know what made you sick."

"What made me sick?"

For a long time, Maria stared at the log roof, and then at the walls capable of withstanding an army's assault. This miniature fort had been built by Bowman and had become the deserters' prison cell.

"Killing your father and all the others who were like him. Killing everything that could have made a difference, until there was nothing left to kill. And then, instead of saving yourself, you saved someone else in your place. For you, changing is a betrayal. They don't understand that it will make you sick. You can't stay here."

Pete was still staring at Bowman on the porch, remembering him standing there back when the Civil War was mowing down thousands of Ferguson brothers every day. Sergeant Arthur Bowman, a soldier in the British East India Company, saving two kids, redeeming himself as best he could, stoically accepting his punishment in the cold for hours.

"Where will we go?"

"It's your country. You choose."

"My country? I deserted it."

Maria laughed.

"Then you can show me the country of deserters."

Bowman put out the lamp and went back into the main house.

Pete put wood in the stove, undressed Maria and lay down on top of her, her soft skin turned to gooseflesh in the cold.

"Old Meeks and all those guys like him, they think deserters are cowards. That if they showed me a real enemy, I'd go off to war."

She laughed again, her breath shortened by Pete's weight.

"I'll show you your enemies."

He inhaled his own breath in Maria's neck and listened to her voice resonate inside her throat.

"You don't have any enemies here."

The first person he talked to was his brother. Feeling strong enough to ride a horse, he suggested they go to see the lake from the hills above. His real objective was to be found halfway up the slope, on an abandoned path that he still knew by heart.

Oliver helped Pete into the saddle. They had chosen two peaceful geldings and they set off slowly amid the sounds of trampled snow, their necks warm under fur collars.

Oliver had become one of those men who mould their country while making their fortune. He was the most authentic American yet produced by the Fitzpatrick family. Their past in Basin and at the ranch had turned him into a perfect businessman. Lylia had consolidated this successful image and she kept their accounts in Carson City. As soon as they had married, two years before, she had encouraged him to move to the city, to move as far as possible from the ranch and the memory of Pete. The brother of a murderer, and a deserter himself, Oliver owed his tranquillity purely to his influence and his money. But the city was growing and the new inhabitants, by sheer weight of numbers, would end up diluting those memories.

Lylia and Oliver had met when he went to ask her to withdraw her testimony. He didn't go into the details, and Pete did not want to know if he had proposed an arrangement or if she had blackmailed him: a wedding as payment for the elder Ferguson's innocence. It didn't really matter. Seeing them together, they looked made for each other, despite Oliver's naivety. His brother had always seen the good in people, where Pete had always suspected the bad. They did not defend themselves from the world in the same way.

The den, as they called it back then, was the other tiny shelter where they had hidden whenever people came to visit the ranch. It consisted simply of some logs in a hollow in the rock, a roof covered with earth and vegetation, a door, a loophole and a stove: more like an animal's lair than a house. Pete led the way and Oliver, as if he had already guessed where they were going, followed unquestioningly.

The two brothers both had to push hard, side by side, to open the door of their former refuge, which was now half-buried and collapsed. The bed was worm-eaten, the stove cloven in two by a fallen beam. They stared in silence at this tiny space where so many memories were concentrated: whole days without going outside; Alexandra's visits, when she would bring them food and books; Bowman dropping by from time to time, making his rounds without stopping to talk, rifle in hand.

They sat in front of the shelter, looking down at the glints in the lake below through the vertical lines of the tree trunks. Pete sat with his head lowered, his elbows on his knees, his hat between his hands. Oliver looked at the end of the tattoo on his neck, the little branches and the two names: Pete and Maria. Pete gave him time to have a good look before sitting up.

"Saying something in a house and saying it outside are not the same thing. When there's a view like this, words are smaller. You have to choose them better so they'll be understood. At the same time, it's like they'll be lost and forgotten more quickly."

He turned to Oliver.

"I'm not going to stay here long. What I learned at the equator is that nothing changes, but that fighting is less absurd than waiting. That you have to change even if you know it won't make any difference. You understand?

"That a problem that's been solved is still a problem that existed.

That remembering and forgetting are not all that different. It's an arrangement between ourselves.

"We'll still be the same, past, present and future together. I'm not here to tell you what's in my heart, but to ask you if you want to hear it or not. It's your choice."

Oliver stood up. The cold air was entering his chest too quickly and he had to move to burn it up. He took a few steps in the snow, turning his back on Pete, then came back and sat next to him. He took his brother's hand in his own and their gloved fingers intertwined. Oliver held back his tears with a courage that Pete could not match.

"What happened that night, in the barn?"

Pete nodded. Oliver put his arm around his brother's shoulders.

"I'm sorry it's in your heart and not in mine. It's your story. But I'm not going to let you leave until you're in better health."

They returned that night. Pete looked exhausted, but the tension had gone from his face. Aileen was waiting for them in the barn, and she was pleased to see Uncle Pete able to ride a horse.

"Tomorrow I'll go with you."

Dinner was more relaxed than it had been the night before, but Pete still seemed to bear the responsibility for breaking all the silences. Between him and Lylia, him and Alexandra, him and Bowman, whose voice Maria was quite sure she had not yet heard. She was fascinated by that man, who put her in mind of a wounded lion. A former soldier, all scars and bad dreams, with his severed fingers, Bowman did not belong in this country, perhaps not even in this world. The ten thousand acres that surrounded him were not enough; he continued to wear himself out by guarding the ranch as if it were a fort and he the last officer. Bowman's anxiety had grown. Maria could tell this from the looks his wife kept shooting at him. Bowman knew, just as Pete did, that the older Ferguson brother had brought back some sort of menace with him. This made Bowman sad, and his silence weighed heaviest on that second night at the ranch.

On the third day, Pete went riding with Aileen, who began by urging her horse to jump the fence that surrounded the enclosure. Then she turned and waited patiently for her uncle. They did not return until late in the afternoon.

All of them, except Lylia, would go out riding with him.

In the days that followed, it was Alexandra who rode along the shore of the lake with Pete. Maria watched them leave, frowning deeply, until they vanished from sight. When he came back, she asked him what they had talked about.

"About you."

"So you're not in love anymore with the woman who adopted you?"

"She is not my adoptive mother."

"Is she jealous of me?"

"No."

Maria became annoyed. "What did she want to know?"

"She wanted me to tell her about our voyage. But as if it were a visit, not a flight."

"Why?"

"Because she thinks only of the future."

"She's a Utopian."

"But it's true. We weren't only running away. We went on a journey together."

"That's a lie."

"She likes you."

Maria became even more annoyed.

They had been at the ranch for a month. The winter was still relatively mild: there were regular snowfalls, but they had been spared the blizzard and the cold had not yet killed any horses. Lylia had gone back to her house in Carson City. Oliver went there more often too. Pete could breathe more easily now; his strength had returned, he had put on weight, and he no longer needed his walking stick. He still had a slight limp. Maria had to admit that this place was one of the most beautiful she had ever seen.

In late November, while they were all gathered in the house by the lake, Oliver announced that news of Pete's return had spread through Carson City. He looked tense. Pete realised in that moment – with a rush of shame and anger – that they had tried to keep his return secret for as long as possible.

"We'll go to see the judge next week," Bowman said, "so that Pete can sign the official papers. It's not just rumours now, so there's no reason to hide here anymore."

Lylia had to force herself not to leave the table. The meal was cut short.

Pete's last trip on horseback was with Bowman. The two of them left one cloudless, windless morning and rode for four hours – across the Fitzpatrick acres and over the mountain – to the courthouse in Carson City. Bowman gave Pete a faster, livelier horse than the gelding he had become used to. He himself rode old Walden, his bad-tempered but still quick stallion, the father of Reunion. Bowman and Aileen were the only ones who rode Walden.

In a mountain pass, on the border between the Sierra to the east and the Nevada plains to the west, they saw one of the ranch's boundary stones. Pete pulled on the reins.

"This is the first one we saw, me and Oliver, when we were lost in the mountains."

Bowman came to a halt beside him and looked down at the smoke plumes rising from Carson City below, the straight lines of its streets and the houses crowded together.

"The city's grown since you left."

"I can tell."

Bowman made that familiar grimace which stretched out the painful scars on his face and whose meaning was hard to guess: was he worried, or angry, or had he just come up with a satisfactory battle plan?

"I'm glad you came back. Even if, along with your Indian girl, I quickly realised that you wouldn't be able to stay long. I don't regret what I did for you and Oliver. I'll always defend the Ferguson brothers."

Bowman reached into one of the saddlebags and handed Pete a

holster attached to an ammunition belt. Inside the holster was an oiled and loaded Colt.

"The city's grown, but it hasn't changed all that much. It's full of gossips, and there are also some members of the Meeks family still living there."

"I know."

Boots digging into the stirrups as they descended, they continued their journey, Bowman taking the lead.

"What happened to Reunion?"

"He died in Mexico. He died to save my life."

"That's how a horse should die."

They left the ranch's land and soon reached the main track. Imitating Bowman, Pete pulled his hat down over his forehead and hunched his shoulders. The sign announcing that they were entering Carson City was now located at the foot of the mountain. The houses here were new, and there were piles of planks and posts in empty lots. Pete hunched even lower when they passed buildings he recognised. The Eagle Saloon and its hotel, the alley where old Meeks died, the Sheriff's office and its prison cell. Bowman slowed down outside a two-storey building that used to be a hotel – Pete had slept there a few times – but had now been repainted and renovated and was home to the Fitzpatrick ranch's headquarters. The front door opened and Oliver came out, wearing a hat and buttoning his long winter coat over his belt and pistol. He mounted a horse that was tied to a post outside the building and looked up. Pete and Bowman followed his gaze. At a ground-floor window, behind a raised curtain, stood Lylia, pale and rigid as a marble statue. Oliver lowered his head and rode along the street with his brother and Bowman until they reached the central square and its park of newly planted trees. Around them gleamed several buildings: City Hall, a few shops, the Land Office, and the courthouse, outside which they tied their horses.

As Lylia had already given her testimony, and the case had been closed, it took only a few minutes for the judge to provide Pete with the documents he needed to sign. Then he gave him a sealed copy of the verdict and a letter officially declaring him innocent, before God and men, of the death of old Meeks.

The good citizens who were waiting outside for them attached no more importance to those documents than did the judge himself. At the head of the group stood Uncle Meeks, the dead man's last surviving brother, and two of his sons. Behind them were other old enemies that Pete had made back when he used to get into barroom brawls, some former employees fired by the Fitzpatrick ranch, and a few small farmers who had moved to the area at the same time as Bowman. They were not armed, but their pockets were full of bottles. Bowman stared at each man in turn. He did not take a step forwards or backwards. The most important thing was to remain silent. Arthur and the Ferguson brothers mounted their horses and rode slowly through the crowd of men, who reluctantly moved out of their way. Pete could see the hesitation on their faces as they considered the men with whom they were dealing: Oliver Ferguson, one of the richest men in the region; Pete Ferguson, one of the most violent; Arthur Bowman, one of the toughest. It was broad daylight, and the three of them were armed. Not only that, but they had not been expected here so early; their presence had come as a surprise. The dozen men watched them ride away, with a few other onlookers standing behind them: the judge on his doorstep, the sheriff at his window.

Oliver accompanied them to the last houses of the city and then drew to a halt. Bowman scanned the street behind them. Pete's horse was as nervous as he was.

"You and Lylia should come to the ranch."

"Nothing will happen to me. You're the one who should get out of town, Pete."

The two brothers shook hands. Bowman and Pete headed back to the ranch while Oliver rode back into town to join Lylia. Pete turned around once to watch his brother disappear at the end of the street, his only protection against a hail of bullets the money that his wife was amassing as quickly as she could. Pete wished he could nail shut all the doors of the houses and set fire to the city.

Maria got used to the cold. Pete worked hard to bring his muscles back to life. She went riding with him on the Fitzpatrick land. Maria, who came from the teeming forests of Guatemala, had never experienced such silence in nature before. Winter was a season of rest. Here, nature slept, its heartbeat slowed, its branches emptied of sap. In these landscapes, the presence of man became more mysterious.

Maria had also put on some weight. She began hiding her belly under as many layers of clothing as she could, until finally Pete noticed. When he asked her, she shivered and blushed.

"This one is holding on better than the others. It's been there for two months. Maybe it likes the cold?"

She had laughed when she said this, but she was clearly anxious.

She left with her hands on her belly, and asked Pete not to put too much wood in the stove. Whenever she could, she went walking in the snow.

Christmas was approaching. Lylia and Oliver came from Carson; this was the last trip Lylia would be able to make before she gave birth. It was time to say goodbye.

Maria had spent enough time with these people now to accept their generosity. Besides, these were not the kind of gifts that put the receiver in debt to the giver, but presents made by rich people, without vanity, and everything they were given would be useful on their voyage. Two sturdy, well-trained horses, branded with the Fitzpatrick diamond, complete with saddlery, and a packsaddle mule. Camping and cooking equipment. Food reserves. And they were true gifts, because the couple had nothing to offer in return.

That dinner was the saddest since their arrival, but sadness was easier to ward off than fear. They also shared a feeling of relief. In the presence of Oliver, Lylia and Alexandra, Pete still possessed the power of making a room feel too small. Around him, the air became rarefied, and they always ended up fighting to breathe it. He had changed and he was the same; without his little Indian woman, the others doubted that he would be able to control himself for very long. Perhaps he wasn't running away anymore, but he still had to leave.

As the sun set over the lake, they went out with blankets on their shoulders to get some fresh air on the porch. The sky was sheared by blades of red and orange, and the last yellow rays outlined the shapes of the mountains. Aileen held Maria's hand, and the Indian spoke to her in Xinca. The girl looked at her Uncle Pete.

"What did she say?"

"She said you are brave to hold her hand, because in her village she is a witch."

Aileen stood up straighter as she watched the sun disappear behind the mountains. She was clearly impressed, but she did not let go of Maria's hand.

"I don't believe you. There's no such thing as witches."

Maria added in English: "In my village, there was another witch, very old and very powerful. When I was a little bit older than you, she told me that one day I would dance with a white prince. I didn't believe her to start with, and then I was very frightened."

Aileen turned to look at Pete again. She had no doubt that he was a prince, but she had never seen her uncle dance. She hesitated, trying to imagine this.

"Did you dance together?"

"You could say that."

Maria leaned closer to Aileen.

"In an ogre's palace."

The girl let go of the Indian woman's hand and moved closer to her father. Bowman said that the weather would be good tomorrow. They all knew it, just looking at the clear sky, but at least Bowman had managed to say something when the silence threatened to suffocate them.

Halfway up the mountainside, they stopped to look at the ranch. The house by the water, the barn, the hut built against the rocks, the horses' enclosure . . . they were all like children's toys from this distance.

"You know what he's going to do?"

"Bowman?"

"He's going to the plains to capture mustangs."

Maria smiled. "And you'd like to go with him?"

Pete did not reply straight away.

"We could go and see what it's like over Utah way. Have you ever seen a herd of wild horses?"

Maria took a deep breath of the pure mountain air. She had learned to enjoy the effect it had on her lungs.

"Let's go."

As they came towards Carson City, they turned off the main track, opting to skirt northwards around the city. Pete would have preferred to go straight through, instead of starting his journey by hiding. But Maria just laughed at his stupidity. He raised his collar and they continued north towards the Salt Lake City track. His grazed pride gradually stopped stinging as they moved away from Carson. He looked at the yellow desert to the east, the snow vanishing at the plains' horizon.

"We make a strange pair of pioneers."

"Why?"

"Because we're not looking for land."

"Deserters are not allowed to own land, gringo. That's their reward."

Their end

Maria and Pete left the county of Carson City in January 1875 with their horses and their mule, leather waistcoats, guns and ammunition. There was nowhere to hide in this vast country of equatorial forests; no matter where they went, they would be found, this disturbing, mismatched couple. Except in one place . . .

The first stage of their journey led them to the prairies, past Utah, Salt Lake City, the Rockies and that land of giant canyons carved out by the Colorado River. In early spring, they arrived in the long stretches of green grass to the south of the Platte River. A few days' ride from Lincoln, where the burned-down Land Office had long ago been rebuilt.

Maria only spoke English when she had to now, addressing Pete in Xinca or Spanish. To her swollen belly, she told stories of her tribes' gods, its legends, its country, its pyramids. Pete's determination to avoid other men had only increased. As had his conviction that he had the right to be an American – a different kind of American from his brother or the Meeks – and to hate his own country, if he wished.

One clear morning, the air smelling of damp grass, Pete lined up a lone bison in the crosshairs of his Yellowboy. Maria was lying on her back next to him, looking up at the sky. They had approached the beast against the wind, and now they were so close that they could hear it breathing. They had spent days crossing the prairie before they found it.

"How many hunters are searching for one last bison right now?"

Pete had laughed.

"Soon there won't even be any left for those who need them."

They had followed this creature for two days and two nights, listening to it low in the evenings, calling out for the herd that it had lost; it was a young male, quick, strong and searching for a female. Maria had sharpened two daggers the night before, by the fire. They had lain down on this little promontory, Maria staring up at the sky, her belly in the air, while Pete took aim. He waited for the bison to lift its head above the grass and look over in their direction, so he could shoot it between the eyes. The animal jumped up, its four hooves off the ground, then fell back into a standing position, staring straight ahead, before its head slumped forwards. Now it became a rock in the grass as the sound of the gunshot echoed over the prairie. The bison died without knowing that it was dying.

The Indian and the gringo plunged their sharp blades into the fur, stripping it off the muscles and unfolding the skin, wool in the air, on the bloodstained grass. Then they butchered the meat. Their blades sliced through all the tendons, between all the bones and all the joints. They used a hatchet to separate the vertebrae, then they cut off the legs, and – fighting the urge to vomit – pulled out the warm, stinking entrails and spread them on the grass around the fur. Like ants gradually devouring a tree, the two of them trimmed the bison's carcass. Maria followed Pete's instructions for arranging the pieces of meat. The flies went into their mouths; the smell of carrion spread quickly over the plain. In the distance, coyotes stood up to sniff the wind, while vultures massed in a spiral above them, the bison's soul ascending invisibly through this tunnel to the sky.

They finished their work late that afternoon. Their hair was sticky with blood, their boots, trousers and shirts covered with a layer of grease, fur and bits of flesh. They undressed, rinsed their hands and faces with water from flasks, and changed their clothes. Pete rolled a cigarette and they sat down to look at what they had done.

The fur was surrounded by the intestines, spread in a witch's circle, and on top of it the quarters of meat were lined up, each of them a roughly identical size, to form a square of seven pieces, side by side. You could see half a head, a thigh, a length of spine, some ribs and shanks. Amid the thrum of flies, the rational aspect of this geometric reconstruction of the dead bison seemed to mutate into something sacred. A temple of the absurd, an answer and some questions, an insane centre to the prairie, now bereft of all markers, stripped bare of its most ancient inhabitants.

"What is it?"

Pete answered Maria in English. "The end of the conquest."

Nostrils still filled with the smells of dead flesh, sticky with their work, they set up camp a hundred feet from the temple of meat, to which all the imaginary tracks on the plain converged. Night fell and they did not light a fire. The horses were nervous, scenting the presence of the coyotes, wolves and vultures drawn by the slaughter. All night Maria and Pete listened to the howls, the barks, the whistles and the growls, the cries of the animals biting and scratching one another around the feast. This went on until dawn, when the sated beasts fled the daylight. The vultures were the last to leave. Pete fired a shot in the air and they slowly moved away, jumping through the grass without taking off, discovering the remnants of the orgy and two of their own kind killed by wolves. The quarters of meat had been dragged away and half-devoured, but you could still make out the shape of the temple, now in ruins, the skin and the lined-up flesh. The next night, it would all begin again, until nothing remained but the bones drying in the sun on the brown fur. For the animals of the prairie too, the last few bison had become rare. This feast had been offered to them without any benefit to man: it was a total loss, an authentic act of generosity.

Maria and Pete got back in the saddle and rode off in search of a stream where they could wash themselves.

In Omaha, Nebraska, they took a train to Salt Lake City. They took refuge in the anonymous din of a third-class carriage. They did not enjoy travelling at that speed, but they were able to gain some precious time. Maria would give birth in a month and, once they left the train, they could only cover about ten miles a day because she needed so much rest.

Returning eleven years later to an American town that had been part of the gold rush meant running the risk of finding it abandoned. But Basin, a small town in Oregon, was still standing when they arrived there in July. If a town did not disappear, it had to grow, and Basin had tripled in size.

They did not go into town, but skirted around it to the cemetery. Previously a wild, isolated place, it was now no more than a hundred feet from the nearest houses; to hide it, a wall was being built. Oliver had sent someone here, two years earlier, with money. The man had been told to move their parents' graves from the farm to the cemetery. He had sent a telegram: the farm had vanished and the graves with it. Even so, Oliver had asked him to buy a concession and to erect two gravestones on it. It was in front of these two bodiless graves that Pete stood next to Maria and gathered his thoughts.

On the old Ferguson land, not the smallest remnant of the buildings remained. The meagre orchard had been torn out and the place where Pete had been born and grown up, where his parents had been buried, was now pastureland. They stopped in the middle of a field where the house had once been and Pete, locating himself by the lay of the land and counting his steps, rebuilt the farm for her with words. Here was the orchard, there was the fence that he had once tried to jump with the old mare, where he had fallen and broken his arm, here was the vegetable garden, there was the well and the barn.

They took a nap in the warm grass, where Oliver and Pete Ferguson used to hide from the Old Man when they were children, where they would lie on the slope in the afternoon sun and watch the clouds move overhead.

When Maria was rested, they continued along the track that led to Crooked River, going past a little cliff, a pile of fallen rocks with the riverbank and the grey water at its foot. Pete told Maria the story of Billy Webb, whose name he had once worn, like a coat of hatred; Billy Webb who had died wanting to prove his courage to the fathers of Basin by going off to kill Indians at the reserve in Warm Springs.

They followed the bank to the confluence of the Crooked and

Deschutes rivers, then joined the rampart walk of Jackson Trail. On the shingle banks, they crossed the widened riverbed and entered the reserve. Heading upstream, they traced the winding course of Shitike Creek and came to a halt before they reached the camps of the Wasco, Paiute and Tenino Indians, the rival tribes forced together by the white men on this cramped little territory, who had learned to cohabit in peace. The white man's world had become their common enemy.

The sky was yellow, the low sun turning the trees and the grass a deep gold. The Indian from Guatemala and the gringo from Basin unloaded the horses, lit a fire and waited.

Hands on her belly, long black hair flowing over her shoulders, Maria watched the small group of horsemen move towards them, armed with rifles. They stopped a few feet away from the woman with Indian skin and the white man dressed like a trapper. Maria walked towards them and spoke in Xinca. The Paiutes looked at one another. A warrior replied in a language that Pete and Maria did not understand. She repeated: "We've come to live here."

The warrior replied and Pete listened attentively, trying to memorise the first words of this new language.

Acknowledgements

For some things borrowed: my thanks to Nicolas Jaillet, who brought back from Mexico the story of the Guardia Blanca – thanks to him, Pete Ferguson and Reunion were able to cross the Rio Grande with dignity – and to Sébastien Rutés, who discovered (also in Mexico) the red sea urchin of falsehood. *Que vive fiction.*

Thanks to my editor at Albin Michel, Stéfanie Delestré, who is a joy to work with.

Posthumous acknowledgments to two extraordinary people, whose autobiographies provided some breathtaking elements of this story. The first is Frank Mayer, whose book *The Buffalo Harvest* gave me Bob McRae, Vimy and the hunters on the prairie. The second is René Belbenoît, a prisoner in French Guiana who made six escape attempts, captured morpho butterflies to survive and was married in the middle of the forest to an Indian woman whose language he did not speak, before going to Los Angeles and working for Hollywood studios. His story, which took place a few decades after mine, is entitled *Dry Guillotine* and is far wilder and more implausible than anything a serious author would invent. Another encouragement to write fiction.

Thanks to my friends in French Guiana, with whom we spent a few months, particularly Mathieu, my oldest friend in the world and companion in my first adventures. The first chapters of *Equator* were written there, in Roura, under endless sheets of rain.

Thanks to Judy and Craig Johnson in Wyoming, and David in Colorado, in whose homes I made the final corrections to this text.

And, lastly, thank you to Abbey – the part of America I love most of all – for this fantastic voyage, begun twelve years ago.

ANTONIN VARENNE was awarded the Prix Michel Lebrun and the Grand Prix du Jury Sang d'encre for *Bed of Nails*, his first novel to be translated into English. His second, *Loser's Corner* was awarded the Prix des Lecteurs Quais du Polar and the Prix du Meilleur Polar Francophone.

SAM TAYLOR is an author and translator. His translations include works by Laurent Binet, Hubert Mingarelli and Joel Dicker